The single mums' mansion

Janet Hoggarth

First published in the UK in 2018 by Aria,
an inprint of Head of Zeus Ltd

9 7 5 3 1 2 4 6 8

A catalogue record for this book is available from the British Library.

ISBN (PB): 9781788548625
ISBN (E): 9781788545686

Typeset by Divaddict Publishing Solutions Ltd.

Printed and bound in Great Britain by
CPI Group (UK) Ltd, Croydon CR0 4YY

Head of Zeus Ltd
First Floor East
5–8 Hardwick Street
London EC1R 4RG

WWW.HEADOFZEUS.COM

For Vicki and Nicola, thanks for saving me.
Single Parents Alone Together! The mansion will
always hold a special place in my heart.

Prologue

What is family? Is it a thing you are born into or a cosy patchwork blanket woven from people who have come in from the cold at a time when you need them the most? I happen to think it is a bit of both. You are born into a blood family, but you gather people along the way, some of whom will feel like jigsaw-piece soulmates that click into a gap in the puzzle for a brief while, maybe even years. Then one day, in the blink of an eye, they're gone, missing down the back of the sofa.

And then there are the permanent ones that have been wedged in the centre of the puzzle for years. These are the people that squeeze you tight when your mind scatters on the winds of change after some dreadful trauma. They hold your hair back while you vomit after a bottle of wine too many. They carry you home from the chip shop when you fall down drunk, sobbing that your life is a mess and your children will be irretrievably damaged by your slovenly parenting. They arrive at your door when you ask them, no matter what time of day or night because they know you need them. And in turn, you fit snugly into the heart of their own pictures.

I'd always hoped my jigsaw was complete. That the husband, three children, friends, family, ramshackle half-finished house, accoutrements of married life, was it. Yet deep down, I could feel a gaping hole in the centre of that picture. A piece was missing and I couldn't quite put my finger on it – did I need another baby? Why wasn't my husband making me happy? Plagued by bad dreams soon after my perfect wedding at which I was cloaked in a white tulle froth of a dress, my sleeping brain would throw up terrifying scenarios of my husband leaving, carelessly tossing the words: 'I've lost the love,' over his shoulder like a crumpled tissue into the waste-paper bin. And I would wake, the words snagging a jagged hole through my heart as I clawed my way back into the real world where he would, of course, be asleep next to me in our marital bed, assuring me on waking that I was being ridiculous. However, my third eye was positively throbbing – it knew something I didn't. But there was no way I wanted my marriage to end. I loved him completely, didn't I? So why did I dream about it most weeks? It felt like I made it happen.

And happen it did. A pivotal jigsaw piece fell down the back of the sofa, in exactly the way I had expected it to. In the aftermath of 'I've lost the love' (yes, he did indeed use that very insult), I think I mislaid what was left of my baby-addled mind. Then, as luck would have it, two jigsaw pieces that happened to be freewheeling along life's superhighway at that exact moment collided with me and out of the ashes of my marriage, a phoenix arose.

Welcome to the Single Mums' Mansion. Names have been changed to protect the innocent.

I

The Heartbreak Diet

My face was reflected forlornly in the drip-splattered kettle, huddled in the corner by the compost bin overflowing with the detritus of this morning's breakfast. A half-sucked toast crust hung like a mini prosthetic leg over the edge where I hadn't quite managed to ram the bugger in. I pressed the button to start the ritual of tea making within my five-minute window of opportunity. The Chugganug was squatting like a rotund Buddha in his inflatable ring, lovingly chewing a board book on diggers, and the girls were upstairs playing shoe shops in my half-empty wardrobe. I had yet to browse their offerings – slim pickings, if I remember rightly – all lined up at the foot of my bed in pairs. The kettle was about to click off when the hammering on the front door began. Chugga watched me run from the kitchen to the door, swiftly dodging the wooden brick truck with the reflexes of a ninja. Oh, how I had laughed when Sam had broken his toe on it two years previously. *Maybe that's why he left?* The hammering stopped and I could make out the shape of a person hovering behind the frosted-glass panels.

The wide entrance hall was home to the red double Phil and Teds buggy, two pink scooters and a faded yellow trike, lined up against the left-hand wall. The pockmarked bare boards were in need of some kind of cheap carpet runner to mask the splattering of silver star stickers from *Barbie* magazine, but as soon as I pondered this the shiny idea customarily burst into a trillion shards of what's the fucking point. Baffled by his urgency, I opened the door, expecting it to be the postman.

Alison barged past me, her formidable bump brushing me as she hurricaned it into the house. The chandeliers above squeaked menacingly on their pendulous light fittings and I glanced upwards, wishing (not for the first time) that Sam had never bought them. I was convinced that, any day, one of those bastard chandeliers was going to plummet to the ground and impale someone. They were a testing reminder of jobs abandoned in this half-finished 'For Ever' house. Sam had given me the chandeliers as a birthday present a year before he left, with a promise to finally decorate the hallway and return it to its former glory as the centrepiece of the Victorian villa. Instead, it was still smothered in the original seventies mustard-yellow and poo-brown flowery wallpaper all the way from the ground floor up through the heart of the house.

Chugga had crawled over to investigate, and I scooped him up into my arms and sniffed the top of his head before I kissed him. I wondered if I had kissed him over a million times in the last sixteen months. I loved his sweet baby scent, and his hair was like a silky scarf upon my lips, apart from when it became matted with puréed spinach, potato and cheese bake.

'Jim's singing from the same song book as Sam now!' Alison's eyes were hidden behind aviators, unnecessary on this dull grey autumn day. I ushered her into the chaos of the kitchen where she skilfully swerved the brick truck, the washing maiden draped with babygrows and small clothes in varying shades of pink, and levered herself down into one of the awkward, yet trendy, bamboo armchairs I had insisted we buy from Habitat. *Maybe that's why he left? He never liked them.*

'What?' Ali removed her shades and her usual aquiline features and annoyingly perfect skin was puffy and blotchy. I grabbed a tissue from the box by the cooker and thrust it at her, curbing the urge to wipe her dripping nose like I did for everyone else in this house.

'Jim said he's going to leave.'

'But he can't! You're just about to give birth!'

'When has that ever stopped anyone?' she snapped, smearing tears across her cheeks. 'Sam left you on Sonny's first birthday!'

'He didn't,' I barked defensively, squeezing Sonny (Chugga) tightly, making him wriggle down onto the floor where he resumed his love affair with the digger book. I have no idea why I was alleviating Sam's guilt. A wife's misplaced sense of duty, perhaps.

'All right, a couple of weeks later.'

'How long have you known? When did he say all this? Tea?'

'Have you got any wine?'

I warily eyed the clock near the back door. It was eleven thirty a.m. but there was a cheap bottle of red already open on the Moomins melamine tray next to the cooker.

'I suppose it's wine o'clock somewhere in the world,' I sighed, and grabbed a glass.

'You're not having one, too?' Alison's voice wobbled dangerously. I had found it hard to enjoy wine since Sam had left. In fact, most things were joyless. In the catatonic weeks that followed his swift exit from our home, I had dropped body weight like sandbags from a rising hot-air balloon. My stomach was perpetually clamped shut and anything I did manage to force down came swiftly out of one end or the other. While out shopping a few weeks after Sam left I bumped into my hairdresser when I was mindlessly skimming through one of those achingly trendy gift shops for a friend's birthday present.

'Amanda! Is that you?' Sally had gasped, pushing her shades up onto her head to scrutinise me in detail as I leaned on the double buggy to prevent the spins taking hold. I couldn't remember when or what I had last eaten.

'Yes.' That was all I could manage to say. I knew if I uttered anything else the waterworks would start gushing. Most days I was perilously close to the edge of Niagara Falls.

'Are you OK? You don't look very well. Are you… ill?' she probed uncertainly, most likely wanting to ask if I had cancer, but not quite daring to. I certainly looked like it, with my twig-like arms and legs and scrawny turkey neck, heartbreak's version of concentration-camp chic.

'No. My husband… he left a few weeks ago.' Predictably the tears started. I flapped my hands by my eyes as if that would somehow quell the tide of grief.

'Put your Pradas back on,' Sally ordered, indicating to my sunglasses on top of my head, a Valentine's gift from Sam a few months earlier. I should have trod on them, ground them under my heel, but I loved them. I still wore my wedding and engagement rings, too. I had tentatively taken them off after a few weeks, but the gap on my finger pulsed like phantom limb syndrome and I had to ram them back on, but they were so loose now that they were in danger of falling off.

Sally grabbed my hands. 'Gosh, you're so cold.' She rubbed them in a vain attempt to warm me up, but it was no use. I spent every day with ice-cold extremities from the sheer shock that I was still having to function, when I wanted to be sectioned and drugged into a coma so that I didn't have to experience the searing pain in my chest and the incessant roundabout of ifs and whys.

'You poor thing. How are you coping? Are your parents helping?'

'They live miles away. My friends Rob and Amy moved in for a few weeks, but they couldn't really stay longer than that, so it's just me and the three kids now.'

'Jeez, love. Three under five. That's hard anyway.'

I know, I wanted to scream. It's so hard that I feel like I am loathing every second of their childhoods. My parenting consisted of a television babysitter while I tried to make sense of my life, operating in a dream-like state, somehow shovelling food into the children while ignoring myself in the process. Bedtime stories were an emotional minefield; anything with a mummy and daddy in them set me off. I never knew the human body could produce so much water.

'Come in and get your hair cut and we can have a chat, yeah?' Sally hugged me. 'Take care, and I'll see you soon.' That had been nearly five months ago. Things really weren't much better apart from that food had finally stopped tasting of cardboard and I had somehow hoodwinked myself with Beardy Weirdy alternative therapies into behaving like someone who was coping. The children now knew Daddy had left (that was fun). I'm not sure whether they really understood – I certainly didn't. Meg didn't talk half the time anyway, so I had no idea what she actually thought. She operated on two levels – screaming and not screaming. Sonny was too young to know anything, but unfortunately Isla, a five-year-old version of Nanny McPhee, noticed everything. One night when Meg wouldn't stop screaming at bedtime and Chugga wouldn't let me go for a wee, shouting through my tears and frustration, I was so frayed I was in danger of unravelling in Meg's bedroom, Isla calmly looked at me from the doorway and announced: 'It's hard without a husband, isn't it, Mummy?'

'Yes,' I had squeaked, unable to stop sobbing at her astute observation. Was this what hell was like? Postnatal depression had been an absolute skip through the daisies compared to this. Isla came over and hugged me.

'We love you, Mummy. I know Daddy does too. He just doesn't realise.' How I didn't expire on the spot after that was sheer willpower on my behalf. I had had dark thoughts about not living, about slipping peacefully away on a cloud of painkillers, but the anchor that drew me back was these three innocent hearts. How could I ever do that to them?

So it was with a sinking feeling of dread that I stood there, illicit wine bottle in hand, awaiting Ali's revelations.

'Please,' Alison wheedled. 'Have a glass with me. I feel hideous enough drinking with this one inside me.' And she nodded her head down to her full-term bump.

'Don't feel bad,' I reassured her. 'She's fully cooked now. A glass won't harm her.'

I poured her a small slug and then thought, Fuck it. Why not? No one ever died from drinking at eleven thirty in the morning. Apart from maybe alcoholics; they might die. I handed Alison her panacea.

'Cheers seems wrong,' I admitted, but clinked with her anyway.

'He's such a wanker,' Alison growled after her first sip. Then she clapped her hand to her mouth. 'Shit, sorry. I forgot Sonny was here.'

'Don't worry. I'm sure his first word will be "twat" anyway. Or "For fuck's sake". Isla already goes round kicking things, muttering, "For sake for sake" under her breath.' I had tried to be so careful with my organic, knitted yoghurt upbringing of the children, but what was the point now their childhood had just been snatched from underneath their tiny feet? Instead I changed tack and joined a different Mummy Gang. Just Get Through the Day Without Anyone Dying – that gang.

I inhaled a sip of wine and as it hit my empty stomach the heat radiated out through my veins, fuzzing my head and relaxing my perennially racing heart. The background sickness also seemed to fade. Maybe I should have been self-medicating from day one? However, hangovers with kids are soul destroying.

'Things haven't been great for a few months,' Alison admitted, draining her glass. I got up and brought the bottle over, topping her up. 'He started acting weird once we had the second scan. I think it hit home that this baby was coming and he couldn't stop it.'

'But he wants her!' I protested. 'It wasn't like you forced him.'

'Well, no, not forced. But I went on and on and on and on until he gave in.' Jim already had a twelve-year-old daughter from a previous marriage. The one that Alison became a part of after Jim's agency offered to represent her fashion stylist work, an old-fashioned *ménage à trois*. 'He never wanted any more children, Mands. He swore he was getting the snip when we got together, and I begged him not to. I didn't want to die with cobwebs in my womb!' I smiled weakly. 'He's been getting himself in a state about money. *How will we afford this baby, the big house, the lifestyle? I will have to go back to work as soon as I am able*. Then he started saying I'd better lose all the fucking weight I've put on. He doesn't fancy fat girls.'

'What? He said that?'

'He did.'

I wanted to punch his face in. 'Do you think he really will leave?'

She shrugged, tears threatening again. I put my wine glass down and hugged her tightly as she gave in and sobbed.

'Ooooh, Grace's kicking – look!' It was the distraction she needed. I pulled back and watched her alien-like stomach as a heel or bottom grazed the insides and protruded like a shapeshifter across Alison's black dress. Growing a baby inside your body never ceased to amaze me.

'I think he's having a nervous breakdown,' she volunteered after Grace settled back down. 'I also think he has a drink problem. He said a few nights ago that no one would ever give me a baby so he had to.'

'I don't know what to say to that. Maybe he needs some help? With his drinking or breakdown or whatever it is. When did he say he wanted to leave?'

'Last night. Cunt.'

'Mummy, are you drinking wine?' Isla clopped into the room wearing an ancient pair of battered fuck-me shoes, interrupting the conversation.

'No, it's Ribena.'

'Why is it in a wine glass then?'

'Er, to make it feel a bit more exotic.'

She nodded. 'What's a cunt?'

Ali spat out the last mouthful of wine, spraying the clean washing.

'I don't know, Isla, but I think Daddy knows. Ask him.'

At three a.m. my phone pinged with a text. Three a.m. was danger time for me anyway. Sleep only graced me with a faint veil every night. The slightest breeze ruffled it – a child coughing, a dog barking, foxes shagging. Alison was in labour. Now I was wide awake, willing the phone to herald more news. Jim said she was in the bath and the labour was fast, already eight centimetres dilated. I wondered if he was drunk. I got up and made a cup of tea, careful not to creak the eighth step as I stole down the steep stairs. Chug's bat ears would know I was up. He could probably feel his belly button stretching as I pulled the cord further away.

As I sat in the cream and mauve living room, I switched on the TV, immediately muting it, staring at the screen while an old episode of *Everybody Loves Raymond* played out in silence. I'd seen it before. I used to watch hours and hours of banal crap to while away the prison sentence of new-born breastfeeding. I must have dozed off because the next thing I knew, yelling belted out from upstairs. Sonny was awake, broadcasting to the world that he was ready to participate in this thing called life. Once he was ensconced in my bed with his bottle, I checked my phone. There was a text from Jim. Grace arrived safely at five thirty a.m. Seven pounds two. No word about Alison. I asked. She's fine was all he said. No words about what a hero she was. I didn't like the sound of that. But I pushed it to the back of my mind as my day spread out before me: another, the same as the one before. The dull ache in my chest, the realisation I was in sole charge of these three and the buck stopped here. What was it Sam announced hours after I had birthed Isla, surviving a gruelling twenty-four-hour labour? 'I don't understand how anyone can leave their wife after they've seen her give birth. I don't get it.' I hoped Jim was having that thought right now and meant it.

2

The Would-be Mansion

My bedroom, the living room and the kitchen were the only parts fully finished in the house. My favourite feature of the living room was the Shrine of Tat. I had curated all sorts of random junk from travelling, weddings, days out, charity shops, and displayed them in a floor-to-ceiling grid-frame bookcase between the two chimney breasts, which Sam had built for me when we moved in. It was an organic collection, swelling each year, as people donated things they thought I might like from their travels. A mini gold-sprayed Vatican imperiously overlooked a diminutive naked clay man with huge bollocks. It was all about the inappropriate juxtaposition.

Originally, when the estate agent handed us a bunch of property details to browse through, this house had been rammed at the back of the pile.

'What's this?' I'd asked her, fanning through all the paper. She was about nineteen and probably still lived at home.

'Oh, that? It's er… a bit of an erm, what do you call it, white elephant, I think Gavin said. But I thought you might like it, with you wanting a project.'

'It's out of our budget, though, and it's massive.'

'Let me see,' Sam had asked, and I handed him the brochure. 'Oh, wow, it's like a mansion.'

'It's a single-fronted Victorian villa,' the girl said. 'It was originally the main house on the road before the others were built around it, when a lot of this land used to be grazing pastures.' She may have been young, but she knew her stuff. 'I think it's beautiful, but it needs so much work and it's been putting some people off. You might be able to make an offer.'

When we pulled up outside the house I was bowled over.

'It towers over the other houses,' Sam observed, obviously impressed, the façade playing to his showy nature. The rusty curly wrought-iron gate was pushed back against a tide of pea gravel, jammed permanently open. Weeds sprouted up intermittently through the shingle, which could almost house a car. A small lawn hid behind the low brick front wall, also overgrown and reclaimed by weeds. The villa boasted a porticoed entrance, the flaking cream pillar sentinels straddling the peeling black front door set to the left of the house, a wide sandstone step laid down before it. To the right of the grand entrance, a roomy bay window protruded with another one stacked directly on top serving the floor above. As part of the seventies makeover, all original wooden sash windows had been ripped out and replaced with aluminium frames, a host of mould creeping round the rubber seals.

'Oh my God!' I cried on being assaulted by the hall wallpaper. 'I need sunglasses!'

The rest of the house didn't fare any better, with outdated décor, damp on outside walls, woodworm burrowing through all the floorboards. The huge garden overlooked a graveyard and would need some serious taming. The stone patio, outside the barely working sliding doors in the Formica-clad kitchen, was badly cracked, the edges of some of the broken slabs at odd angles, like wonky tombstones revealing clods of London clay beneath.

'We would need to tear everything out, apart from the bedrooms – they could be done one at a time – and perhaps we could just tart up one of the bathrooms, as long as they both work. I can have an office for all my camera equipment and show reel tapes.' Sam's eyes were far away, making plans, thinking outside the box. I loved it, but it would leave us with no contingency fund. I felt it was too ostentatious for a first house. 'What do you say, Mands? We could take our time because it's a 'For Ever' house...'

And now I was left living alone with our children in this working mausoleum of our life, not sure whether eventually to sell; trapped because no bank would give me a mortgage – freelance writing wasn't renowned for its riches or reliability – and we were plummeting into the worst recession for decades. I either had to move miles away from my circle of friends and support to somewhere affordable, ripping the kids from their home, or stay, see it through and ask Sam to help me financially. He had moved out into a modern two-bedroomed flat and professed he didn't want to get divorced, yet, leaving me stuck in marriage no man's land, knowing the real end was coming, but not sure how or when.

Sam's old office on the middle floor now resembled a crime scene – one box spewing its contents all over the bare boards where I had ransacked it, ferreting for evidence of why he had left. Old work notebooks, diaries, scraps of paper scrutinised, books pulled off shelves so I could frisk them for clandestine notes or receipts. I hadn't entered the room for months, not since he'd retrieved all his camera equipment, computers and office furniture. The single bed (from his childhood, gifted to us by his dad) remained against the left-hand wall, the bright red and navy check bedspread dulled under a layer of dust like Miss Havisham's decaying shrine, and his wooden bookcase resembled a mouth with missing teeth, the surviving books carelessly abandoned in his desperation to leave.

I found no indication of an affair, but I did find the speech he wrote for his brother's wedding two years before and, stuck to it, a prophetic joke he had scribbled down on a dog-eared Post-it.

What do marriage and hurricanes have in common?
They both start off with a lot of sucking and blowing, but in the end, you lose your house.

Even drowning in my sea of grief, the joke had elicited a sardonic smile.

'All grief counsellors say you should never move straight away after something like this. Stay put and see how the land lies,' my oldest friend, Mel, advised. 'Or move back here with me and we can have a commune!' But I didn't want to move back to Sussex where I had grown up – each of my parents had moved hundreds of miles away and it felt like admitting defeat. I knew I was lucky to have a choice at all, so chose to stay put, all the while hoping for some kind of miracle.

'He's gone.' Ali was sobbing down the phone at seven in the morning four days after Grace's arrival.

Chug was nestled in next to me, his slurping building up to a noisy climax as the milk squirted into his mouth, bubbles bursting inside the bottle as he sucked furiously. I girded myself for the scream that predictably followed the realisation there was no more. I imagined him aged twenty-five, still addicted to milk, surreptitiously drinking it under his desk at work like a crack addict.

'Sorry, Ali, what happened?' The crying kicked in and I cuddled Sonny, wrapping his baby blanket around him so he toned it down to a whimper. He smelled of warm skin and fluff.

Greeting cards can't predict your reaction to motherhood. With their idealised messages depicting bundles of joy and happiness, they flood onto your doormat on a cloud of optimism. But what happens when the father ups and leaves? It's shit enough without that happening. When Isla was born, I felt like someone had purloined my life whilst dropping this howling ball of energy on me until the end of days. Walking aimlessly round Peckham Rye Park with Sam and Isla a week after she'd arrived, I escaped across the road to the pub pretending I needed a wee and broke down in the toilets with sheer terror that I didn't want to do this for the rest of my life. How could I have had a baby when no one had told me how frightening and how relentless it was? Why hadn't I read any books? I had stupidly trusted my mum's rose-tinted version of my blood-free birth where she coughed once and I slipped into the world after her labour was spent reading a book to pass the fucking time. 'I would have killed for you there and then,' she reiterated yearly on my birthday.

As I stared at my pasty sleep-deprived face in the toilet mirror (perilously close to my post-clubbing face, but with irises), I had my first ever real gut-wrenching fright that Sam would leave. I had to step up, had to pretend that I was OK. Walking back out to the sun-drenched park I noticed a bus thundering towards me and fleetingly wondered if it would hurt as much as labour if I just stepped out in front of it. I stepped off the kerb as the bus ploughed on towards me, but reality hit me first and I hastily pulled back, the red blur puffing up my skirt like Marilyn Monroe, shocking me out of my black dog moment.

'You look like you've seen a ghost,' Sam said, and hugged me close when I returned. 'It will get better, Mands. She won't be this little for ever.' But I realised it wasn't just that. Never again would we be just us two. Now we were three and he wasn't just mine any more, I had to share him with a baby. After the turmoil of Isla's birth, Sam had produced a bottle of champagne and a stunning platinum diamond eternity ring and presented them to me in the delivery suite in a touching show of unity and love, prompting the midwives to cry. I still couldn't comprehend how we'd hit the wall in such a short space of time.

'The love will come, don't worry,' Mum had tried to reassure me when fear had me by the short and curlies. 'You can't expect too much after that long labour.'

'But what if it never comes?'

'It will.' It took four months, leaving me wanting and terrified, every day asking myself: Will I love her today? Eventually after a plane ride where Isla howled incessantly, I was steamrollered by a tornado of love that felt completely out of control and just as frightening as its absence. Now I was consumed with it, how would I ever love Sam like I had before? What if Isla died? I couldn't live without her so would obviously have to jump in front of the bus properly this time. And what about the other children we had planned? How would I ever love them this much? I felt inadequate all over again.

'Jim has left us,' Ali wept down the phone hauling me back into the present.

'Gone for good?' I asked tentatively, possibly unnecessarily, but you never know with a woman who has just given birth.

'Yeeeerrrrrrrsssssss.' Fuck.

3

The Birth of Beardy Weirdy

'Have you got anything for stress?' I had asked the man in the health food shop just before Sam left.

'What kind of stress?' he'd asked studiously, his eyes searching my anxious whey-coloured face.

'The worst kind. Stuff going on at home,' I had mumbled, my cheeks burning with shame.

'You need balancing to get you through it.' He offered me some Bach Flower Remedies and then paused. 'I have a crystal that might help centre your solar plexus, stop the anxiety.'

'Yes, anything,' I begged, desperate to quash the seesawing uncertainty pulsing through my chest. He disappeared upstairs and then moments later came down and opened his palm, displaying various yellow stones.

'Pick the one that talks to you,' he said like it was a normal request. I pointed at a satisfyingly smooth teardrop-shaped yellow stone.

'Good choice,' he said kindly.

'How much is it?' I asked.

'No charge.'

'Really?' I questioned, thinking I had misheard him.

'Really. It's from my own collection, so no charge. Lay it here at night,' and he indicated below my boobs. 'Imagine white light around you.'

'Thank you,' I managed to squeak out, the dreaded tears trying to creep up my throat and humiliate me.

'Some men can't see what's in front of them, eh?' he said so imperceptibly I wasn't sure he had said it at all. I looked quizzically at him and he nodded, closing my hand round the crystal. I will never forget his kindness, and so in his honour I named anything to do with crystals, mediums, meditation, spirituality, self-help, anything vaguely witchy after him: Beardy Weirdy.

A month before Sam left, I visited Mel down in deepest Sussex. She still lived in Bingham, the tiny South Downs market town where we grew up. Bingham was pretty in that quintessential English way, cobbles, wisteria, higgledy-piggledy architectural styles ranging from Tudor right through to eighties facsimile Georgian cul-de-sacs. Mel, her husband, Colin, and daughter, Imogen, had gone to live in Dubai for two years when Imo was six months old, because of Colin's work. Mel hated it and was lonely, but they knew it was just for two years and would pay off their mortgage in Bingham. She had not returned to work in recruitment, instead becoming a stay-at-home mum, something she struggled with. I went out to Dubai before I had the children and found her addicted to day-time soaps and gin. She would have her first drink at eleven thirty in the morning.

'Just to take the edge off. Everyone does it here.' By the time they came home and she was pregnant with Ashley, she had stopped drinking altogether and the Shelf of Self-Help appeared in the downstairs toilet.

'I scared myself. I actually had one day where I could not tell you what I did because I was so out of it.' It didn't make sense – she was always so level headed.

'Post-natal depression doesn't make sense, though,' she said when I had questioned her. 'Here you are with this baby that you desperately wanted, and Mother Nature decides to turn you mad as some sort of punishment for bringing another human being into the world via your vagina. It's shit!' Yes, it was, as I found out for myself when a year after Meg was born I woke up feeling normal, having had no inkling I had behaved like a hormonal hag for twelve months.

Sonny was installed at my feet chewing a Matchbox car in Mel's living room, and the girls were scouring through the vast collection of Lego that Imogen and Ashley had spilled out for them. Mel's kids were older than mine, with Ashley now frequenting our former senior school. We had been chatting aimlessly about nothing in particular when out of the blue I blurted: 'I think Sam's having an affair.' It just impulsively shot out. I clapped my hands over my mouth in horror and tears instantly filled my eyes.

'What on earth makes you say that?' Mel had hissed, clearly shocked. 'Surely not Sam, he of the perfect marriage and saintly husband status.'

'I don't know,' I had squeaked, wanting to punch my eyes to stop them leaking.

'Well, you must have some sort of idea. You've never ever mentioned this to me before.'

I took my hands away from my face, wishing I could snatch back the words.

'Think back, Amanda, what sparked this?'

'Oh God.'

'What?'

'It's his eyes. They're not here. They haven't been here for years, not since Meg was born.'

'That's three and a half years ago!'

'I think I just accepted it's what it's like when you have small kids. You lose your way a bit.'

'Yes, I know what you mean. I was a complete nut job when mine were little. But that doesn't mean he's having an affair.'

'I know. Just lately we've lost our connection completely and it's getting worse. I find myself saying the most awful things, just to get a reaction. I've become such a moany bitch. He isn't there at all and it's hideous. It's like he's checked out. And he's changed his aftershave. The one I love has been banished to the back of the bathroom cabinet. He's got this new one I've never even heard of or seen before. He's worn the same thing for over ten years – why the change?'

'I think you're reading too much into it. Your subconscious will have dragged up that scenario as a way to make sense. There could be another explanation?' Mel was always the more sensible of the two of us. Whenever I saw a disaster, she would always pragmatically see the other side, and she loved playing devil's advocate. We were completely different in so many ways and not just physically, with our different hair colours (Mel was blonde to my raven) and body shapes (Mel had tits and arse, I just had arse). I was always a bit on the wild side at school, getting drunk at fourteen, different boys, parties galore; whereas she would be the one cleaning up the vomit from behind the sofa so the parents didn't find out. Even now she was more grounded than me, the proof being she possessed a salad spinner. Only real grown-ups bother with one of those.

I shrugged and was about to let it go when a suppressed memory from my childhood stepped up to the witness box.

'Dad always used to change his aftershave with each different woman he had an affair with. That's how I always guessed. It was excruciating. Remember?'

'How could I forget double French? The only work we did was dissecting what was going on with your dad.'

'I know,' I sighed mournfully.

'Don't jump to conclusions about what "it" is. He could be having his own midlife crisis about work, anything really. Three kids under five is really hard work.'

Later on, I visited the downstairs loo where Mel kept all her Beardy Weirdy books. As I pulled the chain, I browsed the huge selection of spines and, looking back, I realise this was a pivotal moment in my life. I had flicked through this shelf many a time, picking up books but not borrowing anything. It had never occurred to me to read one of them, but a book was practically pulsating with some sort of answer to a question I had to yet to ask myself. *The Journey.*

I grabbed it and devoured the blurb hungrily. The author had cured herself of some sort of cancerous growth by using various healing techniques that had amalgamated into the umbrella term she now called *The Journey*. But how did this relate to me?

'You OK?' Mel asked from outside. 'Thought you may have fallen in.'

I opened the door, brandishing the book. 'What's this?' I asked, my stomach churning. The book felt hot, like some sort of magic talisman. Mel was holding Sonny, his head resting on her ample bosom, obviously a novelty compared to my bony chest.

'Ahhh,' was all she said.

'Can I borrow it?'

'Yes, of course.'

'Thanks, although I'm not sure it will help. She had cancer and, as far as I know, I don't.'

'It's not really about that. Just read it and you'll see.'

Later when I was back at home, after the kids were in bed and Sam was watching TV, I jammed my nose in the book. I couldn't put it down. I never read books any more, which was senseless really because I was a writer and, in the past, could easily read two books a week. But my last published children's book had been three years ago and I had no space left in my overcrowded head for following trends. Myriad unread books were dotted around the house, jammed onto shelves and in abandoned piles on my chest of drawers. I had let reading go like someone might subtly drop that friend that never calls you any more, wondering if they will ever notice. So it was, with great glee, I found myself able to read a book and not fall asleep.

But the glee soon turned to despair because the very nature of the book meant you had to hold a mirror up to yourself, shining a searchlight directly into the black night of your soul and ask some torturous questions. The message in the book opened me up like an origami lotus flower. Be the best version of yourself by laying to rest all the ghosts of the past. Do not expect outcomes, just be with yourself and observe, and forgive, and let go of all the things that no longer serve you. If you do all of this, the present will fall into place and the universe will deliver what you need.

Despite the initial despair, I began to feel alive for the first time in years, as if I had been given a life-saving blood transfusion. I had taken a step outside of my own skin and had turned observer on who I was and how I behaved. As soon as I did that, I could see all my faults laid out like neatly folded clothes. I was needy. I expected Sam to make me happy, and when he didn't I blamed him. I lived in the future and in the past. I tried to control things and people so that I felt better about myself. Everything was always somebody else's fault – period. I assumed what people were thinking about me, themselves, anything. I cared what other people thought about me. People's lives affected my own. The list went on and on. There was some sort of perverse pleasure in looking at how imperfect I was. And that was another fault – not forgiving myself for anything. Jesus, this was going to be a hell of a lot of work. Each journey starts with a single footstep, the mawkish old saying goes, and mine had begun with a trip to the downstairs toilet in Bingham, where *The Journey* set me free. But it all felt a little too late.

Soon after my fateful visit to Mel, Sam and I plunged further into a mire of unsaid grievances, until his no-show at Amy's birthday, where he left me stranded without a credit card or cash, resulting in a blazing row the like of which we'd never experienced before. Subsequently the fateful sentence made its appearance. The one that had haunted my dreams since Isla had been born. 'I've lost the love, Amanda.' I threw up in the toilet next to Sonny's room. The force of the grief was so strong that I wasn't sure I was still alive after he'd spoken. It was frightening how the assembly of words in a sentence can inflict such pain.

4

The Truth Will Be Revealed

I consulted the dog-eared print-out in my hand as I walked down cobbled Bermondsey Street, cool cafés bursting at the seams with Saturday afternoon tourists and locals making the most of the last-minute sunshine before winter arrived. Today everyone seemed to be exclusively living lives that only existed in trendy lifestyle magazines and Sunday supplements. I gazed at a couple with a baby on the opposite side of the road, the man lifting the baby out of the pram and sniffing his bottom as his tiny feet curled up, trying to retain the foetal position mid-air. I felt a stab of jealousy that they were a unit. Her name would be something like Nicola and he would be a Dan. They would have met in a bar five years ago, got married four years later and before the ink was dry on the wedding certificate, she was baking a bun in the oven. Everything was perfect, right now.

'Just you wait,' I muttered. 'Just you wait until you have more kids and lose your way and Dan thinks he needs to find himself.'

God, I wanted to punch myself. I could feel the heavy

cloak of negativity swirling round my body so I bid farewell to Nicola and Dan, wishing them light and love, and spotted the half-hidden sign for the housing estate.

The lack of control over my own future was excruciating. I tried to accept living in the moment: just be, sit in the pain, blah blah blah, but this week, I just wanted a silver bullet. My desperation at having my heart in someone else's hands was compounded by the fact that Ali and Jim were giving it another go; he had apparently come to his senses. I was alone again on my path.

The estate was quite charming, with trees lining a communal square and the autumn sun dusting the grey regulation paving stones with ochre light, softening the harsh concrete. I found the door number and knocked, apprehension playing out through the tips of my fingers as I tapped a soothing rhythm on the sides of my thighs. A tall balding man in his fifties answered the door. He was wearing a white linen granddad-collar shirt and jeans. Red prayer beads hung round his neck and he had a silver stud in his right ear. He looked the part.

'Ah, Amanda, welcome.'

I caught a waft of the obligatory patchouli oil and followed him into his small living room decorated with Indian statues of varying sizes and of differing gods, brightly woven rugs and a couple of those wall hangings with diminutive circular mirrors stitched into them. I sat at the table, which was covered in a purple silk cloth, and he turned to the business in hand.

'Let's do a Celtic Cross with the Tarot.' He offered me the colourful pack to choose my fate. Come on, I coaxed them, show me what you know...

'Have you got a particular concern, or do you just want a general reading?'

'Relationships and work, I suppose.'

He carefully lay the well-thumbed cards face down and started turning them over.

'There's been a split, and it has left you feeling terrible. I see you walking round this huge house sitting in the rooms and asking what went wrong, holding a baby's clothes and crying.'

My blood froze. He was talking about the very first time Sam had taken the children overnight, giving me some respite after weeks of no sleep and constant solitary childcare. I had met Amy in London to go to the cinema and have dinner, and it had all seemed a bit of a novelty, some freedom. But as the day edged towards night and I had to catch the bus back with all the drunks and usual Saturday evening crowd, the sparkle faded fast. All I kept thinking was my babies weren't at home waiting for me and I managed to cry silently on the 176, trying to halt the sobs that were fighting to emerge. I stumbled off the bus and as soon as my foot hit the pavement, a volcano of grief erupted from my mouth. Heaving sobs so violent I had to bend over, I somehow managed to totter down the road to the house and once inside fell on the floor in the hall. I lay there for ages, just howling like a wounded animal. How was I ever going to get used to this? I crawled up the stairs and shuffled to Isla's room where I sat on her sofa, drinking in the pink aura, the cuddlies, the Disney cushions, her cosy bed. I tortured myself and peeked in Meg's room too, her yellow walls plastered in stickers above her bed, her gorilla tucked in under her daisy-covered duvet.

In Sonny's room, I curled up in the rocking chair where I used to breastfeed him. His babygrow hung disconsolately over the side of his cot, unleashing a new wave of sobbing. I had always taken it for granted that I was able to tiptoe into their rooms and freely kiss their sleeping faces. The pain threatened to overwhelm me and I knew sleep would be evasive, so I placed Sonny's babygrow on my face and inhaled his smell and tried to ride it out. I woke an hour later with it still there, freezing cold but much calmer.

'Does this ring true?' the Tarot reader asked gently.

I nodded.

'I want you to stop that wondering, stop tormenting yourself, stop blaming yourself. It is done. You did not cause it. He has chosen a path and is going down it. I can't see if there is anyone else with him on this path... yet.'

I didn't like the way he said 'yet', but then I didn't like the way my gut constantly grumbled at me, gurgling: Listen to me for a change!

'You've gone through a massive period of personal growth also. You were just on that path when the split happened. You haven't wavered. You're facing in the right direction. Keep reading and visiting people, take it all in. All of it will help you become a new you. You have one friend, a Sagittarius, who is on this healing path too. She gave you a book that changed your head...'

Gosh, he was good. I wondered if he could tell what I'd had for breakfast.

'Work's been slow,' he continued. 'But things will pick up. You write?' I nodded astounded. 'Everything with your writing will suddenly kick off in about two years from now. It's going to be a bumpy path. This book you're writing at the moment is just the start.'

I had only just handed in the synopsis to my agent last week, after the entire plot spontaneously downloaded into my head while I was on the school run. I had never experienced that kind of artistic ambush before in all my years of writing, and had to feverishly scribble it down the minute I returned to the house.

'I expect you want to know about romantic ventures in the future?'

I shrugged. What I wanted him to say was Sam would return.

'This card here indicates a man, younger than yourself. He's not ready to meet you yet; he's on his own journey right now...' He stopped like he was listening to someone speaking. A handsome young prince stared back at me from the card. 'Do you know anyone called Chris?' he asked me suddenly. I shook my head.

'My guides are insisting on this name Chris. Very adamant, they are. He's going to be very important to you. It could be the young man.' I racked my brains to try and uncover anyone with that name. 'Anyway, look out for him. There will be a man before him. But you will know he's not him. There's energy for a marriage, too.' I rolled my eyes. I NEVER wanted to get married again. I was technically still married. The thought of not being so was something I purposely ignored. I touched the underneath of my ring finger with my thumb and the gap still felt weighed down with the two rings that used to sit there snugly until recently.

'And accept an invitation to tea. You will meet a new friend, someone familiar from the past. They will become important to you.'

The next day thoughts of Chris, the handsome young prince, evaporated as I sorted school and nursery bags ready for the children's return.

'Mummy!' Meg cried. She was always pleased to see me when she came home, but would then clam up for the rest of the time until she let rip with one of her ineluctable tantrums.

She was a funny one. I gave her a hug, kissing the top of her head. Sam was lugging the kids' blue suitcase. He looked slightly different each time I saw him, like now he had escaped he was shedding skins like a snake and trying on new looks. He was wearing a quilted Barbour old-man-style jacket and navy deck shoes with bright red socks.

'I thought you might want this back,' he said, not meeting my eyes. 'Sorry, I forgot to return it after the summer.' He stood on the front step and hugged all the kids. Sonny clung to his leg and I wanted to scream: See, he needs you!

Later on, I set about returning the case to its home on the top shelf of my wardrobe. I failed on the first attempt, toppling backwards as it fell on my head.

'Shit it!' I yelled, and made a more violent second attempt, ramming it on the shelf and slamming the door against it, hoping it would stay put. That's when I noticed it. The boarding pass, conspicuously white against the dark wood floor. It must have fallen out of the suitcase when it crashed on my head. I picked it up and read the name on there, sinking to my knees as I did so.

'Mummy, Mummy, why are you shouting?' Isla had crept out of her room, her pale face luminous with apprehension.

'I'm not.' My heart fluttered in the base of my throat like a bird trapped in a chimney.

'You were. You said a rude word.' I had developed Tourette's since Sam had left. I loved swearing anyway, the complete satisfaction of launching the forbidden words out into the ether. I do think that instead of Primal Scream therapy, there should be swearing therapy, where you deliver every single swear word you know (perhaps they could teach you some new ones, too) to a therapist in whatever way you like (mine would be shouting like a tazered crack addict) and then afterwards have a cup of mint tea and a digestive. I bet most people would feel a whole lot better after that. Fuckcuntbollockswankshitstabbingfuckstícksdickswipefuckface. And... breathe. I said all that in my head rather than to Isla.

'Just go back to bed, darling,' I spoke quietly, my escaped lunatic voice desperate to make a scene. 'I just hurt myself on the suitcase.' I glanced at the boarding pass once more.

5

Deferred Responsibility

Carrie Stone – that fucking TV chef he had been filming! Bile belched up my throat like paint stripper. I tried to swallow but my tongue dwarfed my mouth and began sprouting claggy sick-flavoured fur. Sam had talked enthusiastically about her in the past when they'd worked together years ago. I stared at the date on the boarding pass – it was the middle of August after he had left, when he said he had gone to visit his mum in Spain, alone. The boarding pass said Palermo. Wasn't that Italy? Wasn't that where we were supposed to go on honeymoon but didn't? I wanted to shred the tell-tale slip of paper, but it was evidence that I wasn't insane, paranoid or a needy ex-wife.

I know about Carrie. She left her boarding pass in the kids' suitcase. You're a cheating snake.

The phone erupted into life in my hand, the ring tone too loud for my ears.

'Hello?'

'What are you doing sending a text like that?'

'What do you mean?' I exploded. Typical Sam, turn it back on me.

'How about not jumping to conclusions.'

'Oh, I see, that's how we're going to play it, are we? It's me being paranoid again. Me being the nutty ex-wife. All in my imagination. WHATEVER!'

'No. Carrie and I are very… new. Look, I'm not doing this over the phone. I'm coming round.'

'I don't want you to.'

'This needs to happen. See you in a bit.' *Carrie and I are very new.* I ran to the toilet and retched, dry-heaving into the bowl. A silent film of him tenderly stroking her face after sex projected across the back of my eyelids as I heaved again. I didn't know what she looked like, so I imagined Nigella crossed with Angelina Jolie, all sponge cakes and sordid sex. I slid down onto the red rubber floor and lay my cheek flat, the rest of my body collapsing after.

'When will the pain end?' I whispered. I just lay there, my legs curled up in a foetal position for ages until I heard a soft rap on the front door. Let him wait. He knocked again, this time a bit louder.

'Amanda, I know you're in there. It's me,' Sam called through the letter box. I peeled my face off the floor and stood up.

'Can I come in?' he asked sheepishly. His earlier bravado had deserted him and instead he appeared shifty. I opened the door wide and turned my back so he had to follow me to the kitchen. They say all the best parties happen in kitchens, but I also think all the worst conversations unfold there, too. I leaned my back against the cooker, and he sat on one of the Habitat chairs and looked at the ground.

'So, you weren't shagging her before?' I asked, not that it mattered. He was now.

'No! She was sort of engaged, then she broke it off with him and, you know, we kind of helped each other with this,' and he waved his hands around the room like you could grab divorce with your fingertips and propel it away.

'And the boarding pass?'

'I don't know. It may have been in one of her bags and fell in there when I got it out to bring back here.'

'So, is this serious?' I asked, twisting the knife into my innards, wincing as I did so.

'Well, who knows?'

'Well, you do.'

'We'll see. It's new.' He looked properly at me then and I defiantly held his gaze until he had to turn away. 'I really am sorry, Amanda. I was going to tell you, but I didn't even know if it was anything worth telling.'

'I asked so many times and each time you treated me like I was a nutter.'

'Because there wasn't anything happening when you asked.'

'Can you leave now? I need to lie down.'

He stood up and I could feel the tears starting in the base of my throat. At the door he turned, the streetlight highlighting his curly lashes and dark eyes. He saved all the soft gazes and twinkling for her now. I got the hard stares and eye rolls.

'Amanda, I know this is difficult, and I am so sorry. I really am.'

'You have no idea how difficult. Bye.' And I slammed the door in his face. Do not cry, do not cry, do not cry.

*

'So it went well?' Mel asked as I recounted it down the phone. 'At least you know.'

'But something doesn't feel right,' I voiced my nagging doubt. He was away at the same time Carrie was in Italy. Chance or cover-up? Did it matter? He wasn't with me. But the scab was itching and I wanted to pick it off.

'Shall I ask the crystal?'

'It has a fifty per cent chance of being right, Mel.'

'Well, it might help you think clearly. Beardy Weirdy to the rescue.'

'Go on then,' I sighed resignedly. 'But we're being ridiculous. Look at what I've become, putting my faith in a spinning crystal on a chain. How can a crystal *know* anything?'

'It doesn't, it just forces you to look at stuff and face it. It's up to you whether you believe or not.'

'Do you believe?'

'I do when it gives me the answer I want!'

I laughed hollowly. 'Me, too!'

'So I'm asking if Carrie went on holiday with him?' If the crystal spun round and round it was a yes. Side to side was no. Obviously it was super scientifically accurate.

'Yes.' I could hear Mel's breathing down the phone.

'The crystal says yes.'

'I fucking knew it.'

'Shall I ask if they have been together before you broke up?'

'Yes!'

'Er, it seems they have.'

'He's a liar.'

'Well, it is a crystal, not a person telling us this, but there is someone who could tell you, if you wanted to go down that road.'

'Who?'

Ten minutes later I was skimming through the address book trying to find his mum's number. There were several crossed-out entries for her, all written neatly in Sam's swirling feminine script. Angela was an old hippie who lived in a refurbished Spanish farmhouse in the middle of nowhere with ten dogs, five cats and wild pigs roaming the scrubland. She also incongruously looked like she had stepped out of the pages of seventies *Vogue*, spritzed with that air of money and style that some people just manage to channel regardless of whether they are born in Chelsea or Romford.

'Angela, it's Amanda,' I breezed, trying to sound confident but all I could hear was a treacherous wobble in my voice.

'Amanda, dear, how are you? I was just thinking about you and wondering how you were doing. How are the children? Are they OK?'

'Yes, they're fine.' And I rattled off a few activities they had been up to and our plans of visiting my dad for Christmas. If I had my way, Christmas would be cancelled for the entire world.

'It sounds like you're all sorted then and coping well...' And the unsolicited question of *what do you want?* hung implicitly on the long-distance phone line between London and Valencia.

I took a deep breath, my heart flailing around in my rib-cage once more.

'I just wanted to ask you something. When did Sam stay with you in the summer?'

I was so sure I heard a sharp intake of breath. And then silence.

'Angela? Are you still there?'

'Yes, dear. Oh, Amanda. I knew this would happen.'

'Knew what would happen?'

'That you would ask me this.' It was my turn to remain silent. I could picture her battling with some sort of moral dilemma at the other end. 'I told him at the time it would all end in tears, that he should tell you. His dad said the same. We all did.'

'He's told me about Carrie, the girl from work, that they've just started dating, but I don't believe him. I think this has been going on for months and that they went away together to Italy and he asked you to lie for him. I think it was going on before he left.'

'Yes, it's true. All of it,' and then she started to cry.

I slammed the phone down, rage coursing through my veins like a class-A drug, my entire body shaking. His whole family already knew…

'Argh!' I screamed unexpectedly, and I grabbed the first thing I could, which happened to be one of the kid's little wooden chairs lovingly bought from John Lewis when Isla was two. I propelled it across the kitchen like I was the Hulk, smashing it into the door. The anger consumed me and, in my bid to trash something else, I stubbed my toe on the sly brick truck, but it didn't even hurt. The toy pushchair was the next casualty, crashing against the sturdy metal dresser that housed my Technics record decks. The crunch it made was as satisfying as bursting a pulsating pimple. I wanted to smash something else. I eyed my nana's beloved Ainsley bone china, daintily arranged on top of the other, corresponding dresser. Don't break me, it seemed to squeak in a Disney voice. I threw open the mug cupboard above the kettle and started slinging mugs at the floor. Sam's favourite orange one, which in his hurry to leave he had forgotten, splintered from the force of my thrust. I gathered up all the cushions from the Habitat chairs, pitched them on the floor and began stamping on them, fantasising they were Sam's head. The kitchen door abruptly creaked open, breaking the spell. I stood there out of breath, trembling amid the carnage of my unbridled fury.

'Mummy,' Isla wavered, hovering behind the door. 'What are you doing?' She sounded terrified.

I had no answer for her. She stared wide-eyed at the mess, taking in the violence committed while she slept.

'It's OK, Baba,' I cooed, using her baby nickname. 'Did I wake you?'

'Yes. I thought it was robbers. I was scared. Meg made me come down. She's crying upstairs.' I felt my anger crash round my ankles, leaving me depleted. Poor Isla, being the brave one again, coming down to check if we were being burgled. I wanted to howl.

'I'm sorry, Baba. I just went a bit nuts. I'm not great today. Remember me telling you Mummy has good and bad days? Well, this is one of those bad days.'

'You've had a tantrum,' she observed sagely.

'Yes, I did.'

'You'll have to clear it all up.'

'I promise I will.'

I took her back to bed and then sat with Meg.

'Mummy, why did you get so cross?'

'Because I have a broken heart, darling. I need to fix it, and I can't yet, so I get upset.'

'Oh.'

'It won't happen again.' However, in my tenuous state of mind it didn't feel like a promise I could keep.

I woke the next day to find Meg standing next to the bed. She thrust a torn-off piece of paper at me. It was a tiny red felt-tip-lined heart, the inside deftly coloured with pink crayon.

'It's your new heart,' Meg said seriously.

I lay back clutching it to my chest.

6

Saved by a Superpower

'Are you sure you should watch it?' Mel asked me. 'Not on your own, anyway. I can come up in the car?'

'Don't be silly. I need to see what she's like.'

'But you might smash the kitchen up again.'

'I won't. My mum comes tomorrow. The house needs to be tidy.'

I wish Google didn't exist. Then I wouldn't know what Carrie looked like. Her name had spewed forth a list of articles, pictures and headlines snaking down my laptop screen. The most recent one was today in the *Guardian*. A review of her sparkly new TV series debuting on Channel Four this evening. It received four stars from the deluded journalist who rated her 'full of pizzazz and a new star in the culinary pantheon'.

Shall I pop in and watch it with you?

Ali texted as well. But I wanted to be on my own.

'Fuck you, Pizzazz,' I muttered as I bleakly waited for the interminable adverts to finish at eight o'clock, peak viewing time. 'She pizzazzed her way into Sam's bed.' Even though the heating was on and I was sitting on my hands, they refused to warm up.

The credits began to roll with a fifties cartoon pastiche of a conveyor belt resembling *The Generation Game* except instead of cuddly toys and food mixers, there were shepherd's pies, lasagnes, roast chicken and various cakes, and as they streamed past the cartoon lady with the red beehive hairstyle she waved a magic wand and they mutated into pimped-up versions of what they were before. Oh, how lovely. I wondered how she was going to pimp up Sam. Then it dawned on me – the new clothes, the shorter hair, how preppy he was gradually turning with each month he had been gone. Carrie, marking her territory.

'Hello, my name is Carrie Stone and I'm going to show you how to turn every day favourite meals into real show stoppers with just a few twists and some imagination.'

OMG!

Ali texted immediately.

She's a fifties throwback. Look at that hair. High maintenance or what! And she's got a massive arse.

Yes, but she also had huge tits. Mine were shrivelled A cups, sucked dry by three babies. Hers were perky and young, two steamed buns to my wrinkled prunes.

She must spend a fortune on hair dye.

Mel texted.

She's not what I had in my head.

She probably got it on expenses, I thought, inspecting the screen when her blemish-free face loomed in, filling the frame, her kohl-rimmed eyes playfully twinkling. It was that kind of auburn that could only exist in a box. No one was born with hair that striking. Her outfit was fifties starlet – black clinging dress with a plunging neckline revealing just enough alabaster cleavage to draw the eyes down. She had this way of winking at the camera and slightly manoeuvring her shoulders upwards when she said anything remotely coquettish, thus thrusting her tits at the camera. She was flirting with Sam while he filmed her and he was undoubtedly trying to conceal a huge stiffy.

I think you're prettier.

Ali loyally texted.

Colin said she's ugly and bet she's crap in bed. Also, that she probably has crabs, genital warts and the clap. Sorry for his crassness.

Mel texted.

Thought it might lighten the mood…

'Now, the first dish I'm going to concentrate on today is roast dinner…'

I switched the TV off; I couldn't watch it any more.

FYI I spoke to your mum yesterday. I know everything.

I sent the text and turned off my phone.

'Welcome to Reiki One. I'm Natalie, your Reiki Master, and I will be taking you on your first journey within Reiki.' Sitting cross-legged in her living room sipping my Women Blend herbal tea, the weekend after Carriegate: rake thin from not eating any solid food for four whole days, emotions rolling inside me like waves towards a beach, I pulled my jumper sleeves over my hands for extra warmth. It had been Mel who had encouraged me to try Reiki months ago. It couldn't have fallen at a more fortuitous time. Two other women, one of whom was Natalie's younger sister, were also in attendance.

'Reiki is Universal Life Force Energy; anyone can channel it. Some people will not need to be attuned, like you are going to be today. You channel it from the universe and it comes out of your palms. You can't use it to influence people; it is only for the greater good. So don't attach any expectations to it. That is the simple explanation.' She then relayed a history of Reiki and what we would be doing today.

'Well, you know all about me, how about we go round the room and explain a bit about how you came to be here.'

The other two women said their pieces about wanting to fulfil something in their lives, and then it was my turn. I wasn't going to go into detail, I decided, I would just say I wanted to embrace a new direction.

'My name is Amanda, and I found out three days ago my husband has been having an affair with a woman from work for the last seven months.' NOOOOOOOOOOOOOOO! It was like I had no control over my mouth. 'Oh, God, I'm so sorry, I didn't mean to say that.' I promptly burst into tears. Natalie handed me a box of tissues.

'I think you have to get it out,' Natalie soothed me. 'Tell us what happened.'

The story crashed into Natalie's calm and neutral living room in North London, bringing with it the wreckage of my marriage, my children's broken hearts and the recent betrayal.

'So, you had no idea he was with anyone?' Francesca, the sister, asked. The other lady called Anna just held my hand.

'Well, no, but yes. All along I didn't want to know, and yet somehow I knew. I've always known.'

'And what did he say when he finally talked to you this week?' Natalie asked me in a concerned voice.

Thursday's events were freshly pressed in my memory, as yet unfuddled by time. I could still summon it word for word. We had sat in the dark car outside my house while Mum gave the children their tea. Sam looked dreadful and I was so, so glad. I wanted him just for that moment to know an acorn's worth of the pain I had been enduring while he blissfully shagged and forged a new life with her. What I couldn't comprehend was how angry he was.

'Why did you have to ask my mum? Why did you have to drag her into this?' he snapped.

'I want to know why you lied to me, why you treated me like I was some sort of utter imbecile nagging old witch the few times I asked if you were with someone else. And then continued to lie when you got found out.'

'I-I er—'

'No, I haven't finished! I want to know why you had an affair.'

'I didn't!'

'You did!'

'We were over. You knew it, I knew it.'

'I didn't know it. I was scared you were with someone, and I was right, and I didn't know why the feeling wouldn't go away.'

'Amanda, it had been dead in the water for ages.' I shook my head. 'It had.'

'For you, maybe. Not for me. I was still here, even if I was a nag and a cow and all the things you said I was. I was still here, loving you, wanting to be in the marriage.'

'Sorry. I just don't feel that way. I loved you, you know I did. It's just not there any more.'

'No, you feel like that about her now, don't you?'

He turned away and shrugged.

'Why did you lie? You've made it all so much worse.'

'Because I didn't want to hurt you even more.'

'I don't believe you. It's not that! You didn't care because you carried on being mean, saying awful stuff in marriage guidance. It's something else. I'm sure your mum will tell me the *real* reason.'

'All right! I couldn't tell you because Carrie didn't want to be implicated in any way just as her show was coming out. It wasn't going to look good, whatever the circumstances, even though we were over.' He managed to slip in that last justification as if it negated the act itself. I got out of the car. This man whom I had loved so fiercely, whom I would have followed to the ends of the earth, fell off his pedestal before my eyes and splintered on the ground, clay feet first.

'Amanda, Amanda!'

I spun round not caring what he had to say.

'You have to believe me when I say that I didn't want to hurt you. I really mean that. We had a good run, you and I. Eleven years isn't bad.' A good run? What was I, a fucking Broadway show?

'I'm afraid I won't believe anything from you ever again.'

'You won't blab, will you? To the press?'

I laughed contemptuously. 'Fuck you, Sam.' I stomped into the house, shaking, my heart pounding in my ears, muffling his parting shot.

'Oh, Amanda, that's pretty awful,' Natalie spoke quietly when I finished. 'He was probably so defensive because he knew he was in the wrong. But you know what, I think the timing of this is great for you. Don't look at it negatively. Yes, it's awful that your marriage has ended, but you have arrived here with all that knowledge behind you. You are being given the chance to become a Reiki person with a clean slate. You are open right now for change and positivity and you have been ignoring your inner self all this time – you knew he was having an affair; you chose to deny that truth. Now with it out on the table, you can work with your truth and higher self and really go to town. You have the chance to be a great healer. All the best healers have experienced some sort of trauma or massive life change.'

'Do you think so?'

'Yes! Come on, let's do a meditation, then get down to work.'

Right then, I loved those three other women. I didn't know them at all, but they held me together and something magical happened: I felt truly and honestly happy for the first time in years. The safety of that living room cocooned me from my past. I was finally living in that present moment, experiencing it with tingling nerve endings in its entirety, listening to everything Natalie said, following her meditation without a wandering mind, and when it came to the first initiation, I was overwhelmed. My beloved grandpa showed up.

'Well done, Mands,' he said in his gruff Liverpudlian accent as I sat on the floor, eyes closed, sensing the gentle movement of Natalie's hands gesticulating behind me. 'I'm proud of you.' He was wearing his brown chequered flat cap, beige cords, his green woolly tank top and white shirt. The clothes I fondly remembered him in. The sceptical will scoff, he's dead, how can he show up? Maybe the mind plays tricks, but my heart felt like it would burst from the authenticity because Grandpa would be the last person to reveal himself at a Reiki attunement – he regarded everything Beardy Weirdy or religious with barely concealed contempt.

We practised Reiki on each other, all of us astounded when it tingled on our palms, flowing out like an invisible superpower.

When the day drew to a close I found that I wanted to stay. Natalie's husband wandered into the living room and switched on *The X Factor*. They were settling down for the night. It was a dark November evening outside and the bite from the cold air burst the cosy bubble of Natalie's flat as Anna shut the door behind her. I stood in the hall, my coat on, Natalie and Francesca facing me smiling, *The X Factor* blaring out behind them. I felt like I could just sit back on the squashy corduroy sofa and blend in with their family, feel safe.

'It was so good to meet you,' Francesca said kindly. 'I really hope everything works out for you. You're amazing. I can't believe you look after three children on your own. I can't even manage our cat!' She gave me a hug and disappeared to watch Simon and his pithy put-downs.

'I wish I could stay,' I said to Natalie, half hoping she would invite me, but knowing she wouldn't. The hours spent in her company had infused me with a sense of invincibility I hadn't felt since I'd been a child. Like I was more than just the children's mum, like I mattered and could make a difference.

'Ahhh, that happens sometimes when you make a big change. It feels hard to leave the place where it happened. But you will be OK once you get home again and start practising Reiki on yourself every day. You might notice people will think you look different. Like you have been on holiday. You might feel things about people and intuitively know stuff and wonder how you do – your intuition is now operating on a higher level. And coincidences will start happening, but know that they aren't coincidences, they are meant to be. And remember the Reiki principles – I have them stuck on my fridge so Andy knows them, too. It's good to be reminded.'

> Just for today, I will not be angry.
> Just for today, I will not worry.
> Just for today, I will be grateful.
> Just for today, I will do my work honestly.
> Just for today, I will be kind to every living thing.

That night, as I lay in bed exhausted to my very core, Natalie's instructions to practise on myself rang through my head. We had to perform Reiki for a whole month before we were unleashed onto the outside world. I followed a self-healing ritual and drifted off somewhere around my solar plexus chakra. Out of nowhere, Ali barged into my head, gripping Grace tightly while Jim tried to prise her away. I didn't recognise their surroundings. 'You can't have her here!' she was screaming in his face over Grace's head.

'Watch me!' he yelled back. Grace started crying. I jumped out of my trance and the vision evaporated like a will-o'-the-wisp. I tried to decipher what I'd witnessed but sleep beckoned and I gladly acquiesced to its rare request. When I awoke, I remembered the dream and texted Ali about it. My phone rang immediately.

'You fucking witch!' she cried. 'How did you know?'

'Know what?'

'Jim has been secretly living with a girl I know. I followed him yesterday and barged my way in. We ended up having a huge fight in the living room and had a kind of tug of war with Grace between us.'

7
Week One in the Single Mums' Mansion

'What made you follow him?' We sat on my sofa sipping calming anti-psychotic herbal tea, Grace wedged between us propped up on one of the chintzy cushions.

'He had started going AWOL again and I just knew he was up to something, so I followed him in my car when he said he was popping to the dry cleaner's yesterday, but he ended up at a tiny place in Brixton where he had a key. I knocked on the door and pushed past him when he opened it. I obviously started screaming in his face.'

'What did he say?'

'What could he say? I shouted, why did he lie and pretend we were back together, and he said he didn't want to leave Grace, but he knew he would have to eventually and was buying some time.'

'What a fucker.'

'I know. I went mental at him, asking who she was. He refused to tell me, told me she wasn't important, and that they were just friends and she was helping him find a flat, that was it.'

'What a crock of shit.'

'I know. I shoved Grace at him and crashed into the bedroom where there were house brochures all over the bed addressed to Ms Hattie Sloan and Mr Jim Bradfield. He had clean suits in the wardrobe and she had the most awful collection of clothes – all drab and grey, with a pair of battered Converse stuffed at the bottom. Jim hates Converse, always took the piss out of me if I wore them, said they were for students!'

'Oh, Ali, what a fucking cunt flap.'

'It gets better. In my rage I pulled back the bedcovers and a massive vibrator was lying half under the pillow.' I cringed. 'I asked what a vibrator was doing in the bed if she was just helping him find somewhere to live.'

'And?'

'He shouted at me: "It's not a vibrator; it's a clit stimulator!"'

I exploded into involuntary raucous laughter and hurriedly clamped my hands over my mouth.

'Oh shit, I'm so sorry.'

'I punched him in the face.'

'No!'

'I know. Bad, bad, bad. He was holding Grace, too.'

'Ali! He could do you for that.'

'I knew I wouldn't hurt him; it was more like a slap.'

'I bet he went nuts.'

'He did.'

'So this has been going on for some time with her?'

'I think so. I know her. She's the Marketing Director at New Look. They're moving in together. He wants to sell our house immediately. She was on her way home from the shops and he rang her in front of me and told her to stay away and that I knew everything.'

‘Oh, Ali. What will you do? He’s making you homeless. And he certainly can’t be your agent any more.’ She dissolved into tears after my clumsy precis. ‘I’m so sorry. I didn’t mean to be brutal.’

‘No, it’s OK, it’s true. I’m going to have to find my own place. The house might take ages to sell and the thought of staying there while it does makes me feel so sad. Grace and I won’t be living in a home… And I’m not sure what I can afford. I need my money back first.’ She blew her nose and wiped her eyes. ‘I hate her, and I hate him. I want to key his car and slash his tyres.’ From the crazed look in her eyes, I thought Ali capable of both.

‘Look, leave them to their clit stimulating, I have a better idea…’

I rarely visited the top of the house. I had used it as my office, writing on a table under the eaves, but writing occurred downstairs at the living-room table now so I didn’t have to heat the room. The radiator was permanently switched off, lending the room a forlorn feel, abandoned and empty, the stale air oppressive. The walls were painted basic white and the carpet was cream dotted with a few indeterminate stains. The only furniture was a plain white double bed made up under one of the windows and two chests of drawers in a recess knocked out of the chimney breast. This had been our spare room for when family visited. The bathroom next door was a sorry sight. The tiles were mismatched where they’d obviously been tiled with a different batch number and some of them were cracked, with tenacious mould festering between them. The loo seat, once white, now yellow, sported a dubious-looking fag burn right in the middle. The brown cork tiles on the floor were peeling upwards round the edges in some places like fungus-infected toenails.

'Please won't you let me pay you for the work you're going to do?' I asked Pete, Ali's dad.

'Don't be silly, woman! You're letting my daughter and granddaughter stay with you in their hour of need. The least I can do is tart this place up for them. It's what I do.'

'Are you sure?'

'Yes! Now, I thought new tiles on the floor. I got these from a man I know – like them...?'

'Close your eyes, Ali. No peeking!' I held Grace in my arms. Meg, Isla and Sonny stood back as Ali walked into the room, guided by her mum and dad. 'Open!'

The stark winter sun streamed in through the two shabby windows. Pete had hung powder-pink blackout blinds above the frames and they distracted the eye from the unyielding bleach-scrubbed mould stains. The walls were now painted a lovely light stone colour with the window wall painted hot pink. Anne had styled the room, leaving the bed under the windows and Grace's white wooden cot at the foot of the bed. In the alcove under one of the eaves my two battered chests of drawers stood snugly pushed together side by side, newly painted dark grey, a basket of nappies and wipes on top, with all Grace's baby books lined up neatly between yellow solid wooden 'G' and 'A' bookends. The bed resembled a marshmallow puff stuffed with pillows of all colours and a chintzy Cath Kidston throw draped artistically over the pink chequered duvet. I could imagine disappearing into the bed and never resurfacing. Chugga obviously had that very same thought as he launched himself like a torpedo, falling short of the bed.

'Lift him up!' Ali laughed, taking it all in, and he fell face first into all the pillows, giggling.

Next to the cot a sizeable round dark brown wicker basket overflowed with cuddlies, rattles, shakers, neon electronic plastic button-pushing toys and a giant Elmo perched on top, surveying his kingdom. Unable to shift her shabby chic wardrobe from her old house up the stairs, Ali had to make do with a clothes rail on the left side of the room, next to the desk, tucked away under the opposite eaves.

'It's perfect. Thank you!' Ali looked flabbergasted and wiped a tear from the corner of her eye. 'I love that view.' Anne had cleaned the window panes, revealing London in all its majestic glory, the London Eye the crown jewel, twinkling as it turned imperceptibly, the city looming up like headstones from the roof-top horizon.

I handed Ali a tissue-wrapped present.

'Oh, wow, a gorgeous crystal. Thank you.'

'It's a rose quartz. Stick it in the top left-hand corner of the room from the door. It will attract love again, when you're ready. And keep you calm.'

Ali hugged me.

'Check out the bathroom,' Pete said proudly.

Across the small landing he opened the door and stepped back so we could enter. Gone were the cracked mismatched white tiles, yellow loo seat, wonky shower door and fungus-infested floor. In its place was a bright shower room with a realigned shower door scrubbed to within an inch of its life. The trendy brick-shaped white tiles were fixed with dark grey grout, echoing the colour in the bedroom. The sink splashback utilised the same tiles and the walls were painted in the stone shade from the bedroom. Real slate tiles covered the floor and the loo seat was one of those old-fashioned black ones, immune from fading or yellowing. Anne had placed a scented candle on the window sill and fresh pink towels hung on the chrome rail above the radiator.

'Oh, Dad, thanks so much.' Ali's voice wobbled with emotion. 'You've made a proper haven for Grace and me.'

'Thanks for adding value to my house!' I laughed, unable to believe the transformation in such a short time. 'Now, if you could just do the rest of the house by tomorrow, that would be fab!'

Anne had brought up ice-cold champagne and we all clinked glasses.

'Here's to our new life in the Single Mums' Mansion!'

8

Familiar Face, New Friend

I fought against the January arctic drizzle, the formidable pushchair my shield against the rain, perfect conditions for the first day back to school after the Christmas break. On any given day when this kind of weather prevailed, I would normally have walked back to the house after dropping Isla at school and then driven Meg to nursery. But, oh no, not today. Today I would walk, because, well, just because a stubborn urge hunkered down and refused to budge. And I needed to start listening to my intuition, believe in myself again, just like Natalie had said.

'Want to go in the car, Mummy!' Meg cried as I announced the new order of events.

'No, Meg, we're walking.'

'It's wet!' she sobbed, and ground to a halt outside school, a sure-fire harbinger of a shit fit brewing. Instead of giving in and trudging back to the car, a spark of anger ignited.

'No, Meg, we're walking.'

'Don't want to walk!' she screamed, and some of the other parents filing past on their way to work looked at me pityingly.

'Look, Meg, I really want to walk. It's not that wet. Jump in the back of the pushchair and I will push you.' Sonny was cosy and dry under the rain hood, so it made no difference to him in his steamed-up plastic bubble. Meg's saucer eyes overflowed with tears and her huge pudding cheeks wobbled as she worked up into a temper, even though I had offered an alternative. Hug her, a voice echoed in my head, just hug her. It doesn't mean you have lost. Even though I wanted to throw a fit myself because no one ever listened to me – and why did everything have to be a fight? – I surrendered to the know-it-all voice and bent down and hugged her. *Just for today I will not be angry.* Her little body stiffened inside her pink puffa jacket; I could tell she felt hesitant. Usually our roles were clearly defined. She would start having a strop about nothing, I would be patient for about ten seconds and then I would irrefutably get cross and sometimes (always) shout and the entire thing would blow up into a mushroom cloud of doom. The scenario customarily concluded with me lying on a bed of nails for the rest of the day wanting to gouge my eyes out because I was a useless twat.

Hugging Meg instead of firing off admonishments was definitely following the road less travelled. She melted into the hug and her muffled sobs slowed. My anger dissolved, tears stung the back of my eyes and my heart filled with love for this little person who was tricky, but actually very like me. I made a pact to start Reikiing the children at bedtime that evening.

'I love you, Meg,' I whispered into her ear. 'Even when you get cross, and even if I shout, I still love you. I always will. Do you understand?' She nodded her head inside her fluffy hood.

'Mummy, can I get in the pushchair now?'

I nodded and my heart hurt for her. I didn't tell her I loved her enough. I started silently chanting the Reiki principles, in an attempt to ingrain them into my psyche, when inside my mind's eye a cine film projected a scene of a nicely spoken woman I used to be friendly with at Baby Music. I could see her children, too, Joe and Neve. The vision was bathed in a sepia tint and she was laughing and hugging the children. I didn't even know her name, which was odd because we had been going to the same music group for a few years, and we were pregnant with our second babies at the same time. Every week we would chat animatedly, but for reasons unknown to both of us, we never ever asked what each other's names were or met for coffee.

'Why am I thinking about her?' I asked the rain as I trundled on down the hill towards nursery. I dropped Meg, giving her an extra hard hug and kiss, and turned round for my return journey home. I looked up from my gloved hands on the pushchair and spotted a tiny figure at the top of the road, wrapped up in a black trench coat, tottering down the hill and I knew instinctively it was her. As she got nearer, her startling blond hair poked out from under her umbrella and her face broke into a smile.

'Hello!' she said brightly. 'I haven't seen you for ages. How have you been? Is this Sonny? Wow, he's big now.' She bent down and peered in through his steamed-up rain hood.

'Yes, I'm OK. How are you?'

'Oh, I'm all right. Lovely to see you, though. I'm just popping down to Lordship Lane to get some bits. Look, why don't we go for coffee one day? We can have a proper catch-up.'

'I'm free Wednesday evenings and every other weekend, or I can meet you in the day. Next Monday after I drop Meg?'

'Oh, me, too, with the weekends. This is going to sound stupid, but what's your name?' she asked, looking embarrassed.

'I'm so glad you said that because I have no idea what your name is either!' We both started laughing, a bit too hysterically.

'Jacqui Snowden. I feel like we're at school!'

'Me, too. I'm Amanda Wilkie. Shall we exchange numbers?'

She pulled out a flash new iPhone from her bag, and I scrabbled around for my Nokia brick in my pocket and punched in her digits.

'Listen, I've got to dash, but I mean it about meeting up. I'd love to hear what you've been up to and how the kids are.' And she leaned in and gave me an affectionate hug and kissed my cheek, then set off down the hill. I'd been home alone about an hour when my phone pinged.

Are you single?

Yes! I thought you might be too!

So did I. When you said every other weekend that's when I realised.

My phone rang immediately.

'Hello,' Jacqui said. 'I'm just walking back home.'

'Where do you live?' I asked.

'At the top of Underhill Road.'

'You must walk right past my house! Have you got time to pop in?'

'Give me your address.'

Ten minutes later there was a knock on the door.

'Come in.' Sonny was having his morning nap in his room and there was a rare air of calm eclipsing downstairs.

'Wow, the wallpaper!'

'I know. It's an original seventies horror story.'

'But it feels in keeping. It's very bohemian. This must have been glorious at one time.' I laughed. 'Gosh, sorry, I didn't mean it like that! I meant back in the day, when it was at its peak. All the cornicing and ceiling roses are amazing. People pay a fortune for them. The developers who did my house had to buy them in.'

'Don't worry, I know exactly what you mean. That's how I feel and that's why we bought it. If I don't have to sell it in the divorce, one day maybe I will get to finish it. First World problems and all that. I know I'm incredibly lucky to have a house at all in my situation.'

I led her into the kitchen at the back.

'Oh, your kitchen is wonderful. I love all that pale blue with the bright yellows. Did you do all this? Gorgeous tiles.'

'Yes, when we moved in this room was massive but a dark cave with no light, so we put the glass doors on the end and opened it all up.'

'My kitchen is a very similar layout but it's in my basement. I didn't do it. It was like it when I moved in last month.'

'You only just moved house?'

'Yes, I'll tell you all about it.'

'Tea?'

'Yes, please.'

While Jacqui inspected my metal dresser openly displaying my nan's mismatched floral bone china, dining plates, vintage cake tins, jars of pasta and pulses, I sorted mugs.

'Your house is so homey and colourful. My kitchen is all white – I love the kids' playroom over there.'

'Well, we hadn't got loads of money so we painted the cabinets ourselves. It's all done very cheaply. The floor's reclaimed boards because the originals were all rotting.'

'You did a good job; I hate DIY. I always manage to cock it up.' I laughed. 'I also loathe ornaments in my house, but you've managed to get everything in its place. My house is bare, very uncluttered. But I like this.'

'Thank you.' I handed her a tea in one of the surviving mugs that had evaded the massacre.

'So, tell me what happened. You're going through a divorce, too?'

I nodded and shared my tale of woe.

'He ran off with that woman off the telly?'

'Yes. I'm only telling you because I can't tell anyone else in case they blab to the press, and I have a feeling you're trustworthy. No one else knows, apart from my friend Ali and my parents and another friend, Mel.'

'That doesn't sound like no one to me.'

'You know what I mean.'

'So, when will the divorce start going through?'

'I only filed before Christmas. My mum gave me a lecture about getting it started before he has kids, which made me want to vom.' I sipped my tea and contemplated opening the chocolate biscuits I'd squirrelled away. 'So how come you moved house? Did Simon make you sell for the divorce?'

'No. I wanted to. I couldn't stay there. It felt too emotional, too many memories. I knew he was shagging his PA – I found the emails – but I have no idea what he's doing now, if he's still with her. He sees the kids but we don't talk about what happened, not after I begged him to stay. He just went.'

'What, he just left there and then? Didn't even explain, or try, or do anything?'

'Nope, just upped and left with a suitcase. Said he would come back for the rest.'

'What did you do?'

'I got down on my hands and knees and held his feet so he couldn't go. It was awful. So traumatic. I've never broken up with someone before. I still can't get my head around it. Now I don't think he ever loved me. He was ticking a box.'

'I'm sure that's not true.'

'I don't know. It's how I felt after I tried to make him stay, just to talk it through. He waited until my sister arrived because I was in a right state, and then he left, completely cold. The kids were crying. My mum and sister didn't know what to do. But at least they were there. I also had people at school saying, "Well, at least you get every other weekend off to do what you want. A nice little break."'

'Fuck me, people have said that to me, too, and I have literally wanted to kick their FUCKING heads in! Don't you think I would rather have my family back together and my children happy than having every other weekend free to drink myself into a dark hole? Stupid fuckers.'

'Who're stupid fuckers?' Ali wandered into the kitchen carrying Grace, her hair stuck up in a shagger's clump at opposing angles so she had clearly just woken up from a sneaky nap.

'Other people who say aren't we lucky to have time off from our kids when they go to their dads.'

'Oh my God, who says that? I will punch their fucking faces in!'

Jacqui started laughing.

'Oh, Ali, meet Jacqui, she's one of us.'

'What, superior beings?'

'Yes!' Jacqui agreed animatedly.

'No, she is also a single mum.'

'It must be catching. How do you know each other?' And so we explained.

'This is so strange because up until a few hours ago, I was the only single mum I knew. Now suddenly I know you two.' Jacqui beamed like she had won a full house at the bingo, only she was far too posh to enter a bingo hall.

'I live in the attic like Anne Frank,' Ali admitted, smoothing down her errant hair. 'Well, until my house is sold, which could be years in this recession.'

'I think that's lovely,' Jacqui said. 'I would love to have someone help me with the kids and share a bottle of wine in the evenings.'

'Well, you can come here any time you like!' I could feel an indefinable difference, as if something had clicked into place.

'Look, I've adored meeting with you girls. I don't have anyone to talk to about this stuff. No one else really understands what it's like, do they?' Ali and I both shook our heads. 'If you're around for coffee, we could meet up and get the kids together? I know my two would love to see you all.'

'We'd love to!' Ali cried, like she and I were a married couple ourselves.

After Jacqui had left, I told Ali about my Beardy Weirdy vision on the way to nursery.

'What are the chances of any of that happening, you witch?'

'But what are the chances of Jim leaving you so soon after Sam left me, and then me bumping into Jacqui, who I never really knew but always liked? What if I had never gone to Baby Music all those years ago? I almost drove home when I was sat outside in the car with Isla because I knew no one, but something forced me to go inside. Natalie said there are no such things as coincidences. This was predestined: we were meant to be friends and then adopt Jacqui. The universe has been silently nudging us together all this time.'

'Like a witches' coven?' Ali marvelled.

'Yes, like *The Witches of Eastwick*. Weren't they all shat on by men and then doubled their power?'

'The Witches of East Dulwich! *Double, double, toil and trouble.*'

9

Lipstick Putting the Bins Out

'Oh my God, it's too early.' I blindly clawed around for my phone on the desk next to the bed before it vibrated onto the floor, the ringing hammering inside my skull.

'Have I woken you?' Sam's voice blasted into my ear. Sonny was curled up next to me, having woken screaming at two in the morning.

'Yes. What's happened? Why are you ringing me at five thirty in the morning?'

'Sorry. I just wanted to warn you that you might get doorstepped. Someone's sold a story to the papers.'

I was instantly awake, the news injecting adrenalin into my eyeballs.

'Who?'

'Carrie's ex.'

'Why would anyone want to doorstep *me*?' I whispered.

'Because technically you're still my wife and mother of our kids, and Carrie is currently riding high as Channel Four's big success. She's got a book deal and another series in the bag. She's a celebrity.'

Excuse me while I flap my pompoms and execute a particularly nifty sideways split.

'No comment,' I said.

'Is there anyone outside?' I asked as Ali peered through the shutters in the front room, all the lights off so no one could see us. I had woken her at six.

'I can't tell; it's still dark. It's so early. It's not like Carrie's a politician, is it, caught with her pants down giving a male stripper a blow job? She's just a fucking TV chef.'

'No, you're right.'

'Come on, let's look on the internet and see what it says.'

'Probably nothing.' However, I was wrong: the scandal was springing up all over cyberspace.

'TV Star Chef Carrie Bags Sexy Married Camera Man.'

Ali read on one website as we sat shivering side by side at the living-room table, the heating yet to come on.

'I don't know if I can read it,' I admitted, feeling mildly nauseous. 'I'm going to make tea. Do you want one?' The children were all still asleep, even Grace.

'Do you want me to read it out to you?' Ali asked.

'No, thanks. I think I'll just ignore it. Maybe I'll give it a go in ten years' time when this is funny and they've got divorced, she's got fat and Sam is bald.'

'This Alex guy sounds very bitter!' Ali commented when she'd finished reading. 'I know you don't want to know, but I could summarise – it's quite interesting!'

'Go on.'

'Apparently he and Carrie were actually going to get married next year. They had a date, a venue, everything.'

'Sam said they were kind of engaged. Very different from actually getting married.'

'Yep! Anyway, he found out about Sam and Carrie when he walked in on her snogging him in the loo at work.'

'No way! He worked with them both?'

'Yes! Talk about shitting on your own doorstep.'

'Poor guy. I bet he was gutted. But still, doing a kiss-and-tell is pretty shitey.'

'I bet they paid him megabucks for it. He looks a bit like Sam, too. She obviously has a type!'

'You're not going on the school run looking like that?' Ali's face creased into a critical frown at breakfast an hour later.

'What's wrong with this?' The kids were eating Nutella on toast and Ali was breastfeeding Grace while I whirled round grabbing book bags and making Meg's packed lunch for nursery.

'You're wearing leggings and a hoodie; the same ones you've worn for two days.'

'I always wear this. It's just the school run.'

'No, it isn't. It might be a fashion show where you're going to be pitched against Carrie Stone, the husband stealer. The wronged wife needs to look glamorous, not like a bag lady. What if there *is* a pap waiting?'

I was torn between my hatred of fakery and the need for some one-upmanship.

'Is this all you have? Where are all your clothes?' One-upmanship won by a slim margin. Ali fingered the pathetic offerings in one of the built-in wardrobes that stood proud either side of the fireplace in my bedroom. The other one was empty, having been Sam's. He'd left behind his black vampire cape from one of our many dressing-up parties and it hung like a solitary funeral shroud above the rolled-up spare duvet.

'Yes. My other clothes are in the shops. There're some jumpers in the chests of drawers.'

'Come with me. This won't do.'

I followed her up to the attic room where she lay Grace down on the crumpled duvet and kneeled on the floor, reached under the bed and heaved out a lidded plastic box rammed with shopping bags, her secret haul of unreturned clothes from photo shoots.

'See what's in there.' She thrust a Topshop bag at me. I peered in and eased out a gold lamé dress; it slipped like mercury through my fingers.

'I think this is a bit much for the school run.'

'Keep it, though. Better for Sainsbury's. Try that one.' Inside the trendy brown paper bag was a pair of grey skinny jeans and a hipster-style, black polo-neck jumper with knitted frills curled round each shoulder, like tiny crimped beetles' wings.

'Yes, wear that!'

I stood before her while she added some blusher, forced me to curl my lashes and apply mascara and smoothed down my hair.

'Right, a bit of lip gloss and you're ready to face the paps. Wear my leather biker jacket, too. That parka is vile.'

'Ooooh, Mummy! You look pretty,' Isla cooed as I rounded up everyone for the infernal hell that was teeth brushing. 'I like your jumper. You look like a ninja.'

'Good luck.' Ali waved me off as I trudged down the drive to take Isla to school, my eyes on stalks, waiting to be ambushed at any moment. We'd practised saying 'No comment' since daybreak. But there wasn't a sniff of any journalists, and again when I returned from dropping Meg.

'You were right,' I said to Ali just before I collected Meg from nursery that afternoon. 'Carrie's no politician shagging a sheep. It will all blow over.'

We got back and Meg hopped down from her car seat and joined me on the pavement outside the house, clutching her gorilla. I locked the car, grabbed her hand, but just as we reached the gate a woman approached me.

'Amanda Patterson?'

I turned to face her. She was very young with blond hair scraped back in a slick high ponytail. She looked like she was about to go off horse riding in her skin-tight black jeans and navy peacoat.

'My name's Amanda Wilkie.'

'Hello, my name's Fiona Walker. I'm from the *Daily Mail*.' I abruptly turned from her and stormed to the house, pulling Meg behind me.

'You're hurting me, Mummy.' I couldn't find my keys. That's when I remembered they were on the hall table. I'd automatically thrown them there when I had brought Isla home. I started ferociously banging on the door.

'I believe your husband left you for TV chef Carrie Stone. We wondered if you wanted to give your side of the story. We'll pay you.'

Just for today I will not be angry. Just for today I will be kind to all living things, even scumbag journos.

'No, thanks.'

'Are you sure. It would give you a chance to say your piece, clear the air. Apparently, your husband and Carrie are just about to buy a house in Clapham with enough bedrooms for all your children.' That lit the fuse.

'Get out of my garden. Get the fuck away from me and my kids. If you come here again I will call the police!' Meg started crying. The front door swung open and Ali stood there with a glass of wine in her hand. She looked nonplussed. Then it dawned on her.

'The paps!'

'No, just scumbag journalists.'

'Here's my card,' Fiona attempted to offer it to me. 'If you change your mind, you'll know where to find me.'

'I said I'd call the police! I won't change my mind.'

'You heard her!' Ali shouted, getting in on the act. 'Get off our land!' She flattened herself against the wall so Meg and I could squeeze past.

'Are you Ms Wilkie's lesbian girlfriend?' Fiona brazenly asked, finagling for a scoop, her Dictaphone held aloft.

'Yes, I am! We're madly in love. Stick that in your paper.' And just as she was shutting the door, Ali threw her glass of red wine at Fiona, soaking her posh navy coat and splashing her in the face. I was too stunned about the house revelation to laugh at the absurdity, and collapsed on the bottom stair in the hallway, feeling like I needed to pull an arrow from my heart as Meg howled next to me.

'Spurned Wife in Carrie Love Triangle Has Lesbian Lover.'

Jacqui read out from the *Mail* the next morning after the school run. Joe, dressed in his beloved Chelsea kit, was very sweetly showing Sonny how to pass a football in the garden, keeping them both out of earshot. Running alongside the sparse feature where a 'source' confirmed we were indeed together, was a series of photos of me and Ali taking Sonny and Grace to the park, their faces blurred out, and a final picture of Ali throwing wine and swearing at the journalist. 'Oh my God, ladies, you can sue them for that.'

'We can't. Ali shouted that she was my lover at the reporter. Straight from the horse's mouth!'

Rob had had a field day.

I always knew you were a lesbian.

He'd texted earlier.

You can join my gang properly now!

'Well, who cares if you're lesbians or not? Let people believe it.'

'We're not, Jacqui. Ali was joking.'

Just then Ali hurtled into the kitchen like a tornado, raging incoherently.

'I want to go round there and throw eggs. I need to smash something. Can I key his car?' she pleaded, her eyes laced with lunacy. She threw down Grace's sheepskin and laid her on it next to Jacqui's feet.

'What's happened? I'm assuming Jim.'

'He just emailed to say he's accepted an offer on the house.'

'Oh, wow, it's sold very quickly,' Jacqui cried. 'What's the problem?'

'He took the first offer, which is stupidly low, without asking me.'

'But it has to be both of you agreeing,' I pointed out.

'The mortgage is in his name and because we were engaged when we bought it, not married, I have no say.' Ali was shaking and pulling her hands desperately through her slicked-back hair. 'I'm fucked.'

'How so?' Jacqui asked. 'Did you put money into the house?'

'Yes, I paid all the money from the sale of my flat into it.

It was a lot. He said my money covered the lawyer's fees, searches and other shit. And also, my share of the payment for renovations.'

'What? You should have made money on that house. It was a wreck when you bought it.'

'We hardly made any money. We put in all new windows just before he left, then the market bombed. We won't get that money back from the sale. He must be keeping some to get somewhere with her.'

'I'm sorry, but none of this is legal. He threw you out on the street, gives you the bare minimum maintenance and now won't give you what's rightfully yours. You have to threaten him with legal action.'

'I'm going to threaten him with something else.'

She whipped her phone out of her jeans back pocket and stalked into the living room. Jacqui and I looked apprehensively at each other.

'This won't end well,' I hissed. We cocked our ears towards the doors to listen in.

'Jim, you can't do this. You owe me my money. I paid the mortgage. It's not legal!' I could hear his indecipherable tinny reply from my chair.

'Well, I'm stopping all visitation rights as of today. You don't get to see Grace.' More tin can raging. 'Fuck you, I can do whatever I like. I'm her mother! I don't want Hattie having anything to do with her. Fuck!' She stormed back into the kitchen, pinpricks of fiery colour anointing each cheek. 'He slammed the phone down on me before letting me know I would be hearing from his lawyer.'

'You can't stop visitation rights, though,' I explained. 'That's also not right. You need to go about this the right way if you're going to get your money.'

'Fuck that! I can't afford to do that. He has all my money. I'm going to go and change the locks on the house and hold it hostage.'

'Ali! That's also illegal! You have to be the bigger person here because he never will be. I know it's unfair, but the last thing you need now is to make it worse by keying his car or posting a turd through his letter box. Revenge is a dish best served cold.'

'How about eggs, though? I could throw them at his car?'

'No! Imagine white light round you to try and calm down.'

'Fuck white light! I need to break something!'

'In that case I have something that might help...'

'How come you have these?' Jacqui asked as we stood facing the fence that adjoined next-door's back garden. Grace was tucked away in the safety of the kitchen in her bouncy chair looking through the glass doors, and Joe and Sonny had commenced a marathon TV session watching a digger DVD.

'When I was terrified of giving birth to Sonny, I went to see a hypnotist. Meg's birth had been so awful I didn't think I would cope at home again, so sought some help to rise above the pain.'

'You are mental, you know that,' Jacqui laughed. 'You could have just gone to hospital and had an epidural.'

'I hate hospitals. I wanted to be at home.'

Ali rolled her eyes. 'I don't get what sponges have to do with pain. Were they for mopping your brow?' she asked. 'Why would you need ten?'

'No, nothing to do with birth. After we went through hypnobirthing techniques I confessed that I thought I was a shit mum 'cos I shouted so much.'

'You don't!' Ali dutifully protested.

'I do! You always miss it because you're upstairs and can't hear it. It's like an airlock up there. Isla once drew a picture of me and I was an angry sneer, no arms or legs, just a red screaming face. I felt shit. So instead of shouting, the hypno lady said I could get these sponges, soak them with water and throw them at the fence.'

'Did you?'

'Don't be stupid. I didn't have time to fill up a fucking bucket, cart it out here and throw sponges. I would only have to clear them up and that added another chore on the ever-present to-do list. I just carried on shouting and hating myself even more.'

'Useful technique then!' Jacqui remarked. 'So, shall we give it a go?'

'I'm glad I didn't key Jim's car. But this just feels silly.'

'The rage will still be there. Best get it out.'

'OK.' Ali threw the sponge like a total wimp and it fell short of the fence, landing with a pathetic plop on the grass.

'That was rubbish! Try harder. Jim traded you in for a younger model, remember, lied to you, is selling the house from underneath you and won't pay you proper maintenance.'

'Thanks. He's vile. I HATE YOU, Jim Bradfield, you fucking cock!' The sponge soared through the air and smacked against the fence, making it shudder, water exploding from it in a satisfying cascade.

'I want to do it again!' Ali bent down into the bucket and retrieved another sponge. 'This is for shagging that slag Hattie Sloan!'

I dipped my hand into the icy-cold water, dug my fingers into a floppy sponge and whipped it out. Who was it for? What was it for? Ali stared at me, eyebrows raised, a smirk skimming the corner of her lips.

'This is for leaving your kids, lying to me, running off with a fifties throwback, killing my sex drive, and forcing me to be a single parent. I DIDN'T SIGN UP FOR THIS SHIT!' *Whooomph!*

'Yeah!' Jacqui cried, clapping her hands in glee. 'You tell him! Can I do one?' She delved into the bucket of truth for her sponge. 'This is for shagging your PA and breaking my heart, ruining our lives and trying to take my money! You won't win, motherfucker! See you in court!' *Splat!*

'Holy fuck, Jacqui! You're going to court?' Ali gasped.

'Yes, in a few months.'

'Shit, that's awful.'

'My lawyer says it'll be OK, so I'm not worried. Moving on. Who's next?'

'What are you doing?' Our neighbour, Philippa, poked her head over the garden fence.

'Sticking it to the men!' Ali said jubilantly.

'Oh, what a good idea! I wish I had thought of that years ago. Go on, do another one. Don't mind me. It can be like some sort of observational study for my course.' Philippa was one of those neighbours that made you feel like you had won life's lottery. Neighbours can make or break your life when you live cheek by jowl, so having 'normal' ones should actually add to your resale value.

Estate agent: 'Yes, we have four bedrooms, two bathrooms, south-facing garden, through lounge and kitchen-diner. But the *pièce de résistance* are the neighbours. Here's the printout about them; as you can see *they're normal...*'

It was yet another example of the universe working its creative magic and softening the blow for my journey into single parenthood. I knew that if the shit hit the fan, Philippa was always next door as back-up. She had recently started training to be a psychotherapist. There was every chance I was a useful unofficial case study, proof that the universe was a two-way street.

'This is for making me go back to work when I was still bleeding!' Ali let rip with a roar when she sent that one flying. 'And this is for telling me crying made me ugly.'

'Tosser!' I yelled as the sponge pugnaciously slapped the fence.

'I think I need to do one!' Philippa cried through the fence. 'Pass me one, please. I can throw it at my side.'

Ali handed her a sopping sponge. We all squeezed together so we could see through the hole in the trellis.

Philippa drew her arm back slowly like a baseball pitcher and carefully aimed to the left of our faces.

'That's for all the untold hurt you selfish men-children cause when you leave women and kids to pursue your own happiness. Makes my blood boil! Argh!' *Whoomp!*

'Go, Philippa!' we cried in unison.

'Oh, that felt cleansing!' She retrieved the sponge and handed it back. 'You girls are amazing, you know that, don't you? You're doing such a hard job. Never forget that. I don't know how you do it. I only have one and that's hard enough. These kids need you to be OK. I'm going to suggest Sponge Therapy as a viable option for anger management. Could be the next big thing.'

10

Blast from the Past

March arrived on a bitter easterly wind and instead of delivering Mary Poppins to our door, Jim's treacherous lawyer's letter landed hand in hand with my showdown at mediation. Like Ishmael hunting down the giant whale, I felt I was stalking my anger with a single weary harpoon. I was angry at everything. Jim for shitting all over Ali, leaving her depleted and with no fight left. Sam for abandoning me with our three offspring to bring up pretty much on my own, then in mediation saying I contributed nothing financially for our entire marriage, baiting me like an injured bear. I bought half the house, you fucking dickwipe! I screamed silently in my head while I clenched the blue celestite crystal Mel had posted to aid my rudimentary negotiation skills.

However, his below-the-belt tactics touched a nerve. I was cross at myself for not returning to work properly after having the kids so I wouldn't be reliant solely on maintenance payments to bolster my paltry earnings. I could go on for days aiming that harpoon, but deep down I knew it wasn't constructive and I was extremely lucky to have a roof over my head after mediation.

Sonny had started at a child minder one day a week, paid for by tax credits, and I spent that time staring into space and trying to keep my flame of inspiration alive for the book idea as well as editing the odd manuscript old freelance contacts threw my way. I needed another job…

'What about DJ-ing?' Ali said one day, when she found me, head in hands at the living-room table, writer's block forcing my recalcitrant brain into headless chicken mode. 'You and Amy are so good at it.'

They broke the mould when they created Amy. She invented quirky, with her bright red hair tumbling down to her waist, a sly shaved strip round one ear preventing the style appearing conventional. Her clothes were mercurial thrift-shop finds teamed with vintage Topshop, some of the pieces thirty years old. She had a good eye for the unusual. No leggings and baggy jumpers for her.

'I haven't done that for years.' I gestured to my dejected turntables buried under haphazard piles of paper, left to gather dust when once they'd gathered disco sparkle. 'Who is going to want an almost forty-year-old female DJ when everything is computerised and played by kids who don't even know what a record is?'

'Vinyl is cool again – it says so in all the magazines. You would be retro in a hipster way. I'd love you to DJ for my birthday. Please? I'm going to have it at that place where I had it last year.'

'Will you play some Spice Girls for me?' Jacqui begged before the party officially started.

'No!' both Amy and I cried in unison. Sam and I had ventured out here a few times on the rare occasions we had managed to escape the house before Sonny was born. It had been a lively new opening on the Nappy Valley high street, a refreshing change from the gastro pubs and throngs of curry houses. It promised trendy salmagundi mezze platters and exotic cocktails created by expert mixologists, while on the decks DJs spun their own brand of musical magic, all the while attempting to seduce the punters into believing they had jetted off to New York for the evening to party in a boxy warehouse with fake Eames chairs, black-and-white hip hop pictures plastering the walls, and smooth concrete floors to dance upon. The veneer cracked as soon as the bar staff opened their mouths and their south-east London twang spilled forth.

Ali looked spectacular in a little black dress and gold sparkling heels. Jacqui wore an alluring clinging red dress, her blond hair blow dried so perfectly she looked like a box-fresh Girl's World.

'Who's babysitting?' Amy asked Ali.

'Babs, Freya's old nanny, agreed to do it. She's the only person I would trust with Grace, apart from you lot, but you're all here!' It was the first time Ali had been out without Grace since she had been born. Isla, Meg and Sonny were with Sam.

I introduced Jacqui to Ursula, Ali's oldest friend, whilst Amy played the first record. As I was doing the rounds an unsettling feeling stole up behind me, prickling the back of my neck and shoulders. My palms began tingling with Reiki, like some sort of Beardy Weirdy warning signal. I tentatively looked round and my heart bounced right up into my throat. Woody was here.

I slipped urgently behind the decks, putting a physical barrier between us. I had no idea how to talk to him. How was he even here? Well, I knew how he'd got an invite – Ali or some of her other friends would have brought him with them – but I thought he was abroad.

'Have you seen—'

'Yes.' I cut Amy off.

'When was the last time you saw him?'

'I don't know.' I did know, though. It had been the day of my wedding. That was the last time I had properly seen him. After that, fleetingly at other weddings with one of his many girlfriends, watching him self-destruct with drink and drugs. My friend Rob didn't like him, even though he wasn't averse to snaffling pills and dancing all night in gay clubs himself. I idly wondered if he'd already spotted him from among his cluster of flamboyant friends hiding out by the sofas at the back.

'It's his attitude. He would laugh while watching Rome burn.' I knew what Rob meant, having witnessed Woody stealing a golf buggy at one wedding when Isla was three months old. He drove it over the golf course next to the hotel where everyone was staying and crashed it into the pond at one in the morning, abandoning it there. We all knew he had done it, but he somehow managed to evade any kind of official reprimand, just like he always did.

Tall and good-looking in a matinée idol kind of way, with dark shaggy hair, bleached at the tips from sailing, and perfectly white teeth, he could have been an actor, or someone famous just for being themselves. He had that magnetic quality that made people stop what they were doing and stare. But the sheen that radiated off him had definitely dulled over the years as the constant partying chipped away at it, so that now he was a faded pastiche of his former glory.

'I wonder where he's been,' Amy said in between records. We'd found our groove and even though it was early on in the evening, people were dragging each other into the space in front of the decks that sufficed as a dance floor, whenever a tune caught them.

'Hopefully, rehab!' I laughed, trying to disguise my unease at his appearance here tonight.

'Well, yeah, you would hope so! I still would, though!'

As the evening wore on and the tempo picked up Amy and I didn't have time to gossip. People thrust drinks at us and we gladly accepted them though we didn't have time to get drunk. The bar manager came over at one point.

'You ladies are great. Do you do this often?'

'Yes, and we're looking for a residency,' Amy enthused, silencing my protests with a sharp kick of her green wedge heel.

'Good stuff. Well, come and chat after.'

'Amy!'

'Amanda!'

'What did you do that for?'

'Because it would be fun. And you need a distraction. You said after mediation that you needed a job.'

'But not this!'

'Why not? You have every other weekend off!'

I couldn't think of an answer, so I chastised her another way.

'Hurry, we need to find Salt-N-Pepa!'

Jacqui had acquired an admirer, a nice-looking young guy out with a group of friends who were all dancing and giving Amy and me the thumbs up every time a floor filler blasted out. Ali was enjoying being the centre of attention, dancing in a massive mêlée of friends and hulking boys who all looked like they had been bussed in from the local rugby club. The evening was flowing nicely until I felt a light tap on my elbow while bending down over my record box at the side of the decks. I stood up clutching a copy of Britney Spears' 'Toxic'. Exceedingly apt.

'How have you been doing?' Woody asked me, raising his voice above the music. He kept his hands jammed in his pockets. I took in his clothes – nice jeans, a navy shirt, work boots.

'OK. How are you?'

'I was really sorry to hear about you and Sam. I was very shocked. Everyone was, *is*.'

'Yeah, well, so was I. It's been shit.'

'I'm not surprised. How are the kids? How old is the little one now?'

'Sonny? He's going to be two in a few weeks' time.'

'Wow. Are they OK?'

'Not really, no. They don't really understand.'

'Can I get you a drink?'

I gestured towards the full bottle of wine underneath the table and the queue of other drinks lined up patiently beside it.

'Ah. OK.' He didn't know what to say after that.

'Look, I've got to go. It's all kicking off on the dance floor.'

'Sure. Great job, by the way. You always were good on those wheels of steel!'

I watched him retreat back into the crowd and Ali hugged him, welcoming him into the inner circle buzzing round her. His best friend, Will, was there with his wife, Sarah, all friends of Ali and Sam's from way back. Will thrust a beer at him and he drained it in one go. I sighed.

'Quick, we need Britney!' Amy shouted, and I jumped to it, ripping the twelve inch out of its sleeve and jigging it onto the spindle, plopping the needle down gently and listening in the headphones for the beginning of the track. Britney echoed out of the speakers and onto the dance floor as more people barged in from the bar area at the front, drunkenly singing the words and sloshing wine down unsuspecting people's backs.

Confusion reigned at the end of the night. The bar emptied its revellers onto the street, bouncers in long black overcoats shepherded the crowds out like sheep, drinks forlornly abandoned only to be scooped up by efficient bar staff desperate to get home to bed or take the party elsewhere.

'Those girls are with me!' I cried to the lady bouncer and she stepped back, allowing Jacqui and Ali to stay. Jacqui was still dancing in a corner, the nice boy nowhere to be seen.

'Are you OK?' I asked as Amy packed up the records and unplugged the iPod.

'What? Me? I'm fab!' Jacqui laughed. 'What we doing next? I love you gals, you're the best. I don't know what I'd do without you, you know that? No one else understands my life.'

'Did someone give you something?' I asked, the absence of irises giving rise to suspicion.

'What? Nooooooooo!' she cooed theatrically.

'Ali? What's going on?' Ali's eyeballs were popping alarmingly out of her head, too. 'Did you both have *drugs*?' I hissed.

Ali started laughing. 'Maybe.'

'Oh, shit. Are you OK?'

'Yes. I want to dance, though. Can we have a party back at the house?'

'I'm going to kill Woody.' I ran out onto the pavement. Everyone was still milling around, smoking and chatting, ignoring the bouncers, who kept trying to move them on. As the cold air hit me, the drinks I had speed-drunk at the end of the evening fired up in my blood stream, walloping me flat in the face. I spotted Woody having a fag with Will, Sarah nowhere to be seen.

'Can I have a word?' I slurred quite badly, blinking to keep my eyes straight.

Woody looked down at me quizzically. 'Sure, what's got your goat?'

'Have you given Ali and my friend Jacqui pills? They're both wasted.'

'You look quite wasted yourself.'

'I'm not!' I protested indignantly, treading on the back of my dress whilst trying to steady myself.

'They're big girls,' Woody said laughing. 'Surely they can look after themselves.'

'Oh, whatever. You're right, none of my business. Have a great night!' And I huffed off back towards the bar to order a cab back home.

'Hey, Amanda!' Woody caught my shoulder and I shrugged him off. 'It wasn't me. I promise.'

'It doesn't matter. I don't care who it was.'

'You did when you thought it was me.'

'I was just cross. And you seemed the most likely person. It's Jacqui's first time out with everyone and she's never done anything stronger than wine before.'

'Oh.'

'Yes, exactly.'

'I think Will gave her some MDMA.'

'Fucking brilliant. And Ali is breastfeeding and shouldn't be doing anything other than wine.'

He looked shamefaced.

'Well, all I can say is it will wear off soon. They hardly had anything. It's Will's, not mine. I have no idea how strong it is. I didn't have any.'

That wasn't reassuring. 'I've got to get them home now.'

'I'll come and help. I can carry the records.'

'No, it's fine.'

'No, it isn't. I feel bad because I knew what was happening. I'll come.' He bid goodbye to Will and followed me back inside, waved through by the bouncers.

'I love you, and I love you too, Wooden,' Jacqui enthused for the millionth time as I made cheese on toast in the kitchen at three a.m., my hangover starting to tear at my head and insides.

'Woody,' he repeated patiently.

'That's what I said, Wooden.'

I glanced at Woody and he smirked, taking a sip of his freshly made tea. He didn't seem drunk.

The low lights underneath the cupboards had transformed the kitchen into an illicit late-night bar where Jacqui and Ali sipped red wine from an already open bottle. Tealights twinkled in the vintage teacups on the dresser and on the shelf underneath my decks.

'Can we have some dance music on?' Ali asked, bopping to a bass only she could hear.

'Oooh, yes, please, can we? Any Spice Girls, though?' Jacqui joined in.

'NO! What about Babs? She might wake up.' Babs had agreed to stay over until seven a.m.

'OK. Can we have some chill-out music on instead…?'

At four a.m., Woody and I put Jacqui in Meg's room and Ali in Isla's.

'But I'm not tired,' Ali griped.

'You will be when you have to make up bottles at seven.'

'I did them already,' she said smugly, giving up on the fight and lying down, surrounded by teddies, a giant Dumbo the elephant standing guard at the end of the single bed.

'Well, you still have to be on duty and you have to express all your milk for a few days.'

'OK, Mum!'

Jacqui was already gently snoring. I was hoping the post-comedown cheese on toast would soak up all the chemicals. I felt responsible for her falling down the rabbit hole on my watch.

'They'll be OK,' Woody assured me, reading my mind. 'I don't think they're going to die in their sleep.'

'Thanks for helping. I don't know how I would have managed to get them, plus all the records, home on my own.'

Woody smiled, melting my stomach. Oh, no! I thought I was numb below the waist and this discovery, instead of instilling me with hope, left me feeling like a flustered sixth-former. *Not Woody…*

'Do you want another tea?' I managed to squeak out, certain he would be picking up clues from the heat I could feel rising up my chest and tingling my cheeks.

'I'll make it. Do you want one?'

'Yes, please,' I yawned, eyeing my bed through the open door.

'Go and lie down; I'll bring it up.'

I hardly heard the tap of the tea being set down on my desk next to the bed. Awakened libido or not, the late hour had me in its grasp.

'Thanks,' I mumbled, the weight of sleep pressing my body down into the bed, strange dreams and visions dancing round the periphery of the darkness, waiting to pounce the minute I surrendered. The bed dipped under his weight as he sat on the edge near my feet.

'I'll drink my tea, then go,' he said quietly, his voice bringing me back to the room.

I opened my eyes to find his directed on me. Immediately, he looked away.

'You seem better,' I said, for want of something to say.

'Well, I had a kind of breakdown a few years ago.'

'Oh, I had no idea.'

'No, I didn't tell anyone apart from Will and Sarah. I was away taking a boat to St Lucia from Antigua for this guy, and I hadn't slept for days. Partying, you know...' I did know. It was all he ever did. I had no idea how he sustained it and where he found the money. 'And I lost the plot. Wanted to jump in the sea to get away from it all. One of the crew had to sit on me. Anyway, I came home and have been staying with Mum in Essex ever since, working for one of Dad's mates in the building industry, doing a bit of carpentry and then sailing the rest of the time. I go out occasionally.'

'Oh. So it must be quite hard coming up to London to see people if they're all still caning it.'

'No, everyone's got kids now. They do it for a laugh now and then, but it's not every weekend, and every day.'

'Do you still go mad?'

'Not like I used to.' He drained his tea. 'I saw that bird Sam's with on telly. Well, it was all over the papers. She was on *Loose Women*.'

'Urgh,' was all I could come up with. I had ignored all the press attention after the big reveal. I knew if I started looking, I would never stop and would be consumed with checking every little thing online. *The Journey* had brought me back to the present every time I was tempted to take a peek; its major message of *Don't Gossip* flashing up in huge theatrical lights inside my head. *Don't put energy where it doesn't need to be. Let the universe take care of things.* The times I had looked with Ali, when we'd had too many wines, always ended up with me almost regurgitating my dinner/breakfast/lunch at the sight of Carrie, renamed 'Thunder Thighs' due to her overly curvaceous bottom.

'What were *you* doing watching *Loose Women*?'

'I didn't have anything else to do. I was just flicking. Will and Sarah have met her.'

I could feel tears sting the corner of my eyes. And this is where it starts, I thought. The slippery slope before I am permanently wiped from people's memories as Sam's wife.

'Oh God, sorry. I'm shit. Sorry. Oh, Amanda.'

The tears flowed properly. I couldn't find the energy to wipe them away and alcohol always made everything worse. Woody jumped up and lay next to me, pulling me in for a hug. He smelled faintly of cigarettes and some fresh citrusy aftershave that plucked a memory from the deep recesses of my brain, a stolen kiss from another life.

'Me and my big mouth,' he whispered into my hair. We lay like that for a while as I calmed down, his presence comfortingly familiar on Sam's side of the bed.

'I'm fine. Sorry for crying. It's still, you know, a bit raw.'

'Don't apologise.' He pulled away and patted my hair away from my face, some of it stuck damply to my cheek. 'I think he's mad.'

I smiled weakly.

'If I was married to you...'

'Woody...' My breath caught in my throat. 'Don't go there.' His face was right in my eyeline, his leonine eyes searching mine. He leaned in and kissed me chastely on the lips. I closed my eyes, a whole brass band marching in my stomach. 'I think you should go.'

'Yes. Look, do you have my number?'

I shook my head.

'I still have yours. I'll send you a text. I'm away for a while next week.'

'Oh, that's good. Sailing?'

'Yes. I have a job out in Antigua for a few months. I'd love to see you before I go?'

I shook my head. His eyes drooped.

'OK. Well, look after yourself, and get some sleep. I can let myself out.' He ruffled my hair and disappeared downstairs.

I heard the front door close quietly as sleep crept up, ushering in the tantalising dreams about Sam and me still being together.

11

King Herod's Wife

'He's living with her, and he never told me,' Jacqui squeezed out between sobs. 'I knew it. The spineless twat.' This was the first time I had seen, or rather heard, Jacqui fully let her defences down. She wore a steely air of sang-froid compared to Ali and me, our bleeding hearts pinned to our sleeves.

Her divorce made mine seem like one of those joyful wet Sunday afternoon films with inclusive smiles, warm hugs and puppy dogs. A wise person once said, if a group of people threw their problems up in the air, they would race to catch their own rather than their neighbours'. The same applies to divorce. As much as I hated my situation and everything it threw at me, I would so much rather deal with it than have to deal with Jacqui's.

'Are you at home? I'm just at Sainsbury's but can come to yours. I'll leave the trolley; I'm still in the veg aisle.'

'No, I'm outside the court having a fag. I can't believe it, Mands. He stood up in court and brazenly said he would tell the truth, and when the judge asked where he was currently living and who with, he said he was living with her.'

'The woman who sent the emails?'

'Becky, yes.'

'Oh, Jacqui. I'm so sorry.'

Sonny started crying and, being ill-prepared, I hadn't brought any snacks with which to plug the building noise.

'Dad, Dad, Dad.' He wanted to get out, but I knew if I scooped him out and let him loose on the shop floor, I would get zero shopping done so I started to manically push the trolley one-handedly towards the baby aisle.

'Do you need to go?' she asked as Sonny turned up the volume when he realised he was stuck fast in his metal cage of a trolley seat. I was always having nightmares about snapping his legs off when I yanked him out of those things like a poor rabbit in a poacher's trap. They hadn't improved since I had sat in them in the seventies.

'No, I'm just about to shoplift some rice cakes.'

'Oh, what, the extortionate apple organic ones?'

'Those very same.'

'I always nick them too, stuff the wrapper in one of the freezers.'

'That's what I do!' We had a brief comic relief before Jacqui remembered she was the wronged woman. I ripped open the rice cakes and Sonny clapped his hands together like a seal awaiting its mackerel fillet. Silence prevailed once more.

'So, Simon is officially living with Becky?'

'Yes. He didn't even seem embarrassed. He had denied everything up until now.'

'You never really explained why this needed to go to court.'

Jacqui was very self-contained. It didn't surprise me, really, as we had only been firm friends now since January and Sam and I were about to hit the first anniversary of our splitting up in May.

'Simon went after half of my inheritance. I received it after he left. All of us sisters got a share of it.'

'But he left you! He isn't entitled to anything after he left, surely.'

'That's not what the court thought. They awarded it to him.' She started crying again. 'How could they? He has a new life and is buying a house. He said he needed the money to make the split fair, to buy this house with *her*! The kids and I are left heartbroken. Joe is in speech therapy because he can't talk properly and won't eat, possibly because his dad left, and I've been called up to the school about Neve because she has been crying in class. He has moved on while I'm still picking up the pieces for all three of us. It's shit. I hate him!'

'Oh, Jacqui. I wish I was there with you. You should have told me. I would have come with you today and taken Sonny to his child minder.'

'I didn't think this would be the outcome. My lawyer said we would win so I thought I would be OK. But seeing him acting all hard done by in the dock made me want to scream across the court how he's ruined our lives.'

'Look, as soon as you can leave, come round. Bring the kids. I can make them pasta and we can just all slump in front of the telly until bedtime. Don't be on your own.' Silence. 'Jax, are you still there?'

'I won't er, be on my own. I'm going out.'

'Oh, OK. Who with?'

'Tim.'

'Who's Tim?'

'That guy from Ali's birthday.' I failed to conjure him up from the blurry memory of that night. 'He's really cute. Loved your DJ-ing.'

'Oh, him! Where you going?'

'For dinner.'

'Wow, on a first date?'

'No, third date.'

'You are such a secret squirrel!'

'I know. I didn't want to say anything in case it was crap. But he's really nice.'

'Well, have an amazing time. Let me know how it goes. I'm working tomorrow but I'm around before I leave for Mel's on Friday.'

The Saturday morning after I'd arrived at Mel's, we headed out to attend an angel meditation workshop. 'It's for people who have a bit more experience, are either already healers or want to be healers. We could give it a go. It might distract you from thinking about your single parent anniversary,' Mel had suggested on the phone before she booked it.

More people had been expected, but it was just us and one other, older lady (who kept giving me filthy looks) that turned up in the intimate room at the top of a Norman church in Western, a tiny picturesque village nestled in the heart of the scenic Downs. There was nowhere to hide at the back and mentally tally up a shopping list or think about lunch. My tummy rumbled hungrily, making Mel giggle.

'Now to welcome your angels into the room, imagine a white light shining down from above.'

Nikki, the lady leading the event, was truly out there. If we possessed Reiki, we had to open up our channels and connect with the universe. I could feel the energy in my hands shoot out and begin pulsing in my palms. 'Notice any subtle differences in your energy field. See if anything is trying to communicate with you.' The whole point of the workshop was to link into the same frequency as angels, which to me, now a card-carrying member of the Beardy Weirdy brigade, wasn't too hard to visualise.

On the Beardy Weirdy scale, this was at least an eight, but I had thought: what the hell, I'm open to anything on this weekend. I wasn't immune to inexplicable feelings or premonitions.

'I've just realised who you are!' the other woman, named Patricia, burst out as we took a break from mind-expanding exploration. We had apparently tuned in to our guardian angels and, despite the subject matter, I felt myself easily accepting its dogma, keeping my mind open to new experiences. This, along with all the other alternatives on the Beardy Weirdy spectrum, served as my somewhat outlandish coping mechanism for facing a situation I had no emotional contingency fund for.

'You were Herod's wife at the Crucifixion!' I looked at Nikki and then back to Patricia, whose eyes had toned down their flinty glare. 'I was Mary Magdalene.'

'Oh, yes, you *were* Herod's wife. I can see you now with your crown,' Nikki agreed wholeheartedly. 'I was there, too. I was one of the priests.'

'I'm sorry. How on earth was I there?' We had suddenly flown from an eight to a ten, leapfrogging over number nine.

'We all were. Well, it's believed in many healing circles that a huge cross-section of people were all in attendance at the Crucifixion of Christ. From major players to bystanders, we all had a part to play.'

'Was I there?' Mel asked Nikki in a thoughtful tone.

'Yes, you were an embalmer. You prepared Jesus's body.' The seriousness with which Patricia disclosed this snippet lent it gravitas I wasn't sure it deserved.

'You don't believe, do you?' Patricia asked me, not unkindly.

'I don't know. How was I there, though?'

'In a former life. Do you believe in past lives?'

'Yes, I do. But to be Herod's wife – that's pretty mad. Why me?'

'Why not you? Do you like a man who can fix things with his hands? Someone who is good at making things out of wood?'

'Yes. My ex-husband was amazing at carpentry. It was a major reason why I found him attractive.'

'There you go. Jesus was a carpenter. Herod's wife didn't want him to die. You like a carpenter; you've carried that love through from then. This may be why you feel so stuck and can't move on from the split. You need to accept what has been before.'

Or maybe it is because I really loved him to the moon and back and just wanted to stay married.

'What do you reckon to all that?' I asked later as we wandered to Mel's car parked down a side street. The gentle heat of spring fluttered on the breeze as we strolled past whimsical walled gardens populated by a few squat gnomes, the brick cottages and statuesque houses all draped with wisteria and climbing roses, their heady scent tickling our noses. I always felt a tug in the very centre of my being when I returned to this part of Sussex, like an ancient mariner must feel the draw of the sea from his bath chair, knowing he will never sail again.

Mel was silent.

'You believe it, don't you? I don't think I do. How could I have been there?'

'Now, don't freak out, but I have a recurring dream that I work in a morgue. I've had it for years!'

'But that doesn't mean anything.'

'I know, but when she said that, I kept getting nasty whiffs of chemicals out of nowhere. It made my eyes sting. And that other woman really did seem convinced.'

'Great, so tomorrow is not only the shit anniversary, I am also the wife of a despot who killed Jesus Christ. I didn't think this weekend could get any worse. I'm probably doomed for all eternity.'

'Oh, Jeez, will you look where I parked.'

I started laughing and thought I wouldn't be able to stop. The car was directly outside an undertaker's.

'Now, if that isn't a sign I don't know what is.'

'So that means I was definitely Herod's wife.'

'And the message is: avoid all men who are good with their hands, just in case your relationship crucifies itself.'

'Amen to that!'

I awoke in Imogen's girlie bedroom. Posters of plastic popstars adorned the purple flowery walls and a violet butterfly duvet cover cocooned me in her cosy single bed. The hilarity of yesterday was forgotten as fear sluiced round the base of my stomach once more. Sometimes it disappeared for days, especially when Ali and I got into a companionable groove and felt like we were winning at life. It was in the quiet moments that it found me, creeping in through the half-open back door, cooing, 'Hey, I'm here, remember me?' I always bargained with it, with the universe and ultimately with myself.

'If I write one thousand words today, take the fear away.'

'If I manage not to shout today, the fear won't come back.'

'If I meet someone else, that will get rid of it, won't it?'

But I didn't want anyone else. Even a whole year later, I only wanted Sam. I knew my window for bargaining with him had closed a long time ago, so all I was left with was my own pathetic game of don't step on the cracks.

I got up and padded softly downstairs to the kitchen in order to make a cup of tea. I didn't want to wake anyone. Sun streamed in through the tiny lead-patterned window at the top of the stairs, dust specks twirling in time with the birds tweeting an unusually loud post-dawn chorus.

'Oh, hello.' Mel was sitting at the weathered kitchen table nursing a cup of tea and reading a book.

'Gosh, I didn't expect to see you here.'

'This is my house!'

'I know. I just thought you would still be in bed.'

'No. I've been awake for hours. I have a meeting with suppliers tomorrow and it's playing on my mind.' Mel's cottage industry of Himalayan salt scrubs had proliferated and now she was branching out into beautifully scented candles, supplying local shops and some well-heeled London boutiques. 'How are you feeling?'

'Oh, you know, the fear's returned.'

'It's bound to today. I think you have to be gentle with yourself, remember you're a queen!'

'Ha. I know. Well, I must steer clear of men who are good with their hands. Oh…'

'What?'

'Something freaky has just hit me.'

'To do with the meditation?'

'Kind of. A man who's good with his hands.' Sweat beaded in my armpits.

'Tell me. I didn't know you'd met anyone. You've been keeping it quiet if you have.'

'Let me make tea and then I'll tell you. It's made me feel a bit sick.'

As I automatically poured water and stirred my tea bag, I heard the kids come downstairs and head to the living room to switch on the TV. I plonked down opposite Mel, the radio rumbled in the background, eighties hits competing for my attention.

'There's this man from years ago. He's one of Sam and Ali's friends from uni, though I know Sam doesn't see him any more. He went off the rails and kind of fell from grace.'

'Have I met him?'

I nodded.

'Was he the really, really drunk one at your wedding, the one who carried you across the dance floor telling everyone he loved you?'

'Yes.'

'He was very good-looking, but mad.'

'Exactly. Well, when I first started going out with Sam, we spent a lot of time with Woody. He worked near me, and Sam and him were good friends. We had a few nutty weekends away with them all, Ali included. After one crazy weekend, he came and met me at work for lunch and confessed he liked me and asked if I felt the same.'

'What?! You never told me!'

'I didn't tell anyone. It freaked me out.'

'Because you *did* like him…'

'Yes and no. He was dangerous and handsome, and he always had different glamorous girlfriends, and on one of those outrageous weekends, he kissed me in a dark corner when we were all off our tits on ecstasy, but I pushed him away.'

'Wow. Did Sam ever know?'

I shook my head.

'Was it any good? What did you say?'

'I said no. The kiss was pretty sexy, actually, hence my fear. He said he knew there was a spark. And I said you can have sparks with all sorts of people but choose not to ignite them. I asked him why he would even think of asking me, with Sam being a good friend, and he didn't seem to care. And that snapped me out of any little secret passion I'd harboured for him. I saw him for what he was, a self-regarding druggy narcissist who was only interested in his own gratification. All his behaviour after that just confirmed it.'

'OK, but why is this relevant now?'

'He turned up at Ali's birthday party, all sensible after a breakdown, seems to be on the up and no longer mad.'

'Don't tell me, the spark was still there.'

I slowly nodded.

'Did he just think he could waltz back in and take up where Sam had left off?'

'No, but I think if I had let him stay the night, something might have happened.'

'Not might, definitely.' Mel slapped her forehead. 'Holy Herod, is he a carpenter?'

'Yes. It's like a red rag to a bull. I never knew he did stuff like that, but I suppose skippering boats you have to be practical, and his dad has run building firms for years. It's in his blood.'

'What are you going to do?'

'Nothing! If that angel workshop flagged up anything, it was to run a mile from men with manual skills.'

'But you don't have to marry him, you could just have sex and see what happens?'

'I know, but what if a disaster occurs?' I wrung my hands.

'It's just sex. You'll be fine.'

'But it's never just sex. Anyway, I think I'm safe. He's away now for months and I won't bump into him.'

'Well, you could do this instead and order someone non-carpenter related!' Mel lifted up the book she had been reading.

'What's that?'

'It's a book on Cosmic Ordering. I got it last week. Mad Nikki told me about it. We could go through it before you leave and both order something! It's Beardy Weirdy, of course!'

'So, what do we do?'

'Well, I've skim-read it. I don't honestly think it needs a whole book, but it's called the Law of Attraction. It's all about how positivity travels on a high frequency, a bit like the angels yesterday. Negativity travels on a low frequency. In order to tap into the positive frequency and attract those things to us that we want, we have to be and think positive. That's putting it simply.'

'Like a magnet? Just attract good things?' I had read about it in *The Journey* and various other books.

'Yes, but more than that, you have to feel it, act like you already have the thing you have asked for. Be very specific. If you ask for a new pair of shoes to make their way towards you, make sure you ask for the right colour, right size, type, etc.'

'And how long does it take?'

'You can set a time limit, or not; it's up to you. But once you wish for it you have to trust that it will happen. Don't keep asking. You wouldn't keep sending Amazon emails when they've told you your book is on its way, would you?'

'So, I'm going to have to play hard to get with my own brain? Double bluff that I almost don't care if the thing happens, but at the same time feel like I already have the thing?'

'Exactly!'

'Come on, let's do an experiment! I want to shag Ryan Reynolds. Can I ask for that?'

'No! No specific people, or changing people's behaviour. You can ask for someone *like* Ryan Reynolds. Write down all the attributes you would like a man to have and ask that he is delivered to your door.'

'Hmm, I think the last thing I need is a man. How about a job? I need a job. Something to do alongside writing, to bump up tax credits, editing and maintenance payments.'

'Write it down and ask then. Put the paper somewhere safe and be grateful when you ask.'

So I did exactly that, folding the piece of paper inside my diary in my handbag.

'And don't think about it,' were Mel's last words on the subject.

12

Cosmic Shopping List

'She wasn't a patch on you,' Rob loyally sucked up over the phone. 'She's not warped; we won't be best friends.' Carrie was officially meeting everyone, like a debutante during the Season. Gossip reached me via the jungle drums almost weekly. It left me distracted and on the back foot, never knowing which friend would report meeting her next.

Amid my distraction I'd taken my eyes off the ball with Meg and she'd slipped somewhere I couldn't reach her. Weekly spats turned into daily hours of screaming and febrile tantrums. Her darkness had won.

'I think she's finally realised Sam is never coming back,' Mel said down the phone. 'And she's feeding off you feeling so stuck.'

One evening at bedtime when I was guest of honour at my own pathetic pity party, Meg just followed me round the kitchen hitting me, my violent shadow. By some superhuman effort, I didn't retaliate but roughly seized her and dumped her in the garden instead. She grabbed a brick from under the patio bench and hurled it at the glass doors. She was four. How did she lift a brick? Ali was generally upstairs dealing with settling Grace when Meg descended into one of her maelstroms, so I was largely left to my very limited devices of shouting and bargaining, which proved fruitless. But this evening was different. There would be no bargaining.

'Right, that's it. I HAVE HAD ENOUGH. I HATE YOU. YOU MAKE MY LIFE HELL. YOU MAKE YOUR LIFE HELL. THIS HAS TO STOP NOW!' The relief was monumental. The fact that I had screamed something gutturally repulsive directly in her face with such force that gobs of spit smacked her cheek was beside the point. Deep down, I knew what the sensible plan was. It was to listen, holding her in a strait-jacket arm-hold until the rage blew itself out, but I had nothing left to offer. It was all I could do. And it was shit. I was shit.

Chug was in his cot crying inconsolably, no doubt scared by the shouting. Isla was in her bed, probably hugging Emily, her lavender heat-up bear. Meg was just crying now, her anger spent, like mine. Someone urgently banged on the front door. I wiped my eyes and stalked off, leaving Meg sobbing. I wasn't cut out for this kind of parenting. Why couldn't it be innocent potato prints and baking fairy cakes instead of a fucking war zone?

Philippa from next door was standing there, an empathetic look on her face.

'Can I come in?'

I nodded silently, too scared of what might slip involuntarily out of my mouth. I ran upstairs and grabbed Sonny from his cot. He was hysterical and desperate for a cuddle. I dashed back down to the kitchen were Meg remained bawling.

'Hello, Meg,' Philippa said in a low sympathetic voice, the voice I imagined she used with her clients. 'What's up?' She grabbed a tissue from the side and handed it to her. When she didn't take it, she wiped her eyes and nose, which were streaming. Meg let her, a miracle in itself. She stopped crying immediately. 'Does she need some milk or something?' Philippa asked as she turned towards me.

'Yes, I'll get it.' I rummaged in the plastic tat drawer where plates, bowls, sippy cups, babies' bottles and random take-away cartons fought for space with the Tupperware, place mats and ice-lolly moulds.

I poured Meg's rice milk into her pink sippy cup and handed it to her.

'We can hear what goes on when we're in the garden,' Philippa said looking me in the eye. 'I'm not judging at all, but do you need help? How is Sam with you about what's going on? Does she behave like this at his?'

'She has tantrums with him, but saves the worst ones for me.'

'That will be because she feels safe with you.'

'She threw a brick at the back door.' Philippa winced. 'I don't know what to do. Who to talk to. My parents think she will grow out of it, but I think it's getting worse.'

'I think you both need help. You're dealing with three on your own, and you have another baby here too and I know you help a lot with her. It's only just a year since Sam left and he's in his new house and all moved on, though I bet he isn't. I bet it's hard for him, too.'

'Good. I want it to be.'

'Of course you do. But you need to help this little girl. I know I'm sticking my nose in, but you sound like you're all in so much pain I had to come and see if you were OK.'

I caved in and the tears arrived.

'I'm such a shit mum. All I can think about is how broken I feel.' At this point Ali wandered into the kitchen, an empty bottle in her hand.

'Oh God, what's happened? Hi, Philippa.'

'Meg threw a brick at the back door and had been attacking Amanda for the last half-hour at least.'

'Mands, why didn't you call up the stairs?' Ali gasped. 'I can't hear anything up there. I had no idea.'

'You're not a shit mum, Amanda. You're just pushed to your edge, and this is the time to sort it out before it gets worse.'

'Oh, Mands, you're not shit. I don't know how you juggle them all and just get out of the house. You have so much to deal with, and you have me here in the way.'

'I want you here,' I sobbed. 'It stops me from feeling alone. I haven't even written any of my book now for ages. There's nothing inside me any more.' Ali came over and hugged me while I sobbed all over her shoulder.

'I've finished,' Meg said, and handed me the empty cup. 'Can I go to bed now?'

When I came back down to the kitchen after putting Meg and Chug to bed (Isla was awake and needed reassuring all was OK) I was wrung out. Philippa was getting ready to leave.

'Thanks for coming round. I'm sorry you have to live next door to this madhouse.'

'You're not mad, well, only a little bit. It makes our lives far more interesting being here.' She smiled. 'Ring your health visitor tomorrow. The waiting list for counselling is long, but I know that some children's centres can get you in quicker. Be sure to tell them how desperate you feel. Because you're on your own, it might speed things up.'

'Wine?' Ali suggested after Philippa had left, grabbing two glasses before I had even answered. 'Do you want to talk about Meg?'

'No. I'm done. All I keep thinking is that she wouldn't be this bad if I was more together. But I'm not.'

'But you seem it.'

'I'm not, Ali. I feel dead inside. I don't feel like I will ever recover from Sam's betrayal.'

'But you do all this Beardy Weirdy stuff. It helps, doesn't it? Your Reiki has helped me! And those crystals you got me, I do feel like they keep me calmer than I ought to be.'

'I feel stuck. I feel like I need something to change. *I* need to change.'

'I think you need to have sex.'

'The thought makes me feel sick.'

'You need someone you really fancy. Come on, let's do some of that Cosmic Ordering. Get your weird spell book out, too, and send out a charm to bring us hot men.'

'But who will want me? Someone with three tiny kids and one of them who's turned feral. I wouldn't want to date me!'

'Shut up! Drink your wine and let's write shit down. We're going to order some men! Then we'll pull a Tarot card just to see who's going to turn up.'

Dear Universe

I would like to meet someone who is really into me for a change, who accepts that I have children, who is funny, good-looking, and is willing to fit into my life. Oh, and they have to have a decent cock.

Light and love,

Amanda

Dear Universe

I would like to meet someone who treats me well, who is a bit of a rock star, exciting, loves going out and having fun. Doesn't mind that I am a single mum, likes sex, has a big cock, likes going out for dinner and is looking for a relationship. It would be good if he was rich too as I have no money. But if you get me my money from the house then that would be even better!

Love,

Alison

'The Hierophant.' Ali thrust the card at me, showing a picture of an older learned-looking man on a throne.

I thumbed through the Tarot Bible, not yet *au fait* with the meanings of all the cards, this being our new obsession in the house. 'Hmm, it could mean someone quite conventional, also someone who is a guru, and quite clever, I think. Maybe you'll meet a brain surgeon?' I shuffled the cards and one fell from the pack.

'It's a sign!' Ali cried. 'The Devil? That's not good!'

'Hmm, let me see...' I read the page. 'The Devil could mean that I might be led astray by someone, or someone is controlling. Or I'll act without awareness of consequences to my actions. It also flags up addictions.'

'You're going to go on a rampage and start having one-night stands and meet loads of bad boys.'

My phone started ringing in the kitchen. It was Amy.

'Love, guess what! The bar where we DJ-ed for Ali's birthday want us to start a residency. Isn't that brilliant?'

13

Be Careful What You Wish For

'No one's dancing! What if no one ever dances and we're left standing here like idiots until two a.m.? What if I have to play "Agadoo"? What if we're actually shit and it's only in the rich fantasy world inside our heads that we're any good at all?'

'Flipping ball sacks, love, will you lighten up! It must be exhausting being you! It's still early, a lot of our crowd are staying in because of the wedding tomorrow. It will liven up as soon as some of the pubs chuck out further down the road.'

'But that twat asked for some awful teenage chart music, something Isla would like.'

'Chill! Look people are just having after-work drinks; no one wants to dance yet. Let's massage them slowly without them realising. I'll put on some old soul classics and Stevie Wonder. You can come in later with the big guns. I've advertised it all over our Facebook page. I reckon some fans will wheedle their way out of the woodwork.' Amy winked at me and placed the needle on a single, looking every inch the cool-headed disco diva in her vintage silver shoulder-padded crop top and high-waisted green flares. The wall of fairy lights draped artfully behind bathed us in a flattering halo, disguising our age, which was rather higher than the clientele's.

Amy was right. I knew all that; I knew how to DJ. It was embedded into my psyche that you never launch your whoppers in one go at the beginning – first rule of DJ-ing. But apart from Ali's birthday I hadn't DJ-ed for years and I think my nerve had deserted me. Hadn't I asked for this, sent out an epistle into the universe for a job I could fit around my writing and the kids?

'Excuse me, do you DJ here often?' I looked up from flicking hastily through my record box to find a sweaty young kid, probably early twenties, possibly drunk, bending over next to my face, his breath a potent combination of stale garlic and beer; I recoiled.

'Yes, all the time. You're in my space, though. Do you mind backing off?'

'Sorry, but I was wondering if you could play some decent house music, not this shit you're playing. No one likes it.'

I unfurled and drew straight up to my full height, taller because of my vertiginous black cork wedges. The dance floor writhed, a snake pit of busting out moves and grooves, hands waving in the air with Jacqui, the undisputed Dancing Queen, bopping right in the centre with her boss from work. Ali was at home babysitting so I could work, but also keeping herself in reserve for tomorrow's big lash – Rachel and Justin's wedding. I wasn't invited. It was one of the many events where people had had to choose between ex-wife and new girlfriend. I lost out this time and I guessed that was how it was going to be from now on as people picked sides. Fighting off self-pity, I refused to be upset at my inaugural paid DJ gig.

'Are you seeing something I'm not?' I asked the sad little boy berating our music, levelly eyeballing him. Amy glanced over from where she was changing records.

'You OK?' she mouthed; the music was too loud for me to hear her from even a few feet away.

'Yes! This boy thinks the music's shit!' I shouted to try and make myself heard. She stepped over my handbag, which had fallen on the floor from its protective hidey hole under the table.

'You think it's shit?' she challenged him.

'Well, no, but we don't like it.'

'Who's we?'

'My friends.' He pointed to some boys whose testicles had yet to descend, huddled by the toilet door, necking beers. They were the only motionless people in this part of the bar.

'Well, I think everyone else here likes it.'

'I want you to play some rave. Get the tunes out. Decent stuff. Not this shitty hip hop disco crap.' I inspected him properly and he gurned so badly his jaw nearly dislocated.

'Listen, pipsqueak, I was raving while you were sat in your nan's conservatory eating Jammy Dodgers. Unless you can be constructive and polite I suggest you go back to your friends and chew your own face off. Goodbye.'

'I was only asking.'

'No you weren't, you were being hostile,' Amy said. 'We're playing what we're being paid to play. If you hate it that much, go somewhere else.' I contorted my face into a snarl until he slunk off, his tail between his legs. 'Nice put down, by the way. Though he looks more like a chocolate Hob Nob kind of boy.'

I soon forgot all about him as we appeared to be having a successful night until a kerfuffle broke out behind. I spun round on my haunches and came face to black-trouser-clad knee with one of the bouncers. He was getting a grip on the raver whom Woody had in a headlock.

'What the fuck!' I jumped up.

'This little shit was taking pictures of your bum sticking out of your hot pants. He was going to twang your thong and those idiots were recording him,' Woody explained loudly.

'I was just messing around.'

'Would you do that to your sister?' Woody reprimanded him.

'I don't have a sister.'

'All right, your mum?'

'No, her bum isn't as good as hers.' He was laughing and I could see Woody flinch. The bouncer grabbed him before Woody could get arrested for death by asphyxiation and marched him out, the dance floor parting like the Red Sea, his chastened gaggle of mates dallying behind through the crowd.

'Hey!' Amy cried as she slipped on another record. Once it was cued up, she slid off her headphones and came over, kissing Woody on the cheeks. 'So you came, then!'

'You knew he was coming?' I looked suspiciously from one to the other. Was something going on with them?

'Yeah, he said he would on the Facebook page. If you actually used Facebook, you would know that.'

'You getting into fights again?' Jacqui laughed, popping out of the crowd. 'Oh, hello. I can't remember your name but I'm sure we've met.'

'He really likes you,' Jacqui hissed in my ear as I monitored the cheese on toast bubbling like molten lava under the grill.

'No he doesn't.'

'He came on his own to see you play.'

'He came with Will.'

'Will left early to go to bed in prep for the wedding. Woody stayed on.'

'That's because he doesn't like to miss a party.'

'Why don't you give him a chance?'

'It will end up in a mess.'

'You don't know that. He likes you. He *really* likes you. Look, he keeps staring at you. I wish someone would look at me the way he looks at you.' I caught his eye as he stood sipping tea with Amy by the decks where she was spinning some nice laid-back Northern Soul. He winked at me, making me blush.

'I'm dead inside.' But my goosebumps begged to differ.

'So you keep saying. But he might be able to give you mouth-to-mouth!' Jacqui cackled. 'You're so hard. I don't know how you can brush him off. I like having the odd night of mad sex with Tim, it breaks up the monotony of being a single mum. You should try it. Didn't you and Ali order men from the cosmos? Maybe this is it? He's arrived.'

'Woody? Nah, you know he's one of Sam's friends.'

'Does he still see Sam regularly? They best buds?' Jacqui asked pointedly, her hands on her hips, her lips pursed like a cross teacher.

'No.' I admitted sulkily. 'But he is good at carpentry.'

'Jesus – ha – you have to let that Herod thing go. You're just putting up blocks. Just see. I'm off to bed...' And she winked at me, just like Woody had. Jacqui had requisitioned the bed in Sam's old office as her crash pad when Meg was in her usual bed. She said she didn't mind the cobwebs. As I shut the door half an hour later on Amy getting into a cab, Woody stood at the bottom of the stairs with his coat on.

‘How will you get home?’ I asked wearily. ‘Why couldn’t you stay with Will? Taxis to Essex will be expensive.’

‘Every available nook and cranny is taken with people staying over from abroad for the wedding.’

‘Couldn’t you sleep on the washing line?’

‘I’m so tired I probably could.’

‘Look, you can stay, but on the sofa, down here.’

‘Are you sure?’

‘I’ll get you a spare duvet.’

14

Wedding Blues

'Amanda! Wake up!'

I peeled my eyes open feeling like I had only just got back to sleep. Ali was towering over me, her hair wrapped in a towel, Grace on her hip, waving what looked like a bill at me.

'What's up?' I groaned. It still felt like the middle of the night.

'I got a tax rebate! It's enough to be able to find a lawyer and fight cunt face for my money.'

I sat upright, grinning. 'Oh, that's so amazing! The universe delivered for you!'

'I know. All I need now is a hot man and I'm sorted. Seems like your Cosmic Ordering worked, too. Woody stayed last night, then?' Ali smirked. 'I didn't know he was your type.'

'He isn't. Nothing happened. There was no room at Will and Sarah's. Everyone's there for the wedding.'

'Did he try and kiss you?'

'No!' I tried to sound as horrified as I could. Too late, Jacqui was up and shuffled into my room, rubbing her eyes, still wearing full make-up.

'Don't listen to her,' she yawned. 'She's gagging for it with him. I think she needs to shag him and get it out of her system. He likes her.'

'*Does he?*'

'Don't sound surprised. I'm not an ugly sister from *Cinderella*.'

'No, you're more like the wicked heart-of-stone stepmother,' Jacqui quipped. 'Making that poor man sleep on the sofa when you have a super-king-size bed that no one has been in since Sam left.'

'Shut the door!' I cried. I didn't want Woody overhearing this.

'Do you and Woody have a thing going on?' Ali hissed. 'I mean, it's Woody!'

'I know. I keep trying to explain that to Jacqui.'

'I suppose he *is* hot,' Ali reluctantly admitted. 'And when he's not off his face, he's got some good chat. But he lives at home with his mum!'

'So?' Jacqui retaliated. 'He seems nice. You can't judge someone just because their life isn't going to plan, can you?' She emphatically stared at Ali.

'Sorry. You're right. Look at me, living in your attic with no pennies to my name.'

'Why don't you ask Woody to help today?' Jacqui went on. 'I bet he would. Then you could gauge how you feel. Like a test to see how he performs with all the children. Especially now Meg is ill.'

Meg had come down with a sore throat and temperature while I was at work. Ali had been up in the night with her and used up the last of the Calpol.

'I think it would be his idea of hell.'

'I disagree,' Jacqui retaliated. 'I'll pop down and see you

tomorrow with Joe and Neve. Neve's got some clothes for the girls – they can play dressing up while we have a gossip. I need to go and spruce up this hair for my date!' Her and Tim's casual friends with benefits arrangement did seem to be working for both of them. Perhaps she was right about occasional sex...

'Look, would you like me to stay?' Woody asked kindly while he stuffed the spare duvet back in its hiding place at the bottom of the wardrobe. 'To help you out. It's not going to be much fun on your own. You might stew about the wedding and forget to feed the kids or something...' He looked at me from underneath his shaggy fringe. I actually felt relief that he had offered. The thought of dealing with Grace and Sonny fighting for my attention while Meg was poorly had been weighing me down. Poor Isla would suffer and probably spend the day being overlooked.

'Well, if you're sure you're not busy?'

'I had an important appointment with *Football Focus*, but that's it really.'

'OK, thanks.' I spontaneously kissed him on his stubbly cheek, catching a waft of his unwashed man scent mingled with lingering cigarette smoke.

'What are we doing first?' he asked, sounding flustered.

'Well, could you go and get some Calpol, for a start?'

After Ali departed, looking totally stunning in a red knee-length chiffon shift dress, it was pretty much nonstop. Meg had to lie down on the sofa and I said they could watch a film, but Sonny kept wanting to get up and run around, annoying the girls. In the end Woody enticed Sonny outside to the garden and played football with him, something Sonny didn't do with me. He loved it and I caught Woody chasing him round and round the bottom part of the garden, lifting him up in the air and making him squeal. It brought a lump to my throat. He missed out on that regular man rough-and-tumble stuff; I was always too exhausted.

Late afternoon, I had a text from Ali.

> You're very much missed. I love you and we all wished you were here. I hope Grace is being good. xx

I didn't wish I was at the wedding, I just wished that it didn't matter.

As bedtime drew nearer, the madness it usually stirred up somehow didn't feel as scary now I had a wingman.

'I'm glad you're here,' I said to Woody as the kids all sat at the table eating a hotchpotch of sausages, garlic bread, cucumber and cheese. Grace had managed a big sleep in the afternoon and was therefore not too grizzly without Ali at teatime. 'I actually didn't know how I was going to achieve bedtime without jumping off the roof.'

'Mummy! Why would you do that?' Isla asked, shocked.

'Sorry, Baba, I was just joking.'

'Woody, are you married?' Isla asked him in her best job interview voice.

'No.'

'Do you want to get married?'

'I'm not sure. Maybe one day.'

'I never want to get married,' Isla declared. 'I think it's stupid.'

'Oh, how come?' I asked, intrigued.

'What if you don't like the person, you know, like you and Daddy? And then one of them leaves? It would make me sad like you, Mummy.'

'Just be friends then,' Woody casually answered, filling in the gap when I was stumped. 'Then you'll have nothing to worry about.'

'Like you and Mummy are friends?' Isla carried on.

'Yes, like us.' I couldn't look at him, so I busied myself with Grace, wiping her mouth until she pushed me away.

'Daddy and Carrie were friends for a long time. But just before they moved into the house, they realised that they loved each other.' Oh, the web of lies we weave…

'Oh, right. That's er… good?' I sneaked a peek at Woody, floundering in the conversational shallows.

'Well, not really. Mummy needs someone, too, to make it fair. It's not fair that Daddy's happy and Mummy's on her own, is it?'

'I'm fine on my own, Isla. I don't need anyone. Who wants chocolate cake?'

Small children's bedtime is akin to warfare against erratic dictators. Just when you think the peace process is complete, they change their capricious minds and the fighting breaks out once more.

'I don't want this cup. I want the pink one.' Scream.

'Dad, Dad, Dad, Dad, Dad!!!!!!' More milk required.

'I don't like this story. I want the one about the parrot.'

'Where's Emily? You said she was in my bed, she isn't. I can't sleep without her!' Dissolves into sobs.

'I want Mummy to read the story, not you.'

'Dad, Dad, Dad, Dad, Dad!!!!!' I want my digger in bed.

'Your phone has been going nuts,' Woody said when I returned from settling Grace with Reiki. 'I think Ali is trying to ring you.'

I checked and had three missed calls from her, so I rang her back.

'Hiiiiiiii! Howya doing?' She sounded wasted.

'All good. How are you?'

'I think I'm shitted. What time do I have to be home, Mum?'

'Before the morning! Why? When does Grace wake in the night?'

'About two, or three, depending… I met someone!'

'Oooh, who?'

'He's a newsreader! He's cute. And he's got my number.'

'That's good. Is there a wedding after-party?'

'Yeah, that's why I rang. He wants me to go. Everyone else is going.' I wondered if Sam and Carrie would be going.

'I met her,' Ali said suddenly sounding serious, tuning into my thoughts.

'And?'

'I love you. And she is not you. I wish you were here.'

I started crying down the phone.

'Oh, Mands, it feels wrong, him here with her because it should be you. We all said so. Everyone felt weird. But they all want you to know we love you so much. Ursula sends you a big kiss and says your cakes will always be her favourite!'

'S-sorry. I'm being pathetic. Why does it still hurt?'

'Because this is the first big thing. And he's moved on. I don't have to deal with this rubbed in my face because Jim isn't in my group of friends, but you do, and that's shite. Honestly, when Grace starts overnights, I will be worse than you; I'll probably slash Jim's tyres or something.'

'Look, have an amazing time. Stay out as long as you want. I will see to Grace if she wakes.'

'Thank you. You're amazing! I'll see you in the morning when I'm dying.'

I slumped back on the sofa, almost forgetting Woody

was there as I sobbed into my hands. 'When will it stop?' I pointlessly raged. 'I hate that I feel like this. I just wish divorce didn't take so long.'

'I'm sorry, Amanda. I don't know what to say.'

'Don't say anything. No one can make it better. Only I can, and I'm being shit. This has to stop.'

Woody grabbed my hand and squeezed it. 'Come here.' And he enveloped me in a hug, kissing the top of my head. I rested my ear on his chest and listened to his heartbeat beneath his shirt. 'Look, you're amazing, and kind, and it's fucking awful that Sam left. I've no idea how it feels and I don't know why he did it, but you're going to be OK. I know you are. And in the meantime, let me take you out somewhere. If you could go anywhere right now, where would you go?'

'We can't, we're in charge of four kids.'

'Pretend! Anywhere.'

I lifted my head and tilted my face up to his. He was smiling and the lava lamp caught the dangerous twinkle in his eyes.

'I'd like to go to Greece and sit on a beach and send my boring sadness away into the sea.'

'Then let's do it, let's go to Greece.'

'For real?'

'For real.'

'You have no money. Neither do I at the moment.'

'I do have money. I'm working back in Essex, doing carpentry and general building work. I've been saving. And I went to Antigua and got paid a wedge to sail that boat to its new owner.' I sat very still. Something untoward was happening. 'Say yes,' he whispered gently. 'Let me take you away. We could go in the summer.'

'Yes.'

The edges of his mouth curled up into a sexy smile and before I knew what I was doing, I kissed him. Softly at first, but when he realised what was happening he kissed me back, making my head swim. The door opened a crack and I'd invited him in.

15

That Wasn't Meant to Happen

'Oh, he was so funny. I didn't fancy him, but he grew on me because I kept laughing at everything he said.' Ali relived the wedding, while Grace clung to her mum like she didn't trust her not to disappear again. We slouched in the Habitat chairs, the nest of oriental bamboo occasional tables topped with coffee, toast, Marmite, scrambled eggs and ketchup. I had spotted the tables in the Cancer Research shop window recently and just had to add them to my menagerie of bad-taste objects.

It was a grey October morning, similar to the one when Ali had barged in a year ago, paving the way for the Single Mums' Mansion. How different things were now, yet somehow the same.

'Why haven't I heard of him if he reads the news?'

'Because it's on some financial channel. Bloomberg, where Justin works. They're friends.'

'Show me a picture.'

He was handsome in a suave newsreadery type of way.

'What's his name again?'

'Dara.'

'That's unusual.'

'Yes, he's half Indian, half English. He's so posh, too!'

'God, you must be like some common oik to him then. You going to see him again?'

'He seemed very keen and it would be nice to go on a proper date. I bet he doesn't ring, though, so it will be a bonus if he does.' Ali sipped her tea and crunched her toast. 'Thanks for having Grace. I can't believe she slept all night. She's never done that.'

'The magic of Reiki.'

'And how was it with Woody?'

'He's Mummy's friend,' Isla piped up from the living room where my three were crunching Nutella on white toast. 'He showed us how to make paper aeroplanes.'

'She has bat ears,' I hissed. 'Be careful.'

'Did you have fun with him?' Ali called through.

'Oh, yes. So did Mummy. We heard her laughing when they were downstairs.' I almost choked on my tea.

'What happened?' Ali whispered.

'You know…'

'Did you shag him?'

I nodded, feeling vaguely seasick at the thought. And not because my vagina was clenching in ecstasy at the thought of the unbridled sex marathon and couldn't wait for it to happen again, kind of sick (with extra butterflies and sweaty palms). This was nausea thinly disguised as creeping regret.

'And? Are you seeing him again? Reveal all! Actually, don't, wait until Jacqui is here and tell us both together.'

In the cold light of day with that bitch hindsight shining her smart-arse torch on the previous night's activities, I wished I had never let him help.

'Are you sure you want to do this here?' Woody had asked me as we ripped each other's clothes off like kids tearing Christmas wrapping paper, one ear trained on the door, listening out for the ritual crying that accompanied most bedtimes.

'Would upstairs be better? Can you lock the bedroom door?'

'No. Upstairs would be even more dangerous. They just come in my room whenever they like.' Write 'Buy lock' on ever-present to-do list.

'Right.' He let out a laboured sigh, lay back against the sofa cushions and dragged his fingers through his tousled hair like he'd just asserted some kind of superhuman restraint.

Even though I knew this was a bad idea, I couldn't ignore the fire within. Putting it bluntly, I wanted sex, and I wanted it now. It was almost irrelevant who it was with. My body had been in hibernation for so long I was practically a born-again virgin.

'Just fuck me. I don't care if they walk in. I haven't had sex for so long.'

'If the lady insists.'

'Just get on with it.'

So he did.

His smell, unwashed as it was, stoked my desire to fever pitch until the inevitable fumble for the condom.

'Where is it?' I gasped, pressing myself against him, reason a thing of the past.

'In my coat pocket in my wallet in the hall.'

'For fuck's sake, this is like *The Crystal Maze*. Have you got to find a time crystal before you can actually shag me?'

Woody burst out laughing. 'Yes! And I have to run around the house collecting as many as I can before we have our allocated session.'

'Well, hurry the fuck up and get on with it. I'll go off the idea and you'll have to start again.'

He leaped up and shoved the door wide. I could hear swearing as he rooted around in his coat. Please don't let one of the kids come to the top of the stairs. His huge erection would scar them for life.

'Ta da!'

'Don't rip it. Have you got any more?'

'No, I don't. I won't!'

I always hated this race against time – can the man get the condom on before the desperate urge to procreate has died a sudden death? Luckily, Woody was adept at the condom game and we resumed play without incident. I forgot all about the usual everyday worries when you're about to have sex for the first time in a trillion years: what if the kids walked in on us? Would I remember what to do or call him Sam by mistake? Would my fanny feel baggy after three children, and finally, would he even be able to find my vagina through the unkempt but lush vegetation that hadn't been pruned since Tony Blair had been Prime Minister? It was splendid. He actually kissed me, something Sam had avoided in the last few years of marriage. Sam's focus always seemed to be the end result. And it was always a good result – we were a perfect fit and had been from day one. There had been no getting used to each other, we had jumped straight in with fireworks from the word go. But over time, it had morphed into scratch-the-itch sex. Get-it-out-of-the-way-before-the kids-wake-up sex. Something I had vowed would never happen to us, just like every parent thinks they will never shout at their kids. It's as inevitable as night following day. I had forgotten how delicious kissing could be before and during sex.

'You're a good kisser,' I murmured as we moved rhythmically now on the carpet instead of the sofa.

'You're not so bad yourself.'

'Fuck me!' he gasped after we had both synchronised our happy endings. 'That was a surprise.'

'What was?' I lay there a bit stupefied, not used to having to chat after an orgasm. Rampant Rabbit wasn't much of a raconteur.

'Just all of it. The beginning, the middle and the end. It was pretty hot. *You*'re pretty hot…' And he brushed my hair off my face and kissed me tenderly on the lips. And that was when remorse rushed in as desire exited stage left.

'Would you like a cup of tea?' I asked, shifting myself away from him so I could escape. He looked a bit put out and I felt dreadful. I leaned down and kissed him on the lips but it now felt perfunctory. 'With biscuits, obviously.'

'Is that a euphemism?'

'Maybe. Or it could just be biscuits.'

'Yes, please to anything.' As I busied myself making tea in my dishevelled red and white stripy top and granny cardie, bare feet rammed into my Ugg boots, he slipped up behind me.

'I'm off.'

I turned around and he was already in his coat, shoes on ready to go. 'What about your tea?'

'Don't worry. I'll leave you to it. I know you're going to be up in the night with Grace and I don't want to get in the way.'

The words weren't there; I couldn't even half-heartedly dredge them up to reassure him he was wrong. He pecked me modestly on the cheek.

'I'll see you around.' I stood there, soggy teabag suspended mid-air on the teaspoon, mouth opening and closing, fishing for the right phrase.

'Yeah, OK. Thanks for helping me out.'

He didn't turn round, just ploughed on towards the front door, and raised a hand in acknowledgement of my appreciation. As the door shut behind him, I guiltily sighed in relief.

Jacqui never did materialise the next day.

'Do you think she's all right?' Ali asked. 'I mean, she had that all-day date with Tim; she was so excited about it. You don't think he murdered her, chopped her up into tiny bits and fed her to Alsatians, do you?'

'No! Have you texted her?'

'Yes, three times. You?

'Twice.'

'Shall I ring her?' Ali suggested it, like using the phone to actually talk to someone was an absurd concept. Which, essentially, it was. You only ever rang your family (or in my case, family and Mel) or when you had serious news, or you suspected the person was dead and just had to make sure. I nodded.

'Jacqui, it's Ali.' I could hear incoherent mumbling from the other line. 'Neve, can you tell Mummy we'll come now? Good girl.'

'Christ, what is it?'

'I don't know, but Neve answered. She said Mummy won't get out of bed and has been crying since they got home.'

16

The Mask Slips

'He's engaged.' Jacqui's eyes were open wounds. We rarely saw her without her face on; she wore it like armour, protecting against persistent childhood memories of bad acne. 'It makes me feel like me,' she once told me. 'I think I look horrendous without it; I have appalling skin.' The fact that she was easily the most stunning woman of everyone I knew said otherwise, but I understood what it was like when you can't see past limiting beliefs that have their roots securely embedded in childhood taunting. I'm not clever; I'm not good at maths; I'm rubbish at sports; I'm not creative; I'm not funny; I'm not brave; people think I'm boring; I'm fat; I'm ugly; my ears stick out (a particular favourite self-imposed belief from my own private collection). The list of what you are not could stretch into eternity. Beardy Weirdy lore would say burn that list and make a fresh one of all the things you really are, and make it good.

Neve peered gravely round the door frame of Jacqui's bedroom, earwigging.

'Can you go and check on the others for me, Neve?' I asked

her. 'I need you to help me here and be in charge. Can you do that?'

'Yes, sure,' she smiled, her face lighting up. 'Do you want me to get everyone some snacks?'

'That would be fab, thanks.'

'She's always listening at doors,' Jacqui said sadly. 'I don't think she can wait to grow up and escape being a child after what happened. She still begs not to go to Simon's, always asking what age she can make her own choice.'

'That's so shit!' Ali cried. 'She's only eight. She should be able to enjoy being a child.'

Grace was crawling across the floor and nosing in the understated and stylish monochrome en-suite bathroom while we flanked Jacqui on her bed of pain, heroines from a Jane Austen novel. The shutters were only half open and a few empty coffee cups lay abandoned on the white shabby chic bedside table.

Ali and I had only been inside Jacqui's house about three times; she always insisted on coming to ours. It was a beautiful semi-detached Victorian villa that teetered over three floors. She had bought it already done up to a high standard, ready to move straight in, but the whole house still felt rather transient. The sprawling basement kitchen was the only room where things were mostly unpacked. Boxes littered the corners of the other rooms, taped up in case their contents opened up a dialogue with any painful memories.

'What's up?' I probed gently. 'Don't tell me you've been in bed since it happened.'

'I have. I'm pathetic, aren't I?'

'Noooooo!' we both chimed at the same time.

'It's OK, I know I am.'

'So, how did he tell you?' Ali asked carefully.

'I met him at two in the Bishop and he was weird from the first moment. Kissed me on the cheek, instead of on the lips. He looked like he wanted to blab something before he got the drinks; he wouldn't let me get them, insisted he paid. Anyway, he said he had something to tell me.'

'Did you have any idea?' I asked while Jacqui steeled herself.

'No,' she squeaked. 'None whatsoever. He just came out with it: "I'm engaged." Like it was normal. I thought it was a joke at first and laughed, and when he just sat there silently looking like he was shitting himself, I knew it was true.'

'What a wanker,' Ali cried. 'How can he be engaged when he has been going out with you for a few months?'

'More than a few months,' Jacqui lamented. 'I mean, I know it wasn't serious, like as in, let's move in together. And yes, I snogged a few other boys on other crap internet dates – we had huge gaps in between seeing each other. But every time we did meet up, we got on really well. I hoped maybe it would get serious, the longer we hung out.'

'So who's the person he's engaged to?' Ali wanted to know.

'An old girlfriend. They had just broken up when I met him at Ali's party. But she got back in touch when I was in Australia during the summer holidays; they dated a bit and then when I came back, he kept me on as he didn't know where it was going with her. Said he couldn't make up his mind.'

'Huh! Wanted to have his cake and eat it!' Ali huffed incredulously.

'Then he said he was busy for ages, when he was actually at a wedding with her, and being at the wedding made him realise he wanted to get married... To her! "Brought it all into focus," was what he said...'

'Oh, Jesus, does she even know you exist?' I asked.

Jacqui shook her head.

'Well, I know you're gutted, but look at it this way: would you want to be his fiancée? If he can do this now, what will he be like later on? Who knows what else he won't admit to?' Ali said.

'I know. I know all that, but it doesn't stop the fact that I wasn't good enough.' And she burst into fresh tears. 'I feel like I'm the consolation prize, the idiot who everyone thinks they can just fuck over.'

'You're not, it just hurts because it feels the same as Simon leaving, the same as the way he treated you. It's almost immaterial that you and Tim weren't serious. It's an echo of what went before so it's bound to regurgitate old feelings that haven't really ever gone away.'

'I know. I'm so scared of being on my own. You two have each other to bolster you up day to day. When the door shuts here, it's just me and the kids. That's why I would always rather be at your house. It feels like a home. This isn't my home.'

'You have to *make* it a home,' Ali insisted. 'We could help you unpack, put pictures up, make it feel more cosy. Your life is still in boxes.'

'It's not just that. I'm tired of feeling broken. And, yes, I'm sick of shagging men, realising it makes no difference.'

'No difference?' Ali asked. 'To what?'

'To how I feel. While I'm with them, the fear, sadness, all the other shit, goes, but it's just putting it off. It's still there. I just want it to go away!'

'But being with someone in that way isn't going to help long term,' I said prudently. 'No matter what we do to avoid grief, it always has a way of catching up with you.'

'I'm so bored of feeling like they just moved on and we're here, picking up the pieces.'

Ali and I nodded in agreement.

'You know I read on one of those fucking divorce websites that it takes four years to get over one. Four fucking years! We're only just over a quarter of the way through that. How are we going to keep going for another three years?'

'We have each other,' I said, grabbing her hand. 'We can all be fucked up together. And please, don't hide away here. It's OK to be pissed off about it all, like Ali and I are. Keeping things stored up will only make you ill.'

'Single Parents Alone Together!' Ali chanted. 'Remember, from *About a Boy*?'

'Ah, yes, SPATs,' Jacqui smirked. 'That's us, we're SPATs now.'

The next day, as I lifted Grace out of the Sainsbury's trolley and into her car seat, I felt an almost audible click happen, like the shutting of a door. I had the uncanny sensation something was about to happen, something big. My Beardy Weirdy radar automatically switched on and scanned the universe for signs of latent activity. My guts churned up: I just wanted a calm week where this didn't happen. I scrutinised the car park like a meerkat in the savannah, checking for potential predators as I hoisted a wriggling Chug out of the seat next to Grace. The horizon looked deceptively clear.

I texted Mel as soon as I reached the house.

Something's going to happen… I can feel it. Not sure what though.

I occupied myself with getting Chug and Grace some lunch, though the act itself seemed futile, both of them expert food dodgers. I had been known to uncover fossilised pizza being ingeniously utilised as a mini duvet on the double bed in the dolls' house.

When Grace was napping and Chug was curled up brainwashed in front of a digger DVD, I checked my phone.

Have a proper look and see what you think it is.

I started texting another long-winded missive and abandoned mid-sentence.

'Can you talk?'

'Yes, but I have to go out in about ten minutes. Meeting with potential stockist in town.'

'London? Why didn't you tell me?'

'Because what are the chances you can dump all three kids and escape up there for a ten-minute coffee?'

'Yes, I know. Sorry.'

'We could pull some cards over the phone, see what's going on?' she suggested.

'Yes. I can feel something bad in my stomach, a kind of dread.'

'Go get the cards then.'

I ran to my bedroom and rummaged round my fold-down desk. I stowed the Tarot cards in a special triangular zip-up bag guarded by a plethora of cleansing crystals. I shuffled them while sitting on my bed, Reiki pulsing out of my palms at the same time.

'What are you asking?'

'What's about to happen.' I shuffled the cards and tried not to second guess what it might be… 'Oh, shit.'

'What? It's not Death, is it?'

'Death would be preferable. It's the Three of Swords. Most commonly known as heartbreak.' In fact, you couldn't get away from it when you studied the picture. A man lay prostrate underneath a giant hovering red heart with three swords viciously slicing it through the middle.

'But what are the other meanings? It might not mean that.'

'OK, a selection of meanings are: getting to the heart of the matter, torn between two lovers, feeling hurt inside, feeling let down, being cheated on – well, that's already happened! Discovering a painful truth. And various others, all on a similar theme.'

'Well, maybe Sam will regret the divorce, beg to come back and you will be with mad boy Woody at the circus.'

'I've not even heard from him since he scarpered from the kitchen last weekend.'

'Do you like him? Be honest.'

'I don't know. One minute I do and feel affronted that he ran off. And then I don't blame him because I brought the shutters down the minute we'd shagged.'

'Yeah. I would run away after that! Well, there's only two things that Sam could do now that would hurt you even more.'

17

A Bun in the Oven

Wednesday nights were my favourite. It was a weekly oasis in the desert of bedtime sand storms. As I opened the front door to Sam, eagerly anticipating an industrious evening of writing (or in reality checking Facebook twenty times a minute) his face knocked me off balance.

'What is it?' I asked before he even spoke. The shorthand of reading someone you know inside out endured.

'Can I talk to you, in the car? Is Ali in?'

I nodded, my resigned heart cowering in my chest, fending off the three inauspicious swords. As he shut the car door, me in the passenger seat staring straight ahead, hands trembling, he spoke.

'I need to tell you something.'

'I already know.'

'How could you already know?'

'Carrie's pregnant.'

'Who told you?'

'No one, it's pretty obvious, isn't it?'

'God, you freak me out with your witchy ways. Yes, Carrie is pregnant. Three months.'

'Congratulations. Thanks for telling me in the car. Makes me feel really great.'

'I'm trying to do the right thing by telling you before we tell anyone else. I haven't told the kids yet. Where did you want me to tell you? In the pub?'

Just when I thought I couldn't break any more. Just when I thought nothing could hurt as much as when he left, in he swooped with the second battalion, trampling over any progress I'd made.

'When will you tell the kids?' I croaked.

'Tonight.' I opened the car door and ran back to the house, hurtling straight up the stairs to my bedroom and throwing myself on the bed. I lay there, ears buzzing, trying to digest his words. A sob crept up from my belly, dragging others with it. I could hear Sam in the hallway rounding up the children. Isla and Meg came in to see me.

'Mummy, what's the matter?' Isla cried, and burst into tears, setting Meg off, too. I sat up against my pillows and hugged them as they climbed on the bed.

'I'm just not feeling well. I'm OK. Honestly.'

'I don't want to leave you,' Isla protested. 'Can we stay here?'

'No, Daddy wants you to go to his. I'll see you tomorrow.'

'Don't want to,' Meg joined in, her cheeks wobbling. 'Can we sleep with you?' Sam appeared right then. I switched the bedside lamp on and scrabbled around for a tissue. He handed me the box.

'Hey, girls! I have pizzas and ice cream at home. I think Carrie had made your favourite cake, too.'

Both girls looked contritely at me; I could tell they

wanted the cake, but deep down they knew it might hurt me. It drove a skewer through my already lacerated heart, a fourth sword.

'Oh, girls, a cake! You love cake. I bet it's amazing. Carrie makes lovely cakes. Remember to say thank you.' And the award for best actress goes to… Sam smiled at me and mouthed 'thank you'. It wasn't for you, I silently seethed.

'How do you know?' Isla asked suspiciously. 'You've never had one of her cakes.'

'I just know. They look amazing on the telly.' Isla didn't look convinced but hugged me anyway. The front door banged and I sank back and howled. I could hear footsteps running up the stairs.

'What do you want? To twist the sword even further?' I gasped between sobs at Sam as he lingered on the threshold of the room.

'Amanda… I feel awful.'

'Good. You can't feel as awful as me. We're still married, Sam!'

'I know,' he said wretchedly. 'It wasn't meant to happen. It was an accident.'

'Well, you should have been more careful if you didn't want another child.'

'I do, but didn't expect it to be now. I wanted to wait until after the divorce.'

'Just go. I don't want to talk to you,' I growled, fighting more tears.

'Amanda, look, I—'

'Just leave me alone. GO AWAY!'

He continued to stare at me, audacious tears in his eyes, his face contorted in some kind of remorseful grimace. I turned my head and he left. Footsteps returned and the door pushed open again.

'I told you to leave,' I cried.

'Oh, sorry,' Ali said embarrassedly, shuffling out of the doorway.

'No, Ali, come in. I thought you were Sam.'

'He just flew out the door. What the fuck's going on?'

'Carrie's pregnant,' I exploded rather loudly, surprising myself and Ali at the same time.

'Oh, Mands.' Ali promptly burst into compassionate tears. 'Oh, you poor thing.'

'It hurts so much,' I cried, sounding like a child.

Ali leaped over the bed and pulled me in for a hug. 'What a dick,' she sighed. 'He's just made his life so much more difficult. You're still married!'

'I know.' I pulled back and grabbed more tissues to stem the snot. 'Have we got any wine?'

'No, we drank it all at the weekend. Let's go to the pub. I'll go and get ready.'

'Ali, you're forgetting Grace.'

'Oh shit, yes, she's downstairs in the high chair. Fuck, she better still be alive.'

'What I don't understand is how he's affording all these kids!' Ali said, waving her sherry glass around as Grace splashed in the bath next to her. 'I mean, four kids is a lot of kids.' We'd decided on the dregs from the Cupboard of Badness next to the fridge where vodka, ouzo, Calvados, tequila and other piquant alcoholic orphans waited patiently for a desperate situation like this.

'She's rich, she must be. Book deals, TV deals,' I reasoned, perched on the closed loo seat sipping a sickly glass of Martini Rosso. 'She's having a moment. You get well paid for having a moment.'

'Do you think she tricked him into it?'

'Maybe. Who knows? I don't care. All I care about are the kids. I think they'll hate the idea of a baby.'

'You know you'll get door-stepped again as soon as this breaks in the press. You better start wearing those clothes I gave you instead of looking like a bag lady. Standards have slipped, Amanda!'

'I will face the press and moon them. Show them what I *really* think of it all.'

Meg and I started therapy in November just before she turned five. It mostly consisted of her playing with dollies or drawing about how she felt, with me remaining in the room along with Elley the extremely young and presumably childless therapist. Sometimes I had to talk about things that had happened, how I parented (like a fucking idiot compared to the perfect non-shouty parent handouts Elley foisted on me where everyone looked like they were auditioning for *The Joy of Sex* manual with beards and earnest do-gooder faces). I honestly didn't get how this was helping, but somehow it did. Her tantrums had abated dramatically. We fell into a little routine where I picked her up from school (she had started in September), took her to see Elley, then afterwards, we would sneak to the French Café at the end of the road for hot chocolate before I returned her to lessons.

'I lub you, Mummy,' she would say every time I dropped her back at school, making me wish I could spirit her away for the day.

'Sometimes having an animal can help young children who have real difficulties expressing themselves,' Elley suggested in one session. 'Would that be an option?'

I knew that Meg loved gorillas to a point of obsession. She slept with Jimbo every night, tucked up in her bed, her arm clutching him fiercely to her chest. But I wasn't going to get a simian playmate for her.

'She was talking about a cat earlier.'

'Yes, next-door have one. She loves it.'

Elley smiled encouragingly at me. I recklessly signed up for the Celia Hammond Rescue Centre the minute I got home.

'We should have a kitten for you in the new year,' the cat lady brightly chatted on the phone. I decided to keep it a secret until the day we went to collect it, to avoid fending off on the hour, every hour 'Is it today we get the cat?' questions. Or unless I came to my senses and realised what a completely foolhardy idea this was. I was not a cat person.

'Jesus! Look at this!' Ali screeched the next morning while I was loading up the terminally busy washing machine. She shoved her phone in my face open in Facebook messenger.

Dear Alison

I am so sorry I never rang you, but I really couldn't make up what happened. Right after you went home, I followed you out to get a cab and was beaten unconscious to the ground by a mugger who stole my phone, and ultimately your number. I woke up in hospital and had to stay in for a few days because my injuries were so bad. I wasn't allowed to present the news for a few weeks because I looked like

Shrek on a bad day. I also didn't want to see you while I looked like this. I scared myself in the mirror. Anyway, rather than go through Justin and have him asking loads of questions, I found you on here. I hope this is you! You look like I remember, even after the head injury! So, what I am asking in a roundabout way, is would you like to go for a drink? My number is…
Dara

'Can you believe it?!' Ali laughed, a sliver of Schadenfreude dampening the revelation. We had joked after a few weeks that maybe he'd had his phone stolen and that was why he hadn't called.

'I hate the thought of *her* with Grace,' Ali seethed, the morning of her third date with Dara. After spearing an aggrieved Jim with some hard-nosed lawyers' letters and threats of being chased relentlessly by the CSA, Ali had finally retrieved her money just before Christmas. But as part of the new deal, Grace now spent every other weekend with Jim as well as a midweek night. 'It makes my blood boil.'

'I know, it's a double-edged sword, but just think of the nice time you will have tonight. You're going out with a lovely man who you like. You *do* like him, don't you?'

'I do, but it isn't the same.'

'The same as what?'

'The same as when I met Jim. There's no stomach churning, butterflies, will he won't he call, will we have sex, or won't we?'

'That's because Jim was married to Diane! It was subversive and naughty, and that makes it more exciting.'

'Not just that. I was mad about Jim from the moment I met him. This feels different. There isn't that instant connection, that shared something that I can't put my finger on. I just knew Jim and I were something. What that something was I don't know, but something… I do like Dara, though, and he is kind.'

'I get it. I really do, and I have no idea how I will ever let someone in again. I knew my first boyfriend was something, but we were best friends for years, but I also knew Sam was something straight after our first date. I just felt it to the tips of my split ends.'

'Gosh, Mands, you and Sam were a proper love story. You know we all used to look at you and think, God, I want that. He loved you *so* much. What happened? Look at us. Are we going to have a happy ever after?'

'Yes!' I cried, grabbing her hands. 'Instead of waiting for it, we just have to live in the moment – *that* is the happy ever after. It doesn't need to involve a man. Time will eventually erase the insanity of loving someone who doesn't love you back – that's why it feels like we need a man to fix the hole they left. But what happens if we're happy on our own? My mum was, after my dad. I don't know whether I will ever love someone like I loved Sam because he is the father of my children. Maybe one day it will be different, but good different, more equal. I didn't love *me* enough.'

Except in the deepest darkest night of my heart, I believed that love doesn't totally die. Like energy, it just burns somewhere else, a snuffed-out soul, seeking pastures new. I felt like the teeniest of flames still flickered for him, and that was what I needed to get over. Not by shagging someone else, but by feeling at peace with who I was and setting that love inwards like my own knight in shining armour…

18

DIY SOS

'Water's pouring through the ceiling!' Ali screamed from the kitchen as I changed Sonny's nappy in his bedroom.

He would be three in a few months' time and continued to refuse to use the toilet. He was also not speaking properly, only using occasional words, and I was still 'Dad'. I knew it was considered normal, but doubts rumbled in the back of my mind. Jacqui said that little boys gleaned their developmental pointers from their fathers – she was having similar speech difficulties with Joe. Sonny saw his dad properly only every other weekend and one night a week. The rest of the time he was constantly surrounded by women, even when he went to nursery twice a week.

I barged into the kitchen and found Ali had placed the mop bucket underneath the leak and moved one of the Habitat chairs from its path.

'The ceiling's bulging,' she observed unnecessarily. As we helplessly stood there, dazed by the unfolding catastrophe, other damp patches emerged like a fairy mushroom ring popping up on a damp summer lawn.

'Fuck, the ceiling's going to collapse,' I cried, finally galvanised into action. 'We need loads of towels.' Ali tore upstairs to the airing cupboard on the middle floor while I shepherded Grace and Sonny away from the potential tsunami and into the living room to watch *In the Night Garden*. 'Get the mop!'

Ali scattered the towels all over the crash site and handed me the mop. I raised it to the ceiling.

'What the fuck are you doing?'

'Helping it on its way.'

I pressed the mop head on the swelling plasterwork, and it didn't take much pressure before it split like blistered skin and a torrent of water smacked down onto the waiting towels. The patch of ceiling that had been harbouring the water followed suit and collapsed onto the floor with a resounding thud. Sonny ran back in to investigate the noise, leaving Grace to crawl her way in. Ali inspected the jagged hole where an exposed joist held up the rest of the plasterboard and a network of brass pipes criss-crossed through the space between the floor above and the kitchen ceiling: the concealed workings of a house.

'There's no more water pouring out. I wonder if it had been collecting there for ages and finally decided to escape? It must be from the bath; it's directly above it. Look, you can see the bottom of it.'

'Shitting cunt sticks. I could ring the house insurance but they just up your premium for shit like this.'

'It's such a shame my dad is out in Spain. He would sort it in a jiffy.'

'I don't know anyone who can do this. It's such a small job, yet it isn't at the same time. It's plumbing *and* building.'

I despondently kicked the bucket, almost upending the contents and adding to the mess.

'I know a man who can,' Ali said brightly.

Three days later, after the hell of forcing children to have showers instead of baths, I opened the front door, a combination of apprehension and culpability whooshing round inside me. Woody was here because we needed his skills, but when he towered over me all tanned, his hair bleached blond at the tips, looking the picture of health after his Christmas sailing trip, my groin executed a perfectly swift U-turn, leaving common sense quaking in its wake.

'Hi!' he said, and leaned in to kiss me on the cheek, refuelling the dormant desire. His aftershave was surely catnip. 'How are you? Apart from having a hole in your ceiling?'

'I'm good. Come through. Tea?'

'Yes, never say no to tea.'

Woody set about fixing everything, starting with the pipes in the bathroom.

'How do you know what you're doing?' I asked as he stood on a ladder, his head immersed in the gap. I passed him tools when he asked me and his hand grazed mine, sending an electric shock right down into my nether regions. Everyone was out, this being the middle of the day and nursery for Chug and school for the girls. Ali was at a baby group coffee morning.

'Oh, you know, I've been doing this on and off in between sailing now for a few years. The gaffer my dad employs has taught me loads.'

'So how much do you charge?' He withdrew his head from the hole and turned to look at me.

'Amanda, you're a mate. I'm not charging you.'

'But I must pay for something! The materials, at least?'

'I have all the stuff just lying around at work. No one will notice. Look, I have to fix the leak and then we'll test it and I can patch up the hole, but I'll have to come back at the weekend and sand it down and paint it so it matches.'

'Well, I am kid-free this weekend. I could treat you to dinner to say thank you. I'm not doing anything.'

'Don't feel you have to. Honestly, it's fine.'

'I want to.'

'Why don't you cook me dinner instead and then we can go out for a drink?'

When he'd finished, I helped him carry his tools out to the white Transit van he'd borrowed from his dad.

'So, I'll see you on Saturday.'

I nodded. We stood staring at each other. Ali would be back in about half an hour. I think I made the first move, and before we knew it, we were grinding on each other up against the side of the van in broad daylight, his mouth kissing my entire face.

'Inside,' he said brusquely. 'Now, before I have an accident.'

We just about made it up the stairs, stopping once on the middle landing to rip clothes off. I urgently pulled him down onto me in the corridor outside the airing cupboard.

'What about Ali?'

'She's out. Just do it.'

'God, you're bossy.'

'Don't waste time talking!' The cheap nylon carpet chafed like sandpaper against my shoulders as I arched greedily towards him while he peeled down the condom.

'You trumped Rampant Rabbit,' I said afterwards, his face hidden in my neck, both of us out of breath.

'What do you mean?'

'He gives good orgasms, but that was amazing. A real collywobbler.'

'That sounds like something my nan would say.'

'What was that?' I could hear the jangle of keys in the front door. 'Fuck! Ali's back early.'

'Hellooooo! I've brought some left-over cake. I see Woody's still here.'

'Fuck fuck fuck. Quick, in my room. Grab your clothes.' We hastily scrambled from the landing and managed to get dressed and downstairs in less than three minutes.

'Hey! Ali, we were just checking the pipes in the airing cupboard,' Woody said nonchalantly, kissing her on the cheek. She stared at me keenly, her eyebrows raised.

'Why is your top on back-to-front, Amanda?'

I lay on my side, sucking in my doughy mummy tummy, watching Woody's hairless chest lift and fall in time with his breath. He was conked out. I envied people who just decided that they would submit to sleep. Childhood sleepless nights had been littered with monsters creeping into my bedroom as soon as Mum switched off the light. Headless chickens and dinosaurs would wrestle for space upon the ceiling and, as I grew older, silent black spectres towered in the corner of the room. The pervading fear that I would be dead in the morning never disappeared.

At some point that Saturday night I fell asleep, only to wake what felt like five minutes later, sweaty and disorientated because someone was on Sam's side of the bed. Woody was watching me.

'Morning,' he said. 'How's your head?'

'Erm, OK, I think. How's yours?'

'Totally fine! I'm as hard as old boots.' He certainly was. He had revealed his own brush with rock bottom the evening before in the pub, after he'd spent the afternoon painting my kitchen ceiling.

'When I came home from the incident on the boat when I nearly drowned, Mum locked away all the alcohol, all the drugs, anything I might take, even the cough syrup.'

'Would you have raided it?'

'NO! She has no idea about drugs. Cocaine isn't heroin. She thought I was going to start bartering with her for my fix of Calpol, selling the house from under her to feed my habit. I didn't. I wanted to sleep and I wanted to change.'

'But you still do them, Woody,' I baldly stated.

'I do occasionally, not every day like my old normal.' He smiled at me and leaned over and kissed the tip of my nose. 'Do you want a cup of tea?'

When the children arrived back that evening, it was obvious something was wrong.

'What's going on?'

Isla stormed upstairs and didn't even say hello, her bags dumped in the hallway.

'She's been funny all weekend. She won't talk to me and she's ignoring Carrie as well. Being quite rude.' Sam's injured tone made me want to throttle him.

'She's upset, Sam. About your baby. What do you expect? A ticker-tape parade?'

'Thanks for the understanding.'

'Sorry, but I *don't* understand. It's not exactly the world's greatest news for any of them. They need lots and lots of time to adjust. And reassurance. They'll feel usurped.' And I know how *that* feels I wanted to add, but just glared at him. 'Acceptance isn't going to happen overnight.'

'I know that!' He sounded frustrated. How did he think *they* felt?

'Maybe Isla can get some help with dealing with it, like Meg is? I can look into it.'

'That would be great, thanks.'

'You're just clearing up his mess, aren't you?' Ali said once he had gone. 'He has no idea how this feels for them. How hard they might be finding it.'

Isla walked into the kitchen and silently handed me a folded piece of paper. It was addressed to Daddy. It wasn't a traditional letter; it was a drawing. In the centre, surrounding a tiny baby, was a broken heart with knives sticking out of it (spookily like the Three of Swords Tarot card). Around the outside of the heart Isla had sketched pictures of herself, Sonny, Meg and me all crying. She stood defiantly in front of me, almost daring me to be cross. I gravely handed it to Ali to look at.

'Isla, if this is how you feel, you have to speak to Daddy about it. Do you want me to give him that letter?'

'Yes!' She exploded into a fit of tears. 'I hate him!'

I hugged her hard and Meg somehow squeezed in, too.

'How can he have another baby, Mummy? He has us!'

'I know. But these things happen when people split up. Look at Grandpa Scotland. I wouldn't have my sisters if Grandma Susie hadn't had them and the thought of them not being there makes me feel really sad. I love them so much.'

Fortuitously, I received a phone call from the rescue centre that very week and while the children were at school and nursery, I visited Pets at Home and stocked up on cat necessities, including a dreaded litter tray. I wasn't keen on anything doing a steaming turd in the kitchen, even if it was a cute fur-ball kitten.

'How would you feel about getting a kitten this weekend?' I asked at teatime.

'Mummy! Do you mean it?' Isla shouted above the screeching of the other two.

Meg immediately burst into tears, sobbing uncontrollably, her face burning red. I feared we were about to experience a force-five hurricane taking down the house in some kind of titanic emotional conflagration. I hadn't anticipated this.

'Oh, Meg. Oh, no. Don't you want a cat? I'm sorry, I should have warned you before.' She jumped up from the bench where she was eating her macaroni cheese and hurled herself at me, a mass of raging tears.

'Mummy, I'm so happy. You've made my dream come true. I've always wanted a cat.' And she continued to sob into my chest. Her reaction set me off and soon we were all bawling our eyes out at the dinner table.

'Oh crap, what's happened?' Ali cried in dismay as she brought Grace through for her tea.

'Nothing, we're all just so happy to be getting a cat!' Isla said, smiling through her tears. 'Mummy, is this to stop us feeling sad about the baby?'

I looked at Ali, who raised her eyebrows.

On Saturday morning, Ali, Grace, the children and I stood in the back room of the Celia Hammond Cat Rescue Centre. Wall-to-wall cages ran all around us, housing all kinds of cats, some in pairs and some solitary. A few were meowing and one or two were cowering at the back of them.

'It's between these two,' the lady explained, and pointed to a ginger cat pacing his enclosure like a tiger in captivity, and a black one who wouldn't look at us. We had been told they were male, about six months old and just neutered. They were still technically kittens but just looked like small cats.

'That one!' Meg cried, pointing at the ginger cat.

'Good choice,' the woman remarked. 'He was found abandoned in a cardboard box a month ago. Someone must have got him for Christmas and no longer wanted him.'

'I wish we could take all of them,' Isla whispered. 'I feel so sad for the ones left behind.'

'Don't worry,' the woman assured her, 'they will all find nice homes.'

'Cat!' Sonny shouted with glee.

'Wow, another word,' I laughed ironically. 'At this rate, Grace will be talking before him.'

The newest member of the Single Mums' Mansion joined the commune. At last Sonny had a boy to play with.

'What will you call him?' Ali asked as we crawled back through the freezing rain in gridlocked traffic, the cat mewing dejectedly from the back in his brand-new portable prison.

'Ginger!' Meg beamed, her cheeks fit to burst with happiness. 'I lub him already!'

'Wow,' Ali said softly next to me, 'I've never seen her so animated. This cat already seems like a good idea.'

Ginger distracted the children from properly noticing that Woody was spending a bit more time at the house as 'Mummy's Friend'. We hadn't officially stepped out on a first date, we'd just slipped into something vaguely familiar, like catching an episode of your favourite TV comedy show then getting sucked into the subsequent ten episodes without coming up for air. We kept it low key if the children were in the house, and he would sleep in the office, where I had now hoovered and changed the bed linen, but the boxes and junk remained shoved in piles. It felt scarily easy and yet constantly strange at the same time. Especially when Sam's unwelcome baby news hit the papers a week later.

Carrie Has a Bun in the Oven!

one of the more original headlines blasted.

TV's Carrie Carrying Married Lover's Fourth Child!

That one made it sound more sordid than it actually was. I was so glad the children were too little to read newspapers or look online. It meant they couldn't be teased about it at school. But it also meant I was fair game.

Uncommonly, the house phone rang at seven in the morning that week. It was Ali.

'I'm in the car outside. Is Woody still there?' I was supervising Grace's Olympic try-outs for the toast javelin while Ali went to work. Sonny was still in his cot babbling to his diggers and the girls were attempting to get dressed without me corralling them in their rooms and forcing school uniform over heads like horses' tack. It wasn't going well.

'What's going on? Have you broken down?'

'No! The press are outside.'

'How can you see? It's still dark.'

'They tried to ask me something. One of them has a camera, too. They want a picture of you looking heartbroken and downtrodden. Bloody prove them wrong!'

'What about Woody? They'll take a picture of him!'

'Who will?' he asked as he wandered into the kitchen in his work gear.

'I've got to go, thanks for the tip-off.'

'The press are outside.'

'To stalk me?'

'No! Me! I don't want the children being subjected to it, or you either.'

'Do you want me to go and tell them to fuck off?'

'No! That'll make it worse. You need to stay here until they leave.'

'I can't. I have to get to work! I have to be in the East End by eight thirty.'

'OK, well, they mustn't see you leaving here. I haven't told anyone we're, you know...' Oh, I hated this! Having to have the 'What is this called' conversation before we're even ready to know what it was ourselves.

'Are you embarrassed about me?' he asked in a wounded manner.

'No!' I didn't sound convincing even to myself and inwardly cringed. I just wanted Sam to find out when *I* was ready to tell him, not when the *Daily Fail* splashed it across page ten. Woody came with so many conflicting connotations attached to him, like fruitless warnings stuck on an innocuous bottle of cough medicine. Do not mix with children. Do not take on a full moon. Do not have when under the influence of mind-altering drugs. Do not ingest with wine. Years of his drug taking and self-obsessed partying hadn't really won him any fans in my camp. Rob hated him and that made it all the more difficult to tell him we were kind of together.

'Shall I leave by the back gate?'

'There isn't one.'

'Believe me, I will find one,' he said in a tone that set me on edge. How many times had he had to do this?

I texted Philippa and asked if Woody could escape through their back garden and out through the front door.

Of course! Tell him to knock on the door and we'll let him in.

Good old Philippa, she just wasn't the curtain-twitching type.

'Will you be OK getting over that fence?' I asked him, worrying he would snap a leg on the imposing Leylandii that bordered the rickety leaning fence on Philippa's side.

'Yep, don't stress. I can jump off the shed roof. It's all good. I'll see you soon. Remember: no comment!' He kissed me on the lips and, like the Milk Tray Man, slipped silently out of the back door into the ink-black morning still masquerading as night. I turned back to Grace and jumped. Isla was staring at me from the doorway.

'Woody kissed you, Mummy!'

I groaned bringing my hands up to my face in the vain hope that they could wipe the evidence clean away.

19

Am I Normal Yet?

As winter ploughed on regardless, even though it was technically spring and bulbs were thrusting their imprudent fresh green shoots up through the ice-tipped clods of sodden earth, foreboding cast its capricious net upon me once more. We were all awaiting the birth of the prodigal child with no star to guide us. Even the arrival of Ginger couldn't quell the building tension in the house, though Meg had really blossomed in the last month as we drew to the end of her allotted free therapy sessions.

'I think the main concern with Meg is that she struggles to communicate her emotions,' Elley quietly explained in one session while Meg coloured in a picture she had lovingly drawn of the cat. 'She also desperately wants to please people, and when she can't, it stresses her and she retreats inside herself, lashing out instead. She has a deeply entrenched lack of self-confidence.'

I felt awful. Elley was right. Meg had been trying to please me from birth and couldn't, because I had been buried under the perplexing shroud of post-natal depression. My eyes brimmed with tears.

'This isn't your fault.' Elley patted my arm kindly. 'What's important is she's coming out of herself now. Spending time exclusively with you here, talking about feelings and parenting, is what she's obviously needed. The addition of the cat has given her a focus point, too. Cats love no matter what; she doesn't need to prove anything to him.'

This rang true. Since Ginger, she engaged more, she cared for him, making sure he had enough food and drink. It was like his very presence had completely recalibrated her. He was beginning to feel like part of our patchwork family.

'Look,' Ali hissed, one night when Dara was round to take her out. 'He's like the Pied Piper.' Jacqui and I poked our heads round the living-room doors from the kitchen, and Dara was sitting in the middle of the sofa, a picture book open in his hands, Grace on his knee, Sonny under one arm, Joe squeezed in next to him, and the girls with Neve on the other side, Ginger in Meg's arms, all craning necks to watch him turn the pages.

'It's his voice,' I whispered. 'It's like liquid chocolate, especially with his posh accent and autocue skills. He could make boiling an egg sound enthralling.'

'It makes my womb contract,' Ali sighed sadly. 'I want another baby.'

'With Dara?' Jacqui asked. She shrugged. 'Hypothetically?'

'Yes. Just looking at him with the children, I want to have that. Be with someone who shares things, helps, reads stories, cares as much as I do about our baby. I never had that. I want to have a chance to do it properly.'

I squeezed her arm. 'I know, and that's what's so shit. Well, see how it goes with Dara. Take it slow, but so far so good!'

Sam had met the news about Woody with scarcely concealed mirth.

'So, you're actually dating him? Like he's your boyfriend?' His eyebrows almost disappeared into his hairline.

'Yes.'

He whistled through his teeth in that way I knew meant he thought I was mad.

'Is he still as nuts as ever?'

'No. I wouldn't let him near the kids if he was. He's calmed down massively and doesn't party like that any more.'

'Glad to hear it. Well, be careful.'

'Of what?'

'In case he does go mad again.'

'What, like you did and leave me with three kids?'

'Oh, yes, I walked right into that one. Ha ha.'

You haven't earned that levity, fuck-face, I silently fumed. *Just for today I will not be angry...*

By ten o'clock that same night, Woody, Jacqui, Will and I arrived at the bar where I normally DJ-ed, free drinks on the house to commiserate Jacqui's divorce being finalised, when Dara and Ali came bowling in after their romantic dinner date.

'Loo, ladies, now!' Ali hissed as she thundered towards us leaving Dara with the boys, an uncustomary glacial expression upon her face.

'So, what's going on?' I asked as we three squeezed into the doll-sized cubicle.

'Dara's moving to Hong Kong.' Ali's face crumpled, tears spurting out of her scrunched-up eyes.

'Fuck, I can't even hug you. My arms are trapped by my sides. Sorry,' I commiserated. 'That's truly shite.'

'It is, especially after he's met Grace and she liked him. All the kids liked him. She held her arms up to him the other day when we were at home. She walked for the first time when he was there in the kitchen, remember?' I nodded. 'Just when I felt like I was moving on, and that shit face didn't have such a hold over me. I really like Dara.'

'I know you do,' Jacqui chipped in. 'But can you keep it up over long distance? Does he want to?'

'He said he does. And he'll be back to visit his dad and sisters. And for work stuff, too. He's got a promotion. The channel is massive over there.'

'When does he go?'

'June.' Ali tilted her head up towards the light and fiddled about in her coat pocket. 'I've got this.' She managed to bend her arm into the centre of the huddle.

'Coke?' Jacqui whispered reverently.

'Not just any coke, eighty quid VIP, the big daddy! This will knock your socks off, make you dance all night, and other stuff! I need a holiday from my head for a few hours.'

'Where did you get it?' I asked, knowing full well. Ali looked at me, a hint of guilt clouding her face.

'Woody. He got it for Dara. But I haven't given it to him yet. I'm too pissed off about Hong Kong.'

'Well, it's a shame to waste it…' Jacqui puckishly intimated. 'What have you girls done to me? I never used to do drugs. Fuck it, I'm officially divorced, I can do anything I like!'

We weaved our way back to the bar area, glassy-eyed and giggling.

'Oh, right. I know what you've been doing.' Woody laughed, his eyes expertly probing for evidence.

'I don't know what you mean, Officer.'

'You're bolloxed! Come on, share the goods.'

'It's not mine.'

At some point the clandestine sachet was passed round and the party started properly, ending up at two a.m. in the dimly lit kitchen with a closing-time mob of complete strangers, one of whom Jacqui was snogging in the soggy back garden highlighted by the intruder lights.

'I'm sorry for dropping that news on Ali,' Dara said sheepishly while I poured us both a glass of red wine. 'It's been in the pipeline for so long, way before I met her.'

'Don't apologise to me. You have to do what's right for you. She really likes you and is bound to be upset. But why did you start seeing her if you always knew you would leave?'

'I didn't know. It was just talks before Christmas. Nothing was certain, and then suddenly everything moved so fast. The timing isn't great. I think she's lovely... and Grace is a little darling. I don't want it to end just because I'm going away.'

'But it's such a long way. It's not like you're going to Paris or even New York. Hong Kong is half the world away.'

'I'll come back often, and she and Grace can always visit. Hong Kong is an amazingly colourful and cultural city. So much to do.' I could tell he was already there in his head, planning his new life.

Will had gone home and come back again, using one of his many 'Great Escape' tactics to tunnel his way back to the outside world.

'What did you do this time?' I asked, mystified by what Sarah saw in him.

‘I got in bed after the pub, fed Oliver when he woke at one, then said I was going to have a cup of tea, got dressed and came out here. I’ve left a half-drunk cup of tea in the kitchen so she’ll think I slept on the sofa. As long as I’m back by five she’ll never know.’ In the death grip of coke mania where my jaw involuntarily clamped shut every two minutes, my brain raced through judgements, trying them on for size like snatching products from the shelves of *Supermarket Sweep*. One minute I thought Will was a lowlife arsewipe, but the next I cast him as a total genius for managing to do what he wanted as well as fulfilling his duties as a husband and father. What did I care? None of it affected me.

‘Do you want half a pill?’ Woody whispered conspiratorially in my ear as I sat curled on his knee in one of the Habitat chairs.

‘Why, do you have them with you?’

He shrugged.

‘Do you always have stuff?’

‘No, I knew it was going to be a big night. I haven’t done anything for a while. Come on, it’ll be fun.’

‘You know I admire you, Amanda,’ Will said unexpectedly. He was sitting on the floor at Woody’s feet, sipping a beer.

‘How come?’

‘How you’ve handled the whole Sam leaving. I think Sarah would have killed me publicly and made my life hell. We all think it was a pretty shit thing to do.’

‘It was.’

‘It’s good to see you’re OK now, with the baby and everything. That can’t be easy. But you seem to be handling it.’

Oh, but I’m not! I wanted to yell at him. You have no idea how much it is still NOT OK.

Woody pressed half a crumbling pill into my palm. I should have thrown it in the bin, or down the loo on hearing Will's rose-tinted potted version of my life, implying everything was equal now because I had a boyfriend. Like the kids weren't hurting almost two years on, so no one had to worry about poor Amanda, even though I was still married to Sam, still wrangling over who owned what percentage of the house to 'make it fair', still having dreams that we were married, happy and in love, only to wake and discover it was all still painted with the same shitty brush. Living in a commune (which I loved and had saved me) was fun but none the less I would gladly swap it all to be raising my family with their father living under the same roof. Did all of that account for my life fitting into a recognisable box you can tick as normal? Just because things appear 'normal' doesn't mean they are. People wear masks and act out elaborate plays to cover up words they really want to say and feel. And right then, like Alice seeking the White Rabbit, I chose to eat the forbidden cake, to blot it all out.

The immediate reaction was to dry-heave in the kitchen sink as it hit my system, landing on top of the building blocks of coke and wine. The next was to drink pints of water to quell the nausea. That didn't work. Neither did dancing, nor wine, so I faced defeat and let Woody guide me up the stairs to bed where he stroked my head. Lying under the duvet, away from the rest of the party, my body relaxed and welcomed the ecstasy as it caressed my heart with a diaphanous sensation of wellbeing.

'I'm battered again,' I murmured, my skin tingling, my teeth clenching. I craved cuddles, which opened up negotiations for inevitable drug-fuelled sex, inhibitions dancing to a tune only I could hear.

20

Another Star in Heaven

'Can you come home now?' Ursula was urging me down the phone at ten that night. The kids were asleep upstairs at Mel's. It would mean dragging them out of bed and into an inhospitable cold car.

'Not really. I'm miles away and the kids are all asleep. It's pretty late. What's up?'

'Ali's dad's died.'

I sat down abruptly on the nearest chair in Mel's cosy living room, an audible 'Oof' escaping my lips.

'Are you OK?' Mel mouthed from the opposite sofa. I shook my head in a stupor, the words rattling against my skull. Pete was dead.

'Oh God,' I groped around for an appropriate response and found myself severely lacking. 'How dreadful. Is she OK? I mean, I know she isn't, but what happened?'

'He just dropped down dead, about an hour ago. Anne called me first because she knew you were away, asked me to tell Ali face to face, before she called on the landline. She didn't want her being on her own.'

'Fuck. Look, I'll see what I can do. I can go and wake the kids. I can be back there by midnight, maybe a bit after.'

'No! That's madness. I'll stay here the night. Er... Jim is here, too.'

'What's he doing there?' I snapped.

Ursula lowered her voice. 'Ali rang him so he could deal with Grace for her.'

'But you could have done that.'

'I know,' she sighed resignedly. 'He's here and Grace is up because of all the commotion. I couldn't ring Ali to let me in – her phone was dead – so I had to bang on your door twenty minutes ago and wake her up. It was pretty hideous.'

'It's so shocking!' I cried, the adrenalin waning, clearing the way for genuine emotions, my eyes stinging. 'God, poor Ali. Does she want to talk?'

'She said not. I think if she hears your voice she'll break down. She's holding it together really well. I ran down to get emergency wine, so we're drinking that.'

'I'll leave first thing in the morning.'

'I think she's off to her brother's in the morning. They're going to see if they can get a flight out to Spain to help Anne deal with it all.'

'OK, well, I'll come back anyway.'

After goodbyes I put my phone down, still in shock, hands shaking, sweat pricking my palms.

'Oh, poor Ali. Not what she needs right now. Not with Dara leaving,' Mel sympathised.

Beardy Weirdies say that dead people reveal their presence by leaving signs – white feathers, coins or by mysteriously moving inanimate objects.

Coins started materialising round the house in the most curious places. One day, soon after Pete died, when I was taking the girls to school, I found a brand-new pound coin by the front door. I didn't drop it. One minute it wasn't there, the next it lay auspiciously on the welcome mat glinting in the weak sunlight pouring in through the glass panels. Odd pieces of Ali's jewellery vanished, only to reappear wedged underneath the edge of the carpet in the attic by her writing desk, nowhere near her keepsake box. Coins surfaced under the living-room table and once in the bathroom. Obviously Ali and I, and in some cases, Woody and Dara, could have been dropping them, but in the run up to the funeral it was like an epidemic. Either that or we all had holes in our pockets and bags.

On the drive down to the burial with Ursula, I'd felt fine, apart from the usual dread of these things. Then, standing in the mud, my pink spotty wellies incongruously matched with my gossamer-thin red shift dress and fake fur jacket, I was bobbing up and down on a sea of completely unexpected nausea. We were bang in the middle of natural burial woods in Hampshire, the dark green ridge of the South Downs protruding like a tombstone through the veil of budding trees behind us. Graveside at Pete's funeral was the most inconvenient place to begin with a delayed hangover. The previous night, Woody and I had drunk a bottle of wine toasting Pete's memory.

'I only met him once. Years ago, when she first bought that flat and had a party. He was there, wasn't he?'

I nodded. 'Yes, he re-plastered the entire flat and put the new kitchen in. Looked amazing. Anyway, here's to Pete,' I cheered. 'Take a rest from building in the afterlife.'

When we went to bed that night, a pound coin rested on the threshold of my bedroom.

A measly half-bottle of wine cannot cause this kind of reaction, I reasoned, forcing myself to concentrate on what Ali's older brother was saying. *Don't be sick, don't be sick, don't be sick.* Hang on, weren't you supposed to say what you wanted in a positive light rather than what you *didn't* want to happen? *Feel well, feel well, feel well.*

Maybe it was all the green juice and Chlorella powder I had necked first thing on an empty stomach. It was probably that, or the apple I had eaten before I got in the car; they can be a bit acidic.

It began to spit and I clutched my coat around me. Fake fur wasn't adequate protection against rain. I would begin to smell of wet dog once the water penetrated it. As soon as I thought that, bile rose sharply up my throat. I swallowed it back down, losing an uphill battle against my saliva glands that had now decided to wet my oesophagus to ease the vomit on its way. Fuck it. I looked wildly around, seeing where I could make a discreet and hasty exit, but was blocked by a row of people behind. Thank God I wasn't front row with Dara.

Ali and the family huddled together by the grave after the coffin had been lowered haltingly into the hole. Everyone was engrossed in Dan's eulogy, his speech caught on the breeze, elevating the words above our heads, birds riding a slipstream. Both Ali and Anne, standing side by side, Ali clutching Grace on her hip, wore bright pink dresses underneath their overcoats, a defiant gesture that Pete would have approved of. He had been a congenial man and wearing black would have kindled his loathing of pomp and circumstance.

Dan was recounting a story about how his dad had once been an amateur wrestler. I had a vague memory of a photograph of Pete in a proper wrestling outfit, like Big Daddy or Giant Haystacks in a bright red back-to-front elastane swimming costume, except he was tall and skinny and ginger.

The nausea was getting stronger. Mercifully, my handbag was empty save for my keys, sunglasses case and my purse. It was usually rammed with receipts and other detritus, but I had culled the lot for a more elegant bag to go with my funeral attire. I pretended to bend down on the ground and ferret around for something in my bag while I heaved silently. Nothing sprang forth apart from water. Then a second wave undulated up my throat; this one was more substantial and splattered the inside of my bag with the mulched-up apple I had eaten at seven a.m. I had successfully managed to be as unobtrusive as I could, due to the fact there wasn't much for my stomach to eject. I looked up, sunglasses still in place, wiping my mouth with a tissue. Just like that, the nausea evaporated as rapidly as it had transpired, leaving behind a leather-clad sick bag.

'You OK?' Ursula hissed in my ear. I hoped I didn't smell of sick. 'I thought you'd fainted. Heavy night?'

'No, not at all. I remembered my phone was on in my bag and switched it off.' She nodded.

Back at Ali's brother's house in Dorking, and after I had rinsed my bag out and chucked it in the boot of my car, a Sri Lankan buffet welcomed the guests back from the burial. Dan's wife's family were Sri Lankan and had very kindly catered.

'Well done, Ali, you're being amazing,' I said, touching her elbow as she poured wine and buzzed around making sure everyone was topped up.

'Keep busy, that's my motto. Everyone's telling funny stories about Dad. It's just what Mum needs.' The atmosphere was certainly unlike any funeral I had been to before. It was more like a party, the small back garden decked out with bunting and vases of flowers on tables covered in chintzy cloths, endless champagne and the delicious-smelling food.

'Your dad would have loved this, too,' I said.

She nodded sadly and carried on flitting.

As a rule, I loved curry, but helping myself to an exceptionally spicy prawn dish, I could feel the clench of my stomach as it prepared to expel its contents once more. Noooooooo! What was wrong with me? The smell of the spices had set off a chain reaction. This only ever happened when I was... Oh, dear God, no! How could this be?

'How late are you?' Jacqui asked. I was sitting despondently on the bottom stair in the hall. Ali had flown to Spain straight after the funeral and Chug was watching his digger DVD, mesmerised.

'I don't think I am late. I had a period this month a few weeks ago. That's why I'm not sure this is what it looks like.'

'You can still have a bit of bleeding when you're pregnant.'

'I know. I had an entire period when I was pregnant with Meg.'

'So, if this is how you are, then you might be more pregnant than you think you are. Just go and do it.'

Jacqui sat on the side of the bath while I managed to squeeze out a wee onto the test stick.

'How long do we wait?' I asked her.

She scoured the notes for the answer. 'Two minutes.'

I jammed the cap on the end and noticed a faint blue line rapidly developing before my very eyes.

'Oh fuck, Jax.' I held up the evidence, my hand shaking.

'Hmm. Looks like you are definitely preggers, then. That line appeared in seconds.'

'What do I do?'

'What do you want to do?'

'I have to tell Woody.'

'Not if you don't want to keep it. It might end up being more painful. Better he doesn't know. Does he want kids?'

'I think he does.'

'Then...?'

'Then, nothing. Oh shite, how on earth am I pregnant?'

'You know about sex, right? And you have done it before and have three kids!'

'Oh, ha ha. Yes! But we used a condom.'

'Every time?'

'I think so, though there was that drug-fuelled party a while ago when I don't remember what happened, I was so knobbled. When Dara told Ali he was leaving.'

'That'll be it.'

We stood in silence. How could I be pregnant at thirty-nine with a part-time sailor-slash-builder's baby whom I didn't love because I still carried a torch for the father of my three children?

'Do you want to keep the baby?' Jacqui asked me carefully.

'I don't know.'

'While you think about it, can we have a cup of tea?'

We trooped back down the stairs, the same stairs we had walked up five minutes ago when I wasn't technically pregnant, when life was a lot less complicated, when I only had divorce worries, children worries and money worries.

As Jacqui clinked mugs I rooted around in my bag for my phone, a text from Sam emblazoned across my screen. I didn't need to open it. I already knew what it would say.

Carrie in labour. I don't know how long we will be. Don't tell the kids. I'll let you know when we've got some news.

21

Brother from Another Mother

It's a boy.

I texted Ali in Spain.

Poor Sonny. He won't like that, will he?

No. I wish it had been a girl. At least the girls already have each other, Sonny is the only boy. And now he isn't. Dreading his reaction.

Are you OK about the baby?

Not sure. It's complicated.

That was an understatement.

How's your mum? What's going on?

Mum is amazing. Going through Dad's stuff very slowly. We

have had lots of tears. I think she's jumped the first phase of grief and dived straight into anger.

Ouch. Keep her away from the mug cupboard!

The entrance to the clinic in Streatham was very discreet and set right back in the sun-dappled leafy grounds quite a way from the busy road. I had to state my name on the gate intercom and wait while they buzzed me through. I was expecting a few protestors, possibly an unsolicited flyer being rammed into my hand depicting dead foetuses. That had been my experience twenty years previously when I had arranged a friend's abortion when we were at university. But today the gate was void of haranguers; all I could hear was the cheerful chirping of the birds in the trees that lined the path down to reception. Spring had most definitely sprung, with colourful bulbs in full bloom. I could see where a mower had culled the swathes of dying daffodils, a trail of butter-yellow confetti the only evidence until next year.

My boobs were throbbing and my mouth tasted like a filthy toilet. Welcome to pregnancy. Only this time dread was heavily layered beneath the nausea, and excitement and expectation were conspicuous by their absence. Only Mel and Jacqui knew where I was today. Chug was at nursery. In two days' time I had to meet my lawyer in town and sign some legal papers for the decree nisi to go through.

The children had already visited their brother in hospital. Carrie had had to stay in because there had been so many complications and Jaimie had had the cord wrapped round his neck and was massive so she had torn quite badly and lost a lot of blood. I did not gloat.

I've never been so scared in my life,

Sam had texted when he relayed the news.

I thought he wasn't going to come out when they said the cord was twice round his neck.

Oh, ye of small memory, I had wanted to text back. Sonny had the cord twisted twice round *his* neck and you didn't know because you had been downstairs scoffing Pringles when you were supposed to be getting the camera. Instead of delivering a slap-down, I texted back:

I hope Carrie recovers soon and you can all go home. You need to ring and tell the kids and arrange for them to visit.

I did hope she recovered soon, because she was going to need to with four kids in the house…

'What was the baby like?' I asked Isla when they returned from visiting in the evening, wondering when pictures of Carrie cradling her precious bundle would emerge on the internet, confirming Sam's apparent joy to the world. Though, if I remembered rightly, he hated the tiny baby phase, the nutty wife phase and the no sleep phase. Good luck this time round! You only know her as Carrie the Sexy Chef. How about Carrie the hormonal harridan with leaky tits and a butchered vagina who issues orders while you have to parent three other kids, and keep her satisfied at the same time?

'Oh, he's so cute. I held him! He has massive cheeks like a chipmunk!'

'I kissed him, Mummy,' Meg told me, cuddling the cat. 'But I didn't like the hospital. It smelled funny. I just wanted to come home and see Ginger.'

'Baby,' Sonny said, and surprised us all.

'He said that coming home in the car,' Isla informed me. 'Daddy cried when he said it.' I picked him up and squeezed him and he punched me in the chest.

'Sonny! No!' I thought my boob was going to explode and I dropped him to the floor. 'Don't hit!'

'Dad!' He burst into tears and flung himself at my feet and attempted to climb up me like a cat.

'You hurt me!' I accused him in a wounded manner.

'Dad! Dad! Dad!'

'Mummy, cuddle him!' Isla cried. Her maternal side burned so fiercely I sometimes thought she was here to nurture me. 'He didn't mean it.' I didn't want to cuddle him as my chest pulsated where he had struck me, but I knew Isla was right. I sat on one of the circular Habitat chairs and pulled him onto my knee where he clung to me sobbing, his breathing jagged and irregular like he had been winded.

'I don't think he liked Jaimie,' Meg said quietly, snuffling Ginger's fur and kissing the top of his head. And so the baton changed hands before me. Meg was able to open up and communicate her thoughts, and Sonny was on lockdown, probably not knowing why he just hit me, but safe in the knowledge that he could because I loved him. The chain of pain continued its caustic journey.

'How do you feel about the baby, now you know about *your* baby?' Jacqui asked me the million-dollar question after I returned from the doctor's for my clinic referral. She had looked after Sonny for me. 'I mean, it's weird, isn't it?'

'I feel confused. I don't want to see him. I couldn't bear

it if he looked like Sonny, but as for not liking him, he's just a baby, it's not his fault he was born and might disrupt my children's lives and cause some major upset.'

'Does it make you want to keep this baby?' We were sitting in camping deck chairs on the unkempt lawn facing the direction of the sun, the acer tree stretched up behind us in the raised bed, its newly unfurled leaves already reaching for the light like our upturned faces. Sonny was right at the bottom of the garden bouncing on his new birthday present that Sam and I had bought between us: the trampoline. He would eat his meals on it if he could. In fact, it was the best thing I had ever bought for the kids. They all loved it. We refrained from telling Sonny it was exclusively his present because I wanted them all to play nicely. Woody had expertly put it together for me.

I sighed and sipped scalding tea. 'The thought that Sam has a new baby that isn't mine, who is my children's brother, makes me feel less inclined to be so black and white about having an abortion. Though if I had a baby with Woody, he would have to move in here—'

'Why would he have to move in?' Jacqui interrupted, turning her head sharply to look at me through her shades so her blonde hair bounced in its loose ponytail. 'Do you want him to?'

'Well, to help with the baby.'

'But do you see a life with him? Ali could help, I could help! You wouldn't be on your own.'

'I do like Woody, but as for it being permanent, I never thought further than next week. But we have great sex, and do have a laugh. Though recently he has been hinting at doing more stuff "as a family". I think he likes the idea of being a dad...'

'Then don't jump the gun. Everything is in its place and you will make the right decision for you and the kids, and the baby. You never know, Woody might run a mile.'

'I know, which is why I want to go on my own to the clinic to see how I really feel.'

'Number thirty-six.' I looked up from my phone where I had been texting Ali. I was number thirty-six, no names so anonymity was assured. The waiting room was ubiquitous beige with a wall-mounted TV gently rumbling in the background. A leafy fern in a salt-stained terracotta pot had been placed below the window, its dusty compost peeling away from the sides in desperate need of water, and a mangy-looking palm tree stood guard to the left of the TV. The grounds beyond the streaky waiting-room window were impressive and I could make out what looked like a towering Victorian hospital building beyond the large well-tended flowerbeds. I imagined teenage girls tucked-in under starched sheets with pale faces, and worried parents by their sides behind every window. But the reality was not that. Most women at the clinic were either my age or in their twenties. I was an irresponsibly stupid middle-aged woman who had managed to get myself knocked up while off my face.

'This way, please.' I followed the sonographer to a small room with a hulking ultrasound machine and a bed for me to lie on. After lots of questions about periods and sexual history, the lady put a condom over the dildo scanner (for want of a better word. I think we were a bit late to the party on the condom front).

'We're going to go through your vagina as I doubt we will see very much through your abdomen. Just try to relax. If you don't want to look, turn away from the screen.' But I chose to look at the screen and tried to stay calm. What if there was nothing there? What if there were twins? What if it had already died because it knew I was dithering?

'Oh, wow!' the doctor gasped. 'You're a lot more pregnant than you thought you were. About nine weeks, from the size.'

'But I've had periods!' She studied my face, like she was trying to work me out.

'It may have been breakthrough bleeding.' On the screen a tiny pulse flashed from a tadpole. My baby. I felt my eyes well up and my heart beat in my throat as I swallowed hard against rogue emotions I failed to find words for.

'Are you OK?' I shook my head. 'Would you like a minute?' I nodded. She slowly withdrew the dildo and left the room so I could slip my knickers back on and straighten my head up. But I couldn't; it remained bent out of shape. There was a heartbeat inside of me, a complete constellation of stars and a milky way silently brewing.

Next, I met a different woman in a different office, even more stark and beige than the clinical waiting room. The man-size box of tissues in the centre of the brown Formica desk was the clue that this room had heard some extremely testing conversations.

'So, you're about nine weeks. And you initially came here for a possible termination. How do you feel now?'

'I don't know! I saw a heartbeat!' I exploded, crying loudly. I grabbed a tissue from the all-seeing box. 'The father doesn't even know, and my ex-husband, though we are technically still married, had a baby two days ago and I already have three children and tomorrow I have to go and sign off my divorce.'

'Oh, my. That all sounds very upsetting! Well, how do you feel about bringing another baby into the situation? Is this something you can imagine now with everything else you have going on? I'm not here to tell you what to do, just help you see a way forward.'

'I can't imagine another baby, no. But I also can't imagine terminating after seeing the heartbeat and how big it was.'

I had always been pro-choice. I didn't believe in telling someone what to do or what was right or wrong. A woman's body is her business. But I had never had to face that choice myself and now, staring down the barrel of the gun, I honestly didn't know what I was going to do. If I had a baby, I entered into a life-long relationship with Woody, not necessarily romantic, but as the baby's father, he would be part of its existence if he wanted to be. I also knew it was foolish to contemplate keeping it in my current situation.

'Would telling the father help you make a decision, or maybe talking to a family member? You know you don't have to tell the father to go through with the abortion. It is all entirely your choice.'

'Yes, I know. Maybe I will tell him. It might help me make up my mind.'

When I walked back to the car, the senior school opposite was emptying out for dinner break, the kids shouting and chasing each other across the playground. Of all those kids, I thought, I wonder if any of them were mistakes? The law of averages must swing towards a resounding yes. Did any of their parents ever regret keeping them? I didn't know how I could love another baby as much as I loved my three. But then I had thought that each time I had got pregnant. The love always finds a way to divide and multiply, just like the cells inside my womb. I didn't love this one's dad like I loved... *had* loved Sam. Would that make a difference? I unlocked the car and slumped in the driver's seat. I gripped the steering wheel and bent my head forward until it touched the horn symbol.

'Universe, tell me what to do, please,' I prayed into my chest. 'I feel lost.'

I remained motionless for a few minutes until my phone pinged in my bag. It was Woody.

> I'll be over by seven. I got paid today so I can treat us to dinner! xx

22

Who's the Daddy?

'I'm just going to say it. I'm pregnant.' I was resting on the pillows against the wooden slatted headboard watching Woody roughly dry himself after his shower. His bum was so pert and muscly, as were his chiselled back and shoulders, and staring lasciviously at him sent violent electric shocks to my groin. I had forgotten that being permanently horny whilst wanting to vomit were kindred spirits of all my pregnancies. I had yet to experience vomiting mid-orgasm, though I suppose there was a first time for everything.

Woody slowly brought the towel down from where he had been furiously scrubbing his tangled mop of hair and turned round to face me, totally naked.

'You're pregnant?' Woody's voice cracked like a teenage boy on the verge of becoming a man.

I nodded.

'How?'

'Well, we had sex and some of your semen must have fertilised an egg and now a baby is growing inside my womb.'

'I know all that! But we've been careful!'

'Not careful enough.'

He sank down onto the bed next to me. 'Christ, Mands. What do we do?' He looked to me for an answer.

'I went to the clinic today to arrange an abortion.'

'What? You weren't going to tell me?'

'Woody, let me finish! I needed to see how I felt. I saw a heartbeat.'

'Oh.' This was so absurd, having this conversation while he was naked. 'And how did you feel?'

'I don't know. I wanted to see what you thought. I *had* thought I would just want to get rid of it, what with this being what it is. But the heartbeat...'

'What do you mean?'

'Well, we're not in a serious relationship, are we?' The words clanged together like heavy-bottomed pots. Woody visibly flinched as if I had kicked him.

'If that's how you feel.'

'Woody, I'm sorry...' He stood up and walked over to the rocking chair, the very same chair that I had fed all three babies in before bed. His clothes were draped neatly over the arm. He was very tidy for someone who looked dishevelled a lot of the time. 'Look, I—'

'Don't, Amanda. I need to get dressed if we're to have this conversation.'

I waited while he pulled on clothes, and I felt so torn. His physicality was what drew me to him, and I assumed this 'relationship' would burn itself out in time. We'd never discussed what 'we' might be but I'd guessed we were dating in the old-fashioned sense of the word.

Once dressed, he perched on the chair, squashing the row of teddies that had been squatting there for years, lined up like in *The Usual Suspects*. I found it excruciating to meet his gaze but I knew I owed it to him so I looked up.

'Amanda, I think I love you.'

Ambushed by tears I hurriedly brushed them away, totally stunned by his choice of words.

'I haven't said anything because I know you don't feel the same way. I know you still love Sam, and I get it – he's the kids' dad. But I can't help how I feel and I don't want to sway you in any way. I can't say this news isn't a total shock...' He paused and looked at his hands as if they could somehow prompt his ensuing words. 'Look, I'm a simple man with simple needs and I never thought I would ever face this moment in my life. But if you're waiting for me to tell you what to do, I won't.'

'But what do *you* want?' I asked him tearfully.

He sighed heavily and cradled his head in his hands very gently, like he didn't want to disturb any thoughts.

'I want you.'

'So, what would you do if I said let's have a baby and stay together? I'm not saying that's what I want, I just want to see what *you* want.'

'I would do it.'

'But would you... *move in*?'

'How else would we make it work? I wouldn't be much help living at Mum's, would I?'

'But what about work?'

'I could commute.'

'To Essex?'

I hadn't even considered Ali and Grace. They lived here and I didn't want to turf them out.

'I guess... Or you have the abortion and we carry on as before.'

That simple sentence, supposed to help bring clarity to this confusing situation, did nothing to draw it to any sensible conclusion. It was almost like my brain refused to hear the word 'abortion' and instead swapped the word round to 'baby', making the syntax more palatable.

That's what I told myself afterwards when I said the fateful: 'OK, let's do it.'

'Have the baby?' Woody's eyes lit up.

'Yes.'

He jumped up and enveloped me in his arms, squeezing me so tight I could hardly breathe. 'Do you mean it?' he whispered into my hair.

I nodded though I was paralysed and too frightened to speak because I actually had no idea what I was doing or saying or who I was any more. If someone had asked me would I ever have a love child with a man I had only been dating a few months, who was an ex-hedonistic nutter, who should have gone to rehab but instead was now going to move into my home, where my kids and Ali and her baby lived and become part of the commune, I would have roared, 'Are you shitting me?' But I had just watched myself agreeing to do it without a loaded gun to my head.

23

Ali's Dirty Secret

'Are you OK, Mands?' Jacqui asked as I stared aimlessly out of the grimy peeling sash window in Dara's flat onto the busy street below, scraping off a few white paint flakes with my thumbnail. It was the day after signing off my almost divorce and I was feeling slightly steamrollered by the amount of life-changing events I was dealing with.

The Knightsbridge location was at odds with the imagined grandeur of the flat. Tea chests hugged the grubby magnolia walls, and one had been dragged back to the centre of the main living room to be used as a coffee table. A battered mauve sofa that may have once been comfy in a different decade was the only other furniture in the echoing tall-ceilinged room. A gangling parched fern leaned hungrily towards the light from one of the cobwebbed corners. A few ghosts of pictures past left faint dust imprints on the walls and a red wine stain splattered along one of the skirting boards and onto the standard beige frayed rental carpet. Ali had reported back it was a typical bachelor pad when she'd visited, but now it resembled student digs at the end of term, devoid of any personality, though I suspected it had had very little to begin with.

People milled about smoking out of the half-open windows or drinking cheap wine out of plastic disposable cups. I had no idea who any of them were – most were from the studio at work, I guessed. Ali, being loud and gregarious, was the life and soul of the living room, getting people drinks and emptying fancy Marks and Spencer's crisps onto foil catering trays. She had been very excited when I'd recounted my surprise news after she'd landed, assuring her at the same time she didn't have to leave.

'We're going to be a proper commune. I can help when the baby comes: do some night feeds, if you want. Oh, it will be so exciting! Will the baby sleep in the spare room?'

I winced. No one went in there apart from Jacqui when she was pissed, and Woody before we had told the children about us. I only visited when absolutely necessary, still unable to face the piles of junk Sam had discarded when he left.

'Maybe... You don't think I'm mad?'

'If anyone can do this, you can. I don't think you're mad for wanting to have a baby. It might be the best thing for Woody and for you. A fresh start.' I tried to grasp onto that thought but as the weeks rolled past towards the scan date, doubt greedily ate away at it. Number one fact: I didn't love Woody. I wondered if, when the baby came, I would magically fall for him like a heroine in a soppy film, finally arriving at a crashing conclusion that there was more to him than just his dashing physique, and appreciate that he was lovely and caring. But the reservations that held fast reared their heads soon after, right at Dara's party.

'Is it Woody?' Jacqui persisted at the flat. 'I know he's being a bit... special.'

'Special!' I squawked. 'He's acting like a total dick. He's forty-fucking-one and he's behaving like this. He needs the fucking sunshine bus to take him away he's being so special.'

Woody was strutting round the floor like a peacock on heat to the appalling chart music that was blasting out of the ancient boom box on the floor, unboxed CDs scattered like lotus flower offerings at the foot of Buddha. He was boisterously clapping his hands and trying to drag Dara's polite friends from their sensible journalistic chats about commerce and business and babies.

'Come on, this is supposed to be a party!' he was crying insistently while sweating profusely and chewing his face off. This was the Woody of old. A switch had flipped in his head and it appeared he couldn't flip it back.

'What's made him go all loopy?' Jacqui asked innocently, tapping her ash into the windowsill.

'Cocaine, I would imagine.'

'He's got some?' She inhaled again, blowing the smoke away from me and out through the other open window.

'I'm only assuming, but I have seen this many times. Him and Dara disappeared into one of the bathrooms earlier and came out all loud and weird. I think Ali has had a few lines, too.'

'No one offered me any!'

'I would get in there quick if you want some, or Woody will hoover it all up in no time.'

'Nah, I'm not in the mood tonight. Wine is good enough for me today!' I wished I could knock back a few large glasses of red. 'I've never seen him go this mad before, though,' Jacqui continued. 'But then we are usually in the same state so I may be wrong.'

'No, this is a different level. I think he may have double-dropped it with some ecstasy.' I shook my head, bewildered that he could act so unfittingly at a party where we knew hardly anyone. The scales seemingly fell away from my eyes and instead of sexy Woody I noticed uneven teeth, some of them stained from continual smoking, and pasty skin perspiring profusely, drops working their way into the ratty hair, in need of a trim. There was also the frantic starey pupil-less eyes and too small T-shirt riding up, exposing a hairy bum crack. Some of Dara's friends rolled their eyes and looked pityingly at me every time he unsuccessfully forced me to dance. I said nothing, there was no point because I felt he hadn't done anything inherently wrong, he was just being himself. I felt naïvely hoodwinked into believing he'd grown up, or maybe it was me that was different: staid, sensible and having a gradual dawn of realisation that I was Doing The Wrong Thing. A phrase played in a loop in my head: *Sam wouldn't behave like this…*

'Do you want a cuppa?' Jacqui asked, lying next to me in my bright airy bedroom the week before the scan, the mid-morning summer air wafting in through the gap at the bottom of the open window. Soothing birdsong bounced into the room but couldn't lift my mood. I was having a really bad turn. Spinning head, bone-scraping exhaustion, a blackness within me that I could not shake and the inability to cope with the children. With closed eyes I Reikied my stomach to quell the roiling nausea. Thankfully Sonny was at nursery and Ali was going to pick him up for me this afternoon. The girls were at school. Jacqui and I were supposed to be shopping for a cheap dress for my fortieth birthday party this coming weekend, but I had to lie down. My book had ground to a halt some time ago, DJ-ing was also on pause until I felt a bit better. I wasn't sure how the manager would feel about a middle-aged pregnant DJ spinning tunes to a mashed-up audience. It would be viewed as either achingly hip or massively uncool.

'No, thanks. Maybe some water?'

Dara was taking Ali out for one last hurrah this evening before jetting off to Hong Kong for good.

'Aren't you sad?' I'd asked her after the leaving party the previous week. 'You do really like him, don't you?'

'Of course I'm sad, but I only see him once or twice a week. It's not going to be a radical change.'

'How has he left it?'

'That he's coming back over in August, and when he's back we can plan when I'll go out there.'

'With Grace?'

'Yes. I have to go before she turns two or I can't afford it. I've saved up enough for a flight but he has said he would pay.'

Being so preoccupied with my own unfolding drama over the last month, I felt strangely disconnected from everyone else's lives. On the surface, Ali seemed to be coping with her dad's death OK, though I had no idea how, and Jacqui and her kids spent most of their time here when she wasn't at work and they weren't at school. 'I wish I could move in. I just can't bear that house. I wish I'd never bought it.' Ali and I had repeatedly offered to help unpack the boxes that still remained untouched, but she flatly refused.

From my bed I could hear Ali upstairs on the phone; her presence in the house was always audible. As Jacqui returned with her tea and my water, fireworks detonated above.

'Yes, Hattie, I fucked him. Twice! Once in the front seat and once in the back seat. Happy?'

'Deary me, who's Ali yelling at?' Jacqui asked, setting her tea down on the bedside table. 'The door's shut and I can still hear every word.'

'Hattie. Holy fuckflaps. She must have shagged Jim.'

'What? She hates Jim!'

I revisited recent events and tallied them up against Ali's uncharacteristic behaviour. She had been in Spain for a few weeks after the funeral without Dara and seemed peculiarly unbothered by his imminent departure. Also, Jim had recently moved into a house with Hattie very near to us. Once again Ali had seemed unruffled. I had wondered at the time if she was stock-piling fertiliser to make a bomb and blow them both up, which would explain her *laissez-faire* attitude.

'It's a thin line between love and hate.'

'True.' Jacqui nodded, putting her finger to her lips as a volley of words tumbled from above.

'Ask Jim! No, I'm not with him. I've no idea where he is.... Do NOT come here! He's not here!'

The attic door flung open and Ali stumbled into the wall on her way down the stairs.

'Ali!' Jacqui cried through the half-open door as she settled back on the bed next to me. The thudding footsteps ground to a halt and the door creaked open. Ali stood in the doorway but wouldn't meet our eyes.

'Oh bollocks, I thought you were both out dress shopping.'

'I feel too shit. What's going on?'

Ali grimaced and shame seemed to creep up from her yellow vest top, flaring across her cheeks, staining them red.

'What did you hear?'

'Everything,' I replied bluntly.

'Don't shout at me... I've kind of been having a thing with Jim.'

'What?!' Jacqui yelped. 'Why? How? When?'

Ali sighed and sunk down onto the edge of the bed, still avoiding eye contact.

'It's been going on since Dad died.'

'Wow. How have you kept that quiet? You weren't even here for half of that time!' I quizzed her.

'Who started it?' Jacqui wanted to know.

'He did, obviously. He was here looking after Grace; he couldn't believe that Dad had just gone so suddenly.'

'But he was so rude to your parents the last time he saw them,' I cried indignantly.

'I know. He said he couldn't believe a good man like my dad could just drop down dead when someone like his dad was still alive.'

'I always knew he had daddy issues!' I opined from the bed.

'Anyway, after that he looked after Grace on and off so I could help arrange the funeral, and one day when we met him in a café he started talking about how he'd made a huge mistake, how he was missing out on Grace growing up. How he was missing me. I even got a text from his best friend's wife telling me she was delighted Jim was thinking of getting back together with me.'

'Fucker! Like you would just jump.'

Ali squirmed uncomfortably.

'You *would* have just jumped, wouldn't you?'

'Well, don't tell me if Sam came crawling back now and begged, you wouldn't say yes.'

'You're forgetting I can't say yes. I'm having another man's baby.'

'That's not what I meant.'

'I know what you meant. I have thought about it. It has gone too far now. I don't know who Sam is any more. It doesn't mean I don't have days when I wish none of this had ever happened, but it is what it is. I can't change it.' Oh, but how I wished I could...

'How did Hattie find out?' Jacqui urged, changing tack.

'She saw a text from Jim to me saying he missed me. But she's suspected before and never rang me.'

'Where's Jim now? Is she coming here to have a fight?'

'He's got Grace in the park while I did admin. I need to tell him she's found out. Hattie's at work.'

'Well, she suspected and then you told her.'

'Yes. She was being vile, though. Saying he would never touch me with a barge pole, that I was disgusting and dirty and a bitch. He was just feeling sorry for me because Dad had died and they were laughing about it behind my back, about how I was falling for him again.'

'He's been playing you both off against each other when she's got suspicious, telling her he's teasing you,' Jacqui said.

'Why can't she see he's messed up, saying stuff like that?' I wondered.

''Cos she's obsessed with him. She's hearing what she wants to hear.'

Ali's phone started ringing. She picked it up. I could hear Jim's irate voice from my perch on the bed.

'Jim, she pushed me. She was being horrid.' Jim ranted and Ali's eyes filled with tears. 'OK, I'll come now.

'He wants me to meet him in the park with Grace and tell Hattie I made it up as a way of punishing her for what happened. She's in a cab from work.'

'You're not going to do it, are you?' I asked, horrified.

'He wants to buy some time while he works out what he wants.'

'But what about what *you* want?' Jacqui asked crossly, picking up her tea and blowing on it.

'Were you still keeping Dara going because you actually didn't know what you wanted?' I said, the love quadrangle distracting me from imminent puking.

'Yes. I like Dara loads, but he's leaving, and Jim was there and mentioned getting back together. And I didn't know what to think. My head was all over the place 'cos of Dad. Then we had sex and it was a bit of a game changer.'

'In the back of the car?' I laughed.

'Yes, seedy, but it was amazing!'

'Where was Grace?' Jacqui fired.

'With Amanda,' Ali said, embarrassed.

'Don't go,' I offered. 'Do you want to get back together if he's not being straight with either of you? Remember how he treated you and sold the house. He made you homeless.'

'I know it all! Look, I've got to go. We'll talk later.' She jumped up off the bed and ran down the stairs and out into the sunshine.

'I feel a mess about to happen.' Jacqui sighed ominously, putting down her tea. 'Nothing good can come of this.'

Ali rushed in at five with Sonny in tow.

'Well?' I asked, stirring pasta sauce on the stove.

'I dropped him in it, told Hattie it was all true.'

'Shit.'

'Yep. Fuck it. Jim's about to restart the war. I can't think about it now. I need to get ready for my date.' And off she dashed. I wondered what fire and brimstone Jim would potentially unleash now. Knowing him, he would take his time to carefully stage-manage some devious plan to derail Ali. Jim liked to be in charge and when he wasn't he didn't play nice.

At two a.m. I was woken by a loud crash from upstairs. A muffled tattoo comprising bells and whistles filtered through the pillow jammed over my head. 'The toy box,' I muttered to myself, and attempted to block out the subsequent sex sounds with ear plugs.

24

This Is Forty

'I'll call Sam,' Ali said calmly as I tried in vain to extricate myself from Sonny's proprietorial clutches in the hallway.

'Dad, Dad, Dad!' Sonny wouldn't let go of my dress and was attempting to burrow underneath the gossamer skirts, possibly to retrace his steps back to my womb. I wondered if he's guessed there was yet another pretender to the throne furtively growing in there, ready to overthrow him once more. The minute I slipped on the gorgeous silver maxi dress Ali had stolen from a shoot for me, Sonny had jumped on me, cat-like. The real cat had been shut in my room with a litter tray and enough food and water to last the day. He had a few days before he was allowed his first foray into the outside world. Meg had made a 'Private Keep Out' notice and taped it to my door. I was certain I was going to be gifted a poo on my pillow.

'I'll keep checking on him, Mummy, to make sure he isn't scared or lonely. I've given him a Build-A-Bear to cuddle.' I was still astounded at the change in Meg, and hugged her tight.

'You're such a good cat mummy, Meg. Ginger is very lucky.'

'Hi, Sam, yes, I'm ringing because you need to come and get Sonny... Because he's been hitting Amanda for the last hour and a half and the party is about to start... I don't care if you're doing DIY, get here, please. Your son is ruining Amanda's fortieth birthday and you need to help out. She deserves it!' She rolled her eyes as she hung up. 'Like DIY is important. I bet *she*'s got him trapped under her massive thumb.'

'Is he coming?'

'Yes, in half an hour.'

Quite a few local friends, and stalwart mums who had sewn me back together in the beginning after Sam's swift departure, arrived bearing gifts, along with my brother and his wife and kids. I was unable to get people drinks or socialise because of Sonny and his vice-like grip. 'Be nice,' I whispered to Rob when he arrived as he hugged me hello over Sonny's head. 'Get all your negativity out before Woody comes.'

'Who, me? Negative?' Rob laughed ironically. 'Look, as long as he treats you right, it's good with me. It's your life. I would always just say be careful, that's all! And if all else fails, marry me and be my beard!'

Ali opened the door to Ursula, who came bearing a massive package wrapped in red spotty paper.

'I can't believe you're the first one to hit forty. What's happening to us? We need to stop time now before it's too late!' She hugged me tight and I sucked in my belly, safeguarding my secret. Ursula was quickly followed by Woody, with Sarah and Will grappling Oliver in a buggy, Maisie trailing behind holding her panda and looking her usual wan self.

'Happy birthday, my darling girl!' Woody cried. He looked like they'd stopped at the pub on the way here. He kissed me on the mouth and tasted of beer. I chose not to look in his eyes in case I discovered something I didn't like. I summoned all my Beardy Weirdy inner strength and set a white light around myself. Today was going to be fine.

Woody had met an old friend one Friday night, someone who might be able to offer him local work. He returned after midnight, clearly wasted. 'I only had one line, honestly. Sean had a whole bag, and I had the smallest one.' Another night he was supposed to cook Ali and me dinner. 'I was in the pub with Will. I'm sorry, gorgeous, we lost track of time. You know I love you. Shall I order a takeaway?'

'What's going on here?' Woody asked Sonny as he clung ferociously to me. 'You're too big to get under there.'

'Dad!' Sonny defiantly cried.

'It's Mum!' Woody tried irritably. 'Why don't you correct him?' I shook my head. Now was not the time. Sonny buried himself even further and I fell against the banisters.

'Come here,' Woody sighed, and grabbed him without even looking at what he was doing. Sonny's fists were bunched around the material of my dress and as Woody pulled him I heard a rip.

'Nooooooooo!' I cried, tears springing instantly. I loved this dress. The top half was embroidered with dainty seashells and silver sequins sewn intricately round the bust, the empire-line skirt billowing forth, hiding my burgeoning bump. For the first time in a month I felt glamorous.

'You little shit!' Woody gasped, dropping Sonny roughly on the floor. I wanted to punch him. This wasn't the first time he had waded in without thinking, or acted short with Sonny. When I thought back to when I first met him all those months ago, his moods had swung unpredictably in such a short space of time.

'Don't say that!' I cried angrily. 'He's only little. You could hurt him.'

'He's three! And he knows what he's doing.' Sarah and Will shuffled past us embarrassed, and out to the kitchen and playroom with bottles of fizz and some Cellophane-wrapped white flowers.

'I've told you before,' I hissed under my breath, 'I tell him off. Not you.'

'Well, what happens when I'm living here?'

'You're not here just yet, are you?' The door banged again and I dragged Sonny up onto my hip ready to welcome the next guest, leaving Woody to join the party already gathering in the kitchen. Amy was DJ-ing and the kids were dancing. I picked out Isla's worried little face through the throng of gyrating children before I turned to see who had knocked.

'Happy birthday!' Mel sang. Just seeing her made me want to start crying. The party suddenly felt like a really ridiculous plan. So many people I couldn't speak to anyone properly. Why had I thought this was a good idea?

'Are you OK?' I shook my head. I was going to be sick. I shoved Sonny at her who started screaming and took the stairs two at a time to the middle-floor bathroom, almost tripping on my dress. I didn't make it, projectile vomiting up the wall and all over the shut toilet seat.

'Oh, Mands,' Mel said softly behind me as Sonny tried to grab me but then realised I was ill. He started bawling his eyes out all over again.

'You weren't like this with the other ones, were you?' I shook my head, wiping my watery eyes in some loo roll.

'Have they said it's normal to be sick like this, even at three months?'

'Yes. I was sick through all the others, but I feel wrong all the time. Like I'm ill. I have days where lifting my head is a struggle.'

'You've got sick in your hair. Come here.' While Mel tidied me up, the door banged again.

'It's Sam,' Ali called up the stairs. 'Have you got Sonny?'

With wet hair and a dishevelled demeanour, I met Sam downstairs. I had always thought we would celebrate this significant birthday together and a poignant pain struck my side. Mel followed me, heading for the anti-bac spray and kitchen roll. Sam was wearing his scruffy DIY jeans decorated with paint splatters, some of the colours dating back to this house.

'Hello, Sam,' Mel said on her way to the kitchen.

'Oh, wow, Mel, I haven't seen you for ages!' He leaned in for an awkward peck on the cheek.

'Yes, it's been a while,' she said non-committedly. 'Excuse me, Amanda's roped me into cleaning the loo!' He laughed like he was at the party. I half expected him to join in with: 'Oh, how like Amanda,' then roll his eyes. At this point, if he had, shortly after I would have been in the dock for murder and the baby would be born in prison.

'Hey, Sonny, you ready to play some football?' Sam cried, scooping Chug up into his arms and kissing him. Sonny was beaming from ear to ear.

'Dad! Yes!'

'Bye...' Sam called out to the air. No one was listening. I followed him out to his car, the exact same one as mine, parked further down the street. I idly wondered if his new house was anything like this one.

'Sonny's fine. I don't know what you're making all the fuss about,' he said, turning round after he had strapped him in the back.

'What?'

'You heard me. I bet the only reason you made Ali phone me was so you could get hammered with all your mates and not have to deal with all three of them. I'm assuming Woody will be there in charge of proceedings.'

'I can't believe you're saying that.'

'Oh, come on, Amanda. I'm not stupid.'

'Don't you think I want my little boy, one of the loves of my life, at my own birthday? Why on earth would I want him sent away? He won't stop hitting me! You don't get it.'

'Get what?'

'This is my fortieth. All our friends, people who we've both known for years, are in that house having a party. He should be there... So should you.'

'I can come. If you want me to come, I'll do it.'

'No!!!' I yelled. 'As my husband!'

'You know I can't do that.'

I walked off, a fresh tidal wave of grief crashing over my head, soaking through all the carefully fixed layers of armour, cruelly stripping them off, leaving me bare.

'I'll drop him back in the morning!' Sam called at my retreating back.

'This is for your blood pressure,' the lady said. I had to slip both arms into an automatic Robocop-type machine with dual airbags that slowly inflated, crushing my arms in the process.

'There's something wrong with the baby,' I said involuntarily.

Woody crouched down on a stool to the side, watching me. He winked.

'Don't be silly,' she reassured me. 'Why would you say that?'

'Because I feel it. I'm too old.'

'How old are you?' she asked me in her Eastern European accent. She was tiny, like a porcelain doll, her hair scraped back into a severe bun, high Slavic cheekbones disguising her real age. She could have been anything from twenty-five to forty-five.

'Forty.'

'Wow, you certainly don't look it. But that's not old. It will be OK.' But how did she know? She couldn't see inside my womb and witness the festering doubt suffocating the developing baby. I could. It was happening and I knew it.

'Don't say that,' Woody said softly, stroking my leg. 'It'll be all right.'

'But what if it isn't?'

'Then we deal with it.'

I smiled weakly at him, reservation stalking down the wafer-thin optimism I had been feeling that morning. I had never felt anything was untoward with the other three when I came for previous scans. I had blindly assumed the best every time.

When it was time to lie on the couch, the urge to run from the room was visceral. The jelly was cold and Woody held my hand, squeezing it when the baby swam into view, its monochrome heart beating like the clappers. I looked intently at the monitor. Everything appeared normal: two arms, two legs, a head, a beating heart.

'Can we shut the door?' the doctor asked quietly.

That was my confirmation. Suddenly the room was humming with people that I hadn't previously noticed, all of them crowding round the screen, murmuring and nodding at each other. No one was pointing out the baby and telling me about it. I was invisible. The doctor silently took measurements. The Eastern European woman had disappeared. I glanced wildly at Woody but he was staring at the screen, a look of wonder on his face. The Eastern European doctor returned and with her was a tall man in his fifties with thick dark salt-and-pepper hair, wearing a sombre suit. He edged in front of the screen and looked closely, bending over so his face was almost pressing on the glass. He turned to look at me.

'I'm Dr Almendarez. Your baby has a heart defect, I'm afraid.'

'How bad is it?' I asked nervily. Isla had a minor heart murmur but she was alive and well. I detected something even more ominous buried under his words.

'It's quite serious. Something that might be able to be fixed with surgery after birth, but there're the other problems associated with it.'

My body existed in the room with the beeping machines, but I was somewhere else. I wondered if I was having a genuine out-of-body experience. I could hear and feel everything so acutely as if I was the room, the air, the beeping, the urgent footsteps in the corridor, the crying baby in the waiting area.

'What problems?' Woody prompted, bringing me crashing back to the bed with a jolt.

'Looking at the foetus, it would appear it has quite a few characteristics of trisomy twenty-one.' When we looked nonplussed by his exclusive terminology, he elaborated. 'Down's syndrome.'

The words winded me.

'You see here, the big toe is further away from the second toe, and the nasal bone is very small. Your placenta is also abnormally large, which will make you protrude more obviously. The heart defect is in keeping with Down's babies, and is in line with this type of Down's being life debilitating. The baby may not live long after birth.'

I didn't see. The baby looked perfect. It kicked its delicate legs and curled into a ball. I turned away, frightened to engage, but it was already too late. The moment I'd known the baby was poorly was the second all previous doubts dissolved and brought keenly into focus how much I wanted this baby to be OK.

'Is it certain about the Down's syndrome?' Woody asked, stepping up to the plate.

'No. They are just pointers and only carry a fifty per cent chance of being right. The baby definitely has a heart defect, we know that for sure, but the severity of the Down's can only be confirmed with another test.'

They both looked at me. What was I supposed to say?

'What about abortion? How soon could I have one if the baby has Down's?'

'Well, you don't know one hundred per cent yet if the baby has Down's,' Dr Almendarez back-tracked. I assumed he was Spanish, and a thought popped into my head – was he Catholic? Did he think I would go to hell if I aborted this baby, even if it was terminally sick?

'I know that. The test you're talking about, is it the one with the needle into my womb?'

'Yes, the amniocentesis. It carries a very small risk of miscarriage but the results will be certain. I think we can fit it in today. Shall I leave you to have a think about options?' He handed me some paper towels so I could wipe my abdomen of the clear jelly.

'Do you think you should have the test?' Woody asked after the doctor left the room.

'Yes. I think we need to know. Woody, I can't go ahead with this if the baby is going to die, or have Down's. It's not fair on anyone.'

He nodded slowly in agreement.

'This will hurt,' Dr Almendarez explained a few hours later, wiping my tummy. No sugar-coating whatsoever. I lay prostrate on the bed; the iodine had stained my vulnerable bump yellow.

'Ready?' the doctor asked me.

The second the gargantuan needle came into view I balked.

'No,' I squeaked. 'It's massive.'

'It needs to be. We have to aspirate fluid from the amniotic sac. Keep very still, please.'

'Come on, Mands. Hold my hand.' Woody grabbed it and kissed my forehead. 'You're amazing.'

'If it upsets you don't watch the screen.'

But of course that was all I wanted to do. I may never see the baby again. As the foetus innocently twitched on the monitor, Dr Almendarez grazed my skin with the point of the needle, then applied some force. It hurt like fuck as he pressed on through the muscle wall and into my womb. My entire being tensed and it was like no sensation I had ever experienced. I felt violated. I was unconsciously crying and only became aware when Woody handed me a tissue. Watching the needle on the screen narrowly miss the baby sent a shiver down my spine.

'Noooo,' I moaned to myself. I couldn't look any more and buried my head in Woody's arm. He stroked my head as the doctor extracted the needle. It was over.

'When will we know?' Woody asked him as he carefully wiped my diminutive bump clean.

'It can take a week, but it may be sooner. I'll leave you in the hands of Maria. She will explain what happens next.'

Time has a way of slowing down so that minutes can stretch into lifetimes and hours can feel like the landscape is being eroded from under your very feet. That was what waiting for the result felt like. Rob now knew about the baby – Woody had summoned him from the hospital when we were trapped having tests. He had had to step in and look after the children while Ali was at work.

'Does Sam know?' he asked me when he dropped the kids back.

'No! And he can never know,' I replied. 'My lawyer said it might screw up my chances of a decent financial settlement.' But the even stranger thing was that the very person I wanted to tell was Sam. I wanted him to hold me, tell me it would be OK, that the baby wouldn't feel pain if it had to go. Sam had always been in my corner for all previous traumas; he always knew what to say. Apart from when he was causing the trauma. All I wanted was to sit in his imagined front room and drink a cup of tea and just be. Pretend everything was normal; I didn't even care if Carrie was there. I didn't understand my own logic, all I knew was that I wasn't myself and I couldn't find her even when I searched really hard.

'What are you doing?' Woody asked, Saturday bedtime. He'd found me staring into the bathroom mirror. I'd been stuck there for ages.

'Trying to see where I've gone.'

'You're right here.'

'I'm not. I'm lost. I don't know where I am.'

'Do you want me to help? What can I do?'

'Nothing. Only I can do it.' He tried to touch me but I flinched. 'Sorry. I think I need to just sleep on my own. Do you mind?'

'Sure, if that's what you want.'

He clearly did mind, but I felt secure in my current situation that he wouldn't challenge it. Playing host to a time bomb gave you special dispensation, or so I thought.

The children crept into my bed most nights that week, like they knew something was up but couldn't put their fingers on it. I was glad of the cuddles and it certainly helped me through my metamorphosis.

The day finally dawned and I was prepared to hear the news; Woody was the father, but I held the cards. I now knew if the baby was OK, but with a poorly heart, I would face it and go full term. There was life blossoming and we needed to see it through. The instinct to protect was fierce and I felt firmly rooted in my decision.

'Will it be today for sure?' Ali had asked as she left for work, dropping Sonny and Grace at nursery on her way.

'Maria, the midwife, said she would call today, but not what time.' Ali hugged me on the doorstep.

'I hope it's good news. Ring me any time.'

Please let me know as soon as you know.

Mel had texted at six in the morning.

Love you,

Rob texted.

Thinking of you today.

Woody had to work in Essex so was over there today.

Gorgeous, whatever happens, I'll see it through with you.

He texted just after six in the morning.

I thought of his face and instead of the descendent tug of desire, my stomach clenched with anxiety. Where was his place in all of this?

I dropped Isla and Meg at school and when I walked up to the house to begin my vigil, Jacqui was sitting on the front step, her bike leaning against one of the pillars.

'Hey, thought you might need some company.'

'Thanks. Tea?' Relief flooded through me.

We sat companionably in the back garden sipping tea, listening to the birds chattering, the early morning dew sprinkled like a careless sea of sequins across the lawn, twinkling every time the wind rustled the trees, parting branches so that obscured sunlight could dance through the veil of leaves. We didn't mention the phone call.

At about eleven, just as the sun arced above the dense treeline, bathing us within its toasty glow, my phone rang. Jacqui put her second cup of tea down on the patio as I answered.

'Hello, is that Amanda? It's Maria from King's.'

'Yes. It's me.'

'Amanda, I have some bad news, I'm afraid. The test results came back positive for trisomy twenty-one.'

25

One Week, Three Endings

'Why did you tell everyone else first? Why didn't you tell me?' Woody was shouting right at the bottom of the garden away from the children. We were tucked up behind the trampoline to find some much-needed privacy. The early evening sunlight had abandoned ship some time ago and sailed round to the front of the house, blasting it with the last warmth of the day. Ali was upstairs bathing Grace and my three were inside glued to Mr Maker and his artistic endeavours. 'Why did *Rob* have to tell me?'

I was cross with Rob, but I knew he was trying to build bridges between him and Woody and had just been expressing sympathy.

'I'm sorry. Rob rang me to see if I was OK just after Maria called. I went to pieces on the phone. He was amazing. I didn't want to talk to you while I was a mess.'

'Well, I'm glad he was *amazing*. Meanwhile you never told me our baby is going to be terminated.' He was yelling in such a crazed way that spittle had gathered in the corners of his mouth, waiting to shoot me in the face.

'Why are you shouting at me? I was going to ring you, but Rob got in there first. He was just trying to be kind.'

'You took your fucking time telling me!'

I burst into tears and walked back to the house. The lawn was so wild now I would need a scythe to slice it before the mower could even get started. I picked up my pace, eager to escape Woody's rage, the grass whipping my ankles.

'Amanda! Don't walk off! Stop being ridiculous!'

I stopped dead and turned round. 'I am not being ridiculous. I have to have an operation and have this baby sucked out of me. Never mind that I am terrified of needles, that I am killing a baby, that I have to deal with this, and all you fucking give a shit about is that I was an hour too late telling you. Stop making this about you, you fucking twat.'

'Right, that's it, I'm off.' He stalked towards me and for an unhinged split second I thought he was going to hit me. He thundered past. I didn't even ask him where he was going; I didn't care.

'I need a favour.' I hated the way I had to use that word: *favour*. They were his bloody kids, too. 'I have to have an operation on Friday, a gyne thing, lady trouble, won't go into it, but I can't have the kids after school. Please can you have them?'

'Yes, of course. Are you OK?'

'No.' And I started crying hysterically. Just tell him, a voice said. No! another one countered. You don't need his sympathy.

'Oh gosh, are you really poorly?' Sam asked, fear creeping into his voice. Probably at the thought of a lifetime of four kids permanently living in his love nest after my death.

'No, it's not serious,' I squeezed out between gulps. 'It's just I'm terrified of operations and needles and general anaesthetic.'

'Look, you will be fine. People have them every day. Dying on the operating table is very rare.'

'I know that. Thanks.'

'I hope you're OK, Mands. Really. Just relax and I'll have the kids as long as you need.'

That was the first time he had called me Mands since he'd left.

'We need to take your blood pressure,' the nurse said in the cramped green-curtained cubicle.

I lay on the bed, wearing a scratchy blue gown, completely naked underneath. The sheets were super starched with proper hospital corners that you could have sliced your finger on. I offered up my arm to her and she smiled benevolently at me. They all knew I was a mess, that I was in here to end my pregnancy. None of the other patients was crying silently while their erstwhile boyfriend held their hand and promised a holiday the following month in Greece.

'Remember I said we could go,' he said quietly, attempting to mitigate the tension. 'Well, I found some bargains. I'll forward you the emails. We can go when the kids go away with Sam.'

Woody had returned the day after his outburst. He had been staying at Sarah and Will's house.

'Sarah said I was being an idiot. You were right, I was making it about me. I'm so sorry.'

I sighed. *Sarah said...*

'Please let me come tomorrow and be with you.'

I needed a holiday. The thought of aquamarine sea tickling my toes as I drank a large glass of red wine distracted me from this constrained cubicle.

When the doctor arrived with the anaesthetist, Woody interrupted them.

'Sorry, Amanda's terrified of needles. She's got herself in a state about it.'

'We can administer one we use for babies and children – they're tiny. And bandage it up so you don't see it.'

'Thank you.' Hysteria bubbled unobserved below the surface, mixing readily with the triumvirate of fear, guilt and anxiety. Thoughts seesawed between the irrational and rational. I felt barely in control and, when it was time to go to theatre, fear finally freed itself from its moorings. I ululated past all the ingrown toenails and wisdom teeth extractions, fluorescent strip lights whizzing overhead like trackside houses on a fast train as the nurse tried subtly to hurry. In the ante-chamber outside the theatre, they had to hold me down.

'Get Joanna,' I heard someone say. 'She's good with situations like this.'

'Now, what's all this fuss?' a kindly-looking nurse asked me. She had the most startling green eyes, laughter creases fanned out from each corner, and she grabbed one of my hands in both of hers and rubbed it. Her Afro hair was braided close to her scalp with a few silver streaks ducking and weaving through the braids. 'We need to stick the needle in, my love.'

'I'm scared. What if I don't wake up? What if God punishes me?' Hearing myself reverentially say the word 'God' rather than blaspheming was a revelation in itself.

'Listen here, God doesn't punish people for things outside of their control. I know you love this baby, but it's very sick and it will make *you* very sick if you carry on.' She cleverly massaged my hand, warming it up for the needle and as soon as I nodded, she expertly inserted it while I turned away. 'Now, that's a good girl. Here's the pre-med. Relaaaaax. I'll see you on the other side.' I gave up the fight as soon as the drugs took a hold. I even sneaked a furtive look at the bandaged cannula. This wasn't so bad…

'Enough now, Amanda. Enough crying.' I was still in what appeared to be the ante-chamber. Joanna stood next to me holding my hand and patting it.

'When's the operation?' I asked her, confused as to why it hadn't happened yet.

'All done.' Joanna smiled and offered me a tissue. 'Your man is waiting for you. We let him stay. My, he loves you, doesn't he?'

I nodded dumbly. 'You mean it's over? I can go home?'

'In a bit.' I blew my nose loudly and Joanna took the used tissue from me.

'Thank you, Joanna. I'm sorry for crying.'

'No worries. You look after yourself. You're going to be all right, you know?'

Angels walk among us, I thought.

I gingerly held the official piece of paper in my hand, staring at it, not seeing it, but knowing it was there. Decree Absolute. Another ending in less than one week. I sat slumped on the floor in Sam's office, recently optioned as the new nursery, watching the relentless rain sheet down outside. Jacqui and Ali had sweetly cut the grass and tidied up some of the garden when I was sleeping off the anaesthetic.

'Where are you? Are you OK?' Ali cried as she searched for me after returning from the shops. 'I got you some

Reese's peanut things that you like.' I had left the office door open so she eventually found me. 'Oh, you're here. What's going on?'

'I'm divorced.'

'Fuck. Oh, what timing.' She kneeled down and kissed my cheek. 'Are you OK?'

'I think so. I don't know. So much to take in.' My mobile rang in my pocket. It was Michelle, my lawyer.

'Have you got the paperwork?' she asked eagerly. 'You're free! You can be a bit more blasé about the baby now.'

'I lost the baby. It was sick and had to go. I had a termination four days ago.'

'Oh, Amanda. Oh, I had no idea. I am so so sorry. That's awful.'

'I know...' And then the full force of it all hit with a brutality that maybe I had been putting off since the hospital. 'I didn't think I would feel like this, but I feel worse than when he left.'

Ali retreated to sit on the bed.

'You lost your baby as well as your marriage. I hope you recover soon.' I couldn't speak I was crying so hard. I felt like I had fallen down a well with no rope. Michelle said some kind things and let me go with a promise to ring when things had plateaued.

'Ali, I feel like someone died. How can it hurt so bad?' Ali re-joined me on the floor.

'Oh, Mands, someone *did* die.'

'Is this what it felt like when your dad died?'

'I don't know. Some days it's OK and some days it floors me and I don't want to get out of bed. But I do. I don't know how Mum carries on.'

'I feel like I will never be happy. Like this will always hurt.'

'It's everything. You got divorced and lost a baby – two of life's most stressful events. It was never going to be a picnic.'

Woody had bombarded me with emails about our Greek getaway, and I couldn't even open them. Every time I conjured up tentative thoughts about being on holiday, I always imagined I was there alone.

That afternoon, when everyone was back from school and nursery, I sat in Isla's room with her and Meg and attempted to read a story but had to lie on her bed and cry. Isla lay next to me and Meg stroked my hair and cried softly alongside my own grief.

'I'm sorry,' I kept saying over and over again.

'It's OK, Mummy. We're here,' Isla soothed me. I heard the door go and footsteps pad up the stairs. Woody appeared in the doorway.

'What's going on here?'

'Mummy's divorce happened today,' Isla explained seriously. 'She's sad.'

'I can see that, but sitting here crying with you two isn't a great idea, is it?'

Isla and Meg looked at him, puzzled.

'I'll be downstairs.' He sounded annoyed.

Woody was chatting to Ali and drinking tea when I ventured into the kitchen.

'What did you mean just then?' I asked him, trying hard to keep irritation out of my voice.

'About you crying?' I nodded. 'Well, it's not good practice, is it, to unload like that on the kids? Upsetting them, too.' Ali took her tea and wandered tactfully out to the living room, leaving us alone.

'I'm sorry for being human and wanting to be with my girls when I feel desperate and the lowest I've felt for years.'

I could feel anger rushing in my ears. Battened-down words determined to escape queued up at the base of my throat.

'Look, I thought I could make a start on the hallway for you this week, get rid of the wallpaper you hate so much. I did promise I would do it when I decorated the baby's room. I can still do it. Refresh the house for you...'

'No, Woody, I want to leave the hallway as it is.'

'But you hate it. You're always moaning about it, saying what an eyesore it is. I could get a nice soothing colour from work. It would look—'

'No! This has come to the end of the road, hasn't it?'

'What?'

'Us. I think we should end it. I don't see the point. I feel different and need to be on my own.'

'Can't we work it out? You're just feeling awful 'cos of the baby and the divorce at the same time. It's understandable.'

'No. I feel strongly that I need to be on my own. I haven't got the space in my head to consider another person at the moment.'

'Wow. You're being so harsh.'

'I'm not. I'm being honest. If you really thought about it, you'd agree. It would have burned out.'

'I disagree. I've never felt like this before.'

'I'm sorry. I don't feel the same way.' I stared at him. I couldn't bear him being anywhere near me. He tried to grab my hand and I pulled it away in revulsion, my skin practically recoiling at the thought of it.

'Is it because I got so wasted at Dara's party? I was just so freaked out about being a dad, something I had never thought would happen.'

'Part of it. Other stuff, too. I'm different, that's the only way I can explain.'

'If the baby had been OK, would this be happening?'

I shrugged. I knew the right answer, but felt the truth was possibly too punitive.

'OK. I'm going. I can't believe you're doing this.'

Really? I wanted to ask. You had no idea I had disappeared from view? I thought it had been obvious. I'd not physically touched him since the morning I woke after the abortion, not even by accident.

'You'll regret it!' he maligned angrily from the hall. 'You'll be alone for ever if you push everyone away.'

Just for today I will be kind to every living thing...

When the front door finally slammed, Ali bolted back into the kitchen.

'Did you just bin him?'

I nodded.

'What a mad day! Are you OK?'

'Weirdly, I don't feel as dreadful as I did earlier. I know I'm being selfish, but I want to be free. There's no tie to him any more.'

'You're not being selfish. If you don't want to be with him then you don't have to. How was he?'

'Sad, angry. He'll get over it if he doesn't go on a bender and start behaving like a total twat again. I think he could do with some therapy, but I know he won't have any.'

Was this how Sam had felt when he left me? After all, according to him, he had lived in misery for at least two years. He must have been practically giddy with glee at the thought of never having to play at being my dutiful husband ever again.

I wandered out into the hall and surveyed the supposedly repugnant wallpaper. Startlingly, it appeared less offensive today. Perhaps my tired eyes couldn't summon the energy required to process such brash colours and whirling-dervish flowers and leaves. I rubbed it with my fingers and for the first time really appreciated the high quality of the finish. There wasn't one scratch or nick because the paper was so luxuriously thick, and you couldn't see the joins between the different rolls. Only a master craftsman could cover the walls so effortlessly that the jungle assumed a life of its own, curling round the heart of the house like the protective briar forest in *The Sleeping Beauty*.

'You know what, I've always liked your loud wallpaper,' Ali said, giving me a hug as I stood staring at the wall, feasting my eyes on it. 'The chandeliers really do complement it and all the cornicing and ceiling roses just add to the charm. It's a talking point. I think all you need to buy is a carpet runner and the hallway will be complete. The same cream as one of the flowers.'

'Thank you.' I hugged her back. 'Maybe get rid of the shit-coloured stair carpet, though.'

'Oh God, yeah, that has to go!'

I could hear something hitting my window. Sunlight filtered through the slats in the shutters. I checked my alarm clock – six a.m. There it was again. It sounded like a bird pecking the glass with its beak. I rammed the pillow over my head but the noise persisted, knocking its way into my brain so it was all I could hear. Reluctantly peeling back the duvet, I eased myself upright and pushed open the shutters whilst sitting on the edge of the bed. Woody stood in the front garden. He motioned for me to let him in. I shook my head and slid open the window instead.

'Mands, I've not been to bed.'

'I'm sorry to hear that.'

'I don't want to split up. I've been thinking and thinking all night. We can make it work.' He started chewing his mouth and he couldn't quite control his jaw.

'Woody, you're wasted. I think you should go.'

'I love you, Amanda.'

'I'm sorry you feel like this. Sonny has just woken up; I need to go. Please don't do this again.'

His hands flapped uselessly at his sides and his face searched mine for an answer. I closed the window and shutters on him, extremely aware that I was the one dealing out the pain and, even though I knew how it felt to be the receiver, it didn't sway me for one second. There was no other option. I lay back on top of the duvet and did something I had not done for ages. I asked myself what was there, in my body, what emotions or feelings.

First up was sadness, then grief, then guilt, then finally, just before Sonny did come in, I felt peace. Just plain, old-fashioned peace. The kind that reigns after a particularly violent storm has left the landscape bruised and torn, with trees uprooted and roof tiles strewn like shaken blossom. It's only after such a tumultuous battering that you really appreciate the tranquillity, the gentle hum of life and the birds finally tweeting again, celebrating their very existence.

26

Greece Is the Word

'I hate him!' Jacqui cried heatedly, sobbing into her warm sauvignon blanc, tears sliding off her chin and into the glass. 'How can he do this so soon?'

Ali and I sat impotently with her in our back garden on the dilapidated taped-together camping chairs the week after Woody's departure, vainly trying to make the most of the dwindling sun before it swooped behind the chimney pots. The grass was already in need of a cut and, so far, no one had volunteered.

Ginger loved the garden and, now he was allowed out, he could often be found shading himself under the sprawling acer tree or sunbathing on one of the patio benches, stretched out like a fur rug. Once or twice I had been ceremoniously delivered an offering of a dead mouse. He had picked me out to be the chief cat, though Meg was his favourite.

'He's rushing into it,' Ali soothed. 'She must be pregnant.'

'I think she *is* pregnant,' I pointed out. 'Either that, or they want a baby very soon and she ain't getting any younger.'

'Or what if it's actually because he loves her more than anything ever in his entire life and cannot wait to get married again, this time to the right person.' Jacqui burst into fresh tears.

'It's only a matter of time before Sam marries Carrie. They already have a baby, so I imagine a wedding is on the cards. It's going to happen to all of us and it's awful. We may not want them back, but it's the final shutting of the door.'

'I know, it's a shock they're engaged, but I think the fact that they're doing it in a month's time is more upsetting. Like he can't wait to let the kids get used to it. I know my feelings don't matter to him, but the kids?'

'He will just expect them to get over it, like he expected you to!' Ali said crossly.

'Leaving me to tidy up his mess again,' Jacqui groaned. 'It's the gift that keeps on giving.'

'We should do something, commiserate,' I proposed brightly, waving my glass round in the air to add a sense of occasion. 'Get shitted. An anti-wedding celebration.'

'How about a better idea? An anti-honeymoon?' Jacqui outplayed me, smiling through her tears.

'Oh Gawd, this is our room?' Jacqui laughed nervously. When we'd arrived via a dusty cab from Kefalonia airport we had been instructed to go to room eleven by a very young girl who was obviously bored sitting at reception. Our home for the week was a traditional white-washed, two-storey guesthouse with maid service. From the outside it resembled someone's home with a beautifully tended garden, starbursts of different brightly coloured geraniums shooting out either side of the terracotta-tiled steps leading up to the reception area. Electric-pink clematis writhed its way across the walls and spread as far as the roof, curling round windows, complementing the deep blue wooden doors and window frames. The scents of lavender and rosemary growing in the clay pots dotted on the steps mingled in the warm breeze. The corridors and stairs were open to the elements but the guidebook had said the area was so safe that no one ever locked their doors. I found this to be true when we had approached the open door of our room without a key, which lay trustingly in the centre of one of the twin beds.

'Well, what were you expecting?' I asked Jacqui happily, drinking in the orange terracotta-tiled floors, the tiny windowless bathroom on the left as we entered, the twin beds with the ubiquitous satin-edged blue blankets and sheets instead of a duvet – a mini blue table separating them – a wooden wardrobe and dressing table with a mirror, and adjacent to the bathroom wall, a Barbie-sized kitchen complete with a hot plate and utilitarian fridge. It was all I could afford from my carefully hidden rent account that Ali paid into. It had been last minute and dirt cheap. Jacqui had offered to pay for both of us to stay in more salubrious surroundings, but I had refused.

'For it to be a little bit bigger. For it not to be so basic. It's like the place I came with Tara when we were students.'

'All right, Princess Jacqui! We're just sleeping here. Chill – we have a balcony. Look, why don't we go and see what the other room is like next door; it's open too. It's on the corner of the building so it might be bigger?'

'Oh, please, can we have that one instead?'

I'd forgotten that Jacqui never roughed it. This had been her first easyJet flight. ('I only ever turn left, darling.')

‘What do you mean, there’s no free booze?’ she had asked suspiciously when I explained why no one was asking us what we wanted to drink half an hour into the flight. ‘Of course there’s always free booze!’

‘Not on easyJet!’

‘Well, why didn’t we book BA then?’

‘Because they were too expensive! We can *buy* the booze on board.’

‘Why didn’t you say that?’ Tragedy averted.

This new room was about a metre wider, a decent-sized window flooded the slightly larger kitchenette with late afternoon sun. The bathroom was also marginally roomier and boasted a window, so it was less like showering in an airless coffin.

‘Oooh, we could swing a cat now.’ Jacqui clapped her hands and sat down on the bed nearest to the floor-to-ceiling metal-framed French windows, the gauzy marine-blue curtains billowing in the breeze.

‘Let’s hope no one is actually booked in this room.’

‘You snooze, you lose!’

Agia Efimia was a little seaside village nestled in a natural horse-shoe bay at the foot of black pine-covered mountains and was served by the azure Ionian Sea. I had wanted to visit this island ever since I had read *Captain Corelli’s Mandolin* aeons ago. The story had spoken to me in such a way that I had to reread it three times. I think it was because the heart-breaking pathos linked hands with the unadulterated humour of the main characters in a way that mimicked everyday life for anyone, anywhere, experiencing life in general. Real life, horrific as it can be, always manages to shoehorn in some humour, no matter how small. At Sam and my wedding, his sister read aloud a famous soliloquy from the text, expounding the joys of love and marriage. This pilgrimage felt like I had come almost full circle on my journey to recovery.

Ali had already booked to go and see her mum in Spain, which had turned into a complete and utter soap opera in itself. A week before the school holidays, I stumbled in from a run, hot and sweaty and starting to feel a lot fitter. I noticed how my thighs no longer chafed and I could fit into my skinny jeans once more. A small victory against the recent events that faded further into the past each day.

'Fuck off, Jim! That's so below the belt.'

Ali's voice was bellowing from the kitchen. She was shouting so loud I actually thought Jim was in there launching insults at her.

'She lost the baby!' she screamed at full pelt. My ears burned at the words and I tore into the kitchen from the hallway, slamming the door open. Ali was on the phone by the kettle and spun round the second I barged in, killing the call.

'What's going on?' I asked sternly.

'Oh, God, Mands. Fuck.'

'You told Jim about the baby?'

'Yes.' Indignation showed its colours on her inflamed cheeks.

'Why? It's none of his business. Who else did you tell?'

'Ursula. Sorry, she was so suspicious at your birthday because you weren't drinking. She guessed. I just told her so she didn't start a rumour!' That now made sense. I had received a lovely card from her after my birthday thanking me for the party and wishing me luck for the rest of my fifth decade, sure that it was going to be my best. She knew.

'You could have said I had cystitis. That was the official excuse!'

'I know. I forgot in the panic of her questioning me. You know what she's like!'

'So, when did you tell Jim?'

'It was when I was having the thing with him. I said I might have to move out and we were just talking about me moving back in if we got back together. It wasn't gossipy. I was just saying it as something that was going to affect me.'

'But you knew I said you could stay. You were just blabbing! He didn't need to know.'

'I'm sorry. So sorry. He was going to tell Sam you were hiding your pregnancy from him to get more money.'

'What? Why? Was this to get at you?'

'Yes. It's his way of getting revenge for everything. He wanted Grace to go to Majorca with him and Hattie but I had already booked to take her to see Mum and he wanted me to cancel, even though it's the one thing Mum's looking forward to. He also wants to have her one week on, one week off. But won't actually be there to look after her most of the time. He would be at work! It's a fucking power trip. He knows the best way to get back at me is through her.'

'Right, enough! Give me your phone.' I could hear the rushing in my ears, with which I was well-acquainted, heralding a white-knuckle ride.

'No, don't ring him, please.'

'Give it. I need to talk to him.' Ali slowly handed over her phone.

'Ah, changed your mind, have you?' Jim sneered contemptuously.

'Hello, Jim. It's Amanda.' Silence. 'I believe you're using my misfortune to bully and blackmail Ali into handing over Grace.'

'Oh, Amanda, you know I would never do that. She's got the wrong end of the stick.'

'Just how wrong did she get it? So wrong that you were going to tell Sam I was pregnant when in fact that actually isn't true. My baby died, Jim. DIED! And you were going to use this information to garner one over on Ali when in fact what you should be looking at here is what is best for Grace. She isn't a fucking pawn to be pushed and pulled between you.'

'Look, Amanda, I know what you're saying, but Ali won't let me have her. I was desperate. I needed to—'

'What you needed to do was think about the fucking ethics behind what you were about to do. A baby DIED. My baby! And over here in this house, I gave a home to *your* baby when you made her homeless. So, if anyone has any right to give you shit about your treatment of Ali and your ridiculous parental rights, it's me. Don't you ever, EVER pull a cowardly stunt like this again or I will come round there and pull your fucking balls right off. I will make life so fucking shit for you that you will wish you never crossed me.' I handed the phone back to Ali, shaking. She stood before me, now ashen-faced, catching flies with her mouth.

I pushed open the glass doors, lurching out into the garden, and sank down onto one of the benches.

'Oh my fucking God, Mands. That was amazing. He will be shitting his pants now.'

'Please, can we never speak of this again? I'm unimpressed you told him, and I need a few minutes to calm down.'

'Oh, yes. You have no idea how sorry I am.'

'Do me a favour. Next time when I say don't tell anyone something, don't tell them. It will make life so much easier.'

'Would a shot of tequila help?'

'Yes.' Ali brought out two shot glasses and we downed them silently.

I remained on the bench for about an hour, watching the birds swoop and glide to and from the lawn like First World War bi-planes executing daring victory rolls. The anger dissipated and I felt bad that I had snapped at Ali. I knew she was a motor-mouth and Sam was bound to find out about the baby some time via Sarah and Will. But he would find out in an innocent way, not someone poisonously flagging up that he could have given me less money because I was deceitful. When I came out of the shower a beautiful blue and white embroidered beach dress was lying on top of my bed. A Post-it note was stuck on it.

I'm sorry. I love you loads. You do so much for us. Ali and Grace xx

27

Eat Chips Drunk

'What are you doing?' I mumbled still half asleep, hair slicked to my scalp from last night's oppressive heat. Our air con consisted of opening all the windows and hoping to create a natural wind tunnel. It hadn't really worked. Jacqui stretched her arms up to the ceiling, silhouetted against the light streaming in from the balcony windows.

'Yoga.'

'You should have woken me up. I've never done yoga.'

'There's not enough room for both of us.'

'There is outside.'

Ten minutes later, we stood barefoot on the front lawn, both wearing leggings and vest tops, shaded from the sun by the guesthouse and the surrounding cypress trees.

'Normally I would use a mat, but we'll have to improvise on the grass. Look out for bugs.'

Jacqui guided me through one of her typical sequences, my legs trembling holding some of the more challenging postures. Parts of my body that never saw the light of day were being pulled and stretched beyond their comfortable limits.

'Right, now we're going to come down into Savasana, the corpse pose.'

I could see someone watching us out of the corner of my eye. They were standing at the top of the steps leading up to the reception. I rolled down to lie straight on my back like Jacqui for the final pose.

'Close your eyes and let everything leave your head, feel the weight of your body on the grass. Let your breath go...'

I felt myself submit to the uneven ground, my feet flop out to the sides and the sun caress my face as it rounded over the rear of the building, its rays dappling the sharp waxy Mediterranean grass between the shifting shadows of the trees. Crickets hummed in the dense undergrowth and birds tweeted in the cloudless sky. As peace stole over me, I remembered something I had mentioned to Woody ages ago about a holiday in Greece. 'I want to send all my sadness out to the sea.' The email link to this little guesthouse had been one of his parting gifts to me.

Jacqui's voice snagged me out of my contemplative state and we sat up, bowing whilst cross-legged, wishing each other Namaste.

'Wow, Jacqui. I loved that. My body feels alive. Why aren't you teaching yoga?'

'Strangely, or rather not so strangely, it's something I have been thinking about for a while.'

'Why not just do it then?'

She shrugged. 'I guess I've felt so broken and rubbish for so long that I thought who am I to teach anyone anything.'

'Healer, heal thyself! That's why I learned Reiki, to help me, but I've helped others, too.'

'True. I feel like I need to get today out of the way, and then see how I feel.'

'How do you feel now?'

'Hungry!'

As we walked lazily back up the steps, the person who had been watching stepped out of the office at the side.

'Good morning! Were you beautiful ladies doing yoga?' She had a hybrid Greek/American accent and her English was faultless.

'Yes, we were,' Jacqui answered her.

She looked a bit older than us, a few more laughter lines etched round her inquisitive brown eyes and dark salt-and-pepper hair piled stylishly into a loose bun on top of her head. Her long black and yellow flowered halter-neck dress was nipped in at the waist, giant silver hoops hung from her ears and her wrists were adorned with myriad silver bangles that clashed like an irregular simulacrum of the nearby lapping waves every time she moved her arms. She was mesmerising.

'I love yoga, but I have to drive to Assos to do it and I don't always have the time.'

'If we're in a state to do it tomorrow, please join us,' I said, then slipped a furtive sideways glance at Jacqui to check if this was OK. I could tell she was as equally charmed.

'Yes, please do,' she urged. 'My name's Jacqui, and this is Amanda. Are you the owner?'

'I am. Mrs Kourakis,' and she held out a slender hand for us to shake. I was already in the throes of a girl crush. 'But please call me Remi. Yoga tomorrow sounds good. What are you up to today?'

'Well, Jacqui's ex-husband is getting married today and we're going to have our own anti-wedding party!' Her inclusiveness already made her feel like a friend.

'What a brilliant idea! I'm also divorced. A bit of a scandal, living here.'

'Me, too!' I eagerly joined in the party.

'Do you want to come in and have some coffee before you start your day? I just made some.'

Remi's sprawling apartment underneath the building had double doors leading onto a secluded garden, hidden away from balconies and prying eyes. I popped my head out and breathed in the redolent herbs planted in deep blue terracotta pots on the rather pleasing stone-flagged patio. At the end, bordering next door's irregular brick wall, a sizeable vegetable patch bloomed with plump runner beans, potatoes and what looked like fennel and bristly artichokes. The rich russet-coloured soil was obviously dense with vital nutrients, unlike our sodden London clay back home.

'Oh, wow, I love your home,' Jacqui said breathlessly. 'Where did you find all the art?'

The white-washed open-plan living area and kitchen walls were covered with a medley of contrasting canvases. Some were abstract blocks of colour with texture painstakingly ground into them, thick insistent marks tempting you to run fingers over the deep grooves. Some smaller ones bore more figurative paintings of nudes set against brightly coloured backgrounds. The terracotta floors were identical to those in the rooms above, but the furniture was anything but perfunctory. Vibrant glass and wood medicine cabinets stuffed with curiosities from India and possibly Morocco were placed side by side with ornately decoupaged and lacquered dressers that could have hailed from ancient China, upon which gilt-framed photos were displayed, quite a few of the girl from reception yesterday. The two chunky navy-blue sofas invited guests to sit down and squash the motley African print cushions arranged artfully along the back of each one. Mirrors of all sizes were dotted round the walls, reflecting back light, opening up the room even further. I loved the doors of the kitchen cabinets, all coated in dusty blues and reds, with ceramic hand-painted handles. It was my dream décor.

'I painted the canvases,' Remi admitted modestly.

'You're an artist?' I gasped, my crush instantly elevating into stalker-like echelons.

'Well, I try to be, but organising this place is my main job.'

'Do you sell many?' I asked.

'I do a show in Fiskardo once a year and every few years I hold one in Athens. But people know where to find me, and I have a website. Come, let's sit in the garden and you can tell me all about yourselves.'

'So, you're here to wash away your sorrows?' Remi surmised from our scaled-down tales.

'That would be correct,' Jacqui laughed, curling her hair round her fingers.

'You've come to a lovely place to do it. I came here after my divorce from my ex-husband. We had lived all over – he's Greek-American and his job meant we travelled. One day he just decided no more. Karys, our daughter, was only eight and I knew I didn't want to live in America. I'm from here, but Argostoli, the capital, so we returned to stay with my parents while I decided what to do.'

'Oh, how stressful,' I sympathised. 'Do you still see him now?'

'Of course. He comes regularly to visit Karys, who is off to university in Athens in September, and she in turn visits him. We make it work.' I wondered if one day I would reach acceptance of my own circumstances. That kind of peace still felt a little out of my grasp.

'So where do you recommend for our day of excess?' Jacqui quizzed. 'We want to sunbathe, eat, drink copious amounts of wine and maybe have a boogie.'

I woke stiffly curled up in a ball on top of my crusty beach towel, the light teasing my eyes open. The beautiful embroidered dress that Ali had given me was now grey and blue with dubious stains spoiling it. I was still wearing flip flops. My mouth was so dry I had to forcibly peel my tongue from the roof of my mouth, removing a layer of skin cells. I had somehow acquired a twinkly silver ankle chain and a hefty blue-stoned ring on my wedding finger. I dragged myself up to sitting and with relief found Jacqui curled up next to me, her large sunglasses on, mouth open, dried spittle in one corner. Her nose was sunburned. She also sported a blue ring on her wedding finger.

The pebble beach had served as a suitably castigatory bed; I rubbed my back as I tried to remember what had happened. It had all started off so civilised when we'd bunkered down in one of the marina bars after a day of eating and sunbathing, but once we'd imbibed that second bottle of wine we flew a little too close to the sun…

'Have you seen those cute boys over at the bar? They keep pointing at us.'

'At you. No one would point at me, unless I've revealed one of my apologetically saggy tits by accident.'

'Shut up! Of course people would point at you! You're amazing.' I didn't feel amazing right then. I felt three sheets to the wind and could hear my own voice slurring, so to a casual observer I must have appeared completely wasted. The most recent visit to the loo had also revealed that the beach-proof, waterproof, nuclear-war-proof mascara and eyeliner were in breach of trading standards.

'Oh fuckity fuck, they're coming over.'

'Where's the emergency lip gloss?'

Earlier in the day, Jacqui and I had visited the authentically Greek place Remi had recommended. It was aptly called the Paradise Beach Taverna and overlooked a bucolic little stretch of coast bearing the same name. Paradise Beach wasn't in breach of anything – a small white pebbled cove lined with weather-beaten olive and fir trees, plaited trunks curling towards the ocean, bleached silver by the unremitting sun.

Already a bit tipsy after our lunchtime wine, we set up camp near the edge of the sea, thus ensuring navigating the pebble shore for a swim wasn't akin to an agonising barefoot Lego run.

'I can't actually believe Simon gets married today. I mean, it doesn't feel like it. I don't want to sit and cry. I just want to be here on this stunning beach and swim in the sea, let the ocean hold me and wash away all the crap.'

'Good. Then that's what we'll do. I have wanted to send my sadness out to sea for ages. I can Reiki it for us when we're in the water.'

'Aren't you supposed to be a clean channel when you do Reiki? You're a bit pissed. What if you open up a channel into the underworld and sell our souls to the Devil?'

We waded cautiously out into the sea so we were up to our waists in the crystal-clear water; tiny fish darted between our legs, startling us.

'I think we should float,' I announced. 'Come on. Let's get our barnets wet.'

'I'll get sheep hair!'

'Tough. If you want the ocean and the universe to hold you and take away the pain, you have to show willing. Sacrifice the hair.'

Breathing deeply, I dived into the water and resurfaced further out and unable to touch the ocean floor. Ever since I had watched *Jaws* in 1981 from behind my nana's chintz-covered replica Louis XIV sofa, I had had a fear of deep water. Even swimming pools could sometimes unnerve me. But I would always swim in the sea, not too far, just enough to feel I had accomplished it, all the while trying hard not to imagine my limbs being violently torn off by an undetected predator.

Jacqui emerged next to me, treading water.

'Hold my hand,' I instructed her. 'Now let's float on our backs.' It took me a few minutes to relax and not keep sinking, then the Reiki really flowed.

'Your hand's burning,' Jacqui said, seemingly from miles away.

The sea buoyed us up in its saline embrace, stroking our bodies, fanning out our hair like mermaids. My edges gradually dissolved the longer we floated; I couldn't even feel Jacqui's hand in mine and after a while I felt in union with the ocean.

'Argh, get off!' Jacqui unexpectedly screamed, flailing her arms and snatching her hand away, splashing water into my face, forcing me to take in a mouthful of briny seawater.

'What?' I spluttered, water in my eyes almost dislodging my lenses, hysteria mounting. 'Are you OK?'

'Fucking seaweed! It scraped my leg and freaked me out.'

We looked at each other and started laughing uncontrollably, practically choking.

'I've just weed in the sea,' I gasped. 'Seaweed!'

'Me, too! It's all warm!'

'Come on, let's go back.'

'Did you feel different?' Jacqui asked as we dried off on the shore. 'I did... *do* feel different. I feel empty in a good way.'

'Me, too. I felt like I wasn't afraid. A bit like after giving birth and you realise death will be a piece of cake after that hideous invagination.'

Jacqui made a sound like someone had kicked her in the stomach and sat bolt upright, pushing her sunglasses onto her head.

'Slagger, why are we here?'

'We escaped after the party on the boat because it all got a bit creepy. You said you wanted to watch the sun rise on another day.'

'I snogged that boy, didn't I?'

I nodded.

'He was hot, though, wasn't he?'

'Yes, very.'

Jacqui let out a loud guffaw, then slapped her forehead. 'Oh, no, we promised Remi we would meet her for yoga this morning. I don't even know what time it is.'

I rummaged round in my bag and pulled out my phone. 'It's nine fifteen.' I still felt faintly drunk.

'What's this ring?' Jacqui asked, thrusting her wedding finger at me.

'We got married on the yachties' boat, remember. The captain got us rings and made us kiss.'

'With tongues? I hope you're taking my name!'

*

Before the week faded over the cloudless horizon we set about exploring local beauty spots. I indulged my *Captain Corelli* fascination by imagining that Agia Efimia was part of the legend and inspiration for the setting when Louis de Bernières delved into his research. It certainly resonated with me and that felt good enough.

'Do you think we will ever feel OK about being divorced?' I asked on our last morning, before yoga.

'I know that I feel better now than I did before I came,' Jacqui admitted. 'I feel like I've shed a skin. This was just what I needed to distract me from Simon's wedding. I know I would have probably been fine, but to do something so amazing instead of sitting at home moping has made the whole thing a real treasured memory. Thank you.'

'I didn't do anything.'

'You did. You brought me here and baptised me in the sea. You practised yoga with me every day and you made me see it's something I'm good at. I think I *will* do that yoga teacher course. I'm signing up as soon as we get back. It's about time I stopped thinking life will feel better when this happens or that happens or when I meet someone. Life is happening now.'

'You're so right. I needed to let my hair down, be me again. I wasn't me when I was with Woody. I felt like being with him just gradually highlighted how much I missed Sam. He so wanted me to love him and I just couldn't. I think Sam and Carrie having their baby made me feel so left out, so wounded that he could have a child with someone else, that when I was gifted one in return, getting rid of it felt wrong.'

'I totally get it. I kind of knew that. Did you have a name for the baby?'

'No. But I think he was a boy. I just felt it. I found it strange seeing all the babies on the beach this week. It made me feel sad because I know I probably won't have any more kids now. It's all downhill to the menopause.'

'Oh, don't say that. I can't believe we've got divorced and then the next thing to look forward to is that! Well, I think the universe helped you come to a decision.'

'I think you're right, I couldn't have coped with an extra baby, a man I didn't love and my own three kids. I would have lost the plot.'

Jacqui grabbed my hand and squeezed it. 'You know we all would have helped. You would never have been on your own.'

On our last night we asked if we could take Remi out to dinner at the Paradise Beach Taverna as a thank you for being such a wonderful host.

'Here's to you lovely ladies. Thank you for treating me.' We toasted with tumblers of the taverna's finest red wine poured from a rustic clay carafe. Fairy lights loosely looped like strings of pearls amid the grapevines emulated the dense splattering of stars that stretched far above the sea beyond the patio.

Even though it was a balmy evening, a slight nip in the air rolled off the ocean, its waves swishing gently on the stones below. Our divorces had been picked back to the bare bones over dinner, lots of incredulous gasps and cries of 'Fucking wanker!' peppered the easy conversation. But I was keen to know one more thing before we paid the bill.

'You don't mention anyone else in your life apart from Karys, your parents and friends. Has there been anyone else?'

Remi took a large gulp of wine and sat back in her chair. 'There is, but it's complicated and not many people know about it.'

'He's married?' I asked, painfully aware I felt disappointed in Remi.

'He is, but it isn't what it seems. His wife is very ill, she has motor neurone disease and is in the final stages of it. She is in a hospice in Argostoli.'

'Oh, no, how tragic,' Jacqui cried. 'How long have you been together?'

'Well, we're not exactly together. We haven't, you know, consummated anything. I have known Nikolas for about six years.'

'So, you're just friends?'

'We were for a long time. However, we realised we were in love about a year ago, but he feels in respect for his wife we have to keep it like this.'

We all took a minute to digest the tragic paradox of Remi's situation. I sipped the last of my wine before speaking tentatively.

'But one day, you can be together?'

'Maybe. I have no idea really. That's the ideal, but until it happens, which is in itself heart-breaking, I won't know.'

'How did you meet?'

'He owns the gallery where I exhibit in Fiskardo. Please don't think badly of him; he is a kind man and has been living with this disease in his life for some time. He has been amazing to Cassia, so dedicated, caring for her and their children and running a business.'

'I don't think anything!' I said, hastily banishing the disappointment as quickly as it arrived. 'He must be worth it.'

'He is. I think he may be the kindest man I have ever met.

He wasn't expecting this and neither was I. I made a vow that I would never marry again. But I feel different now. He has made me see you can recover after divorce, and you change who you would go for, too. Kind is more important to me now. And maybe that's something I can instil in you both – only accept kind.'

'I feel wrong saying I hope it works out for you,' Jacqui said despondently. 'But you deserve happiness, too.'

'Let's not be sad,' Remi said brightly. 'My life is what it is; I made this choice, so there's no complaining. This is your last night.' She tapped the table authoritatively. 'We're celebrating! I think you're both beautiful, amazing women and I am so happy you came to my guesthouse. Live life, don't wait for it. You really are very lucky, remember that.'

28

Free Bird

'I think you need to clear out Sam's old office,' Ali instructed the day before the children returned from their holiday with Sam. 'Jacqui said she would come down and help; Neve and Joe aren't back until next week.'

'Is this some kind of intervention?' I laughed, sipping my tea in the sunshine the morning after returning from Greece.

'Yes! But not really. You said how much you wanted to get on with your book after everything that's happened, and the room isn't needed for anything else. I feel bad that I'm sleeping in the space you used to work in, and clearly writing at the living-room table isn't working.'

'I like it there!'

'Only because it's close to the biscuits! Come on, we could do it in half a day and get some paint and decorate, like a TV make-over programme. We can move your writing desk from your bedroom and buy one of those office chairs from Ikea.' Ali's infectious enthusiasm roused me from my blind spot about the room, and what might have been.

'OK. There's things I haven't looked at for years in that

room, a lot of Sam's stuff that I think he's forgotten about, as well as wedding photos.'

'We'll sort it, don't worry. We can have a pile of his shit ready for him to deal with when he drops the kids tomorrow. You won't even have to look at it.'

Jacqui cycled down the hill, and brought with her a cheeky bottle of cava.

'We can declare the room open when you move in!'

We tackled the boxes of arbitrary crap – old video tapes of Sam's, one of which was of our wedding, an old printer that actually worked, so I kept that, and so many technical books on filming, editing, camera work, lighting, storyboards.

'Chuck it in there, Slagger.' Jacqui pointed to another box.

I flicked open the lid and unearthed our wedding photo album and collection of pictures from when we were young, before kids. I winced.

'What is it?' Ali asked as she peered in. 'Oh. Do you want me to look?'

'No, it's OK.' I pulled out the maroon album, wiping the thick layer of dust from its cover.

'Is this a good idea?' Jacqui asked cautiously.

'Yes, I need to look.' Turning the stiff white pages was like revisiting someone else's life. In one of the pictures Sam looked fresh-faced and nervous, standing waiting for me in the orchard.

'Wow, you looked so beautiful,' Jacqui said. 'That dress…'

'Where's the picture of you and me?' Ali asked and, as she said it, I turned a page and there it was. Ali was tearfully hugging me just before I climbed awkwardly into Rob's vintage Beetle, my dress billowing up around my armpits like a giant marshmallow. 'I love that picture.'

'Oh God!' Jacqui squeaked. 'Is that Woody and Ursula?'

Woody was dressed incongruously in a suit, his arm casually draped round Ursula as they posed with glasses of champagne in front of the fake Gipsy Kings. He looked devilishly handsome and I felt a faint pang of regret.

'And Will and Sarah,' Ali pointed out in another photo. 'We were all there. Look how young we looked.'

'What will you do with the album?' Jacqui asked eventually. 'I think I kept mine for the kids.'

'I'll do that. Put it in my wardrobe until I can bear talking about it with them.'

I didn't look at the other photos and donated them to Sam to make a decision about.

By Sunday night, when the children returned, the dumping ground of Sam's old office had been transformed into a writer's den. The walls were painted navy blue and grey, the bed was decked out with a new white broderie anglaise duvet cover filched from one of Ali's catalogue shoots, and I added some extra bright red geometric patterned cushions from Ikea to accent the over-all design of the room. I had yet to hang any pictures, but I had bought a red and cream kilim rug also from Ikea, to conceal the uneven woodwormed floorboards. The bookcase had been wiped down and I had stuffed it with my grammar guides, dictionaries and Beardy tomes. My antique fold-down writing desk with all its nooks and crannies fitted perfectly and a cheap wooden office chair completed the look.

'Gosh, I can't wait to sleep in my brand-new room!' Jacqui said, winking at me.

'Writing room by day, brothel by night.'

She punched me hard on the arm.

*

'Amanda, it's Sarah. Do you think you could ring me back, please?'

A month into my new life as a dedicated writer I returned to my desk to find an unsettling voicemail waiting for me on a Monday morning. I didn't want to return her call; I had a nasty feeling it was about Woody. I sat at my desk and tried to pick up where I had left off, but I couldn't jump back in; the words weren't forthcoming and the voicemail played in my head. I decided to listen to it once more and try to decipher the tone of Sarah's voice. Oh, fuck it, I should just ring her.

'Sarah, it's Amanda.'

'Oh, thanks for ringing back. How are you?'

'I'm good thanks. Working mostly, at the moment. You?'

'I'm at work, actually, so I have to be quick.' *You* called me! 'Woody's been in an accident.'

'Is he OK? What kind of accident?'

'A car accident; he was driving…'

'Oh God, was he off his face?'

'Twice over the limit, coming back from a night with us. He and Will had taken coke, too. It was the morning after, but I have no idea when he stopped drinking before he drove home.'

'When?'

'Sunday morning. We found out last night. His mum rang. He's obviously survived and is OK, but he's busted his leg and hip very badly. He had to be airlifted to hospital. He needs pinning back together.'

'He didn't kill anyone, did he?'

'No. No one else was involved. He's feeling terrible and very sad.'

'What an idiot.'

'Yes. I think he knows that.'

'Why did you ring me? I mean, thanks for telling me, but I can't really do anything. We're not together any more...'

'I thought, or maybe Will did, would you visit him?'

My kneejerk was to slam the phone down and block her number. I had already deleted Woody's.

'What good would that do?'

'Cheer him up.'

'But he brought this on himself.'

'I know.' She sighed heavily. 'He's been a wreck since you two broke up, what with the baby and everything.'

'Please don't bring the baby into this and make it about that. He has a problem and he needs help.'

'We know. We were hoping you could talk to him, suggest he went to NA or got some counselling.'

'I can ring him and see how he is but he has to want to sort himself out. I thought he had calmed down and just did it every now and then.' God, I was so naïve.

'He had completely stopped after his sailing incident, then started occasionally going out again and sometimes dabbled. Then, when he started seeing you and we all began going out a lot more, I think he slipped back into old habits. Then when you got pregnant I think he freaked out. Will told him he had to kick it into touch when the baby came, and he said he would, and he did calm down massively, but then you broke up.'

'You knew all along he was coked off his nut and we were having a baby?' I roared, rage overthrowing any kind of niceties. 'Were you all laughing behind my back? No wonder he suddenly went all weird and shouty.'

'No! It wasn't like that. I was so worried. Will wouldn't let me tell you. He said he had never seen Woody so happy and so together in years. You were good for him. He wanted to stop for you.'

'He has to do it for himself, not me, not for a baby.'

'I'm so sorry, Amanda. I know it's a lot to ask, but please will you ring him?'

I slowly breathed in, to stop me saying something awful, something along the lines of, *Look at your own life*.

'I will ring him, but I'm not visiting him. Send me his number.'

'Thank you.'

I sat for about half an hour just listening to the pressing silence, the buzzing of my omnipresent tinnitus my sole companion. I was not responsible for Woody's darkness. I felt angry all of a sudden. I just wanted him out of my life; I had moved on. For the second time I speculated whether this was what Sam had felt when I wouldn't let go without a fight, when I insisted on trying to make it work, when I begged, when I cried, when I said I would change – did he just look at me and feel revulsion at my desperation? I shook my head; this was different. Woody and I were together only a short while. Sam and I had been married, brought a family into the world, we had more meat on the bones of our relationship; it had been worth fighting for. It was awful Woody was in a bad way, but it wasn't my responsibility.

'Hello, Woody?'

'Amanda.'

'Er, yes. Are you OK? Are you in pain?'

'Only in my heart.'

'Does your leg hurt?'

'It's not my leg, it's my hip. Do your research.'

'Oh, er, sorry, Sarah said it was your leg, too.'

'I may walk with a limp afterwards.'

'At least you'll be able to walk.'

'Yes.'

'Look, I'm sorry about your accident.'

'Me, too. Will you visit? I know it's a long way, but I'd like to see you.'

I gulped. Fuck.

'No, sorry. I'm not going to. I don't think it's a good idea.'

'Nice to know you care.'

'Look, I do care, but not like that. Have you thought about getting some counselling?'

'What? To get over you? You've got a fucking cheek!'

'No! About your drug habit and self-destructive behaviour.'

'Oh, just fuck off—'

I terminated the call before he could say anything else. I blocked his number with shaking hands. That conversation just confirmed it – no more men.

Before the week was out, there was another romantic casualty in the house…

'I can't believe I was just about to buy the last available flight. I texted him to see if the timing was OK. We'd discussed the visit when he was over a few weeks ago. It was all going ahead. He was going to pay half because we'd left it too late and they were so expensive. Anyway, he called me when he got the text.'

'Oh, Ali, what a fucker.' And also no surprise really…

'I know! He just said, I think we both know this is going nowhere. I'm never coming back, and this isn't fair on you. Please don't waste your money on visiting.' She stood leaning against the door as I wrapped myself up in my duvet, reluctant to get out of bed for my morning run, the bouncy new routine on writing days when the kids were with Sam or at school. Ali resembled a mad professor with her tufty shagger's clump, horn-rimmed spectacles perched on her nose and her monochrome men's paisley pyjamas.

'So clinical.'

'He did say sorry,' she conceded, 'and all the usual crap people say when they're binning you.'

'Oh God, did he say: "It's not you, it's me"?'

'Yes! Why do people say that?'

'Because it makes them feel less guilty. Anyway, you seem OK. Or are you just putting on a brave face?'

She remained silent as a single tear slipped out from under her glasses.

'I don't know. It's not about him, really. I just don't want to be on my own.'

'Get in bed!' I whipped the duvet aside and scooted over to make room for her. 'Look, I liked him and he was fun, but you want someone who wants to be in the same country as you. So you may as well be on your own, right?'

'I know all that. It was the planning things, the stuff to look forward to, the knowing I had a distraction from my life, from thinking about Dad, about how awful it is for Mum, how Grace has no grandpa.' Ali's hands flew up to her eyes and angrily wiped the tears. 'That's why I had the affair with Jim – I hoped it would end with us living together as a family again, something to build on when everything else was just so sad. Now it just emphasises how broken my family actually is. And the icing on the fucking cake is I have no boyfriend either. It's all shit!' I held her while she wept. I wished I could help, but as I found out with grief, you just have to be in it, allow it to blast you with its presence.

'How can *this* be my life? How can I be living in a house share with a baby and not have my own place where my mum can come and stay? I keep thinking things will be better when... But what? When I have a flat? I will never be able to buy one now, not even a studio flat. The money I got back from Jim got sucked into Dad's funeral and fixing my car, and what's left isn't enough for a deposit. I don't earn enough to even get a mortgage and renting somewhere round here would use what's left in no time. Work has practically dried up now I have no agent. Mum's in a pit of hell dealing with Dad's finances, trying to sell the house, move back here. Everything just feels so unstable. I wish he hadn't died. It's left a hole in all of our lives.'

'Your mum is always welcome here, for as long as she likes, you know that.'

'Oh, fuck, you must think I'm so ungrateful, saying all that about living in the attic and how shit it all is.'

'No, I get it. You're having a really awful time at the moment. Of course the natural thing is to want your own home. But to keep thinking things will get better when this happens or that happens isn't helpful. You'll spend your entire life waiting for the next thing to make you happy. This is your life: whether it's what you planned or not, it's where you are right now. It won't always be good, but it won't always be this shit. Life is hard and then sometimes it isn't. Grief also makes you mental. You can't try and outrun it: it always catches you in the end. Maybe slow down, be on your own, see what you want. Why not start with getting a new agent? You did so well on your own after Jim dropped you, but I think you need someone in your corner again.'

'How did you get to be such a guru?'

'I'm not a guru!' I protested. 'I'm just a stupid twat who has read a lot of books and done some courses. I'm still a bloody work in progress. Just watch my reaction when Sam gets engaged. I'll probably have a meltdown and torch their house!'

'You won't. I bet you'll be with someone by then.'

'What makes you say that?'

'Because you don't want to be with anyone and like being on your own, therefore Sod's law says it will happen.'

'I do love it at the moment. I feel light as a feather, free as a bird!' And I playfully kicked the covers up with my feet.

29

So, You're the Ex-Wife...

Can you drop the kids at mine later? I'm stuck at work.

'Is he mad?' Mel said when I showed the text to her and Ali. 'I'm not driving back home tonight. Colin's in charge.'

'You know what he's like. If *he* thinks the weather isn't bad, it isn't bad.' It had been snowing solidly for three hours, transforming our little corner of south-east London into Svalbard.

I'm not going anywhere. Have you seen the weather?

My phone rang immediately.

'Look, why won't you drive?' Sam asked tersely, no 'Hello', no 'Are you OK?' Straight to the point.

'Because the roads are horrendous. Have you looked outside?'

'It's just a bit of snow.'

'It isn't. It's a blizzard over here and I slipped all over the road going to nursery; it's too icy.'

'But you've got the massive Volvo; you'll be fine.'

'I won't!' But there was a more insistent reason why I didn't want to schlep all the way over to his house; I didn't want to meet Carrie or see their house, plastered with photos of their happy life with my children posing as a counterfeit perfect family. I felt more moved on than I had in the past two years, but that was a step too far right now. Carrie could stay in her box until I was ready to open it...

'Fine. I'll see if Carrie can come over and get them then.' He put the phone down before I could object and I waited for the inevitable text.

Carrie is on her way. Please make sure the kids are ready to go. She's bringing the baby with her.

Oh, rub it in, why don't you! I wanted to type back: Perfect fucking Carrie being brave and battling over to our house through the blizzard with baby in tow.

'Carrie's on her way,' I blurted out to the girls in the kitchen.

'What? Has she seen the weather? There's virtually no visibility out there,' Ali said. 'Plus, you nearly went up the kerb on the way back from nursery.'

'I know. He wouldn't listen. I don't think it's as bad in the centre of town where he works.'

'You've never met Carrie,' Mel said astutely, pulling her scarf round her neck. Even with the heating on it was a bit chilly in the kitchen.

'Oh, fuck, you have to put some make-up on!' Ali cried, and started flapping. 'Now! You need a spruce up.'

I checked in the mirror above the dresser. I looked my usual hassled make-up-free self.

'Go on, upstairs, get some slap on,' Ali ordered. Mel looked on amused at the fuss. 'And put a different jumper on. That one's got all sorts of shit all over it.'

'Kids, Carrie is on her way – can you get ready, please? School bags, coats!'

'Carrie's coming here?' Isla asked, poking her head out of her bedroom where she was playing schools with her Sylvanians.

'Yes. She'll be here quite soon.'

'Mummy, is this the first time you've met her?'

I nodded. Isla came out of her room and wordlessly hugged me. I hugged her back, my breath catching in my throat. How did she *always* know? I dashed into my room and rummaged through my sad little make-up bag. Cover-up on a zit, some blusher, mascara and I brushed my hair. At least it wasn't too grey at the roots. I had touched them up a few weeks ago. As instructed, I changed my jumper for a clean black one, and added a pair of dangly silver star earrings for good measure. Hi, I mouthed to myself in the mirror. I practised a forced smile and hand shake, remembering Dad's advice – a bone crusher always ensures you will be remembered, and potentially feared.

'That's better,' Ali smiled at me. 'You look fresh, not trying to impress. Very natural.'

'You know she'll be more shit scared than you,' Mel sagely pointed out. 'Don't forget, it's her first time meeting *you*, the revered mother of his original family, the first wife, the one she has to live up to.'

'You think?'

'Oh God, of course,' Ali agreed. 'I shat myself the first time I met Diane. She was so nice to me; I felt so bad afterwards because she was a real person with feelings. Before that she was just someone Jim used to bitch about and shout at down the phone.'

'Sonny, quick, get ready.'

'Want Daddy,' he sulked. His speech had come on leaps and bounds since the summer, and I now had a real name: Mummy. No more 'Dad'. However, along with the speech came a torrential downpour of tantrums.

Then my phone rang.

'Carrie's had a crash round the corner from your house. She can't get the car back off the pavement; it's gone over the edge into someone's front garden.'

'Oh dear. Are you coming to get her?'

'Yes, I'm in a cab, but the traffic is bad. This blizzard is nuts.' It was on the tip of my tongue to sneer: I FUCKING TOLD YOU SO! Instead I smugly kept quiet, my dignity intact. 'Are you still there?'

'Yes.'

'Would you be able to go and get her? She's in a bit of a state. No one is in the house so could you bring a pad and paper so she can leave a note about the fence?'

Snow was falling so fast our footprints were blanketed before we'd taken the next step, smothering all sounds bar the occasional muffled siren. No one was out.

'I feel like we're in an apocalypse or something,' Ali said. 'It's so eerie.'

The car had visibly skidded going round a corner and mounted the pavement, slicing through a fence and grinding to a halt just before it hit the bay window. The car wasn't obviously damaged but the fence was scattered across the front garden. I knocked on the driver's window and the glass slid down to reveal Carrie's naturally pale face. She looked like she had been crying. The baby, wrapped up in a dotted grey snowsuit, was on her lap bashing the steering wheel with his pudgy fists. He turned to look at me with his unblinking inquisitive eyes and for a split second I saw Sonny. Then he was gone and a baby with overstuffed hamster cheeks and a perfect cupid's mouth stared at me.

'Hello, thanks for coming.' Carrie looked so much younger than on the television with her perfect skin, except for the dark circles under each eye, the war wounds of every new mum. Her vibrant red hair was stuffed under a trendy grey bobble hat and she hadn't painted on her trademark seductive black flicks sweeping off each eye. In fact, she was rather plain in a natural kind of way.

'Are you OK?' I asked frankly. What an out-of-body experience. Did I really care if she was OK? I actually didn't know. It didn't feel like it was supposed to feel. I was expecting to hate her, bask in the superior knowledge that I was the wronged woman and she was the evil bitch who stole my husband. Instead my mind refused to acknowledge her part in the whole tragedy, gifting her a Get Out of Jail Free card.

'Yes, just about. I wasn't even going very fast when I went round the corner. The car skidded out of control. I don't think I put it in Winter mode on the gear stick. I hate this car; it's too big and computerised.'

'Here's a pen and paper.' I passed them to her through the window and she hastily scribbled a note to the house owners. Her hand was shaking and her writing was messy, slanting to the right in direct contrast to Sam's graceful calligraphic script.

'Sam said he'd come and collect us from your house. Is that OK?' She looked at me nervously, her eyes blinking so many times I began to mirror her. Two red pinpricks bloomed on her pallid cheeks and she bit her lip.

'Yes, no problem.'

We made it down the hill without slipping, our previous journey now completely eclipsed by the unrelenting snowfall. Carrie was fearful of falling with Jaimie in her arms so Ali held on to her to keep her steady.

'I'll just run upstairs and get you a nappy and wipes,' Ali offered when we got in the house, shaking snow from our clothes and kicking wellies under the radiator in the hall. Carrie had come without a bag.

'Would you mind taking him so I can get my shoes off?' Carrie asked me apologetically.

I nodded and reached out for Jaimie, who continued to stare at me. He turned to try and reach Carrie, but she was bent down undoing her boots. He let out a howl and Isla and Meg appeared at the top of the stairs.

'Oh, Jaimie, why are you crying?' Isla cooed and walked down to meet him. Meg hung back. He held his arms out to her and I let her take him. 'It's OK. Mummy will be free in a moment. Come and see the kitchen. We have lots of toys and we have a cat. He's called Ginger and he's so friendly.' I felt shut out. I understood the children had a secret life I knew nothing about, apart from when probed, so witnessing Isla play mummy to her adoring baby brother was a lot to digest. Sonny clambered down the hall to see what the noise was and stopped dead when he saw Carrie. He looked from me to her as she finished taking her boots off.

'You're not Mummy,' he gruffly said to Carrie, his lips set in a grim line, his pudgy cheeks aflame. I wanted to kiss him.

'I know, darling. Your Mummy's there.'

Carrie looked at me and pulled an awkward face.

'Shall we go and find Isla?' I suggested in my over-cheery, let's-ignore-how-bizarre-this-predicament-is voice.

'Isla is so amazing,' Carrie enthused. 'She is like a second mummy to Jaimie. He totally loves her.'

Meg followed silently behind me and loyally grabbed my hand.

'Yes, Isla is very caring,' I admitted, while at the same time feeling like my heart was being ripped out through my mouth. I didn't want Isla to be a second mummy to anyone; she was only seven. Don't tell me things I already know; I'm her fucking mummy! I roared in my head while on the outside I was a graceful swan with artfully applied make-up and a benevolent smile.

As we entered the kitchen, Mel was perched at the butcher's block, sipping a coffee and admiring Jaimie, who was playing with Isla's hair.

'This is one of my oldest friends, Mel,' I introduced Carrie. 'She's staying the night, though may well be trapped here longer than twenty-four hours.'

'Hello, Mel, pleased to meet you. I'm sorry to be crashing your girlie evening,' Carrie apologised. 'We'll be gone as soon as Sam gets here.'

How long will that be? I wanted to cry. With my aversion to phoney small talk I wasn't sure how to fill the gap until he arrived.

'So, Carrie, what's your new TV show about?' I didn't give a shit about her next show. My mouth had forgotten to ask permission from my brain before it spoke.

'Oh, gosh, well, it's er... about cooking for families. I actually have to, er... ask you a favour...' I looked in panic at Mel and she widened her eyes in alarm, but before Carrie could elaborate, Ali bustled in with the nappy and wipes.

'Here you go. Is the portable changing mat still in the kitchen drawer?' she asked me.

'Yep, I'll get it.' And I jumped up, glad to have a purpose and useful distraction from whatever social hand grenade Carrie was about to lob. I had no idea what favour I could possibly do for her.

'Come and clean his bum in here,' Isla suggested. 'You can do it on the rug, it's softer.'

'Oh my God, what do you think she was going to ask you?' Mel hissed as soon as Carrie was out of earshot in the living room.

'I have no fucking idea.'

'What, what?' Ali quizzed us, out of the loop. I got her up to speed. 'Maybe she wants a threesome now she's finally met you! I told you make-up was a good idea.'

'All clean!' Carrie had returned without us noticing. 'Isla's practising her changing skills.'

Fuckity fuck, I wondered if she'd heard us gossiping, but Sam timed his entrance perfectly, causing a diversion.

'We're in the kitchen,' I shouted, gleeful to see his face at the room full of women, only one of them in his camp.

'Oh, hello.' With an air of insouciance, he kissed Carrie on the cheek. Quick as a flash, my Beardy Weirdy radar detected some latent activity. A diamond ring flickered across the back of my mind and I saw Sam propose to Carrie. I monitored my feelings and found them to be stable and apparently unbothered by the vision. Though I knew my bloody emotions were most likely prevaricating and by tomorrow I would be smashed in the face by some kind of delayed reaction. Sometimes it was hard to tell if I had moved on or was just pretending. He then kissed Mel and Ali and stopped in front of me. I shot him down with a gimlet stare.

'Thanks for helping out,' he said breezily, and patted me on the arm instead, like I was some serf. 'Right, the snow is insane. The cab couldn't make it all the way up the road. Are you sure you put the car into winter mode?' he aimed at Carrie.

'No. You know I hate that car. Why can't it just do it automatically? I forgot.'

'How could you forget? It's bloody snowing outside?'

'All right! I just did, OK!'

My, oh my, trouble in paradise. I tensed my stomach muscles so I didn't let out an unfortunate chortle.

'Well, if you "forgot" hopefully that means we can reverse it out of the garden and back onto the road and I'll get us home.'

I glanced surreptitiously at Carrie to gauge her reaction. She turned her gaze on me and shot me an ever so slight conspiratorial eye roll.

30
Double Wedding Bells

'I need to talk to you.'

'It's OK. I know what you're going to say.'

'How can you know?'

'Because I'm a witch and saw it in my crystal ball last Wednesday.'

'What do you mean, you saw it? God, you were never this weird when we were married.'

'Yes I was. I just never told you. So, you're getting married.'

'Holy fuck, you're creeping me out. Last Wednesday was the day I asked Carrie's dad for her hand. How did you even know?'

'I just did.'

Ali was earwigging. It was hard not to. The conversation was taking place at the kitchen sink, where I had been scrubbing a particularly crusty pan from the kids' dinner as she was following a workout DVD on her laptop, propped up on the butcher's block. Her post break-up fitness regime was in full swing.

'Well, I wanted you to know before we told the kids this weekend.'

'When will you get married?'

'In the summer some time. Look, there's something else.' This I hadn't predicted. 'Carrie and I need your permission to let the kids appear in her new TV show.'

'What?' I whispered, stupefied.

'We decided that instead of waiting for the TV production company to approach us, we would form one ourselves with a producer and pitch the idea to them of Carrie presenting a family show, centred round her getting married, making her own wedding cake, creating family favourites and feeding her whole brood.'

'But they're not her kids,' I hissed.

'I know they're not her kids, but they're my kids and we're getting married so she will be their stepmum. It's a modern family. Most people are in blended families now.'

'And if I say no?'

'Well, I hope you're not going to.' He laughed tautly.

'What if I am, what will happen to the show?'

'It won't happen. It all hinges on the kids appearing and the girls being Carrie's bridesmaids.' Bile tickled my tonsils. 'But the main focus will be the food. The kids are just to show a different side to Carrie. So her fans can see tiny snippets of our family life...'

'I've got to go.' I couldn't listen any more and switched my phone off.

'Don't waste any more tears on that man!' Ali ordered from across the kitchen, placing her weights carefully down on the floor. 'Be strong.'

'That's not why I'm upset. I always knew he was going to get married. He wants the kids to appear in Carrie's next show as part of their blended family prepping for the wedding.'

'Oh, fuck. I'm so sorry. Trust him to turn his wedding into a money-spinning scheme.'

'What should I do?' I knew Mel would give me the best unbiased advice from her position as all-knowing sage. Jacqui and Ali were all for telling Sam to shove his TV show up his arse and fuck the consequences, but I had niggling doubts. 'I have been avoiding him since he asked me and said he has to leave me alone for a while. He just doesn't get how upsetting it all is. Just because I've met Carrie and didn't stab her in the head with the bread knife doesn't mean we can all go on a Center Parcs holiday as some modern blended family!'

'Hmm, there's two separate things going on here. Sam is getting married. And then his younger and successful wife wants to play mother to your three kids on her TV show, creating this image of caring stepmother while feeding them nutritious food all the while writing cookbooks and making her own wedding cake. I don't understand why you're so upset!'

'I know, when you say it like that, I need to give myself a break.'

'You do. It was always going to be hard when Sam got remarried, but he's foisting this other huge thing on your shoulders, too. The first thing you can't do anything about, but I suppose this one you could potentially fuck up for both of them and that's why you need to look at your motives.'

'Ha, I knew I should have spoken to you straight away.'

'He went about it all the wrong way. He should have asked you first before he pitched it to the TV company.'

'I know, that's what I said! But he said I would have said no. He's a total cunt! Apparently, Carrie was going to ask me when you were there during snowgate, and that was before they had pitched. She was the one who wanted to do it properly.'

'Well, you kind of have to respect her for that. Brave lady asking you in your own home surrounded by your close friends.'

'Except she didn't, did she? She chickened out, probably because she knew Sam would kill her.'

'You're not going to want to hear this.'

'Go on…'

'This show is how those two make money, how they put food on the table and that includes giving you money as part of the divorce. What happens if that money dries up? What if this show is massive? You could ask for a cut of the profits. Or you could swallow it all gracefully and just think I don't need to be attached to this circus. He can do what he likes with the children because they're half his. Ask *them* if they want to be a part of it.'

A few days later, just as I was setting off for the French Café with Chug, I got a card in the post. I thought it was another Christmas card until I opened it. It was a pretty design with bunting spelling out 'Thank you' on the multi-coloured flags. Inside it read:

Dear Amanda,

Thank you so much for granting us permission for the children to come on board with the new project. I appreciate how hard it must be, now I am a mother myself. I completely admire you for the way you have handled everything and how you parent the children, always putting their needs first. It really shows and they love you so much.

Best wishes,

Carrie

I wondered how long it had taken her to think of what to say, before I shoved it on the butcher's block and headed out. Halfway through word bingo at the café, my phone started ringing. It was Ali.

'I just did something awful.'

'What?'

'I just keyed Jim's car.'

'What the fuck happened?' I hissed once I'd got home and after I plugged Sonny into the TV to buy some time.

'I was in that interview with the boss of the agency. She was lovely, really enthusiastic about my portfolio, and when she got to the pictures of Grace in that Mothercare shoot I styled a few months ago – remember when they were a baby short?' I nodded. 'Well, she stopped dead.'

'Oh God, what?'

'She said: "Oh, I know that little one, she's my friend's stepdaughter. Well, she will be her stepmum properly after the wedding."'

'Fuck me. What wedding? Does she know you're Grace's mum?'

'No. I didn't say anything. I didn't know what to do because I actually couldn't speak.'

'I'm not surprised. Are you OK?'

'Obviously not or I wouldn't have keyed Jim's car. Why didn't he tell me? What's wrong with him? He knew I would find out eventually. Sounds like Grace is going to the wedding so he would have had to tell me at some point.'

'What else did that woman say?' Disheartened, I slumped in one of the kitchen chairs sipping tea; Ali's hands were shaking so badly she had to put her mug down.

'Nothing, I didn't ask anything. If I acted nosy then she would know I was Grace's mum. I mean, she must *know* Grace's mum is called Ali and here was someone called Ali with pictures of her in her book.'

'How did you leave it?'

'With her offering to represent me! She's one of the best new agents, up and coming. She said she even had some jobs she thought I would be good for, actual campaigns, not just crappy editorial.'

'Fuckshitbollocksdickwipeknobend. So you said no?' I covered my eyes at this point, not sure I could cope with the next dilemma.

'I said yes. I need the work!'

'Will she drop you if she knows?'

'Business is business. I didn't tell her I was represented by Jim for years. I said I had always been on my own, but felt the need to further my career. I never mentioned Grace at all. She doesn't need to know.'

'So how come you keyed the car? I mean, I know why, but surely the rage was gone by then.'

'No. I fucking hate him! I get a new agent and he's fucking that up for me before I even start. And now he's getting a happy ever after. Why does it have to work out for him? I don't want to know about his life, but it feels like I'll never be free of him rubbing his amazing life in my face.'

'You won't. He's Grace's dad. That's what's so shit about your position.'

Ali sipped her tea, her hand a bit steadier.

'And you have no idea when the wedding is?'

'Nope, could be next week, for all I know. When I got off the bus, his car was parked by the Co-op. So I just ran my house keys down the side facing the road, to look less suspicious, then legged it back here. It honestly made me feel so much better. I proper gouged it too. It actually looked like a lorry had grazed it by the time I'd finished.'

Ali's phone pinged ten minutes later as I was putting a wash on and she was prepping Grace's dinner for later.

'Oh God, look!'

Going to be late dropping Grace. Some bastard scraped my car so have to drop at garage. They said they might be able to do it now.

'Eye of newt and tail of dragon…'

'What are you all doing?' Neve asked, pink lipstick smeared all over her lips, missing them entirely. It was the Saturday after cargate.

'Spells!' Ali cried. 'Now, where was I?'

'Eye of newt?' Jacqui suggested, sloshing her wine round in her glass. 'Does anyone actually say "eye of newt"?'

'Can we join in?' Isla asked, eyeing the gristly ham bone resting on the work surface, peeking out of the butcher's greaseproof wrapping paper.

'Yes, please, can we?' Neve begged. 'We can be witches' assistants.'

'No, either watch the film or go upstairs and play dressing up, or you can go to bed early.' Their faces fell. Grace was already in bed and Sonny was jacked up on sugar with Joe in the living room watching *High School Musical* – his latest obsession. Diggers were yesterday's news.

'Have you got the T-shirt?' I asked Ali. 'Jacqui, can you light all the candles – I think we need to get in the mood.' I had already switched off the overhead spotlights. The girls disappeared upstairs and we set to work in our coven of three.

'How have you got Jim's T-shirt?' Jacqui asked, distastefully fingering it like it was a dead animal pelt.

'It was just in a bag of stuff and I never threw it out. I did mean to give it to him, then forgot.'

'You need to wrap the ham bone up in the T-shirt, put it in a plastic bag, tie the bag with string then everything goes in that Tupperware box with three cups of salted water.'

'That's it?' Ali asked, sounding disappointed. 'This is the "Get Over Your Ex" spell?'

'Then we leave it for a week, and next Saturday at ten a.m. we bury the bone in the garden like a dog.'

'No eye of newt?'

I shook my head.

'Can we do another spell?'

I thumbed through my book to find one we could all join in with.

'Create your own destiny?'

'Oooh, yes!' Jacqui clapped her hands. 'I want to do that.'

'We all have to take showers, but I think we can forgo that. I can cleanse us all with my sage smudging stick.' I produced my sage bundle tightly bound by string, used in Beardy Weirdy ceremonies to banish negativity and cleanse particularly grungy auras.

'We need a chopped-up apple, some cucumber, two white candles, paper and pen and a mirror.'

After I had wafted burning sage around us and lit the white candles, we all had to inhale the crisp smell from the cucumber and apple and focus on what we wanted to achieve in the future.

'Do we write them down once we know?' Ali asked.

'Yes, and then we'll go over to the mirror and chant and read aloud what we want.

'Ready?' The other two nodded after we'd finished our memos to the universe. I held up the book and we began in unison.

'I will travel from the depth to the light. I am my own universe – capable of all things. I create my own destiny.'

'You go first, Jacqui.'

'After my yoga course I would like to make a success of teaching and start up my own local group. I would like to meet someone but just for fun, to go on some dates and see what happens. I will do this in the future.'

Ali spoke next.

'I want to do well at work so that one day I can stand on my own two feet and leave the attic. I need one big client at work who keeps rebooking me for regular shoots. I would also like to let go of the anger about Jim and try and move on so I can meet someone else. I will do this in the future.'

'I want my book to get published so I can finally earn some proper money. I will do this in the future.'

I had delivered the first draft to my agent a few weeks previously and was anxiously awaiting rewrites. Pressing send had been a momentous occasion. It had been written in such frenzied drawn-out fits and starts that I was unable to gauge which way it was going to go. 'Come on, let's go and burn everything in the magic chimenea and send it out into the ether.'

At ten a.m. the following Saturday, Ali reverently carried the ham bone wrapped in newspaper to the back of the garden, both of us wearing our parkas to shield against the drizzle.

'Where shall I bury it?'

'Near the acer tree? There's some earth underneath where nothing grows.'

Ali got down on her hands and knees and hacked away at the soggy leaf-covered soil with the trowel until the hole was big enough, and placed the putrid bone in its shallow grave.

'Goodbye, Jim. Hello, new life. I hope Ginger doesn't dig you up!'

31

Emergency Christmas Brownies

'I don't want her to go,' Ali grizzled into her medicinal wine at Christmas Eve lunchtime. All four kids were sitting watching TV, coats on their knees, bags packed like evacuees, ready for their first Christmas with their dads.

'Just imagine it's the same as when Grace goes for a weekend and we can do whatever we like,' I reasoned.

'But it isn't! It's Christmas Day tomorrow. The first one without Dad! At least Mum is with my brother and his kids. I couldn't face being with another family.'

'No, me neither.' I had turned down my brother's kind offer of Christmas with him, but felt the same. Watching my niece and nephew open their presents would probably tip me over the edge, knowing that Sam and Carrie were playing happy families and possibly filming footage for their sparkly new TV show.

'I just wish we could block out the day and pretend it isn't happening.'

'Funny you should say that; I've had a cunning plan…'

*

'Brownies for breakfast?' Jacqui asked. 'But it's Christmas Day. We should be having champagne and scrambled eggs and smoked salmon.' She poked her brownie with a disdainful finger. 'If I'm being forced into a no-kids Christmas then it has to be top class!'

'We can eat all that after,' Ali said, grinning mischievously. 'These are *special* Christmas brownies.'

'What's so special about them?'

'They're *hash* brownies. Space cakes. They get you high…' I laughed.

'Where did you get them?' she asked me suspiciously.

'I made them. Woody hid his weed stash in my writer's desk. I found it by accident a few weeks ago when I was looking for the window locks.'

'I wonder what else he's stashed around the house?' Jacqui asked, closely inspecting her brownie. 'I bet there's all sorts.'

We cleared away breakfast, spoke to our parents and siblings on the phone and waited.

'Should we drink more?' Ali asked after half an hour. 'I can't feel anything.'

'Patience comes to those who wait…' I said, and poured us all another glass of champagne.

'I want to lie in the grass, feel the energy of the earth,' Jacqui babbled, swaying from side to side, staring out of the glass doors.

'But it's freezing,' Ali giggled, scoffing her fourth mince pie in a row. 'Do you really want to go out there when we can stay in here and eat?'

'Yes, come on. Let's get our coats on and lie in the garden.' House music was blasting out of the speakers in the kitchen, my iPod plugged into the PA system. Ginger had hidden in Meg's bed since breakfast, terrified. Jacqui had made us do yoga earlier but I fell over on my head when we started doing sun salutes because my legs buckled, so we stopped. That was when she suggested lying down outside instead.

'Let the earth hold you. It will be grounding and stop you falling over.'

'I feel like I'm sinking,' Ali said. 'What if we can't get up because we're so spackered?'

'We will get up. Chill,' Jacqui said. 'Wow, you know what, I must eat space cakes all the time. It opens up your crown chakra. I can feel the universe sending me lots of love.'

Waves of pleasantly buzzing pressure undulated from near the top of my head down, across the shoreline of my body to the rocky outcrop of my toes ensconced in my Ugg boots, which by now felt like squashy hugs insulating my feet.

'Do you think Uggs are called Uggs because they are actually the manifestation of the designer's idea of a hug for your feet?'

'Oh. My. God! Yes!' Ali squealed. 'Of course. I never thought of that. We should write to them and say we've worked it out.'

'They might send us three free pairs,' Jacqui slurred. 'Fuck, I'm fucked. It's got even more now.'

Lying there, spaced out, I had a niggling feeling I had invited something to happen but couldn't put my finger on what it was. Everything had slowed down dramatically since the brownies had set to work. What felt like hours were in fact minutes. I had looked at the kitchen clock when we traipsed outside to the garden and it was only eleven in the morning.

I don't know how long we lay there. Jacqui was trapped in a loop of: 'I love you guys, you know that, right?' And we kept repeating, 'Yes we know.' Occasionally Ali would blurt out: 'I'm battered' and then laugh hysterically. I wanted to hold Chugga and kiss his fluffy head and breathe in the comforting smell of his baby-soft skin. As I was thinking of the kids and how much I missed them, the sound of a siren invaded my head. Was it part of the tune on the iPod? I thought I heard a crashing sound. I promptly sat up.

'What's that?'

'No idea,' Ali said dreamily. 'I can't move.'

'Girls! Are you here? Where are you?'

It was Philippa from next door, her voice bouncing out from in the kitchen. Someone had turned the music off. Oh God, I just remembered what it was I had invited: it was her, James and Daniel for champagne. I think I sent a text, replying to their Happy Christmas one when I was out of my head.

'Here, in the garden. Get up, you two! We have to look normal.'

'What are you doing lying on the wet grass?'

'Some yoga.'

'Did you know your holly was on fire in the living room?'

'What?' I jumped up now, somehow finding the wherewithal to act like a person in control of their life.

'Yes, I called the fire brigade. I'm afraid they broke in but I think the door isn't too badly damaged.'

'Oh my God,' Jacqui whispered. 'How did the holly set on fire?'

'You left candles burning on the mantelpiece. James and I were hammering on your door and could see through the window the holly just set alight before our eyes. We rang you, but no one was answering.'

'My phone was in the living room.'

'Are the owners out here?' a man's voice called from further in the house.

'Yes, she's here,' Philippa shouted back.

I walked unsteadily to the back door, brushing leaves from my grubby parka. A tall man in full fireman's uniform strode purposefully towards me, his limbs making regular sweeping noises against the heavy-duty fabric. I felt paranoid that I was about to get dragged over the coals, my children taken into care and some kind of court fine for wasting emergency services' time.

'You know you're very lucky we got here in time and that your neighbours alerted us. What were you thinking, leaving candles burning when you weren't in the room?'

'I'm sorry, Officer. We'd had a bit to drink and thought it would be good to come out here to sober up and we just forgot about the candles.' I urgently stabbed my palms with my nails to halt the giggles fighting to emerge as I suddenly imagined the fireman's head inexplicably morphing into a giant ice cream.

'Well, you won't be the first person to make that mistake.' He looked from me and then to Ali and Jacqui behind me. He must have been in his late twenties. He was very handsome and his raw masculinity was actually quite intimidating as we stood there, make-up free with untamed hair, pyjamas on underneath our coats. He saved lives and was a hero. I felt like a useless worm in comparison. The wave of giggles subsided.

'Haven't I seen you three before?'

'No, we would have remembered you,' Jacqui said boldly. I was taken aback. She never said stuff like that. He coloured ever so slightly pink on his cheeks; it was quite endearing.

'Anyway, come and see the damage.'

The smell hit me first: weird chemicals from the foam. There was some charring on the mirror, up the wall and on the ceiling, but in reality, there was very little damage. The worst was the front door. It was wide open, but not off its hinges.

'What am I going to do about the door?' I wailed. 'The house isn't secure, if it's broken.'

'You can call an emergency locksmith. They'll be working today. I have a number in the truck.' Two other older firemen walked through the lounge to gather equipment.

'Here's the info.' The young fireman handed me an 'After We've Gone' leaflet. 'Look, there's no real damage. You're safe to have the gas and electricity on. It was just the holly on the mantelpiece. Nothing else has been touched. You had it there all week?' I nodded. 'Yeah, it gets dried out, especially with central heating and the fire. It's ideal tinderbox material.' I felt stupid.

'I hope you ladies enjoy the rest of your day,' he said, returning from the truck while the other two carried off the extinguishers. Philippa followed them out giving us a parting wave.

'We will. Thank you,' Jacqui smiled at him, and winked as he purposefully handed her the locksmith card.

'I know where I've seen you. At that bar, DJ-ing. All three of you were there. I remember because, well, I just did. Happy Christmas. Maybe see you girls down there again?'

'Thanks so much for saving us,' I said gratefully. 'So sorry for being annoying. Happy Christmas!'

'You got that number?' I asked once they'd left, leaving me to sort out the door. Jacqui handed me the business card. 'I think Andy liked you, Jacqui.'

'Andy?'

'The cute fireman.'

'Nooooo, don't be silly. He was way too young. I could be his mum.'

'Yeah, if you'd had him at eleven! Seriously though, why else would he have written his name and number on the back of the card and given it to you?'

32

The Spare Man

'Mummy, we're filming the show this weekend! We're going to be on TV!' The promise of stardom overshadowed the glaring realisation that Daddy was getting married. I think Sam had sold it to them in some kind of conflated package for that exact purpose.

'How exciting!' I enthused, while secretly hoping that Sonny pulled one of his monstrous shitfits clean out of the bag, imploding Carrie's soufflé showstopper.

'You just need to meet someone now,' Isla said that bedtime after the TV show announcement. 'I wish you would.'

'Why?'

'To make it fair. It's not fair that Daddy gets to be happy and remarried. You need to meet a husband.'

'Would that make you happier?' I asked curiously.

'Yes!' Meg practically shouted.

I looked from Meg's earnest cherub face to Isla's long solemn one and tried to bring Sonny into this, but he was brumming his Hot Wheels cars up and down the end of the bed. We were cosied up in my bedroom, snuggled under the duvet, Meg in the middle of attempting bunches for the fifth time, pulling my hair out from the roots, making my eyes water. I had several clips in my fringe, one of which was a unicorn with a missing horn.

'But if I met someone, he wouldn't be a new daddy for you. You already have one.'

'We know,' Meg said like I was stupid. She pulled my right bunch tight with her little fist and tried to pull it unsuccessfully through the twist she couldn't quite hold with her fingers. Ginger sensibly lay on the rug by the fireplace; he knew what happened when the hairbrushes came out.

'Isla, can you show me again?' she asked, clearly exasperated. Isla patiently held my hair and guided Meg's hands so they could make the twist work and pull through the bunched-up hair. 'Thank you!'

'Mummy, we just want you to meet someone because it's nice to have a Spare Man around.'

'A Spare Man?'

'Yes, someone to do things with. Go to the park. Have days out.'

'But we don't need anyone to have days out. We have nice days out and we're OK. I don't need anyone… We have Ali.'

'Sonny does. And we do,' Isla explained simply. 'Daddy said Sonny is going mad in that house with all those women.'

Red-hot rage shot up from my stomach. 'What?' I squeaked, then smiled serenely for I knew I had to act indifferent or I wouldn't eke any more titbits out of them.

'Well, you know all the tantrums Sonny has here? And the smashing stuff? Well, at Christmas he started it at Daddy's, too. And Daddy said it's because he's in a house full of women.' And not because his daddy had another baby boy so soon after he left, who gets to live with him permanently. No, it couldn't be that. My pulse throbbed in my temples.

'And Daddy thinks I should meet a man, does he?'

'No. That wasn't his idea. That was ours!' Isla said proudly. I wanted to cry. Of course I wanted them to be happy, but a man? Meg looked at me and attacked the left side of my head, grasping the hair tightly so the roots stretched out of my scalp and tucked forcefully into her fist.

'Where am I going to find a Spare Man?' I asked them, wincing from the pain.

'Ask the universe!' Isla said openly, throwing my own words back at me. 'You're always telling Ali to do that.'

Mel had given me a new book for Christmas, *The Four Agreements*. Once I'd finished it and completely and utterly absorbed its message, I stuck an abbreviated version of it to the fridge under one of our multitude of novelty magnets.

'What's this? More Beardy Weirdy?' Ali asked, inspecting the two pages of computer-printed life goals.

'Yes, but achievable, not ordering men from the cosmos or thinking happy thoughts to attract one million pounds. I'm now choosing to live my life this way. Hand in hand with Reiki, as it were.'

'OK. Let me see…

> Be impeccable with your word – speak with integrity and only say what you mean and don't gossip against yourself or others.

'Well, where's the fun in that?

Don't take anything personally – nothing others do is because of you. If you are immune to the opinions and actions of others, you won't be a victim of needless suffering.

'But what about if someone punches you? You're suffering then!

Don't make assumptions – communicate with others clearly so you avoid misunderstandings, drama and sadness.

'OK, yes, that makes sense.

Always do your best – enjoy the action without expecting a reward.

'Come on – you can't expect to do a job for the love of it and live off fresh air. This guy lives on another planet.'

'Read all the blurb. It's not as simple as that. I sent it to Jacqui and she's going to try it, too. I reckon we start doing this and eternal happiness and success will be ours; we can take over the world. Ancient Mexican people called the Toltecs lived by them.'

'It sounds like something you would get Brownie badges for,' Ali scoffed. 'Where are these people now?'

'They died off.'

'Classic! No wonder they all died out. They were so busy doing jobs and not getting paid that they all dropped dead from starvation!'

'Shut it. Sometimes things die out naturally because they're too innovative for the time. The world is ready to hear this now. Watch and learn.'

'I'll stick to ordering off the universe, I think.'

Late February, standing at the sink vacantly washing up burned cheese pizza pans, a familiar sensation washed over me. My skin prickled all over my back with pins and needles, my hands and feet throbbed rhythmically. I was absolutely positive a person was standing directly behind me, someone tall and well built, like a man. This had happened fourteen years previously while I was sitting on a plane home from Greece. I'd been convinced I could sense a man behind me then, but when I poked my nose through the narrow gap in the seats, there was just a corpulent old lady with bifocals reading a John Grisham novel. I had been sure I was going to encounter someone significant that evening. I hadn't been wrong – I'd met Sam.

I stopped scrubbing the pan. I wanted to turn my head and see if there was anything there. Instead I closed my eyes and reverently asked who it was. Could the Spare Man be about to make an appearance? My shopping list of Spare Man characteristics was secretly stashed away in my desk upstairs. (My favourite point was he had to laugh at the same puerile things I found funny or it just wouldn't work. I'd dispensed with romance. My overlying theme was that kindness had to be paramount.)

When will I meet you? I silently asked. I waited for a sign – anything – that I could flimsily latch on to.

Ali barged into the kitchen, the door slamming wide open against a chair with a violent thwack!

'Fuck's sake!' she bellowed. 'He's getting married this weekend!'

Spare Man vanished in a panic from whence he came.

'How do you know? Who told you?'

'Alice, my agent.'

I ripped my rubber gloves off and reached into the depleted wine rack beneath the butcher's block. I wished for the trillionth time we were cash rich and, after curing world poverty, could fill the crusty damp cellar to bursting with posh bottles of red wine and vintage champagne. I poured us both a glass of red plonk.

'Well, Grace was in the bath earlier and Alice rang. She jumped straight in with, "I know you're Jim's ex, and Grace's mum. Why didn't you tell me?" I said I didn't think it mattered, that we had a business relationship. I also said I desperately needed an agent to help me get more work, being a single parent, blah blah blah. She and Hattie must have chatted and put two and two together.'

'What did she say to that?'

'She said fair enough. She said she would have done the same, especially as I had no idea before going to the interview that she was Hattie's friend. I obviously wouldn't have put in the pictures of Grace if I'd known, would I?'

'No. So she's not going to drop you?'

'She said not. Said she'll try and get some more work with Next. The jobs I did last week got good feedback so she's pleased. They want to use me again. If I get in with them, it would be regular.'

'What a legend. So how did the wedding date come up?'

'She could hear Grace splashing in the bath and asked how she was. Then she said she'd see her at the weekend for their wedding. I felt like she'd punched me in the stomach.'

'Fuck. I'm not surprised. Did you act normal?' I fleetingly

wondered what kind of retribution the bathroom had suffered at the hands of the news.

'Yes, you would have been so proud of me. No freaking out. Though that may happen now.'

I pushed her wine towards her and she downed it in one, a tiny rivulet dribbling down her chin. She slammed the glass down on the work surface, wiping away the dribble with her hand.

'Fucking twat. I bet she's a flower girl or something. I can't believe it; I still have his engagement ring in Grace's keepsake box.' She looked like she was about to cry, but thought better of it. 'This weekend, please can we go out and paint the town red? I need to forget Grace is at *his* wedding. I can't go too far as I'm working the next day. Did you know there's a new late-night place opened called the Adventure Bar? Apparently it's crazy, dancing on tables and people having sex in the toilets. I think we need to check it out.'

You could hear the music two blocks down when we stopped to get some cash out.

'Evening, ladies,' said the heavy-set bouncer all decked out in black as he pulled the door open for us. The beat of the bass echoed rhythmically in our chests and our noses were assaulted by a sweet sickly smell. Years later, Ali would claim that if we spun her round in a game of blind man's buff and pointed her unknowingly towards the Adventure Bar, she would be able to tell where she was from its characteristic olfactory delights of vomit, mingled with flaming Sambucas and cheap perfume.

My armpits instantly started to prickle from the heat and as we walked further in, we started shedding layers. The space was open all the way through the length of the entire building to the back, down some vulgar night-club chrome steps to an impressive bar stretching along the whole right-hand side. Disco lights flashed, highlighting a group of men immediately to the left of the door. They were sitting at two high round bar tables also edged with chrome. They seemed pleased to see us and one of them fervently beckoned Jacqui over.

'We've got jugs of cocktails and lots of spare glasses, if you girls want to have some.' An earnest-looking chap, wearing a shirt and geek glasses, pointed to the tables laden with giant pitchers of fluorescent-looking liquid and scatterings of supposedly clean glasses. A warning immediately flashed across my brain: what if they'd roofied the cocktails and were stationed by the door claiming unsuspecting victims? 'It's Mark's thirtieth. Help him celebrate!' Mark waved from the second table. He looked like a clean-cut boy-band singer. The others were a mix of young guys let out on the town after an intensive librarian conference. We were safe.

The Adventure Bar Small Talk Tennis Tournament opened around the tables. As everyone picked up their rackets I felt a tap on my shoulder.

'What's your name? I saw you come in but was stuck over by the corner.' He was very tall and I had to tip my head back to see his face. He had short dark hair, stubble grazed his jaw and he was wearing a trendy lilac dogtooth shirt.

'I'm Amanda. I didn't see you. Do you come here often?' He laughed and his eyes crinkled endearingly. I hadn't meant it as a pick-up, it was just my hackneyed opening shot.

'No. I've never been here before. It's my first day in London. I just moved down yesterday from Birmingham.' After chatting aimlessly for the best part of an hour, I realised I didn't know his name. So I asked.

'I'm Chris,' he said, just as my drink went down my throat the wrong way.

'Everything OK?' he asked as he patted my back to prevent asphyxiation.

I nodded. 'I have three kids,' I choked out, my motives unclear at this point.

'Oh. OK. Can I get your number?' It threw me. The kids were supposed to be a deflection.

'Why?'

'So we could meet up again? Go for a drink?'

'I only do dinner.' Which wasn't true, but tonight I wasn't in the mood for making anything easy.

'Well, we could go to dinner. Where's good round here?' I mentioned the expensive French place to be facetious.

'OK, we can go there.'

'Don't be silly, I was kidding.'

'So you'll give me your number?' I was impressed I wasn't putting him off.

'Really?'

'Really.'

I rattled it off. By now he was the only one left of his friends. Jacqui had disappeared ten minutes ago to meet Andy the fireman after his night shift, and Ali was waiting patiently with her coat on.

'Can I get a kiss goodbye?' he asked, and shot me a sly grin. He was very cute.

'No. Sorry, you have to have a date to get one of those.'

'Just on the cheek then?'

I gave in and offered up my cheek and he swung round and kissed me gently on the lips.

'I'll call you!' and he was up out of his seat and through the door before I could protest.

33

First Date Nerves

'Glass of red?' Sam looked at me from under his brows as we stood side by side at the bar. We were on a date. It was so skewed and familiar yet alien all at the same time, rather like existing in a parallel universe.

'Yes, please.'

'Get a seat, I'll bring them over.'

I wanted to laugh; the place was deserted apart from the crusty old gimmers at the bar, and a couple of builders in their plaster-covered work clothes. This place was a bit of a last bastion, ungentrified old man's pub stalwartly clinging onto the squelchy red floral carpet and nicotine-stained beige walls, with a few chocolate-box framed paintings by Constable. It still sold pickled eggs, and not in an ironic hipster way.

Just before Sam had left, Rob had offered to babysit as we attempted to inject some missing spontaneity back into the daily grind of three children under five. We rarely left the house, just the two of us. There would always be a crowd or a reason to go out: someone's birthday or Christmas drinks.

It would never be to reconnect and talk to each other, remind us why we got married and found each other irresistible all those years ago. So that week before Sam stung me with 'I've lost the love', when the grumbles of discontent were too loud to ignore any longer, I had begged him for a date. This pub was what he'd come up with. The writing was on the wall but I had been blind.

'God, I've not been in here for years. Didn't we come here once?'

'Yes, I think it was where you were going to tell me you wanted to leave, but bottled it.'

'Ha, funny.' Not it wasn't. The chasm between us widened further still. 'How are the kids?' Argh, small talk.

'Well, Isla is dating a sixteen-year-old from the sinkhole estate. Meg is smoking crack most days, and Sonny's started collecting knives. They're the same.'

'Are we not going to have a serious conversation?'

'Yes, but don't ask me questions about your own children when you're going to see them tomorrow.'

'Are you on your period?'

'FYI you are banned from ever asking me that again.'

'I was kidding!'

'No shit, Sherlock. Now why don't you just tell me what is so important you couldn't tell me in the car outside the house like you normally do.' I found I was drinking my wine much quicker than usual and my heart rate had picked up its pace in anticipation of whatever bombshell he was about to drop. My instinct was to prepare for the worst.

'Well, you know we were going to get married in August?'

I nodded.

'Well, we're not any more.'

'Not getting married?' For some reason this made me want to laugh like a drain.

'We *are* getting married, but we've had to bring the date forward because of the TV show. The schedules have been rejigged and they want the wedding segments filmed and done before the summer.'

'Can't they just film it when it happens in August and splice it together?'

'But they want it to go out over the summer. We're filming the main body of it all now.'

'OK, so when's the new date?'

'The last Saturday in May. It's a bank holiday weekend.'

'OK. Why does it involve me?'

'Well, because we've had to move the date so far forward we've had to find a different venue.' I had no idea where the first one was, and I didn't want to know. Because I knew I would Google it and play Top Trumps against the beautiful wedding we'd held at his dad's house in the country. 'And the only place we could find was my dad's house.'

'What?' I squawked. 'You can't; that's where we got married. It's the same!' The gimmers and the builders swivelled their heads away from their pints and pickled eggs to stare at me. I hadn't meant to raise my voice, but the disbelief that had thundered into my guts propelled me onto my back foot and I lost control.

'It's not the same. They've redone the barn and it'll be in there.'

'But you'll be able to see where we had our first dance on the patio to the fake Gipsy Kings.'

'You won't. It's not even close.' A hairline crack appeared in his nonchalant façade, a faint glimmer of shame flickered behind his eyes.

'I can't believe it...' I whispered. 'Nothing is sacred.'

'Look, I'm not apologising. I can't help it, the schedule changed and it's all last minute.'

'There must have been somewhere else free. Anywhere but where we got married.'

'There wasn't.'

I drained my wine, but my hand was shaking so badly I spilled some down my chin and it dripped onto my cream jumper.

'Do you want another one?'

'What, you mean there's more? I thought the meeting was over.'

'Have another drink. I do want to talk about the kids, too.' While he was at the bar, the parallel universe split in two, exposing a memory I had until now deemed too painful to revisit. However, the scenario it was too futuristically reminiscent of was staring me in the face, tracing a familiar path fourteen years apart. Tomorrow I was going on a first date with a man whose face I could not recall, just like my first date with Sam. Since Chris had texted and arranged the date over a week ago, his likeness had faded fast like an unfixed silver photograph exposed to sunlight; only the essence of him remained. I knew he wasn't unattractive and he was tall and dark, and I remembered the kiss he stole as he left the Adventure Bar.

September 1997, and I'm walking ambivalently towards the now defunct Virgin Mega Store on Oxford Street, to meet the DJ who had nervously rung me, asking for a date after I had helped him select tunes at the thirtieth birthday party five days previously. As I reached my destination a man jumped out of a doorway and hugged me to his chest.

'Oh, thank God you're not a hosebeast!' It was Sam, and I burst out laughing.

'A hosebeast?' He pushed his glasses back up his nose. They must have slipped when he launched himself.

'Ugly. You're far from it. Sorry, I was just panicking because I couldn't remember what you looked like.'

'Charming!'

'Oh, that came out wrong. Sorry again. Shall we go and get a drink? Where do you want to go?'

'I thought Riki Tik's in Soho.'

'Oh, wow, that's where I was going to suggest too.' I scrutinised his face, inspecting it to see if he was attempting to create a fake persona to fit with mine and charm me into bed. I decided to give him the benefit of the doubt.

What followed was possibly the most perfect first date anyone could ever experience. No wonder I was so traumatised when he left – nothing had ever lived up to all that potential. I think I was still waiting for an action replay all those years later. Or I could have just been looking back in anger, bitter that the dream had soured. After a drunken kiss in Waxy O'Connor's, the cavernous Irish pub on Rupert Street, we decided it was still too early to go home, both desperate to devour more of each other. The only place still open was the Häagen-Dazs ice-cream parlour in Leicester Square. We ate ridiculous sundaes, spooning them into each other's mouths, giggling and pulling stupid faces. I felt like Audrey Hepburn in *Roman Holiday*, living an entire life in one night, fighting against the inevitable rising sun, not wanting to break the spell.

'Come home with me,' he whispered after the clock-watching waiter declared us in love. 'Just to sleep.'

I knew he was the one for me. I could feel it embedded in my skeleton, within my DNA, the knowledge solidifying in the morning on the bus to work as he tightly gripped my hand, while I wore his Nigel Hall baggy grey jumper to shield me from the walk of shame into the office. I had inhaled the faint traces of his Acqua di Giò cologne for the rest of the day, my work colleagues laughing at my lovesick demeanour. His parting words on Tottenham Court Road had been: 'Isn't it amazing we found each other?' I would love for eternity that beautiful boy who fed me ice cream and held me all night without the promise of sex.

Tears stung my eyes and I hurriedly blinked them away. Sam slid a large glass of red before me.

'You OK?' he asked, fear skimming across his face, obviously terrified I was about to unleash some kind of hysterical diatribe.

'Fine. The kids?'

'Oh, yes. Well, I was wondering if on the day of the wedding, you could have them for the evening.'

I shook my head, more in bewilderment at where I found myself. If I could tell that younger me on that magical date what was yet to unfold, that years later this darling man would ask me to have our three children on his wedding night so he could enjoy screwing his new wife unhindered by responsibility, would I have done anything differently?

'Is that a no?'

'It is, yes. A step too far. I will be busy the weekend you get married. I will be going out.'

'Oh. I could get someone to drop them off at yours.'

'I said no.'

'Just go!' Ali cried at me as I hovered on the threshold of the house, my feet already pinched in my fuck-me red stilettos.

'You look gorgeous.' I was wearing a high-waisted denim A-line skirt that laced up from halfway down my back and a see-through custard-yellow short-sleeved blouse with miniature zebras printed on it. Ali had picked it out of the jumble sale piles of clothes I had hurriedly discarded on the floor in a tantrum.

'I don't even want to go,' I complained, hoping she would let me off with an elaborate sick note.

'Look, if you hate it, just leave. Chalk it up to experience.'

Good luck.

Jacqui texted as I tottered down the road, my shoes already beginning to rub.

I am not shagging him! Dinner dates before that happens. I AM MY WORD.

I was adamant about Being Impeccable With My Word.

My phone rang.

'So, how are you feeling?'

'Shit. Mel, I feel nothing. Last night was so weird. Sam isn't the man I married. I don't love who he is now. It's like he changed so gradually I never noticed. He feels dead to me and that opens up a whole new grieving process.'

'Listen to me. I am saying this for your own good. Do not think about this right now. You are going on a date. You have no idea what this evening will be like, but don't taint it before you even get there. Relax.'

'Thanks. I needed that. I'm so caught up in feeling nothing for Sam that I don't think I can feel anything for anyone ever again.'

'You will. Enjoy your date. I'm going, so pull yourself together, woman!'

I slipped my phone in my bag as the pub veered into sight. For the first time that evening my stomach fizzed with nerves. What did he look like? What if I just wanted to leave? This was only the second official first date I had ever been on in my life. How would it live up to the other one? I pushed open the swing door and walked to the front of the bar where he'd texted he'd be waiting. I couldn't see him and anxiously swept my eyes from one side of the pub to the other, cringing when a mum from school waved at me from across the room.

'Can I get you a drink?' He stepped from behind me. 'Sorry, I was in the loo.' He smiled at me and I sighed in relief. He wasn't a hosebeast.

34

I Am Not My Word

'There's a mum from school here,' I said covertly as he handed me a glass of red wine. I thought it might break the ice, introduce the children into the conversational arena in case he had forgotten I was a mum. He glanced indiscreetly round the pub. 'Don't stare! She'll come over!'

He looked so much younger than in the sliver of recollection I had dredged up and I wondered if he was thinking the exact opposite, and what was the requisite amount of time to stay in order to be polite. In spite of any misgivings, we fell into easy conversation covering all topics, even the prohibited ones outlined under Common Dating Law.

'So how did you and your girlfriend break up?' I pried when I had almost finished my wine, the alcohol rendering the first dating commandment obsolete. Thou Shalt Not Enquire About Past Break-Ups… Chris took it in his stride.

'Well, we basically never had sex.'

'Oh, right, how come?' Had they been part of the Let's Wait brigade, only copulating once a ring was firmly in place?

'She was a prude and I think she didn't like sex, at least, not with me.' Commandment two and three broken. Thou Shalt Not Slag Off Your Ex. Thou Shalt Not Talk About Sex.

He had been in a long-term relationship from very young and it had fizzled out but they had clung to the wreckage for a few more years of misery, neither wanting to admit defeat.

'When she ended it, I was upset, but decided to change my life. I started running and lost four stone.'

'You were fat?' You could not tell at all. He was very trim and muscly.

'Yes, Fat Chris existed. I keep an old railcard photo as a reminder in case I ever slip into bad habits. I'm not going back there.'

'Wow, good for you. How long have you been single then?'

'Two years.'

'And when you were with Laura, you never wanted to get married?'

'God, no way! That should have been a sign really. We never lived together in eight years.'

'And do you think you want to get married now?'

'Why, are you asking?' The edges of his lips twitched imperceptibly as he tried to keep a straight face. He enjoyed watching me squirm.

Strike four. Thou Shalt Not Discuss Marriage.

'Er… no. I was just wondering. I was married. I'm divorced now.'

'Would you get married again?'

'I honestly don't know. I think the children would like me to!'

'How old are your children?'

'Sonny's three, Meg is six and Isla is seven. You don't mind about someone having children?' I just wanted to clarify that fact before I wasted any time liking him, assuming there would be a second date.

'No. I'm not naïve enough to think people won't have pasts.'

'But I bet you didn't set out to meet someone with a family in tow.'

'Well, to be honest, a few months ago my best friend dared me to go on a dating website, so he set it all up. But the women they were matching me with weren't for me so I jumped off pretty sharpish.'

'What, older women with kids?' I laughed.

'Well, I stated no kids in my search and I did have an age preference up to late thirties. But when you meet someone in real life and not on a screen it's completely different. You've finished your drink. Do you want another one?'

'I'll get them.' Standing at the bar I realised I really liked him. There was no fakery, no blustering bravado, just two people connecting with the ease of old friends. I couldn't imagine us running out of things to say.

'So, how old are you?' I asked curiously, the age-gap red flag flapping.

'Thirty-one. It's rude to ask a lady her age!'

'I'm forty.' His eyebrows shot up while the rest of his face remained tactfully impassive.

'Right. You don't look it.'

'What does a forty-year-old look like, then?'

'I obviously knew you had three children, but assumed you'd had them quite young. I was expecting you to say you were a few years older than me, maybe.'

'Does an age gap bother you?'

'Not at all.' He looked me directly in the eye without even hesitating. If he was playing a game, it was a good one because

I couldn't tell. We talked about work – he was a computer programmer – about the waiting game with my book to find a publisher, about food, holidays, the children. And then he told me something that was a game changer.

'I don't live in London full time. I live with Mark only a few days a week. The rest of the time I live in Birmingham. I'm going to move down permanently at some point, though. The night I met you was my first proper weekend in London.'

'Oh, how come you do that?'

'I moved back to live at home two years ago. Work were very good and set up working from home for me as long as I commuted in three days a week. But some weeks I could work from home the entire week. My dad became very ill with early-onset Alzheimer's and it got so bad Mum couldn't cope on her own. I'm the youngest, unmarried and single, so it seemed obvious that I should move in and help out.'

'Oh my God. What a lovely thing to do. You just put your life on hold?'

'Kind of, yes. Dad would be awake in the night, wandering the house. He's strong and Mum needed me there to get him back in bed. He had no idea where he was and could get cross and shout. It wasn't very nice.'

'So, he's still there now?'

'No, he moved into a home before Christmas. He was on a waiting list for ages, hence why I needed to move back in. He should have been in a home before then because he was so ill.'

'I think that's an amazing thing to do.'

'Not really. Someone had to do it.'

'No, a lot of people wouldn't. What kind of state is he in now?'

'A bad one. He has no idea who anyone is or where he is. I can't visit; it's too… upsetting. Seeing what he's like now after knowing what he's really like. I find it stressful.'

'Of course you do. You've already done so much to help. I don't know how you coped.'

'You just get on with it, don't you?'

I nodded. The way he talked about what had happened was without any trace of expectation, or reward, not wanting a medal like some people expect when they heroically take the bins out once a week or empty the dishwasher at the weekend.

'Do I have your permission to rip off your skirt?' Chris towered over me still wearing his white vest, reminiscent of Bruce Willis in *Die Hard*, while I perched befuddled on the edge of the bed, his giant erection comically bobbing about near my face highlighted in the amber glow from the bedside light. I thought I wasn't going to do this.

'Yes, just do it!' Was that even me talking?

'Lie back so I can get a grip on the zip.'

I did as I was told and Chris masterfully grabbed the material either side and yanked the jammed zip apart, tearing the top of the skirt in the process. He pulled it down from my waist and I shimmied at the same time to aid it on its way. Before I could even worry that I wasn't sticking to the final commandment: Thou Shalt Not Have Sex On The First Date, Chris was executing the condom fumble with the finesse of someone who was badly out of practice. It took three attempts for the slippery bugger to fit properly. There was no point asking me to take over – I was even more useless. I had obviously missed the sex-ed demo at senior school when we all had to dress a banana for a safe shag.

He was an excellent kisser, setting the bar high for the ostensible main event and, despite the condom jitters, what followed was hardly the work of an amateur. We managed to find our rhythm almost immediately.

'When was the last time you had sex?' I asked as I lay next to him, his arms fitting comfortably round me while I tugged at his chest hair, trying to wind it round my finger. It was a novelty being in bed with a hairy man; Sam was like a prepubescent boy with no body hair and Woody had very little to play with.

'Over two years ago. I was worried I wouldn't last very long.'

'You're doing well then! I'm impressed with your stamina.'

'It's not over yet.' He raised his head from the pillow, a mischievous glint in his eye. 'I reckon I can go all night.'

We worked our way through a small packet of condoms and the headboard repeatedly struck the wall for four hours. I thanked the universe it was an outside wall.

'We should go to sleep now,' I yawned after the fourth time. 'It will be time to get up soon.'

'Did this answer your question?' he asked me, bashing the pillow with his fist to try to plump some air back into the flattened feathers.

'What question?'

'You asked me before we left the pub if I had a high sex drive. I think that was when you were properly shitfaced. Then we snogged in the doorway outside by the bins.'

'Oh God, I'm sorry. I do remember now.' I always had to shoot my mouth off when I was drunk. 'It does answer my question, though...'

In the morning I made us both a cup of tea while Chris got dressed and I felt even worse than I had anticipated.

'Don't look at me.' I half-hid behind the open front door, an icy draught blasting up the front garden, ruffling my scabby dressing gown. I didn't want the reality of the morning after to blemish the memory of the date. The shards of light hurt my eyes, and I wanted to shut the door in Chris's face so I could crawl upstairs, forage for codeine in the overflowing bathroom cabinet, and collapse under the duvet. He bent down and kissed me softly on the lips.

'Thanks for last night. I had a great time. I'll call you later.'

'No you won't!' I laughed. 'And it's fine.'

'What? You think I'm not going to call?'

'Yep. Don't worry about it.'

'Oh.' He looked genuinely hurt. 'Do you not want me to call?' This had never happened before.

'If you want, but don't think you have to say that because of what happened.'

'I want to see you again.'

'Oh, OK. Call if you want then. But I bet you don't.'

He turned and started walking down the path. 'Bet I do!' he shouted over his shoulder, his feet crunching on the gravel as he pulled up the collar on his black peacoat against the early morning drizzle.

How's your head?

Chris texted at lunch time.

Told you I would ring.

This isn't ringing. It's texting.

35
Voice from the Past

Four dates in and I remained stoically on the fence. How could this be? My usual pattern of behaviour, within this given time frame, is I may have furtively participated in a wedding day dream, possibly imagined how many children we might have, most likely pictured the idealised For Ever house I may have cobbled together from places I have visited, and then giggled about all of the above with friends over a bottle of wine.

But we're not in Kansas any more, Dorothy. That was the past and the past was a foreign country. I never graduated from the school of casual dating; I am an all-or-nothing person in most areas of my life. (Why have one child when you can have three?) I either dated someone and we ended up together for ever (how many for evers is one girl allowed?), or I was single and had a few consensual dead-end one-night stands. Woody was, so far, the only anomaly. Would Chris be the next one?

'It's understandable to feel hesitant,' Jacqui said the afternoon of my fifth date. 'We've all been burned, and I think we're still on the road to recovery. It's not even three years, which I know some people will think is a long time, but it's so hard to extricate yourself from a mind set when it wasn't you who wanted the marriage to end. For us, it was a shock, an instant plunge into the grieving process. For the men who left, they had been planning this for a while and all three of them had someone lined up who absorbed all that pain. The excitement of the new – the new sex, the new life, no kids twenty-four hours a day, time for themselves – while we were literally left holding the babies and all our broken hearts.'

Jacqui and I sat cautiously on my frail gaffer-taped-together camping chairs. This summer surely had to be their swansong. It was the tail end of March and the sun was verging just above the line of still-skeletal trees, the buds waiting patiently for their starring moment in a few weeks' time.

'You've only been on four dates, stop thinking you should be feeling a certain way. Just enjoy it for what it is. If I'd analysed what was going on with Andy we'd never have got past that first date.'

'I know, I know. The last time I was in this situation I met Sam and that had a clear trajectory. I have no idea where this is going in my own head. I've ticked all my boxes: been married, had kids, bought the house. He's at the beginning of his journey. He's younger. Why would he want to be with someone who's got a T-shirt for every experience?' I shook my head in bafflement.

'You're not sticking to the Four Agreements – Stop Making Assumptions. He may not want to get married and he may never want kids, but be happy to bumble along with yours. Be in the moment. Not everyone wants the conventional trappings of modern life.'

But by the time the fourth date had arrived the previous Wednesday evening, I had got myself into a bit of a pickle because on the third date he had announced his imminent move to London, for ever. I hoped he wasn't moving because of me. My anxiety coincided with the return of the dreams that had plagued me during the worst part of the divorce. In them Sam begged to come home, declared he still loved me, and was desperate to fix our relationship. The dreams were so realistic. The reconciliation was such hard work, real back-breaking graft at forgiveness. So much so that on waking, I was suspended in a preposterous bubble of belief for about a minute, until reality cruelly popped it, leaving me strung out for the best part of the morning.

Sitting on the plush expensive seats at the back of the cinema, I could feel Chris's hand itching to hold mine but I'd constructed an exclusion zone around me and leaned away from him, unable to eat my popcorn, loathing the film, which was some dire Matt Damon romance sci-fi tale.

'That film was weird, wasn't it?' Chris said as we walked back to his car parked behind the Greenwich Picturehouse.

'Yes, odd.' I just wanted to go home; my hands were purposefully stuffed in my pockets. We talked pointlessly about the film on the journey home and when he pulled the car into a space outside the house, I had unclipped my seatbelt and leaned over to kiss him briskly on the cheek before he had even turned off the engine.

'Thanks for taking me. I'm really tired tonight. Going to get an early night. See you soon.'

He looked nonplussed and nodded. 'Hope you sleep well.'

I bolted out of the car and had to refrain from running so I didn't appear rude. He drove off as soon as I disappeared into the house and I burst into tears, falling dramatically to my knees in the hallway right at the bottom of the stairs. As I lay on the scuffed floorboards, the stale smell of sweaty feet emanating from the shoe basket nicely complemented my misery.

'What's wrong with me?' I wailed pathetically into the dark. 'Why aren't I fixed yet?' I felt frightened of nothing and everything, and I wanted to be on my own because it felt safe and uncomplicated. When I was with Woody, a kind of shorthand had existed. He knew me from before, and as a mum, and as Ali's friend. I didn't love Woody and even though it had ended like it had, an easy companionship smoothed out any initial awkwardness. Chris and I had no shorthand. We had yet to write it. I wanted him to be Sam, for us to have those cliquey in-jokes, shared memories, years of experience and knowledge of each other. What I needed was a just-add-water partnership with all the trial and error removed. I wanted to know I could just stop waxing my pubic hair, let my legs grow some stubble, wear tracksuit bottoms for three days in a row, pick my nose, swear like a builder, not wear any make-up – ever – and he would still fancy me. I wanted an end to the pretence of dating; age and marriage had rendered me impatient and it was easier to disengage.

'I hear what you're saying,' Jacqui sympathised when I tried to explain the jumbled-up mess in my head that day in the garden, 'but I think you need to give him a chance. He's a good egg.'

'I know he is, but I don't think I fancy him, even though he's a Perfect on Paper Man.'

'He's pretty good off paper, too! And he's not a carpenter.' I smiled. 'Look, go on this date tonight. I think you need to have sex and reconnect. Try and stop the eternal loop in your head. Read through *The Four Agreements* and have a glass of wine. You don't really want this to be the final date, do you?' I shrugged. I honestly didn't know. 'Look how far you've come

– we've all come – in such a short space of time. I think you need to remind yourself of that.'

'You're right. I wrote a diary during the darkest part so I could get all the madness out of my head. I don't think I've ever properly looked at it. Maybe I should.'

'Come on, why don't we find it? It will probably shock you how much you've moved on, help you get some perspective.'

22 May 2008
Week two. Pain still wrenching my heart. I want to die and not wake up. I vomited on the school run today, in the gutter. Cried all the way without the kids noticing and then just puked. It's half a life, no life. No sleep, no joy, just pain. Even Sonny, who is so small, brings no joy. It's an excruciating slog. A woman came up to me on the way back from school and pointed out my skirt was about to fall down. I didn't even know. My bones are sticking out, nothing fits. Sam doesn't want to come back. I am praying he will see he needs his kids. I pray most minutes when I can remember. Dear Universe, please let him come home.

'Oh God, that's how I felt,' Jacqui said wretchedly. 'It's so awful, so heart-breaking. Where did you go up to?' We sat on the edge of the bed in my office. The diary, which was just a non-descript ring-bound blue notebook, had been rammed in a drawer with cards and pictures the kids had made me throughout the years. Even my handwriting looked deranged with grief, barely managing to graze the lines, words spiralling into each other messily as my hand tried vainly to keep up with the torrent of raw agony surging from my whole body.

'Until I ran out of space. Some of it is absolutely insane, about magic spells I cast, Tarot readings that proved he would return, dreams of him coming home. I literally latched onto anything for months and months, refusing to believe he'd gone. Look.'

25 June
Dearest Universe, please bring my husband back. My body hurts all the time for him. I hate everything. Though sometimes I am OK, and I have no idea how I am. I think it's the universe supporting me until he returns from his time in the wilderness. I will forgive him everything, even if he's slept with someone else. I know I was a nag and a total cow. I know I was negative and moany. I'm on a journey to change, not for him, but for me, to be my own hero. Living in the now helps, but the thought of him never being here, never loving me, makes me want to die. I cast a spell from my book, I hope it works.

'I made him a book, too, in one of our empty wedding albums, of all the photos and letters and keepsakes from our time together. I had a box stuffed with so much stuff it was actually insane; it was like a museum of our relationship. Even a letter from his dead granny thanking me for some nail varnish. He was so far up on a pedestal, I felt like everything needed to be documented.'

'Where's the book now?'

I shrugged. 'It was beautiful. I handmade all the decorations inside and linked all the letters and memorabilia with corresponding photos in chronological order from our years together, up until the Christmas before he left. I left space at the back to add future photos for when he came home. I was so deluded, but then so were my friends. Amy helped me, as did Rob – they were almost as traumatised as me that he could leave the kids. My mum came and stayed for a week and looked after the kids constantly so I could finish the book. It took me two weeks to eventually get it all together. Even Amy was convinced it would work. How could it not? She said I needed to wrap it in velvet to contain all its magic powers inside, like a mystic talisman. I gave it to him on 1 July, sent it to the flat he had rented, via a courier. Rob organised it for me from his work account. The courier returned it: no one was in at seven in the morning. Now I knew he left for work at eight. He made up some excuse about staying the night at his brother's. It was a crock of shit – he was at Carrie's flat. Even then I was blind to it.'

'So, did he ever get it?'

'Yes, I left it for him one day when I went away to see Mel and he came to get more of his stuff. He never said a word. When he dropped the kids back, I asked him what he thought. He was so shifty. He hadn't even opened it. Looking back, how could he? It was like the Taj Mahal, a monument to our so-called "love". He was already shagging Carrie and making plans for their life together. That's when he said he was never coming back. It would *kill* him to play the role of the husband, and that he would save the book for the kids when they were older. I felt like he was leaving all over again, though a part of me lived in hope for a long time. It was weeks of effort for nothing because he then "lost" the book when he moved house.'

'Fucking hell. What a total dickhead. I bet he threw the book away.'

'Probably. I remember when he said the word "kill" I thought I would crumble. He really had no thought on how words affected me, or anyone really. So self-absorbed in his own pain of having to be a husband, and how horrific it was.

He used to be so lovely, but that's what happens when you cut off from love, stop trying. In jumps all the things you hate about the person but overlooked because you loved them.'

'Chris isn't like that,' Jacqui said confidently.

'How do you know?'

'I can tell. Someone who sacrifices their time like that to care for a parent who is so sick wouldn't give up like that.' I nodded in agreement. 'Ooh, what's this?' A CD slipped out of the back of the diary and onto Jacqui's lap.

'Oh, it's one of the Tarot readings. This guy was really good, spooked me. I'm pretty sure he mentioned something about a man I would meet.'

'Let's listen!' I loaded it into my ancient portable CD player. I fast forwarded the man's voice till we reached the part where he talked about future relationships.

'This card here indicates a man, younger than yourself, he's not ready to meet you yet, he's on his own journey right now... Do you know anyone called Chris?'

'Oh my fucking God!' Jacqui screeched. I shushed her.

'My guides are insisting on this name Chris. Very adamant they are. He's going to be very important to you. It could be the young man... Anyway, look out for him. There will be a man before him. But you will know he's not him. There's energy for a marriage, too.'

I stopped the CD.

'You're going to marry him!'

36

The Fifth Date

I felt some distance was needed; we should get our passports stamped and leave the familiarity of this leafy south-east London neighbourhood. I needed to see Chris with a fresh set of eyes, away from all the places we had previously visited. So I decreed we would meet at Waterloo, under the multifaceted clock that hung magnificently from the cathedral-like ceiling, stars in our very own old-fashioned black-and-white film, and then go to the Southbank to have a sundown drink and see where it took us.

Mel had rung me to deliver a verbal slap before I left the house.

'Listen, that medium could be talking about Sam's new marriage, or it could all be bullshit. Don't be swayed by it.'

'I honestly don't feel like we're going to get married. I'm certainly not madly in love!'

'Do you think *I* was madly in love with Col when I first met him? God, no! Even now it waxes and wanes after twenty-odd years. But I decided to give him a chance.'

'But you're happy.'

'Yes, and that's a choice in my head. Love is also a choice so choose wisely.'

The entire way on the Tube I seesawed between trying to live in the moment and wanting to run a mile. With leaden hands covered in a sheen of clammy sweat, I stood on the escalator and emerged into daylight, leaving the chaos of the ticket hall behind me. I wiped my palms on my trench coat as I walked towards the meeting place, clumsily clipping shoulders with a few agitated people, shaking inside from lack of food and nerves. He jumped out at me from behind a newsstand, tall, dark and extremely handsome, and I melted like an ice-lolly, there and then under the clock at Waterloo.

'You look lovely,' he said, his eyes sparkling, so different from when I had last seen him, face puzzled as I'd slammed his car door and desperately scarpered back to my house. He grabbed my hand and gently pulled me in for a kiss. It was a real knee-trembler and just what I needed. 'Let's go and catch the sunset on the river.'

The date was ethereal, in the same vein as my first date with Sam. I wasn't just dazzled by Chris's good looks, there was something more tangible there, too. We talked and talked, conversations falling over each other in their eagerness to be heard. He was very different from anyone I had ever dated. His kindness was so apparent, it radiated from him and I couldn't imagine him being mean. Maybe this would be a new dawn for both of us...

After a delicious sushi dinner (another first for him – along with sex Laura hadn't liked sushi, which apparently also paved the way for not trying hummus, olives, guacamole and various other 'exotic' foodstuffs), he walked me into Soho over the illuminated Jubilee Bridge because he could somehow tell I had an urgent need to exorcise some ghosts. We visited the writers' pub, The French House, and kissed like blithe teenagers at the end of the bar until closing time, racking up an impressive collection of glasses.

'You know the children will always come first, don't you?' I said boldly, trying to put him off, or test his mettle depending on which way you viewed it.

'I wouldn't expect anything else. They should always come first.'

'But what if you get sick of it, and realise you want to be top dog, want someone who can give you more?'

'I just want you. I don't care about anyone else. Stop trying to put me off – it won't work.'

We headed back to mine in a black cab and beat the impressive first date's sex marathon into submission. When I woke in the morning, not even my piercing hangover could dampen my spirits. Everything felt slightly different: a Technicolor world existed where once it had been dull black and white. I had actually forgotten what it felt like when you were standing on the rocky precipice of falling for someone. The adrenalin rush, the topsy-turvy tummy, the laughing inside to yourself, the lack of appetite, the constant yearning for nakedness and intense sex. My body was dusting itself off, preparing to welcome in the rusty emotions swirling round that had prised open my battered cynical heart.

'Thank you for last night,' Chris said as he bent to kiss me on the lips. I prayed my stagnant morning breath wasn't too toxic. 'I'll text you later.'

'Bet you don't.'

'Bet I do.'

*

'He's having a baby.' Jacqui stood on the doorstep, a week before her fortieth birthday, holding the handlebars of her bike, her knuckles white from the effort, tears streaming down her face. It was lightly spitting and her anorak hood pulled tightly round her head made her look like an extra from *ET*.

'Oh, fuck. Come in.' I held the door open and she dragged the bike in and dumped it dripping in the hall. I gave her a hug; she smelled of fresh air and leaves. Jacqui kicked her wet trainers off and followed me through to the kitchen where Grace and Sonny were having their lunch. Ali was at work and washing decorated every available hanging space. 'Tea?'

'Yes, please. Do you have any Beardy Weirdy cake as well?'

'I do, yes. An apple and walnut wheat-free one.'

Jacqui nodded enthusiastically.

'When did he tell you?'

'Just now. I was riding in the park before going to a yoga class and he rang me.'

'Well, we did kind of think it was going to happen, didn't we? We thought she was pregnant before they got married.'

'She was.'

'Oh. I'm assuming she lost the baby.'

'Yes, at three months, which is why they're not telling anyone until the last minute. I need a fag.'

'Smoke out the back door.' I helped Grace with her yoghurt to speed things up. I never knew a toddler so uninterested in food in my life. She could go for days without anything substantial. She shook her head as I tried to get the last few mouthfuls down. I pulled her out of the high chair and set her free into the playroom.

'So how pregnant is she?'

'Five months.'

'And everything is fine?'

'I guess it must be. When he told me, I was just riding along feeling at peace with it all, with the divorce, with the new direction I'm going in, with the yoga journey. I've found myself not daring to be happy because every time I think I'm OK, something comes along and unhinges it all and I feel no more moved-on than that day I was crawling at his feet, pleading for him not to leave. But today I was like, right, embrace it all. It's OK!'

'And then he unleashed a whole load of shit.'

'Exactly. When he told me why they'd left it so long, it was like he wanted me to feel sorry for him in some way, to have a heart-to-heart. I did say I was sorry to hear that, but it was good the new baby was healthy, etc., but he then went on about how the miscarriage had been the most dreadful thing that had ever happened to him.' Jacqui shook her head in disbelief and inhaled deeply on her cigarette, blowing the smoke out into the drizzle. 'I wanted to say, how about the day you left me and the kids, all of us howling our eyes out, begging you not to leave – how was that not a hideous day? You have two children here who need you, who never wanted you to leave, but you couldn't wait to escape. He has no idea what they feel. Since the wedding, Neve's become more withdrawn, and we're back to her refusing to go to his, some weekends.'

'What about Joe? His speech seems to have improved a lot.'

'Oh, he loves his dad and just wants to be there. Fuck knows what they'll be like when they find out about this. He wants me to be there when he tells them this Sunday so they can have some support if they feel upset.'

'On Mother's Day?'

'Exactly! What a fucker!'

'What did you say?'

'I said I would be there when he dropped them off in the morning, and he could tell them at the house. Fuck, I feel like I'm facilitating his life.'

'You are; we all are. All three of us nurse these children's broken hearts. The men have no idea what emotional tsunami they unleashed when they left. It doesn't stop after they leave; time isn't an automatic healer. While they're getting on with the "real marriages", us starter wives are parcelled up in a box, roughly gaffer-taped so our feelings, the children's feelings, can't escape and ruin the new paradise.'

'Yes! That's exactly it! But what happens if the gaffer tape starts peeling off?'

'Well, that's when they'll face what they did. Realise when they reach a bump in the road with the new improved wives that marriage isn't a sprint, it's a marathon. Sooner or later everyone hits the wall. It's how you deal with it that matters. Running in the opposite direction won't win you the race.'

'I've not invited Andy to my birthday party.' Jacqui lit another fag from the end of the previous one. 'It's my family, old friends and you guys.'

'Does he know you're having a party?'

'He does, and he's cool with it. I want to end it, though.'

'Because?'

'Because it's going nowhere. It never will. He's so much younger.'

'Chris is much younger.'

'Yes, but he seems older and he's besotted with you and he feels like an equal. He's also not going travelling. I'm not sure I would want to carry on if Andy wasn't going away. It doesn't gel like I want it to. Doing all this yoga and being in a different mind-set has made me realise it's OK to be on my own. I never thought like that before. After Simon left, I was desperately trying to fill the void with another human being. But it never helped. Learning a new skill helps, though.'

'Why don't you wait until your birthday?'

'No, I think I need to face forty as I mean to go on. Single, working towards being a yoga teacher, and OK with it. The kids will be disappointed, especially Joe. They were always playing football and messing around in that blokey way boys do. I need to be with someone for me, not them. I'd better go. He's coming round tonight and I want to wash my hair. Don't want to look like an old bag. Leave him with a happy memory!'

A few weeks later and a month before Sam married Carrie, Royal Wedding fever hit the country and the single mums' mansion in a flurry of Union Jacks and bunting. Ali and I had planned a midday tea party around the wedding of William and Kate, inviting everyone we knew to arrive in their very own wedding attire. We made a legion of different cakes, including a chocolate wedding cake topped with a Sylvanian Panda bride and groom. The kids woke before seven in the morning, all frothing at the mouth about the forthcoming party. Isla, Grace and Meg wore floaty bridesmaid dresses Ali had procured from a shoot, and Sonny wore a shirt and trousers.

'I'm a pageboy, Mummy.'

'Have we missed anything?' Jacqui cried as she bustled in through the front door wearing one of Neve's dress-up tiaras and a scarlet princess tulle dress we'd found at Absolute Vintage in Shoreditch. Neve was sporting a beautiful white party dress and Joe smiled awkwardly from behind Jacqui, wearing a smart shirt and trousers instead of his usual Chelsea kit.

'I binned my wedding dress when I moved house. I didn't want it contaminating the new place,' Jacqui had explained when I said I was going to wear my dress. Because Ali never made it down the aisle, she had to source a white dress especially for the occasion and chose a lace knee-length frock from Topshop. I still loved my gauzy wedding dress. Microscopic crystals had been carefully embedded in the gossamer silk over-skirt that covered the tulle meringue and bodice. It unfurled memories of nervously getting dressed at a friend's house, waiting for Rob to drive Dad and me in his turquoise Beetle to the orchard where Sam was waiting.

'She's just got in the car. We couldn't see the dress,' Ali informed Jacqui.

'We need champagne. I'll sort it.' By the time Kate arrived at the Abbey, Ali, Jacqui and I were guzzling fizz, Ali and I sitting on the sofa making the sandwiches on a production line using one of the benches as a table, while all the kids ate croissants cross-legged on the rug in front. How terribly British.

'Oh, that dress!' Jacqui cooed. 'She looks so regal.'

'Look at Pippa's arse!' Ali guffawed. 'Bet that makes all the front pages!'

'Yes, good arse,' I agreed. By the time Kate had joined William at the altar, we had abandoned the sandwiches and were watching totally spellbound. Even the kids were entranced.

'Oh, he just said "I love you".' Ali abruptly stood up, knocking over a plate of cucumber sandwiches waiting to have their crusts removed, tears streaming down her face. 'I can't watch.' She grabbed her champagne and stormed out to the kitchen. I could hear her blowing her nose. Grace ran out to her. After a few minutes, she returned, Grace on her hip, her face blotchy from crying. She wouldn't sit down, hovering by the door in case it overwhelmed her again. 'That should have been me,' she admitted during a boring hymn none of us knew. 'My dad will never walk me down the aisle now, even if by some miracle I actually meet someone nice.'

'You'll meet someone,' Jacqui assured her. 'Just stop looking so hard.'

'I want to live with someone properly, not just be Anne Frank in the Attic. God, this wedding has made me question everything. I want what they have! I want to be a grown up.'

Chris turned up halfway through the ceremony.

'I thought you were coming at midday?'

'I wanted to come now,' he said in the hallway eyeing my dress. 'Wow, you look beautiful.'

'Thanks.' I felt rather bashful and overdressed as a blushing virginal bride in front of him. This was only his third outing as Mummy's friend. The day before Sonny's fourth birthday last weekend, we had all optimistically visited Hyde Park. We had started off cautiously hopeful with Sonny perched on Chris's shoulders with him foolishly uttering the fateful sentence: 'I don't know what you're worried about,' and closed with Sonny having a colossal meltdown at Hyde Park Corner about an apple juice drought, Meg almost fainting from low blood sugar after the snacks ran out, and just when they were tucked up in bed so some serious snogging could take place in the living room, Sonny projectile vomited spaghetti bolognese all over his bed and wall. Chris didn't bat an eyelid and cleaned up the garlic-stinking sick while I hosed down Sonny.

'It's actually no different to dealing with my dad on a bad

day,' he admitted when I protested about his baptism of fire. But how many incidents like this would it take before he realised the kids weren't just for Christmas? Inevitably they would grow up, and someone at some time was bound to sling shot the emotive words: 'You're not my real dad!' There I was again, racing ahead, living in the future...

The wedding party followed a similar trajectory. Apart from Ali's tears, it started off sedately. Chris mixed guests a lethal pear vodka cava cocktail as they arrived, and by about tea time the occasion had descended into drunken anarchy, with cake strewn all over the mottled lawn, the piñata's dolphin head swinging portentously on the washing line, its ransacked body trampled underfoot, discarded wrappers and spat-out sweets mulching in with the cake, creating a sugar-infested bog. The crystal silk layer on my dress had accidentally ripped off like a satisfying sheet of sunburned crispy skin and, even though I had sworn every single adult to secrecy about Chris and me, I proceeded to snog him about ten times in full view of the children.

'Is Chris your boyfriend?' Neve asked me, after one particular public display of affection.

'Noooooo! We're just friends.' Her raised eyebrows told me she wasn't convinced.

I sat bolt upright on my bed of nails, my mangled wedding dress twisted back to front, a cloak of shame almost choking me. Sonny was burrowed under the duvet, his arm proprietorially across my midriff, his pudgy fingers hooked into the red-wine-stained tulle.

'Mummy, why was Chris naked in your bed last night?' Isla was standing next to the bed looking at me inquisitively.

'He wasn't.' If I sounded like I was in control, she might just believe me.

'Why did you shout and used the F word?'

'Because Neve barged into the bedroom without knocking.'

'She said she could see Chris in the bed.'

'He was in the bed, but he wasn't naked. He was having a lie down before he went home.'

'Oh, OK. Was he having a sleepover?'

'Yes, kind of. Isla, don't ever open my door if it's shut without knocking, OK?'

'Yes, Mummy.'

I lay back down. Sonny was now awake.

'Mulk, Mummy. Where's my mulk?'

A party bomb had exploded in the kitchen and garden. The forlorn bunting hung lopsided from the acer tree, half-heartedly flapping in the gentle breeze, having somehow untied itself from the fence. The lawn was in need of a good hoovering. Tissue paper, cake, crisps, plastic cups and empty bottles formed an impressive carpet of detritus from the garden to the back of the kitchen. It must have rained in the night because all the food we'd lazily left outside now looked like bloated corpses dragged from a river. The wedding cake icing had washed away in the downpour, along with the two Sylvanians, who were probably tragically drowned somewhere by the raised flowerbed, star-crossed lovers united in death.

I delivered Sonny's milk and returned to the garden to find Jacqui smoking, sitting on the bench in the sun wearing one of my T-shirts and nothing else, and Ali on a beanbag with a wet flannel on her head, squashing her shagger's clump.

'What was that shouting about at eleven? Neve said you told her off.'

'She walked in on me and Chris rolling around. I was fully clothed, as you can see; the zip's stuck. Is she upset? I'm so sorry.' My head felt detached from my body, like a helium balloon full of frozen peas, rattling around.

'She's fine, though you may want to say she's not in trouble. We all know she's a bit of a nosy parker.'

'Of course I will.' I wished someone would whip me with the damp bunting.

'That seems to be a habit of yours with zips. Wasn't Sonny in the bed?'

'Yes. I hate myself. Nothing really happened – it was just a fumble. Chris came up to help me get my dress off before he went home. I was hideously drunk.'

Back inside I attempted to tidy up.

'Listen, I don't have long until Sam's wedding and my party.' I began wiping down the fronts of the kitchen cupboards, wine splatters and rivulets on every single one, while waiting for the kettle to boil. 'I've asked Ursula if she wants to join us but she must be in a K hole or something. It's not like her to ignore a party.'

Ali didn't answer me as she got up and began loading the dishwasher. Every single plate, bowl and cup had been used.

'Do you know if she got the email I sent a week ago? I know she's away this weekend. Rob, Amy, Mel, you and Jacqui are coming. A few of my oldest mates from years back are on holiday that day, but I thought Ursula was free. She always emails right back.'

Ali turned round, a plate in hand, rubber gloves on, geek specs sliding down her nose.

'I don't think she knows how to tell you.'

'Tell me what?'

'She's going to Sam's wedding.'

37

It's Not You, It's Me

'Why's she going?' I choked out, my ears fizzing, the backroom tinnitus clamouring to be heard, overpowering all other sounds.

'Because Sam invited her. He invited everyone, Mands.' Ali's strained voice reached me via a far-off tunnel.

'I knew he'd invited Rob, and he said no. Apparently Sam said he was disappointed and hurt by his decision. Rob thinks the friendship's as good as dead and buried now.'

'Well, he's not the only one who said no. I said no, too.' Ali's face blushed from her chest upwards, spreading like ink drops in water.

'What!?!' I shrieked. 'Why the fuck did he invite you?' I bellowed, gulping for air.

'Mands, please calm down. I said no. God, I knew you would freak out, that's why I didn't tell you. I wasn't ever going to tell you. Jacqui!'

Jacqui dashed in, abandoning her fag. My hands gripped the work surface, the cloth scrunching into a hard ball.

'Breathe. Come on, head down below your heart.' My legs went and I sank like a stone to my knees, burying my head in my lap, taking deep breaths.

'Where's my phone?' I gasped, my inner bunny boiler muscling in.

'No, don't do it!' Ali cried. 'You'll make it worse.'

'It can't feel any worse. I need to ask him why.'

'I said no to the invite, just leave it.'

'Would you leave it if Jim had asked me to his wedding?' I growled menacingly. 'Would you?'

'Fair point,' Jacqui agreed. 'You would have keyed his car. Oh, wait, you already did that.'

'Why don't I get the sponges?' Ali tried desperately. 'You can throw them instead?'

I found my phone on the living-room table where Sonny, Joe and Grace were all watching some inane cartoon. The girls had retired upstairs to do hair and garish make-up. Texting with shaking hands was time consuming: I was deleting as much as I was making headway with words.

'Fucking cuntingly fuck's sake, I can't even fucking type!' I vented, having to grapple the urge to hurl my phone into the garden to smash it into smithereens.

'Let me type it for you,' Jacqui offered. 'Give it here before you break it.'

Why did you think it was a good idea to invite Ali to your wedding? Apparently you've invited the same congregation as our one. Nice work.

'Anything else? Like what a twat he is?'

'No, just that. How he answers will define what level of twat he is.' She pressed send.

'So, was Ursula ever going to tell me?' My stomach had turned in on itself, nausea rinsing round what little space was left.

'I don't know; she just didn't know how to tell you. She's only going because everyone else is going. It's free booze and food and a disco.'

'Why do I feel so upset? I feel properly devastated.'

'Because this is the final hurdle. Ali and I didn't have the wedding shoved in our faces. We didn't have friends invited. We didn't have the same people going to a replica of our wedding in the same venue. It's like he just chopped you out and inserted Carrie in a cut-and-paste.'

'He doesn't even see half these people any more. I see them more than he does. It's like rent a crowd.'

'Remember, it's going to be on TV. People will love that idea, of riding on the coat-tails of Carrie's success, to be able to say "I was there",' Jacqui reasoned. 'And he needs to look popular, believe his own hype of happy ever after and what a good choice he made in leaving you. It's all about the external. It probably doesn't help you're still wearing your wedding dress.' I glanced down at my spoiled tulle skirt, the sneering Disney Dream Princess without a traditional happy ever after.

'It just hammers home how little he ever thought of me, still thinks of me.'

Waiting for a reply was more tense than standing in St Peter's Square craning our necks to catch a sight of the white papal smoke. My phone rang, surprising me; I was expecting a text.

'I didn't invite Ali,' he blasted out into my ear, the words slicing through the buzzing.

'Then why did she say you invited her?' I looked at Ali who silently mouthed, 'What the fuck?' at me and scrabbled around for her phone, charging on the worktop. 'Because you forgot that you did?'

'That's ridiculous. Anyway, I can invite who ever I want to my wedding.'

'I know that, I'm not a total idiot. The whole thing feels horrendous to me. You're just recreating our wedding with the same guests and everything.' Overcome with humiliation, all of my own making for insisting on the text in the first place, I knew being angry with him was hopeless. He was right, he could invite anyone, but it didn't stop me feeling small and insignificant, like a trial run before the real deal.

'Look, it wasn't my intention to make you feel like this, Amanda. I know the venue isn't ideal but that's just life. Don't blame them for being invited or being my friends. One day you'll get married again and some of the same people will come to your wedding.'

'I'm never ever getting married EVER again! And I'm not blaming them for coming. What I'm angry about is no one has the fucking decency to warn me they're going to your wedding, so I find out today, dressed as *your* fucking bride after a party.' I cut him off before he could say anything else. 'I hate myself. I wish I'd never spoken to him. Now I just look like a mental case.'

'No you don't. *He*'s the mental case,' Ali said, shoving her phone in my face. 'Read that.' It was an email from Sam dated 29 March.

Dear Ali

How are you? Long time no speak. How is Grace? Every time I see her she seems to be growing taller. She'll be bigger than Sonny soon. As you know Carrie and I are getting married at the end of May, on the 28th to be exact. In an ideal world I would love you to be there. Do you think there is any way you could come, or is it too delicate? Everyone else will be there, so it should be a total blast. I understand your loyalties are elsewhere.

Hope all good.

Love Sam x

'Oh my God,' Jacqui voiced what I was incapable of. 'He's deluded. That's an invite. Not on posh paper with a wedding list attached and rip-off hotel details, but it's an invite all the same.'

'When he said he hadn't invited me, I had to find that email. I only just deleted it last week, so it was still in the trash. I'm so glad I found it! Or maybe not, Mands?'

I pressed the bile back down with two hardy swallows.

'Yes, I feel a bit less mad now, though not much. I feel so upset with Ursula. How could she not tell me? And how did Sam think I would never find out he'd invited you? It's like he exists on his own version of the truth. Do you think he even remembers marrying me?'

'Ursula was being a dick about it,' Ali admitted, slamming the dishwasher door, setting it off on its first cycle of the day. The work surface by the sink was still crammed with dirty glasses, plates and bowls, ready for the next round.

'I can't stop her going – it's her choice. That's not why I'm upset. It's because she didn't tell me and I found out like this. I hate the creeping about behind my back, like I don't deserve the truth.'

Later that afternoon Jacqui finally prised my sullied wedding dress off me with a pair of scissors and some elbow grease. My hangover rolled over me like a thick fog, making everything seem a lot worse.

'You'll feel better after some sleep,' she said, stroking my hair while Chug lay next to me, worried.

'Are you sick, Mummy?'

'No, Chug, I just need a cuddle.'

The jungle drums alerted Ursula and pretty soon my phone was pinging out regular Morse code signals. Sam decided to get in on the act.

> I would have liked Ali at the wedding but knew it wasn't good practice. Please do not make it out to be more than it is.

He must have revisited old emails to cover his tracks. Chris also texted me several times, but I had no energy to read the messages. I switched off my phone and Ali very kindly marshalled everyone for the bedtime routine. I let Sonny remain in bed with me where he drifted off to sleep and I lay staring at the ceiling, knowing I was solipsistically slipping somewhere I hadn't visited for a while. Hades. Why couldn't I just get over it? I wasn't homeless, a refugee or a battered wife in an abusive relationship. I knew my privileges and should just move on. Why did I take things so personally? I tried to focus on *The Four Agreements* and Mel's wise words. Sam didn't do any of this to consciously hurt me, but knowing and feeling were two different things. I knew it would pass eventually, so I battened down the hatches until it did.

On Bank Holiday Monday, Chris turned up unannounced on the doorstep.

'I've been worried to death about you. All you had to do was say you were OK, you know.' His lip was twitching.

'I'm sorry. I switched my phone off and then, I dunno, I never read my texts.'

'Let me take you out. Where do you want to go?'

We walked to the French Café at the end of the road. Ali took all the kids to the park so we could talk. I stirred my tea and buttered my toast. I had barely eaten since the party, though I really fancied this sourdough toast. The French Café, with its facsimile log-pile wallpaper, televised flames flickering on a monitor in a replica fireplace, displays of deliciously iced cakes and pastries, the best coffee for miles and the ambient French jazz tinkering away in the background, never failed to lift my spirits.

'So, what's happened?' Chris eventually asked me, his brow creasing with concern. I should have just texted him instead of obsessing over my own pitiful situation. 'Is this because Neve walked in on us in bed?'

I laughed hollowly. That worry seemed so trifling now.

'No. I found out Sam invited Ali to his wedding – she said no – and Ursula, who is actually going. For some stupid and naïve reason, I thought he was having a small wedding. But it is in fact some huge do, with most of the same people that attended my marriage to him. Add on that Meg and Isla will be bridesmaids kind of ices that wedding cake for me. I knew I would feel shit at some point, but not this bad. I think I've had my head in the sand about it affecting me and those two things kind of dragged it back out.'

'Oh.'

'I know it must seem trivial after all the crap your mum is going through with your dad.'

'No, that's not what I meant. That's quite a lot of stuff going on in your head. No wonder you feel like you do. Is there anything I can do?'

His kindness was touchpaper to my self-pity, kick-starting the tedious waterworks. I grabbed the toast's serviette to wipe my eyes, but proceeded to smear strawberry jam across my face.

'Come here.' Chris grabbed a fresh napkin from the empty table next to us and wiped the jam off my nose and cheeks. 'How long until the wedding?'

'Less than four weeks.'

'Well, maybe you should just take it easy and stop punishing yourself for feeling sad. I think you're allowed to be upset Sam's getting married.'

'I should be over it. I really should have moved on by now – I obviously haven't moved on as far as I thought, though. Argh, I'm so bored of this still being a thing in my head.'

'What's with all the shoulds? Why are you putting a limit on when things ought to have stopped bothering you? If Sam had died would you be so hard on yourself?'

'No, I guess not.'

'This wedding is hopefully the last thing he can ever do that will hurt as much as this. Look at it that way.'

I nodded in agreement.

'You are so different to other men,' I said. 'Oh, that was meant to stay in my head. Sorry.' He laughed. 'You remind me of my friend Mel.'

'Is that a good or bad thing?'

'Good. She's pragmatic, too. In fact, you're her birthday twin.'

Back at the house, before anyone returned from the park, we lay on the sofa and Chris tentatively kissed me.

'I can't do this right now. Sorry.'

'No, I'm sorry. I should have held back.' He squeezed my hand.

I rested against the cushions and studied his guileless face, searching my closed one for some kind of clue.

'Chris, I don't think I can do *us* right now. I haven't anything to give.'

His face sagged. 'You want to take a break, or you want to finish for good?' His brow creased again. This felt like shooting Bambi.

'Yes. I need to be on my own. I'm just not ready for anyone. I feel like I'm leading you on.'

'I don't mind waiting until you feel ready.' He looked at me hopefully.

'No. I need a clean break to get over this bump in the road. I'm so sorry.' Tears started falling and I brushed them away.

'Oh, OK. I think you're lovely, and the kids are great. It feels such a shame. You're really sure?' I nodded, unable to speak.

We hugged and he left me trapped in my self-constructed Underworld, Eurydice to his Orpheus, uncertainly facing my darkness alone. *Be your own Orpheus,* popped into my head, *and stop being such a drivelling twat.*

38

Letting Go

'Ali! Come here!' I couldn't believe what I was seeing on Facebook. I needed another pair of eyes to verify I wasn't hallucinating. Ali bounded up the stairs from the kitchen and burst into my office, apprehension written right across her face.

'What? Are you OK?'

'Look!' I pointed to a message on screen. It was from someone I used to work with back in the mists of time, but was now a publisher at a major house with her own list of books. I couldn't remember when I'd last seen her. Before I had married Sam, I think.

Dear Amanda

I just wanted to say I have read your book and totally loved it. Your agent sent it to us after the Bologna Book Fair and all of us here think it's fantastic. We will hopefully be making an offer, through your agent of course, but I couldn't wait to tell you how wonderful we think it is. Now we just need to sell the idea to the sales team but that should be easy. I look forward to dealing with you.

With best wishes

Vicki

'Argh!' Ali screamed. 'That's so fucking amazing! Congratulations!'

We started leaping round in circles holding hands until books began jumping off shelves and crashing onto my desk, knocking over my pen pot, randomly scattering them everywhere like Pick-up Sticks.

'Is it too early for fizz?' Ali asked.

'So lovely to see you again. Come in.' Natalie, my Reiki Master, opened her front door the following day and I stepped into the familiar sanctuary that was her home. It had been Mel's idea to come and see her, to further my quest for a Zen mind and be my own champion.

'It feels like I was here just last week.' The piquant smell of incense laced the air and I followed Natalie down the corridor, past the living room, until she pushed open a door just before the bathroom straight ahead.

'What has it been, over two years?'

I nodded.

'This is where I do one-to-one treatments.' The sparse room had a high vaulted ceiling, a Velux window casting down a generous shaft of sunlight onto a multi-coloured woven rug that complemented the cool grey walls. An ornate carved dark wood framed picture of Buddha hung on the left wall above the treatment couch. A small Shaker-style wooden desk faced out of the other window into next-door's overgrown garden. Natalie pulled out the ergonomic chair from under the desk and motioned for me to sit in the royal-blue compact armchair.

'So how have you been?'

'On a rollercoaster!'

As I reacquainted Natalie with the lurching drama that was my life, I felt like I was hearing it for the first time, too, and it sounded shamefully self-absorbed.

'Sometimes we can get so caught up in Our Story; what has happened to us, who did what to whom, and I'm not saying that you have, but a lot has been going on: with the lost baby, the wedding, living with Ali, dumping Chris, your book deal, that we sometimes keep too close a hold on certain things and forget to let them go.'

'I do feel very bogged down with so much stuff fighting for space in my head. I literally cannot think straight.'

'So you're here today to unblock everything then? To get some clarity and let old stuff go that no longer serves you.'

'Exactly, but I need someone else to hold the process.'

Natalie began by burning sage and smudging it over my aura and all around us. She then pulled the bed away from the wall and into the centre of the room. Relaxing music played in the background and, cocooned in a womb of blankets warmed by the streaming sun from above, I instinctively closed my eyes, drifting off somewhere else while Natalie stood behind my head. I could feel the heat pulsing out of her palms lightly resting on my crown chakra; ephemeral images flitted across my mind. I had the unearthly sensation someone was tenderly holding both ankles in a kind of reassuring embrace, grounding me. I could feel

Natalie's hands resting on my heart chakra in the centre of my chest. How could she be in two places at once? The hands were still holding my ankles as Natalie moved to my solar plexus, just below my ribs. I flicked my eyes half open so briefly it was almost pointless, but long enough for me to notice there was no one standing at the foot of the bed.

'All done,' Natalie said softly quite some time later. 'Stay lying for a bit. I'll pour you some water.' I heard the door open and close while I wriggled my toes and teased my body into life. When Natalie returned I was sitting on the edge of the bed still feeling a bit dozy. 'Ah, sleeping beauty, how was that?' She handed me a glass of water.

'Thanks. Can I ask you something?'

'Go ahead.'

'Was anyone else in the room?'

She smiled knowingly. 'Did you feel them?'

I nodded.

'There was an angel standing at your feet. They know you've had a tough time.'

'What were they doing?'

'Grounding you. Your root chakra was completely blocked and if that's blocked, then everything stays in your head and you feel scrambled and out of touch.' She smiled at me. 'Did you have a name for the baby? When I was on your heart chakra, all I could see was the ultrasound scan.'

'Michael. Wow, I never had a name for him, but I didn't even have to think. I always knew he was a boy, though.'

'Maybe have a little ceremony for him when you get home, let him go. Bury his name in the garden, something like that. It might help with all the jumble in your head.'

Natalie hugged me on the doorstep.

'Your anti-wedding sounds amazing. Embrace it all and have fun!'

That evening, when the kids were in bed, I dug out my notes and free maternity packs from the annals of my bottom drawer in the office and I burned them in the magic chimenea. I wrote Michael inside a hand-drawn heart and folded the piece of paper around a small jagged rose quartz crystal. Down at the bottom of the garden where the trampoline resided, I found a spare patch of earth next to one of the bushes and buried it there, drawing the Reiki symbols over the freshly turned soil. The children's laughter from the trampoline would keep him company.

For the first time in months, I slept like the dead, not even waking when Chug climbed in bed some time in the middle of the night. That morning, before the school run, still snuggled under the covers he finished his milk and turned to me.

'Mummy had a baby in her tummy.'

'What? No I didn't.'

'You did, Mummy. It's gone now.'

39
Anti-Wedding Party

'I got you a present.' Jacqui handed me an intriguing square package firmly wrapped in brown paper. She had stopped over last night and all three of us had smeared on Lazarus-style face packs that claimed to resurrect our youth. Jacqui cracked open a bottle of cheap fizz at breakfast and we dined like queens, though sadly not in the garden because it was tipping it down.

'Let's hope it's as shit as this in the countryside,' Ali laughed. 'You had amazing weather for *your* wedding. Open your present!'

I ripped off the paper and pulled out a chunky canvas.

'It's by Remi!' I cried.

'Oh, it's beautiful,' Ali admired. 'So original.'

'Thank you, Jacqui. I love it.' The canvas was Remi's interpretation of Paradise Beach, an image cast with rich blues and golds and the twisted silver tree trunks of the olive trees. There was a postcard of the harbour from Remi tucked inside the back of the frame.

*

Dear Amanda,

I hope you have fun at your anti-wedding. Please don't get married again today, remember you are already married to Jacqui. Hope you like the picture and it makes you want to return to Paradise Beach. Also, when you wake up, a shot of brandy should do the trick, and a strong coffee!! Try not to sleep on the pavement.

Lots of love,
Remi xxx

Various texts flooded in, like absentees' telegrams during the best man's speech, family and friends offering support and orders to drink champagne. I thought of the children and my heart clenched: Isla's anxious face as she had left with Sam's dad the day before, worrying that she would ruin the filming by crying and getting upset. Sam's father hadn't known how to act at the handover. He'd escorted the children out of the house as quickly as possible. 'I'm sure it is awkward for you,' I wanted to say. 'But how the fuck do you think *I* feel knowing my children will be performing happy families to all the same people from wedding round one?'

'This is a bit like your wedding, isn't it?' Jacqui said. 'Champagne breakfast, then cocktails in town followed by mega-posh dinner and back here for a tragic disco in the Adventure Bar and hopefully a snog!'

'I would like to snog an usher,' Ali said. 'It's been ages since I had any action.'

'Well, as bridesmaids, I think we get to shag the best man, don't we?' Jacqui asked hopefully.

'Sadly, that role lies with Rob and unless you are both gay men, you don't stand a chance.'

'Has Chris texted you?' Ali asked, sipping her fizz.

'No, of course not.'

'I just thought he would today, that's all.'

'I'm glad he hasn't. I did actually like him and so did the kids, but my head isn't right.'

'I still think you're mad. Men like him don't grow on trees!' Ali said sadly.

'But it proves nice men *are* out there, just that the timing was all wrong. I'm better off on my own for now.'

'I'll drink to that!' Jacqui clinked glasses with me. 'Here's to being single and fabulous.'

Dinner was so fun. The Criterion in Piccadilly fussed and bowed to us, its gilt-edged Midas palace glamour, marble columns, chandeliers and old-school charm fitting for the occasion. I had booked it on one of those bargain websites where you're somehow offered a three-course meal for fifty pence. The universe was shining its hallowed disco ball down on us that afternoon because our French waiter was gay and fancied the kilt off Rob, who was decked out in full Highland dress.

'Do not tell anyone, but I have got you all sides for free. *Bon appétit!*' He also managed to 'find' some delicious *petits fours* to go with the free coffee and dessert wine, and when Rob told him it was my anti-wedding, he threw in complimentary glasses of champagne.

'You've got to love the gays,' Rob cooed, flamboyantly blowing kisses as we left our waiter with a sizeable tip.

'Take this,' Rob goaded me in the Adventure Bar, ever the devil on my shoulder. 'Go on! It's your wedding, to me! I knew I would get you in the end – I've waited long enough. I took mine an hour ago and I need a playmate.'

'Why are we taking drugs?'

Mel was tucked away in a corner with Jacqui, putting the world to rights, Ali was dancing with Amy on the tiny dance floor, and I was lurking with Rob by the bar at the bottom of the steps, clutching a pill in my sweaty palm.

'Because we're in this godforsaken place and need to block it out!'

'It's not that bad.'

He dramatically rolled his eyes. 'Oh, no? Where are the gay people?'

'Somewhere else.'

'It's full of breeders! I'm used to clubs raining men. Anyway, it's grown on me now I've come up on the pill. Take yours and we can have sex.'

'Rob! No.'

'No to which part?'

'All of it.'

'But I like you,' he joked. 'You're my favourite of all the breeders. No one would have to know. Didn't you say people shagged in the toilets here?'

I was about to join in the banter when the words caught in my throat. A tall dark man appeared at the top of the stairs and waved.

'What's up? You look like you've seen a ghost,' Rob laughed.

For a split second I thought he was Chris and my heart really did skip a beat. But he skirted round us and joined the noisy group behind. I stared at the back of the man's head and contemplated the pill, hesitantly bringing it up to my lips.

'Yay! Take it!' Rob encouraged, desperate for a cohort.

'Do you know what, you save it for later.' And I sensibly handed back the party banger. 'Let's do shots instead.'

*

I woke on top of the duvet still wearing my black tulle party dress, my temples throbbing and feet swollen from dancing in high heels. I was glad I wasn't Ali. She and Grace had to fly out to Spain at lunchtime to visit her mum.

My phone pinged from underneath the pillow.

As it was my wedding and the kids are all desperate to see you, would you mind coming and collecting them later on?

I lay back and sighed. Sam was officially married, finally making me the first wife. I had expected to feel something, possibly upset, but I just felt like it had all happened to someone else. Knowing I couldn't put off seeing his house for ever, I agreed to his request. So, it was with the largest of sunglasses, the shortest of dresses and the brightest of red lipsticks that I headed over to collect the children.

Pulling up outside for the first time, I was struck by numerous similarities. It wasn't detached or set back from the road like my house was. However, the same white shutters shielded both upstairs and downstairs windows, and the masonry was painted a similar off-white. Two potted sculpted olive trees stood proud either side of the exact same turquoise front door. Maybe I was just seeing things that were so ubiquitous in this part of south London, where Victorian houses were almost painted by numbers. I rang the bell, nerves giving way to sweaty palms. Carrie opened the door and fleetingly looked startled.

'Oh, hello! Sam didn't say you were coming.'

'He asked me earlier to collect the children.' I nosily examined the stripped wooden floors and dark grey walls either side of the corridor leading to a huge kitchen at the back, flooded with light from bi-folding doors.

'Oh, right. I don't know where they are. Do you want to come in?'

'I'll wait here, if that's OK.'

Carrie retreated into the house and I watched as she flitted desperately from room to room trying to find the children.

'Sam! Amanda's here! Where are you all?' she shouted up the stairs. Had it been one octave higher it would have verged on hysteria. 'Sam!'

'Hey, we're here.' Sam's voice eventually drifted down from somewhere upstairs. 'Just getting their things together.' Carrie didn't know what to do then because she must have felt my gaze on her as she hovered around self-consciously at the bottom of the stairs, wringing her hands.

'How was your weekend?' she eventually asked after returning to the doorway, a rictus grin possibly masking regret at such an ill-served first shot. I was taken by surprise; what could I come back with? How did your wedding go?

'It was fun. Lots of friends and stupid antics.' She looked relieved I was playing by the rules.

'Oh, I'm glad. I hope you had a lovely time. You deserved it.' She smiled at me, a real genuine smile, igniting her eyes at the edges, smoothing away the apprehension that I remembered from last time we met. She wanted me to like her, I could feel it. I returned the smile, the sunglasses putting me at an advantage.

'I did have a really good time. Thank you.'

'Good. I'll go and hurry them up.'

'Mummy!' Meg cried. She bolted from the foot of the stairs and jumped into my arms, her cheeks buoyant with her Cheshire cat grin. She was wearing a fancy pink party dress of the kind she would normally balk at. She felt like a crinkly Cellophane-wrapped bouquet in my arms. Sonny held tightly onto Sam's hand and looked like he had been crying. I bent down to kiss him and he grabbed my neck.

'Snuggle, Mummy.'

I picked him up after Meg had untangled herself.

'Hello, Isla, you got all your stuff?'

She nodded.

'Say goodbye to Daddy then.'

'Bye, kids. Thanks for being so good and doing your wedding duties so well. I'll see you when we get back.'

Sonny waved from my arms and Sam kissed his head, close enough for me to smell his unfamiliar aftershave. Everything about him seemed distant now, almost like we had never existed as a couple or shared a life together. The proof was the children, but as I stood on his doorstep, one toe grudgingly dipped in his new life, he felt so far removed from that boy in the Häagen-Dazs shop fourteen years ago. How can someone change that much? Maybe it was me who had changed. I thought of the tatty Post-it note hidden away in my desk drawer, waiting for me to do something with it. Maybe some time in the future I would have it framed and give it to him as a present, let him know we could once more be friends. It would have been funny to offer it as an inappropriate wedding gift. However, I hadn't reached that point yet. Perhaps his fortieth birthday in a year's time would be perfect.

What do marriage and hurricanes have in common?
They both start off with a lot of sucking and blowing, but in the end, you lose your house.

40

Take a Chance on Me

'I took inspiration from your Shrine of Tat,' Jacqui told me Friday morning after yoga when I complimented her on the transformation of her living room. 'It brings the place to life a bit more.'

She had added some of Remi's calm abstract paintings, potted orchids on the fireplace, Venetian mirrors on one wall, and on the shelves running the entire length of the room, she had arranged her books in rainbow colour order, interspersed with family photos and a few sparse ornaments. The boxes had finally been unpacked as Jacqui allowed her house to take on a life of its own. Even her garden had metamorphosed. Straggly plants and over-stretched bushes had been dug out and a serene carpet of lawn, velvety to the touch, spread from the stone-flagged patio down to the sizeable shed at the bottom. Buddha statues, outdoor candles and a mini rock garden planted with diverse cacti and succulents added a peaceful air to the previously neglected dumping ground. Her house had finally turned into a family home.

My phone started ringing, piercing the tranquil air.

I mouthed: 'It's my agent,' and walked to the window to take the call.

'Good news, we've managed to bump them up and get more money. If it's OK with you, I'll agree to the terms...' And he reeled off rights and all the legal stuff I pretended to know about in minute detail.

'I have a book contract, sealed and dealed!' I reported back to Jacqui. 'It's official!'

'Wow! That's great news. You'll finally get paid, too!'

'More importantly, I feel like a real person with a job. No more faking it till I make it.'

'What a shame I'm away this weekend or we could have a toast. Wait till Ali's back next week and we'll open some fizz.'

I ordered take-away pizzas as a treat that night. The four of us sat on the rug in the living room having a celebratory carpet picnic, toasting to my success with lemonade.

'Chris likes pizza,' Isla announced unexpectedly. 'You should have invited him, too, now you're a proper author.'

'He's busy.'

'Are you still friends with him?' she asked suspiciously. 'We've not seen him for ages.'

'Erm...'

'Will we see him again?' Meg asked hopefully. 'I liked him. He wasn't like that other man.'

'Woody,' Isla said assuredly.

'Yes, him. He was shouty.'

'Shouty,' Chug echoed, his mouth full of pizza. Evading answering, I playfully pinched his chubby cheek and he laughed, chewed up cheese cascading out into the rug.

I dozed off in a carb coma during the millionth showing of *Finding Nemo* and awoke to a crashing sound from upstairs followed by howling. Meg was sitting next to me sucking her thumb and cuddling her favourite Build-A-Bear. I jumped up, taking the stairs two at a time to find Isla in a heap on the middle landing at the bottom of the steps outside the bathroom with Sonny rolling around next to her crying loudly.

'Which one of you is hurt most?'

'Me!' they both cried, turning a simple accident into *Sophie's Choice*.

'Isla, where does it hurt?' I asked as I scooped up Sonny and carried him over to her. I could barely hear her through his histrionics.

'My ankle.' I knew it was no use asking Sonny because he was in a state and refused to make sense.

'Sonny, shush. Let me see Isla's ankle.' He clung to me like a monkey, making it hard to bend down and inspect. Isla had eased herself onto the step and laid her leg out in front. Her ankle looked OK but her face was drained of colour.

'Can you move it?' She shook her head, crying when she tried to swivel it side to side.

'What happened?'

'I was going to put Sonny to bed for you and I carried him up the stairs.'

'All the way from down there?'

'No, once we got up. I brushed his teeth, then he wanted to be carried to your room, but I fell on these steps and dropped him, and my ankle twisted.'

'Sonny's OK, though?' I tried to establish. 'He didn't bump his head or anything?'

'No, he just slipped onto the floor, that's all.' I prised Sonny off me and managed to get Isla standing. Meg was now watching curiously, clutching her bear, still sucking her thumb.

'Can you put weight on it?'

'Kind of, but it hurts lots. Is it broken, Mummy?'

'No, I don't think so.'

'Why does it hurt so much?'

'Because you probably sprained it carrying Sonny – he's a little lump. I'll get some Calpol.'

Once I had got everyone ready for bed and a bag of frozen peas on Isla's ankle, I texted my sister-in-law Sarah, who was a nurse, and asked about anything else I should do. She rang immediately.

'Is it swelling? Have you put ice on it?'

'Yes to ice. No to swelling. But she's in bed now. Should I check again?'

'Yes, go and look.'

Isla was awake with the night light on and the blind drawn.

'Can I see your ankle?' She pushed back the duvet and I moved the peas wrapped in a flowery tea towel.

'Oh. It's puffed up and starting to go a funny colour.'

'Take her to A and E,' Sarah said without hesitating.

'Really?' I groaned.

'You could go in the morning, but if it is broken, you don't want it to shift in the night. It's best to go now.'

'I'm on my own. Ali's on holiday, Jacqui's away and Sam's on honeymoon. It'll be hell if I drag the others with me.'

'Neighbours? You've nice ones, haven't you? You'll have to carry her from the car. Can you manage? You could call an ambulance, but it seems mad for this.'

I texted Philippa, then James, when she didn't get back to me.

We're at my mums, sorry!

James texted back. I tried Rob.

'Hellooooooo, what's the crack?' he asked, sounding merry.

'What state are you in?'

'I've had three beers.'

'Where are you?'

'At home, contemplating clubbing.'

'How do you feel babysitting while I go to A and E?'

'Are we going on our own?' Isla asked fearfully as soon as Rob said he would head over.

'Yes.'

'But, Mummy, what if I can't walk very far.'

'I'll go and get you a wheelchair.'

'But I'll be on my own while you do.' I looked at her pale face. Fuck it, I would call an ambulance and face the flack.

'Chris could come?'

I shook my head.

'Why not? I know he would help.'

'He's probably out.'

'Ring him, Mummy. Please.'

'No, Isla. I know, I'll call a cab and see if the driver will get us the wheelchair.' I left Isla in bed and went to settle Meg. As I was explaining to her that Rob would be in charge, I heard Isla speaking.

'Yes, Mummy wanted to know if you would come to the hospital with us.' I could hear a small tinny reply.

'She thinks I've broken my ankle and we're on our own here. Rob is coming but Mummy can't carry me to A and E.'

I jumped up and ran into her room, snatching the phone from her hands.

'Hello?'

'Hello, Amanda. It's OK, Isla told me what's happened. I'll be over as soon as I've got a cab.'

'No, it's fine. I'm so sorry, Chris. I had no idea she'd rung you.' I glared at Isla in disbelief.

'I reckon I'll be half an hour. It's no trouble.'

'Seriously, you don't have to. I'll get a cab to A and E when Rob gets here. I'm so embarrassed.'

'Don't be silly. I'll come. Isla asked me to. I'll see you in a bit.'

'Is he coming?'

I nodded. 'Isla, why did you do that? I said I would get a cab.'

'Because we need a Spare Man. I did tell you…'

I was about to admonish her when butterflies swiftly popped from deeply hidden cocoons in my tummy. *Oh no…* I stole a glance in Isla's chipped circular mirror above her bookcase. A swamp creature glared back with unwashed hair, pasty skin and a juicy custard-cream zit on her chin. The doorbell rang.

'Noooo,' I wailed, pressing a tissue over the just-squeezed volcano oozing a sticky conflation of pus and blood.

'Cut yourself shaving again?' Rob laughed as I let him in. It had started to spit outside and glutinous-looking clouds hung heavy in the sky.

'Yeah, ha ha. I squeezed a toothpaste zit. Now it looks worse and Chris is going to take us to the hospital.'

'Chris from the wedding party?'

I nodded.

'Oh, yes. I liked him.'

Everyone liked Chris.

'Go and make yourself look pretty then. You can't let him know what you really look like!'

I just about had enough time to plaster on some make-up and administer emergency dry shampoo before the doorbell rang a second time.

'Hey, are you OK?' Chris asked as he walked in the door. He smelled of rain and some gorgeous citrusy aftershave. *Oh no...*

'Yes, I'm good. I'm so sorry we've ruined your night. I hope it wasn't anything important.'

'Just work drinks with Mark and the boys. Where's Isla?' I led him upstairs to her room where she was waiting fully dressed on the bed. 'Can I see your ankle?' Isla pulled her socks down so Chris could inspect. 'Yes, it doesn't look good. Can we drive there?'

By the time we reached the car park it was full so I tried a side road further up the hill. It was sheeting down and we had no umbrella. Isla had brought her raincoat and I wore my trusty parka, but Chris only had a light jacket.

'I'm so sorry – you're going to get soaked.'

'Stop stressing. It's just a bit of rain. You ready, Isla?' She nodded and he carefully picked her up from the back seat and held her in his arms. My stomach flipped. We walked down the hill, rain flying in our faces, unable to speak in case we drowned from the ferocious influx of water. Chris never stopped once to rearrange his grip; he just purposefully ploughed on against the monsoon while I trailed in his wake.

'That way!' the staff ushered us towards Children's A and E as we entered, dripping rivulets of rainwater all over the blue entrance-hall floor.

'Bloody hell!' Chris exclaimed. 'It's like Butlin's Holiday Camp in here!' Every available seat was taken, not by sick children, but by whole families including grandparents, babies and children of all ages, some eating snacks, some doing colouring, one family even had a cool box and were handing out foil-wrapped packages to everyone in the vicinity. 'Why aren't they told to go home?' he hissed. 'It's mental.' After checking in we found a spot on the floor up against a wall and I laid my damp coat down for Isla to lie on. Chris sat on the other side by her feet. Informative signs and posters were pinned to every available space advising the waiting-room collective about correct hand-washing procedure, binning tissues and when not to come to A and E.

'Mummy, how long will it take?'

'I have no idea. At least a few hours, I would think.'

Isla placed her head on my lap and closed her eyes.

'You going to sleep?'

'The lights are too bright.'

'Thank you for coming,' I said to Chris, feeling properly awkward now the drama had abated. 'I actually don't know how I would have done this on my own.'

'No problem.'

'Aren't your arms killing you from carrying her all the way from the car?'

'They're OK. She's not that heavy.' He shook the excess water from his hair onto his lap and wiped his face with his hand.

'Shall I get you some paper towels?'

'Hey, we're not here for me. I'm big enough and ugly enough to look after myself. I can dry off later.' I wanted to lean over and kiss his cheek. *Oh no*...

'How have you been?' I asked diffidently. 'It's been ages since I last saw you.'

'A month. I'm good, thanks. I went home to get the last few things two weeks ago. I think Mum was sad it's so final, but I need to start my new life here. I like this part of London and I like living with Mark.' It felt strange that I didn't know what he'd been up to as we sat here sharing this mostly parental experience.

'That's good that you like it.' Sitting on the dirty floor of A and E, while people scurried past us at head height calling out names and brandishing files, felt like the only place I wanted to be right then. I sneaked a sideways peek at him; he caught me and winked, setting fire to my face. *Oh no...*

'Chris, are you and Mummy still friends?' Isla asked eventually after a particularly scary episode when a toddler screamed the place down and then vomited right next to the picnicking family.

'Er, yes, we're still friends.'

'Well, how come we haven't seen you?'

Before either of us could answer we were called to a triage room. Chris picked Isla up off the floor and carried her through to the paper-covered bed. When we'd explained the accident and her ankle had been inspected we were told to sit back down and we would be called for an X-ray.

'Are you OK carrying her, Dad?' the nurse asked after a short wait. 'We've run out of wheelchairs.'

'Yep, no worries. Tell me where to go.' Chris didn't bat an eyelid and waited outside when I accompanied Isla into the X-ray suite.

'They think Chris's my dad!' she laughed.

'I know. How funny.'

'How did you get on?' Rob asked when we returned home after midnight.

'She's got a fractured ankle. We need to go to Fracture Clinic on Monday to get it set.'

'Oh, good job you went then. Sonny woke up crying for you, so I just gave him rice milk. I hope that was OK. He's in your bed.'

Rob left, abandoning dreams of cavorting in a gay club, and sensibly headed home. Chris carried Isla straight up to bed, her leg encased in a temporary plaster cast; she was asleep before we had even left the room. Downstairs in the hall he started fiddling about putting his wet shoes back on.

'What are you doing?'

'Going home.'

'Oh.' Crushing disappointment overwhelmed me from the tip of my head down to my soggy toes.

'That's OK, isn't it? You don't need me for anything else, do you?'

'No, no, of course not. I just thought you might want a cup of tea...'

'I'd love a cup of tea, but it's very late.'

'Come on, stay for a bit. At least let me make you a drink.' I walked into the kitchen, making a beeline for the kettle, hoping he would follow me. He rested his bum against the opposite work surface, crossing his arms, silently watching me as I filled it from the tap, splashing myself all up my T-shirt because of my tremulous hands. I flicked the switch and opened the cupboard directly above, rifling inside for cups and teabags.

'I've missed you,' he said so quietly it was almost drowned out by the kettle's energetic bubbling. I turned round to face him.

'But you don't really know me.'

'That's the thing, I feel like I *do* know you. I know you like Reese's Peanut Butter Cups. I know that you don't like it when I kiss your neck because it tickles. I know that you love dancing as much as I hate it. I know that you're kind and are a good mum. I know that you thought you'd die when Sam left, but you carried on anyway. I know that hangover sex cures your morning-after headache. I *think* your favourite word is fuck, but don't quote me. I know that you hope reusing plastic bags and washing them out will save the planet. Oh, and *Friends* is the only TV show you watch.'

'You gleaned all that from a few months' dating?'

'I'm observant and I listen. You do say fuck all the time, though.'

'Did you also know I am a complete nightmare and terrified of commitment?'

'Then how come you made Isla break her ankle so you could lure me over here?'

'I would never do that!'

'I know. I'm messing with you. She broke it on purpose because she could tell you were secretly missing me.'

I play-punched him in the arm. 'Would you have ever got in touch if Isla hadn't rung you?'

'You'll never know.'

'But—'

He leaned forward and pulled me to him, planting a tender kiss on my lips. I drew away and looked him in the eye.

'Chris, what if I fuck this up again? I don't want to hurt you.'

'I'm willing to take the risk.' And he solemnly punched his heart with his fist. 'Are you?'

Before I could say anything, Mel's sage advice echoed in the back of my mind, making me smile: *Love is a choice, so choose wisely.*

Epilogue

'How on earth did you fit all this in that room?' I asked incredulously as the hallway gradually stacked up with various boxes, suitcases, an entire clothes rail, a dismantled cot and assorted bulky Ikea baskets rammed full of toys, shoes, belts and numerous scarves.

'That's not all of it. I still have the stuff from under the bed and my duvet and pillows. There's all the towels, plus my hat stand.'

'When did all this stuff multiply and have babies?'

'I sneaked it in under the cover of darkness when you weren't looking.'

'What time is the man with the van coming?' Ursula asked, dumping a black bag on top of the suitcases. 'You seriously need to have a clear out when you get to your new flat.'

'The man's here!' Neve cried excitedly through the front door as she ran from her lookout post in the front garden where Isla and Meg were guarding the pushchair and Grace's tricycle.

The sun blessed us with its presence that day, shining down on Ali as she prepared to strike out on her own, just her and Grace in a new home. It was the week before Halloween and talk was already turning to thoughts about Christmas, a couple of months away.

'You'll come for Christmas Eve, won't you?' Ali had already established. Jacqui was going to be in Australia visiting her sister, and Anne, Ali's mum, was moving over permanently to live round the corner from Ali's new flat. The sale of Anne's house in Spain had fortuitously gifted Ali the deposit she needed, allowing her to rent a place in Penge, not too far from me.

'It's going to be weird not living with you,' she'd said that day in September when she'd told me she was moving out. 'It's time, though. I really don't want to go, but I want to be in the real world, have my own space to meet someone. Mum needs me to help her adjust, too. She couldn't afford to buy round here, but I think us living near each other will soften the blow. Grace needs her own room, too. She's growing up and we're getting in the way. We need to get out of your hair.'

'Your mum could have stayed here for a bit.'

'Don't be mad! You'd have killed both of us after a week. This is the start of a new chapter. And it's the start of something for you, too. It's about time you got your house back so that you can think about your future and write your next book.'

'I need to get used to living on my own again before I think about anything else.' I needed time to decompress from all the fun we'd had, all the laughter, tears and madness.

After an hour of steady toing and froing, the attic room had been pared back to its original empty shell. Along with a few of Grace's pencil scribbles adorning the walls, and dust marks lining the blank space above the chest of drawers where all Ali's books and *Vogue*s had been stashed, the indents in the carpet pile were the only remaining evidence that the room had been stuffed to bursting with another person's life. Ali and I stood side by side gazing out of the windows across the hodgepodge of rooftops and chimney pots that tumbled Lego-like towards the London cityscape beyond, its sharp jagged edges piercing the crisp blue autumn sky, the early stages of the Shard rising up from between the handful of soon-to-be-dwarfed skyscrapers.

'You saved my life,' she said quietly. 'I would have died of a broken heart, or committed murder.'

'Me, too. You saved me as well. All three of us saved each other.'

'I'm going to miss this view.'

I rested my head on her shoulder. 'You can come back and see it any time you like. Keep your key. I'll never forget your dad working so hard to make this your cosy little nest. He did such a great job. That seems like a lifetime ago.'

'Mands, we'll see you at the flat?' Jacqui called half an hour later from the front garden, still sporting yoga gear after teaching her new Saturday morning class in her living room-cum-yoga studio. Grace clung to Neve's hand, looking a bit lost without Ali. 'You got the champagne?'

'On ice. We'll be up in half an hour. I've just got to decorate the cake.'

Grace started to cry. Neve picked her up and I walked over to see if I could help.

'What's up, Gracey?'

'Want to stay home. Don't want to go.' Fat tears rolled off her sizeable cheeks and splodged onto her red sweatshirt, leaving dark blobs.

'You're going to your new home with Mummy. Neve's going to help you unpack, then we're all coming up in a bit. I've made cake.'

'Want stay here. This is home.'

'Oh, Grace, you'll like it, I promise.' I hugged her and Neve carried her to Jacqui's car, parked out on the road. Ali and Ursula were already unpacking at the flat. I crunched over the path and back into the house where Chris was sitting on the bottom stair, the newly laid hard-wearing biscuit-coloured carpet now running up through the heart of house instead of the vile river of poo, paid for from my first wage cheque.

'You OK?' he asked gently.

'Yes. But I think they're going to find it hard living on their own. Grace has only ever known us. She thinks Isla, Meg and Sonny are her siblings. She'll miss them.'

'Kids adapt and Ali will get used to it. Come here.' I sat on his lap and he kissed the back of my head. 'Let's go out for dinner with the kids tonight, my treat.'

'You don't have to do that.'

'I know. I want to.'

I turned and kissed him on the mouth.

'Ewww, Mummy, gross!' Sonny had crept up on us from the kitchen.

'Chris said he would play football with us,' Joe said hopefully, hovering by the doorway, holding a ball eagerly in his hands.

'You better go then,' I said to them, standing up. 'You've got half an hour until we leave.'

'We better make the most of it. Come on, boys.'

As I added the finishing touches to the chocolate welcome-to-your-new-home cake, Isla and Meg fighting over the icing bowl beside me, I peered through the open glass doors at Chris playing on the grass with Sonny and Joe. Chris was shielding his eyes against the low sun as he posed ready for action in a makeshift goal cobbled together from a cracked terracotta flowerpot and a green plastic watering can. The acer tree had begun its annual changing of the guard from green to red, heralding the garden's steady decline into hibernation.

'Goal!' Sonny shouted triumphantly, grinning from ear to ear and high-fiving Joe. Chris collected the ball from the patio where it had rolled, and caught me staring. He winked and bounced the ball, turning to jog back to his spot.

'Let's see if you can get another one before we go,' he challenged.

'Do you think Grace and Ali will like their new home?' Isla asked, licking her finger.

'I think so.'

'Who's going to live in the attic now?'

'No one.'

'Not Chris?' Meg piped up, her chin smeared with chocolate butter cream.

'No, he lives with Mark.'

'But what if he wants to live here?'

'We're happy with how things are.'

'But might he move in one day?' Isla asked hopefully. 'Like Carrie and Daddy?'

I smiled at her concerned face. Isla the old soul, needing everything to be fair in love and war.

'Maybe, darling. We'll have to wait and see.'

Acknowledgements

Without sounding like an Awards Ceremony speech, there are a few people I need to thank. Firstly, my four parents for supporting me in my darkest hour, as well as my brother and sister-in-law and two sisters. I would have been totally lost without all my friends who held me together on a daily basis. Special thanks to Sharon, Heather, Rachel, Andy, Tasha, Jane, Austin, Nick, Claire, Katie HT, Katie N, Pippa, Tamsyn, Anna, Louise, Andrea, Adrienne, Fi, Shelley and Isabelle. Thanks to Charlie, my agent, who took me on when I was on skid row. He believed in *The Single Mums' Mansion* from day one when it was a sketchy idea based on an anonymous blog I had written to keep me sane during my divorce. Thanks also to my husband, Neil, because he thinks he's the unsung hero behind the scenes in all of this. He is actually, I couldn't have written it without his support. Thank you Katie, Susie, Vicki and Andy for reading an early draft, spotting mistakes, and Vicki for making me tone it down (or we would now be in prison). Finally, thanks to Sarah Ritherdon at Aria Fiction for expert editorial advice, and everyone working at Head of

Zeus for giving my book a home and making it real. I am very grateful indeed.

A special note to my kids: This is all fiction. End of.